SISTERS
OF SHADOW
AND LIGHT

BOOKS BY SARA B. LARSON

Defy
Ignite
Endure
Dark Breaks the Dawn
Bright Burns the Night

SISTERS OF SHADOW AND LIGHT

SARA B. LARSON

**TOR
TEEN**

A Tom Doherty Associates Book

NEW YORK

SISTERS OF SHADOW AND LIGHT

Copyright © 2019 by Sara B. Larson

A Tor Teen Book
Published by Tom Doherty Associates
120 Broadway
New York, NY 10271

www.tor-forge.com

Tor® is a registered trademark of Macmillan Publishing Group, LLC.

The Library of Congress Cataloging-in-Publication Data is available upon request.

ISBN 978-1-250-20840-8 (hardcover)
ISBN 978-1-250-20839-2 (ebook)

Our books may be purchased in bulk for promotional, educational, or business use. Please contact your local bookseller or the Macmillan Corporate and Premium Sales Department at 1-800-221-7945, extension 5442, or by email at MacmillanSpecialMarkets@macmillan.com.

First Edition: November 2019

Printed in the United States of America

0 9 8 7 6 5 4 3 2 1

For Kynlee and Adeline . . . my sweet girls.
My prayer is that you will love each other the way
I love my sisters. It won't always be easy,
but it will always be worth it.

Love seeketh not itself to please,
Nor for itself hath any care,
But for another gives its ease,
And builds a Heaven in Hell's despair.

—WILLIAM BLAKE

PART 1

SISTER OF SHADOW

THE BEGINNING

I have loved the stars too fondly to be fearful of the night.
—GALILEO

The night my sister was born, the stars died and were reborn in her eyes.

Mother refused to talk about it—the one night she wished to forget, but never could. When she did say anything, she recalled how the heat had been unbearable, rising from the sun-baked earth, sweltering in the way only a midsummer's night could. Windows had been flung open in futile hopes of cooling off the citadel that was our home, but instead only admitted an achingly dry breeze, like the hot breath of a Scylla that inhaled smoke and exhaled fire. Mother's labor came fast—too fast. Lucky, or providence, that Mahsami made it in time.

They'd tried to shoo me away, but I was only three years old and tenacious and soon they were too absorbed in the impending birth to be concerned with me. Perhaps I would have been better to go.

My first memories were from that night.

One was of my mother, lying on that bed that had always dwarfed her, hair as dark as raven's wings limp against her head, face wan and lips the bloodless gray of a corpse, while Mahsami bent over her straining belly. Mahsami—or Sami as I called her—once told me that some women cried, wailed, even screamed in labor, but not my mother. She remained silent.

Mother never spoke of what came next, but Sami did. Once. After a particularly tense supper, when it was just me and her left in the kitchen to clean up the day's mess, I'd dared broach the subject and she'd been too tired or too upset to deflect my curiosity as she normally would.

Something was wrong from the start, she'd told me that night, firelight flickering across her lined face, her voice a soft hum over the clink of the dishes I continued to wash, fearing she would stop if I did. *It was as though your mother's body wished to be rid of the baby, but your sister had no wish to be born.*

Her birth was a battle that was swift and brutal and nearly took my mother's life, Mahsami had confessed. A strange bitterness had coated my tongue, as if I could taste her residual shame. She'd felt personally responsible for the near tragedy. But, through whatever skill she possessed, and by the blessing of the Great God, when the moon reached the pinnacle of its arc, spilling milky light over the citadel, Sami pulled my sister from my mother's womb.

That was my second memory. Sami, sweaty, blood-splattered, but triumphant, holding aloft a baby that was more ashen than alive with the same hair as me—as dark as damp earth—plastered to her skull, her skin wrinkled and wet. And completely, chillingly silent. As silent as my mother.

Mahsami told me how she'd placed the baby on Mother's belly and rubbed her back, patting and crooning, encouraging her to cry, and fill her lungs with life-sustaining air. When none of it seemed to work, the midwife lifted my sister up and slapped her across the rump. She cried at last, her eyes opening for the first time.

And *that's* when my mother screamed.

We were in the citadel, so we didn't see the night sky, didn't witness the pulse of darkness that obliterated all light—including the stars—at the moment my sister cried and turned her burning eyes on my mother for the first time.

But Sami heard about it later.

Sami had been in such a talkative mood, I'd summoned my courage once more to ask the question that had haunted me more than the others. *Where was* he?

No one knows and there's no use wondering. He's gone, Zuhra, she'd replied bitingly, hard with old anger that wasn't necessarily aimed at me, the gates to her memories slamming shut at my cursed inquisitiveness, *and that's all you need to know about him.*

That was my third and last memory from that night. My mother staring at the baby in Mahsami's arms—refusing to take her—and asking, *Where is he? Where's Adelric?*

That name had burned its way into my memory somehow, the way my sister's eyes had burned fear into my mother's heart. A name that was banished from our home, as it only engendered loathing and bitterness. I tried to be loyal to my mother, I tried to cling to her hate and make it my own. But there were times, on rare afternoons spent wandering the empty citadel when my mother was occupied and wouldn't catch me, when I stared up at the ancient statues and the molded hangings and carved ceilings of the Paladin—the beings who had once lived in our world, whose abandoned home we inhabited—and I couldn't help but wonder.

Wonder what had happened to him—why he'd left us at all, but especially *that* night. Wonder why the hedge that had been shorter than the iron fence surrounding our home suddenly grew taller than three men standing atop one another overnight, so that we awoke to a wall of green surrounding the citadel where we lived, blocking the iron gate, isolating us from everyone but each other.

And, of course, wonder how my mother had ever fallen in love with him in the first place and followed him here. For Adelric, the name I was forbidden to remember but couldn't forget, was a Paladin. Like the statues I stood beside and imagined were real, like the carvings in the ceiling above me that I tipped my head back to stare at with my plain hazel irises, trying to envision a father with eyes like jewels that glowed with power, riding his gryphon. I knew he was one of them, even though Mother never admitted it, never acknowledged what Inara's *uniqueness* could never let any of us forget.

Inara—Ray of Light. My sister who had the power of the Paladin in her veins—and her eyes. When it became obvious that my father wasn't coming back, my mother grudgingly named my sister—a hopeful name for a child that seemed to only ever bring shadows to my mother's face—and finally took her to her breast.

I was the only one who looked into Inara's face and smiled. Mother said it was because I had been too young to understand and that I grew up accustomed to her. But *Mother* was the one who didn't understand, who paled when Inara looked at her, whose gaze dropped when her daughter's burning eyes met hers. I knew Inara was different, I knew her eyes marked her.

But she was my sister, and I loved her.

And there was nothing I wouldn't do to protect her. No matter what.

ONE

Sunshine filtered through the gauzy curtains, as soft and warm as melted butter, its glow smoothing over the tattered edges of the well-worn but carefully tended furniture that my mother and I were perched on. The "morning room" was one of the few in the enormous deserted citadel that was free of dust—that looked how I'd always imagined a *normal* home might look. A bit shabby, perhaps, but at least it was clean and bright, unlike so many of the other rooms I'd managed to sneak into. Those were dark and shadowed and cold, the hidden past of this place buried under a thick coating of grime and disuse. But here, where Mother insisted we spend the majority of our lives, muted daylight reflected back at me from the gleaming wooden surface of the table next to our chairs.

I dutifully plunged my needle through the dingy-white fabric—push, pull, tighten, repeat; a garden of flowers blooming across my lap, coaxed into existence by my fingers and the thread—but my mind was outside. My heart fluttered beneath the trappings of propriety my mother insisted upon—the fitted dress, the demurely coifed hair, all of it—as the wings of the birds I could hear trilling in the *real* gardens below fluttered, carrying them upon the eddies and whirls of wind. They caught that wind and rode it into the clouds. The birds could escape this place, but not so for the rest of us.

"Focus, Zuhra," Mother murmured, catching the direction of my gaze and the stillness of my hands.

With a suppressed sigh, I turned back to my needlepoint. Though I believed myself fairly skilled at the task, the results of my efforts were still lacking, since we had only whatever cloth and thread Mother and Sami had hoarded throughout the years for my "work" that wasn't needed for other more pressing uses. The Paladin who had once lived there must have left in a hurry, since so many of their belongings remained. But that was long ago . . . and not even their superior (according to Sami) fabrics could withstand time *forever*. So many wasted hours spent trapped in that one small room, bent over useless decorative pieces, already yellowed and aged before I ever began creating them, for a dowry that would never be needed, for a wedding that would certainly never transpire. I wasn't certain I ever wished to marry, but even if I did, how Mother figured that would be possible so long as we were trapped in the citadel was beyond me.

"May I please go outside? Just for a bit. With Inara." I didn't raise my eyes to hers, too afraid she'd see how desperately I wished to be gone from this room and her piercing gaze. Her eyes scorched me far more deeply than Inara's ever did.

"Finish that piece and then you may."

My frustration was hot in my throat, strangling me as surely as this meaningless existence steadily choked the life out of us all. "*Why*? Why must I finish first? What is the point of *any* of this?"

Mother stiffened; I saw her spine straighten in my peripheral vision. She was a small woman, shorter than both me and Inara, but her tiny frame housed a fiery spirit I knew better than to provoke. She reminded me of an Ixtacl, the little rakasa—the Paladin name for "monster"—that lured prey in with its large brown eyes and whiskered face, and then ripped them into shreds with the bone-cuttingly-sharp claws hidden beneath the soft fur of its paws. I knew better than to mention the comparison to Mother, or even Sami. She would have been furious at me for reading about the monsters that had once plagued our land but had now fallen into legend and myth. I did mention it to Inara once. She'd paled and begun muttering in the way she did when she was agitated, making me immediately regret it. I kept my observations to myself after that.

But I couldn't help but think of the Ixtacl again as Mother's own hands grew still, waiting for me to acknowledge her waiting glare.

Here come the claws . . .

I finally looked up, our identical hazel eyes meeting and holding. I was practically her spitting image, save for the gray streaks in her hair, and my olive skin that must have been gifted by my father. Mother was moon-pale, a stark contrast to her inky eyelashes and star-streaked night-sky hair, whereas I merely had to spend an hour or two outside before my skin began to brown. *Like a chicken being roasted by the fire,* she'd scolded me as a child, scrubbing my skin with valuable lemons to try and bleach the sun from it. She never bothered with Inara's skin, perhaps because she knew my sister would merely brown right up again from all the time she spent in her gardens. Or more likely, because she preferred to spend as little time with her younger daughter as possible.

If Inara noticed or minded, she was unable to tell us. But *I* did.

"She is alone out there all the time. I only want to be with her, *help* her," I began before Mother could, "just while the sun is up. I can work on this tonight, after supper." I held up the needlepoint, nearly two-thirds finished, as evidence—as a promise. "Maybe she could even join us."

"You know better than to suggest such a thing. We can't afford another accident like the last time," Mother snapped. Despite myself, my gaze flicked to the singed edges of our curtains.

"She didn't mean to—"

"She never does," Mother returned. A hint of garnet flushed her cheeks. "*You* are the only one that has any hope of leaving this place. You must be prepared for that opportunity when it comes."

"By sewing decorations for a home I will never be mistress of—because it doesn't exist?" I barely kept my voice from rising, but had no such luck with the boiling unrest within me. It surged through my veins, infiltrating my muscles like Netvor venom—another type of rakasa I'd read about in that same forbidden book. Supposedly the strongest Paladin had pierced themselves with it in very small doses for a burst of speed and strength in battle. "No man is ever going to come waltzing through the hedge, seeking my hand in marriage, Mother. The hedge won't allow it, first of all. And second, you know as well as I do that no man would ever wish to try!"

"You don't know that. Perhaps a young man from the village—"

"The villagers either hate us or are *terrified* of us."

"Not of *you*. They're scared of *her*!"

"Why don't you say her name? Why don't you ever say *any* of their names?"

Mother deliberately lowered her darning, her already stiff spine lengthening until she sat arrow-straight, poised to strike. Normally I would have backed off immediately, afraid of incurring her wrath. But something had been building inside me all week alongside the heat wave that transformed the citadel from an abandoned fortress to an oven that baked unrest instead of bread.

I pressed, "They're scared of *Inara*, who wouldn't hurt a spider. *You're* even scared of her. Her own mother."

"That is *enough*." Mother's voice was sharp enough to cleave stone, perhaps even the immovable hedge, but I barreled on, words and grievances I'd swallowed and buried for months, *years*, rising up and tumbling out, lifted on the surge of my discontent the way the birds had been lifted by the updrafts of wind in the courtyard.

"You treat her as if it's *her* fault that her father is a Paladin— that she reminds you of him!"

Mother lips whitened. *"What did you say?"*

Now that the words were spoken, the careful dam I'd built within cracked, spilling all my harbored thoughts out. "You act like it's a huge secret, but we *live* in their citadel. I've walked these empty halls with *their* statues and *their* tapestries watching me, *mocking* me and my ignorance, every day of my life. Inara is more Paladin than she is human and we all know it!"

"You have *no idea* what you're talking about."

"Did his eyes glow the way hers do?" I continued right on over her, despite the warning bells clanging dimly beneath the crash of blood tumbling through my body. "Did she inherit that from Adelric?"

The name reverberated as though I'd punched the air out of the room. My mother's mouth opened then shut again, shocked beyond words and sounds. But rather than the explosion I expected, that I had grown accustomed to from her, the flash of rage dissolved into something worse, something darker. In the space of one blink to the next her fury shattered and she crumpled in on herself, her fingers clenching her own needlepoint into a mangled mess. The exhilaration of my own daring ebbed out of me, leaving me shaken and empty.

"Go," she said at last, stony and quiet, to her lap.

"Mother," I tried haltingly, already sickened at what I'd done. She was implacable and distant and exacting, but she was still my mother. I stood and reached toward her, but she flinched away.

"You wanted to go to Inara, so *go*." It was a half-whispered hiss of a command.

The door opened and I glanced over to see Mahsami walking in with a tray of sliced vegetables and some sort of broth steaming in a pot. Other than a random goat or chicken, she was the only living being that the hedge had allowed to pass through its dangerous grasp—and only on occasion, when things were dire. She could have escaped. But shortly after Inara's birth, she'd chosen to move into the citadel—temporarily, she'd claimed, to help care for the baby.

She hadn't left us yet.

Her shoulders were now sloped with age and her fawn hair had lightened to white in recent years, but her gaze was sharp as ever when she glanced back and forth between the two of us.

"I brought some refreshments," she offered, hefting the tray as evidence.

"Zuhra was just leaving."

Sami's eyebrows lifted, but she didn't comment as I stared at my mother, willing her to look up to see the apology on my face. Instead, she punctiliously unclenched her fingers and smoothed out the fabric of the stockings she'd been darning, acting as though nothing had happened. But I didn't miss the crimson stain on the gray material she quickly tried to cover up, from where she'd punctured herself with the needle.

"Yes, I was," I finally agreed, turning away, my blood like sludge in my veins. "I'll be in the garden with Inara."

I'd gotten what I'd wanted, but my victory somehow felt like a defeat.

TWO

The shadowy hallway was a shock after the brightness of the morning room. The worn soles of my leather shoes—old Paladin ones found stashed in a closet—made a soft slap against the stone floors. I moved quickly through the hulking innards of the citadel, eager to reach the main door and fresh air—and my sister—beyond. The oppressive heat rose up while the emptiness pressed down as I passed shut door after shut door. I'd never understood how the *lack* of something could be felt so acutely, I only knew it *could*, because that pulsing, aching hollowness was a constant companion on the rare occasions when I was able to wander through the citadel alone. When Sami or Mother or even Inara was by my side, the sensation melted away, chased off by their voices or maybe just their mere presence. But when I was by myself, slipping through the endless hallways and stairs, a single being traipsing through a place intended to house hundreds, sometimes the sensation of *vacancy* was enough to send a chill skittering over my skin.

Brushing off the familiar but still unsettling feelings, I tipped my chin at Terence, the name I'd given the Paladin statue that stood, unmoving, at the top of the stairs like a sentinel, feigning a bravery that didn't quite reach my soul. I should have been used to the statues scattered throughout the citadel, but no matter how many times I walked past their glittering lapis lazuli eyes, I couldn't shake the feeling that the stone likenesses of the beings who had once truly walked these halls were still watching me as I passed, somehow marking my presence in their domain. No one had ever said how old the citadel was, but it *felt* ancient. I'd often wondered if it had been hewn directly from the mountain it perched beside eons ago, long before Mother, or Adelric, or Gateskeep, or possibly even Vamala itself. Had the Paladin merely claimed it as their own once they arrived here, to save us from the rakasa? I didn't know . . . would probably *never* know. That *not knowing* was like an itch beneath my skin, unreachable and, at times, unbearable.

When I finally reached the grand entrance, with its soaring ceiling high above and the massive door that led to the main courtyard straight ahead, a sigh of relief silently slid past my lips. But even outside the citadel, I couldn't escape the feeling that I was being watched.

I slipped out the door, into a wall of heat and glaring sunshine. To my left, the dilapidated stables where the Paladin's gryphons had once lived hunkered against the north side of the citadel. To my right were the orchards and gardens were Inara worked and lived. And surrounding it all was the hedge. It loomed across the courtyard, a hulking monster of vines and thorns. Averting my eyes from it, I hurried toward the orchard and Inara's gardens beyond. Though I wished to spend all my waking time with Inara, that meant being outside from sunup until the shadows of sunset stretched across the courtyard, and part of me didn't blame Mother for staying indoors at all times. As much as I longed to be with my sister, I couldn't stand the sensation of the hedge hovering behind me; a presence so real, so tangible, at times I would spin around expecting to find someone standing there, watching me, only to face an empty courtyard—save for the impenetrable wall of vines, our living captor.

I'd wanted to ask Mother if it had always been that way, even before *he* left, before it grew into this monster. Had the hedge always been this . . . menacing? Or had he done something to change it that night—something beyond just increasing the size of it? *Itch, itch, itch,* beneath my plain, human skin. More *not knowing* . . . because I didn't dare. I knew better than to broach the subject of *before.*

Inara kept her gardens closer to the citadel itself, on the south-east end of the grounds, where the sun shone longest—when the sun shone at all. Gateskeep was surrounded by sky-scraping peaks and cliffs, including the one the citadel had been built on, that were most often enshrouded in choking clouds and creeping fog. It was normally gray and waterlogged, even in summer, other than the occasional week of unbearable heat and sun, such as this one. I had no doubt that if I'd tried to grow the fruits and vegetables, we would have starved years ago, especially during the winter. But Inara had a way with plants, no matter the weather. With *all* living things, really. Well, all those that weren't afraid of her.

I headed toward the boxes where she grew the vegetables and herbs in the spring, summer, and fall, winding through the small grove of trees, their branches already heavy with fruit, early even for Inara's abilities to have coaxed out a harvest.

I found her bending toward one of the tomato plants, her long hair falling over her shoulder like night spilling across the evening sky, muttering in that way of hers, the cadence rising and falling, but most of the sounds unintelligible. The sun was hot on my back, as it had been all week. An unaccountably cloudless and blistering snap of weather, especially for the beginning of June.

"It's a beautiful afternoon." I spoke softly, hoping not to frighten her. She paused, her fingers briefly going still, but when she didn't respond, returning instead to her work, I gently touched her elbow.

Inara jerked and straightened, spinning to face me. Even after all these years, my gaze was immediately drawn to her eyes before anything else—to her irises that glowed like the blue flames closest to the fuel of a fire. Her burning, ever-changing, fear-inspiring eyes.

Paladin eyes.

"Can I do anything to help you?"

Inara cocked her head to the side, staring at my mouth as I spoke. I repeated the question, even as her uncomprehending gaze traveled over me and then moved on. If she'd been lucid, she surely would have questioned my inappropriate attire for working in a garden. Mother and I had spent hours upon hours repurposing many of her finer dresses to fit not only my height, but also what

Sami claimed were the modern styles—insisting I be dressed to catch the eye of a potential suitor at any given time, no matter how much I protested the ridiculousness.

Inara, on the other hand, was mostly given Mahsami's extra clothes, leftovers from the Paladin, or the more drab offerings from Mother's closet and left to have her ankles (and half of her calves) on display beneath the too-short skirts.

We had no income to speak of, except for the meager funds Sami could sometimes acquire through selling off objects from the citadel, so new clothes were scarce. For some unfathomable reason, Mother's drive to see me well dressed didn't extend to selling more, though the massive structure was replete with antiques and valuables of all sizes and worth—including an obscene amount of diamonds, some probably near to priceless. But the fact was, even if Mother *had* asked Sami to go to market more often, the hedge wouldn't have allowed it. It opened for Sami—and *only* her. And only when things were so grim our very lives depended upon it. Mother, Inara, and I had to wait inside the citadel.

"Help," Inara finally repeated, loudly, almost a shout. I tried not to flinch. *"Help."* She shook her head, a short, jerky movement. "Two. Four. Six. Four. Two."

"Yes." I glanced past her to the rows of tidy boxes where all of her plants grew, some leafy and wide, others stretching tall and thin with vines that snaked up wooden stakes. The air was full of the loamy scent of earth and vegetables. Most often, Inara spent her time trying to keep the plants from drowning, but not this week. "Do you need help harvesting anything? Or weeding?"

She turned back to her boxes and the words turned unintelligible once more.

I watched Inara silently for a moment, as she bent to prod at the soil at the base of some stakes that were leaning a bit, grown too heavy with beans, before moving forward to stand beside my sister. I'd forgotten to braid her hair that morning, but luckily it didn't look as though she'd ripped any of it out. She did that sometimes, especially if she was cooped up too long in the citadel. She'd grab at her hair, even her face sometimes, as if trying to claw away the roar in her head. But in the gardens, she kept her hands in the soil and on her plants, leaving her hair and face untouched.

She was her most lucid when she worked in the garden, which was why I wished to spend time with her there. Inside the citadel when I approached her, she wouldn't even respond to me. There was only her incessant chanting and muttering, pacing and jerking, her hands trembling. It set Mother's nerves on edge, but far from annoying me, Inara's inability to communicate made me hurt inside, a wound that I couldn't pinpoint or heal, but that ached constantly. At times worse than others—such as the nights when Mother refused to even acknowledge her younger daughter at supper.

Out here, Inara really *looked* at me sometimes, and on her best days, she even spoke of her plants in brief spurts. There were times when we actually had what *could* pass for a normal conversation. That's when the chasm inside me felt the smallest and hurt the least. I prayed today might be a good day; that would at least make the sour tang of guilt at the back of my throat easier to swallow.

"Nara . . . these strawberry plants look like they're wilting."

She didn't look up from the beans, so I slowly reached out and touched her elbow again, drawing her attention. When her blue-flame eyes met mine, I smiled and repeated what I'd said, while gently tugging her toward the plants that indeed appeared as if the sweltering heat were a bit too much for them.

"Can I do something to help?"

Inara was fifteen, three years younger than me. Though we were the same height, where I had inherited some of Mother's softness—my hips were wider, my breasts larger—Inara was leaner, almost too thin. "One, two . . . three . . . one, two, three, four . . ." she mumbled, with a shake of her head.

"Tell me how I can help. Do you want me to fetch more water?" I'd never been able to figure out what the counting meant—but it usually was something she did when she was agitated. I glanced past her to the well, where a few empty buckets were piled haphazardly. An underground river ran below the citadel, and our well was dug down deep enough for us to gather water from it. Just outside the hedge, at the edge of the citadel, a huge waterfall suddenly broke free from underneath the structure, crashing to the earth far below us. It was depicted in multiple paintings and tapestries in the citadel—and though I'd never seen the waterfall myself, I knew them to be accurate because I could *hear* the waterfall on this side of the citadel.

But she ignored my offer to get water and stepped forward, reaching out to the plants.

"Four . . . five . . . five, six . . ."

Her fingers brushed over the brown-tipped leaves and the tiny buds where miniature strawberries had already begun to form with the gentleness of a mother's soothing caress. Her eyes fluttered shut and her hands stilled . . . and then Inara stiffened with a sharp intake of breath as if she'd been stabbed.

Unbridled elation coalesced through my limbs, laving every trace of guilt away. *This* was worth almost any cost—even the hurt in my mother's eyes and the bloodstain on her stockings. "Thank you, thank you, *thank you*," I whispered my gratitude to the Great God as the blue fire that constantly burned in Inara's eyes suddenly flared beneath her skin, racing through her veins—her cheeks, her neck, down her arms to her hands.

The very air changed when her eyes opened once more, so bright I couldn't look directly into them. There was an acrid hint to the previously dry breeze, reminding me of the smell from striking flint with rocks to start a fire. I could even taste it on my tongue, a bitter, sharp tang.

Magic.

Paladin magic.

There was no other explanation for what my sister could do, for the way the strawberry plants immediately straightened, the previously curled, semi-brown leaves unfurling into full greenness, as if woken from a slumber and stretching toward the sun and their full potential. Even the tiny strawberries grew before my eyes, turning a shade closer to red as Inara brushed her glowing fingers over them.

And then, with a groan, as if it took no small amount of effort, she pulled her hands back and the blue fire in her veins dimmed and then vanished.

When I looked into her face again, her eyes had dulled, the fire dimmed a bit. Inara blinked once, and then cocked her head as if listening for something. I heard nothing except for the nearby waterfall and the sound of leaves being rustled by the breeze that had turned fresh again, the bitter scent of her power gone with the disappearance of the Paladin fire in her veins; but I knew Inara suffered under the weight of a roar that remained silent to me. When she sighed, I couldn't help but do the same, spurred by the sound of bone-deep relief issuing from my sister.

Then Inara looked directly at me, *truly* looked this time, and *smiled*—the first I'd seen in . . . a while. "Zuhra?"

My answering smile was accompanied by a tightness in my chest that somehow seemed attached to my eyes. I blinked rapidly to hold back the moisture that threatened to escape. *This* was why I begged to come out with her, why I cajoled Sami into getting more and more seeds for new plants on the rare occasions that she was able to venture to the market, why I prayed for inclement weather—or for days without rain. Why I preferred winter to summer, even though it was cold and dark and miserable and we rarely left the citadel, because that was when Inara had to work on keeping her plants alive *inside* the citadel, to encourage the vegetables to grow with almost no sunshine and very little warmth, which meant using her power far more often and greater amounts of it, too. And when I got Inara to tap into that magic, to help her plants, I got *this* in return. A handful of minutes with my sister in the summer, and sometimes a couple of miraculous *hours* in the winter, before she disappeared again, as surely as the fire in her veins always retreated back to her eyes.

Inara looked past me to the citadel, to the windows of the sitting room. "How long has it been?"

"Not that long," I assured her, even though it actually had been over a week since she'd been this lucid. She'd tried to explain it to me once, years ago, about the roar in her head, the constant noise that drowned everything else out and threatened to drive her mad.

For some reason, when I got her to tap into her power, it abated and I got my sister—my *real* sister—to myself. Even if it was only for a few minutes.

There was so much to say, and yet I couldn't decide where to start. There were never any guarantees of how long we had.

"Where's Mother?" It was always the first question she asked, after wondering how long it had been. I forced myself to keep my gaze on her, not letting it trail up to the window where we'd both sat plying our needles for most of the day. My answer, too, was the same as always.

"Inside. She's mad at me again," I quickly added to keep Inara from dwelling on the fact that Mother avoided her as much as possible.

"What did you do now?" Inara pulled her gaze away from the empty window. Her words were slightly off. Mother claimed she was difficult to understand, but she was trying her best. I knew it wasn't possible for us to comprehend how hard it must have been for her to learn language in such brief spurts throughout her life. Her lucid times had lasted longer as a child; I remembered reading stories to her for hours when she was little enough to sit in my lap, pointing out pictures to her, having her try to mimic my words. But as she grew older, her eyes got brighter and her lucid times began to shrink. In my opinion, it was a miracle she could speak at all. And if that meant expending a bit more effort for us to understand her, well, that was nothing compared to what she endured every minute of every day.

"She caught me reading one of the Paladin books again," I admitted. "I snuck it out of the library. I thought she'd gone to bed, but apparently not. She noticed the candlelight beneath my door and walked in on me before I could hide it."

"Did you find anything out—anything useful that—"

The eager questions cut off abruptly. Her eyes widened, her mouth falling open at something behind me, her face going pale beneath her sun-browned skin.

I spun around and screamed, stumbling backward.

There was a stranger in the gardens.

A *male* stranger—standing next to one of Inara's trees.

My first irrational thought was that Terence had somehow come alive, but it only took one frantic beat of my heart to realize he was no Paladin. His eyes didn't glow. And statues didn't come to life. I'd hoped and feared that for too many years to believe otherwise.

"Pardon my interruption, but I was hoping you could help me. I've traveled some distance to visit the Citadel. We'd heard it was abandoned, but . . . obviously . . ." He gestured toward us. "Do you work here—can you direct me where I can go to inquire about lodging?"

I stared. My blood roared beneath my skin, my mouth gaped open. A stranger. There was a *stranger. Here.* Right *now.* I'd never seen a real, live male before, except for vague, time-smeared memories of my father. But this . . . this . . . person was standing there and he was talking and the hedge . . . *The hedge had let him through?*

The hedge didn't allow *anyone* through. I still remembered the terror from the last time a group of soldiers had tried when I was ten; their shouts, the smoke from the torches they'd wielded rising above the immovable thorny beast that surrounded us, their screams when they'd tried to cut it down and the hedge had attacked. No one had come since then. No one had dared.

Then where had this . . . this *man* come from? Was that what he was? For some reason "man" didn't seem like quite the right word. He appeared closer to my age than Mother's or Sami's.

After all these years—after all of Mother's dreams that I'd never claimed for myself—she'd actually, unbelievably been right. The hedge had allowed a boy through.

As the disbelieving silence drew out, he cocked his head to the side, then his eyebrows lifted a bit. Was he . . . confused? I belatedly realized I had mirrored his movement. Maybe that wasn't the best thing to do. I straightened my head again so fast it sent a sharp *ping* up my neck.

He cleared his throat and his voice was so *different* from mine or Sami's or Mother's when he started to speak again. "I realize I may be—" His gaze had been on me at first, as I stood closer to him, but then it flickered to Inara and he *stopped*. Stopped talking, stopped moving, perhaps even breathing.

It was like having Sami dump a bucket of icy water over my head during the winter months when I needed a bath but firewood had to be saved for more vital uses than warming water. It was unpleasant but effective at forcing me to act quickly. His reaction to Inara was that bucket of water sluicing over my astonishment at his appearance, propelling me to respond.

"Who are you?" My words were halting and uncertain and furious all at once. My legs were strangely stiff—from panic? From shock?—but I forced them to move, to carry my body in front of Inara, blocking my sister from view, though it was already too late. He stared through me as if I weren't even there, as if he could still see Inara's burning eyes through my skull. "Who *are* you?" I repeated, my voice rising. An unfamiliar sensation gripped me; I was hot and cold at once, my pulse a rickety thing, my blood careening through my body. Hope and fear clashed in a tangle of confusion.

Then Inara touched my arm—as I often did to her—and stepped up beside me. "Who is he, Zuhra?" Her fingers trembled but she stood shoulder to shoulder with me, the picture of courage—of *poise* . . . if one ignored the dirt crusted around her nails, laced in the grooves of the skin on her hands, the streak of it across her cheek, her ill-fitting clothes, bare ankles, her hair cascading over her shoulders, loose and wild in the breeze.

And her glowing blue eyes.

"I don't know," I murmured below my breath.

The stranger couldn't take his gaze off her, which raised my hackles, the way our cat Louie's ears flattened and his hair rose when he was agitated. But I couldn't quite quell the curiosity that also swelled.

"Why are you at our home?" Inara asked, more loudly this time.

He blinked and visibly straightened, as if just realizing that he'd been staring at us—at her—in a daze for far too long. He was tall and angular, as if someone had stretched him a little bit further than they'd intended before he finished growing. His clothes were loose on his narrow shoulders and hips, but they looked fine enough, as if he'd purposefully had them made that way, rather than not having any other options like me and Inara. I scrambled to make sense of his sudden appearance in our garden. Sami was the only person the hedge had allowed through before. Why now—why *him*? My heart ricocheted off my ribs.

"I'm sorry, my *manners* . . ." He shook his head, cheeks flushing as he folded his frame forward into a bow. "I am Halvor Roskery, a scholar and traveler." He straightened and pushed one hand through hair the color of dust, somewhere between light and dark brown with a suggestion of auburn woven through.

Halvor Roskery. My fingers twitched at my side; the rough fabric of Inara's skirt brushed my skin.

"And . . . you are?" he prompted, his gaze still trained on my sister.

"Inara," she said, her name coming out short, almost clipped. The tension radiating from her only amplified my own; she was shaking so hard I almost took her hand in mine to steady her.

"I'm Zuhra." It was so quiet in the courtyard . . . could he hear the thundering of my heart? "We're Inara and Zuhra Montieth." He'd told us his full name—was that what was expected? Mother had taught me needlepoint but failed to explain how to introduce myself. Montieth was her last name, from before marrying our father. She always told us she used her surname because he left us. But I suspected it was because he had no surname—no Paladin did, from what I'd gathered in my subversive research.

"A pleasure to meet you." He—Halvor—inclined his head once more, his eyes still on Inara.

"Why are you here?" I knew it wasn't polite, but my limited time with Inara was wasting away by the second. And he had yet to spare me a second glance.

"Zuhra . . ." Her fingers sought mine and I clenched them tightly.

"No, she's right to be suspicious." Halvor mistook Inara's reaction as scolding, rather than seeking comfort. "I'm sorry."

"Sorry?" I echoed.

"I am going about this all the wrong way. You must understand how . . . unexpectedly thrilling this is, though."

"Thrilling?" *Stop repeating everything he says!*

"After years of study and planning and traveling, I'm finally *here*. I made it. And not only did I find the Citadel of the Paladin . . . I found . . . well . . . *you*." He gestured to Inara.

"You traveled for *years* to come *here*?" I tried to hide my shock at his casual naming of the citadel, but he didn't even seem to hear me. So few wished to speak of the Paladin in any tone other than fear or anger—but he sounded . . . awed.

The way he looked at Inara went beyond wonder, however, his expression bordering on worshipful. "In all my preparations and hopes, I never *dreamed* . . . I mean, to find *her—here—*alive and in the flesh. I'm sure you're accustomed to it, being her . . . governess?"

"What? No, I'm her *sister*."

"*Sister?*" he repeated, eyes wide. "That's not possible."

"I assure you she is."

"But . . . you're a human. And she's"—Halvor paused and looked to Inara once more—"she's a Paladin."

THREE

It took me two beats of my beleaguered heart to respond, but finally I bit out, "You've made a mistake. And now you must leave."

Halvor reeled back as if I'd lashed out with my hands, not just my words.

Mother's plan of marriage for me had always seemed ludicrous—impossible, even; but suddenly there was a real, live potential suitor standing in our garden. With a remarkably square jaw, and a shadow of stubble, and he was so much *taller* than me . . . But all of Sami's warnings through the years echoed in my heart, beating next to my own memories of the times soldiers or mobs had attempted to break through the hedge, while we huddled together inside the citadel, praying for our captor to also be our protector.

I had to shut away my own hopes in order to protect my sister.

I turned away from Halvor to face Inara, who had cocked her head to the side in that birdlike way of hers, watching him appraisingly. Already her eyes had grown brighter. It was to be one of her shorter episodes then; our time was running out. And I didn't dare let him see my sister descend back into her other world—the one where no one could reach her.

"Come, Inara, we must go inside. Sami is looking for us."

"She is?" Inara turned to me, confusion flitting across her face. Was it because of the sudden claim or because I was losing her already?

My belly burned as hot as the fire in her eyes, fueled by frustration at this strange young man for showing up *now*, the first time I'd had my sister back in a week, stealing my preciously rare time with her.

"Please, forgive me. I am sorry if I've offended you somehow. Master Barloc has chastised me endlessly for my overeagerness, but—"

"You haven't offended me, but we have to go," I cut him off, without looking back.

"Zuhra . . . I don't believe he intends us any harm." Inara's voice was quiet, too soft for him to hear.

"He will cause it whether he intends to or not." All the years living sequestered in the citadel, just the four of us . . . what would happen now? It had been blessedly peaceful for almost eight years; no soldiers, no attacks on the hedge. But once he spread the word about what he'd seen, the rumors would flare up again, as would the alarm, the hate. Sami had warned me that the different peoples of Vamala believed the Paladin to all be gone from our lands— and they were glad for it. Better that they never learn of Inara's existence, especially since we couldn't leave the citadel regardless. Only the villagers of Gateskeep had any idea that there was *possibly* a half Paladin living at the citadel, and they kept it to themselves (so long as we kept to ourselves), wishing only for peace, according to Sami, and pretending we didn't exist as much as they were able.

I took Inara's hand in mine and tugged her away from the strawberries that were now lusciously fat on their branches, hanging low like a woman's swollen belly just before her time. Like the pregnant queen I'd seen in the book of fairy tales we'd read as children, when she was lucid. Inara resisted, but only a little.

"Good afternoon!"

The pleasant call took us all by surprise and I whirled to see Mother striding toward us, what she clearly intended to be a welcoming smile wreathing her face. I hadn't seen her smile in . . . quite some time. It didn't look right, as if it had been so long since she'd attempted it that she couldn't remember how to do it properly. Her lips stretched wide over her teeth, and her expression was eager, but her face lacked all the warmth of a true smile.

"Good afternoon, Madam. I apologize for my unannounced arrival, but we believed the citadel to be abandoned. To find it occupied has been a pleasant surprise." Halvor bent into a bow once more, this time aimed at her. My gaze flashed from Mother, to him, to Inara, and then back again.

"That's quite all right—we're always happy to receive guests. Isn't that right, my dear?" Mother looked to me with another attempt at a smile, but her eyes sparked dangerously. I understood her unspoken warning perfectly: this was my chance.

"Oh . . . um, yes . . . of course," I stammered.

"What has brought you to our gate?" Mother turned back to Halvor. "I don't recall you from the village." This was a risk, as she hadn't been to Gateskeep herself in at least fifteen years. But then again, no villager would have believed the citadel to be abandoned. They knew all too well that we lived here.

"I am a scholar, Madam, apprenticed under Master Barloc—expert on the Paladin."

He was so eager to share his enthusiasm, he must not have noticed how my mother stiffened, her smile fading the moment he mentioned that forbidden word.

"He has dedicated his life to studying them and their impact on Vamala. Together, we decided to travel here, to visit their—"

"It is unfortunate, but you have made a mistake." All pretense at welcoming him withered under the ice in Mother's voice when she cut in.

Halvor stuttered to a stop. "No . . . I, ah . . . I'm quite certain this *is* their—"

"And now you must go." Mother's gaze turned flinty when it flashed to meet mine, skipped right over Inara, who had watched the entire exchange silently, to land back on Halvor. She grabbed him by the bicep and using every bit of strength in her tiny body—which I'd learned more than once was surprisingly considerable—began to drag him away from us, back to the courtyard.

"I apologize if I have said or done something to alarm you, but

I assure you I mean only to *study* the Paladin's citadel. I mean it—and you—no harm!" Halvor protested, even as he allowed himself to be pulled away. Though he did throw a pleading glance over his shoulder.

"No need to apologize. You are leaving. *Now.*" Mother's voice carried on the parched breeze as she marched him away from us.

"What's happening? Who is that?" Inara's voice was very small, unsure. I was losing her.

"I don't know," I answered truthfully, deliberating my options. I hated to lose any time with Inara, not knowing when I'd get more. But, acting on an impulse I didn't fully understand and wasn't sure was wise, I added, "Stay here," and hurried after them. I'd told him to leave as well, only moments before, but the hint of desperation when he'd said he only wanted to study the citadel had unexpectedly struck a chord deep within me. A *scholar* who meant us no harm . . . who also happened to be an *expert on the Paladin* . . . and Mother was dragging him out of my life before I'd even realized I didn't actually want him to go.

Mother didn't even glance back, practically breaking into a run in her desperation to be rid of him as quickly as possible.

Who was this Halvor Roskery and why had he come in search of the citadel, when nearly all of Vamala had seemingly forgotten what the Paladin had done for them, and over the years had grown to fear them and the power they wielded? Fear, left to fester, turned to hatred, and according to Sami, that certainly was true when it came to the legends of the Paladin.

But not to Halvor. He'd been *more* than eager to come here. He believed Inara to be a full Paladin and rather than fear or loathing, I'd never seen such excitement on a person's face before.

For some unfathomable reason, the hedge had allowed him through; Mother had forced me to spend my life preparing for the day this very thing happened. And now she was making him leave?

Heat rose from the baked soil in unbearable waves, the dry earth stirred up into eddies of dust by their unrelenting charge toward the hedge and the gate still visible between the greenery. No matter the weather—drought or floods, heat or cold—the hedge never faltered, never wilted, never grew. The wall of greenery hid thorns as long and sharp as fangs that ran along every inch of the branches and vines beneath the lush leaves. Anyone intending to try and pass through it quickly learned of the threat beneath the beauty. An elegant, deadly prison warden.

The dark iron of the intricately wrought gate was a deep shadow cutting through the blinding glare of the unfaltering afternoon sun. Still visible—still accessible. Mother quickened her pace, and for the first time, I noticed Halvor resist her ever so slightly.

"Please, Madam, if you'll only allow me to explain—"

His voice carried over his shoulder, a whisper of words that I barely caught as I rushed to reach them before he was gone forever. But she jerked his arm forward, pulling harder than ever.

"Mother, wait!"

She flinched at the sound of my voice, but ignored me, doggedly pressing onward, almost at a run now, as if fearing the hedge would close over at any moment. I broke into a sprint—to do what, I wasn't sure. I only knew I had to stop her, had to stop *him*, before he was gone forever. She'd spent years forcing me to sew and prepare and plan for a wedding that I'd believed impossible; and now the first time a boy was allowed past the hedge, she was throwing him out because he'd dared speak of the Paladin, without even giving him a chance. Had it all been a lie, then? A clever ruse intended merely to keep me busy?

How did she intend to force him out, though, I wondered? If she had to drag him all the way to the gate, the hedge would surely block his exit, as it had never allowed her to leave. I could only hope that remained true and then the hedge I'd hated for so long would become my unwitting ally, buying me the time I suddenly wanted.

But they hadn't come close enough to be the cause when the hedge suddenly moved, rushing to close over the gate, hundreds of leafy, thorn-covered vines spreading across the dark iron like a stain, an otherworldly emerald blood blooming across the only view I'd ever had of the path leading to our home—and the older gentleman charging up it toward us.

"You there! What are you doing with my pupil?"

"Master Barloc! I'm sorry, I *had* to go ahead—"

The older man—Master Barloc—and Halvor spoke simultaneously, but it was too late. I'd no sooner made out the craggy features of the other man's face; the squint to his eyes, as if he'd spent too long reading books in low light; the gray-streaked hair he had tied back at the nape of his neck; his surprisingly wide shoulders underneath a dusty traveling cloak; when the hedge closed him out—and all of us back in.

Including Halvor Roskery.

FOUR

"*No!*"

If the hedge had been capable of fear, surely my mother's bellow of rage would have forced it to shudder and retreat. Instead, it resolutely stayed shut, blocking off Halvor's exit.

I stared at Mother's back, at her white-knuckled grip on Halvor's arm, and then the impenetrable wall of green beyond them. Had she gone too close to the gate—or was it because of the gentleman on the other side, refusing him entry?

"What have you done? What sorcery is this?" The older man—Master Barloc's—shout reverberated through our stunned silence; the hedge could block his body, but not his voice. "I demand the release of my pupil at once!"

"*We* did nothing. Your *pupil* is the one who trespassed."

Master Barloc, perhaps encouraged by the barrier, ignored Mother's unmistakable wrath and blustered, "He did no such thing. Halvor merely came to investigate what has long been told to be an *abandoned* property—"

"This is *our home*—"

"—and has unwittingly been taken hostage!"

"*Hostage?*" The word burbled out of my mother's throat as if she were choking on her own incredulity.

"I didn't see her do anything to control it," Halvor called out, though he sounded more than a little alarmed at the wall of green that had cut off his exit. "She seems as upset by it as you are!"

"What is going on?"

I spun to see Inara hesitantly moving toward us, her eyes wide and bright—too bright. We were going to lose her again at any moment.

"If this is truly your home, I demand you remove this—this *abomination* and let me in at once!"

"That is beyond my power, or I can assure you I would have sent your 'pupil' out to you first!" My mother spat back.

"Zuhra?" Inara's voice was small, my name a plea. I stretched my hand out to her and she hurried forward to take it. Her fear was a palpable thing; her fingers clenched over mine as her gaze darted toward Mother, Halvor, and the hedge that trapped him here—with us. With her.

"Then you leave me no choice." Master Barloc's ominous threat was followed by the sound of steel scraping against hardened leather. Was he carrying a sword? What kind of a scholar *was* he?

"Sir, I wouldn't—"

Mother was cut off by the sound of his sword hacking into the hedge, followed immediately by his yowl of pain. For, as I assumed she had been attempting to warn him, this was no ordinary hedge, and when attacked, it attacked back. Viciously.

"Witch!" Master Barloc screeched, the low thud of his sword falling to the earth a punctuation to his accusation. *"Paladin witch!"*

"I am *no such thing*," Mother hissed. If she'd been a snake, she would have been coiled as tightly as possible, ready to strike. I'd seen one once as a girl; curled up, tail quivering, making that unnerving rattling noise. Mother had been with me, luckily, and yanked me back before it could bite either of us. Louie the cat had appeared in the courtyard the very next day, as if the hedge had been aware of the danger I'd encountered, and I'd been given a very long lecture on the agonizing death that came from a snake bite. A death that it would seem my mother wished to inflict on Master Barloc now, if only she had the capability.

"She did nothing, Master," Halvor added again. I didn't miss the brief glance over his shoulder, toward where Inara and I stood. Did he think *Inara* was responsible?

"Some scholar you are, if you weren't even aware of the capabilities of this hedge," my mother scoffed. "Surely the stories of others' failed attempts to break through had to have reached you at some point on your pointless quest?"

Rather than responding, the older man merely howled, "What did you *do* to me?" from the other side of the hedge.

"*You* did this to yourself. Go to the village, they will help you." Mother finally released Halvor.

He rubbed at the spot on his arm where her fingers had dug into his flesh. "We heard rumors about a hedge as big as a wall. But we didn't know it was *dangerous*. Or capable of . . . ah, movement." Another furtive glance at Inara.

"It *burns*," Master Barloc moaned.

"Ask for Gina at the inn, she can help you. But you must hurry if you wish to stop the poison in time."

"It's *poisonous*?" Halvor had inched forward, as though he wished to assist his master somehow, but abruptly stopped, staring at the hedge with newfound fear, and instead took a step backward toward the citadel.

Inara's grip on my hand grew tighter and tighter throughout their exchange and she'd begun to shake her head and murmur. "It's . . . it's coming . . . no, *no*. Five. Four. Three . . . Three, two . . . no, *please* . . ."

I squeezed back, only half-aware of Master Barloc's continued threats, as my focus was pulled to my sister. "Fight it, Nara. Stay with me."

The whites of her eyes were visible all around her blue-fire irises.

"Stay with me," I whispered, even as she pulled her hand from mine and backed up.

"No . . . no, no, *no* . . ." Inara grabbed at her hair, her fists clenched against her temples.

"What's happening? Is she all right?" Halvor turned from the hedge to us, his gaze immediately drawn to Inara.

"Ssh," I murmured, ignoring his baffled questions as I gently touched her forearms, trying to keep her from hurting herself. "It's okay, Nara. It's all right."

But it wasn't all right.

Because when she finally let me pull her arms down, removing her hands from her hair and face, she was gone again.

And Halvor wasn't.

FIVE

The four of us stood in the courtyard, the massive hedge towering over us, staring at one another. Well, three of us were. Inara had retreated into herself, into the world of roaring and noise that stole her from me—from us—and was murmuring to herself, her burning gaze darting around, seeing, absorbing, but not *truly*. She'd tried to explain it to me more than once, in the winter when we had more time, how she *could* see and hear us, but how hard it was to focus, to make sense of what she saw, or what we said to her, over the cacophony in her head. The roar that consumed all her sense and made it practically impossible for her to function.

Halvor glanced at my sister. "Is she—"

"It's nearly sundown." Mother stepped forward, her hands clasped together at her waist. "You may spend the night in a guest suite, but tomorrow you must go."

"You're going to let him stay?" The words were out before I'd even realized I'd thought them. I quickly clamped my mouth shut at the sharp look Mother gave me.

"What choice do we have? He's trapped here, same as us."

"*Trapped?*" Halvor echoed. "What does she mean? I thought you said this was your home? Please, let me go to my Master—let me help him. If he's poisoned . . ."

"There's nothing we can do," Mother snapped.

Halvor flinched, but didn't argue.

"In the morning, perhaps things will be different." Mother

turned on her heel and strode back toward the citadel. Our home—our prison. "Come along, boy."

Halvor stood still for a moment, uncertain.

"You better go," I urged him, gently taking Inara's arm. She jerked at my touch, turning my direction, but her gaze went right through me. "I'll see you at supper."

He finally did as I bid, throwing one last glance over his shoulder at the gate that was still obscured by the hedge. Master Barloc's howls and whining had grown fainter by the minute, indicating he'd finally taken Mother's advice to seek help from Gina—a wise choice, as the thorns were indeed poisonous and depending on the amount of punctures and length of time given for it to spread, could even be fatal, as one unlucky villager had discovered years ago. I'd been too young to remember the details of what happened, but the shouts of the mob that gathered after the man's death outside the hedge still haunted my nightmares.

Only once Halvor had followed Mother through the door and disappeared into the citadel did I breathe slightly easier. Now to find a way to keep Inara occupied and away from Halvor until tomorrow. When Mother somehow intended to . . . what? Hope the hedge would change its mind and let him out?

The sun indeed had sunk below the green wall that was our living captor; shadows reached toward us with spectral fingers, stretching closer and closer as the light disappeared. I shook my head and gave Inara's arm a coaxing tug. "Let's go back to your garden. I think we'll have strawberries for dessert tonight."

I couldn't make sense of her garbled response, but she let me pull her forward, so I pretended she understood me. We headed to her garden, while I tried to put the idea of Halvor Roskery staying at the citadel out of my mind for as long as possible.

That evening I walked into the dining salon, hardly able to believe the change. How had Mother managed to pull this off? We always took every meal in the "morning" room where we usually spent all of our time, leaving the much larger room closed and draped. One never would have realized that looking at it now.

Candlelight glowed from elaborate candelabras on every surface, including the massive table that dominated the center of the room, stretching from one end all the way to the other. It could easily have sat a party of fifty guests, perhaps even more. I'd never taken the time to count the chairs. This room, like so many others, had been off-limits. And while I made the effort to sneak into the library whenever I could, to slip a book or two beneath my skirts, spiriting them away to hide beneath my bed until I dared to read them, this one had held no allure to me. There was such an air of sadness to rooms like this one; those meant to host laughter and music, tables heavy with food and drink, and instead left desolate, dusty, and forgotten. Abandoned.

Just like we had been.

But now, the cloths riddled with moth holes covering all the furniture had disappeared, and the wooden surfaces gleamed in the flickering candlelight. I glanced at the one nearest me, almost fancying I would be able to see my own reflection in the dark wood.

"Zuhra, at last." My mother's voice carried through the dining salon with a bit of an echo, emphasizing the size—and emptiness—of the room. "Please join us. Mahsami has been waiting to serve us until you arrived."

I ignored the barb in her words and forced my legs to carry me forward to where she sat at the head of the table. By all accounts, Mother should have been dwarfed by the table and the rows of empty chairs running along either side of it, like sad, diminished sentinels standing at attention to a day long gone. But instead, she looked like a queen, reigning over her kingdom, however small it might be. Especially in the dress she'd chosen to wear. It was made of a rich purple brocade accentuated with flounces of white lace, which had somehow been kept from yellowing.

I didn't think I'd ever seen it before, but then with a suddenness that made me halt, a flash of memory rose unbidden. Little more than a glimpse; of Mother standing in the courtyard, a smaller version of the hedge behind her, wearing that dress, her dark hair long and free, blowing in a breeze, her arms stretched out toward me, and smiling. A *true* smile, beautiful and warm.

And the man beside her—tall, broad, with hair like sun-drenched wheat, and his *eyes*—

"*Zuhra.*"

I blinked and realized both Mother and Halvor were staring at me.

My father. Seeing Mother in that dress had given me a memory not only of her, but of Adelric—whose face I had lost until now. The Paladin who had the same glowing blue eyes as Inara.

The chair scraped against the stone floor when I pulled it back, echoed by Halvor's as he stood when I reached the table. He gave me a slight bow while I quickly took my seat. I flushed, unused to not only the presence of a boy, but also having him bow to me, as if I were someone of importance—someone worthy of deference.

But I didn't miss the way his gaze flashed past me to the door then back again before he sat down once more, a trace of disappointment crossing his face.

Mother nodded with a flick of her wrist and Mahsami materialized as if summoned from the darkness itself beyond the reach of the candlelight, pushing a cart heavy with serving dishes. I couldn't begin to fathom what she had scrounged up to put together such a feast. Certainly not our usual thin soup, accompanied by whatever vegetables Inara had managed to grow for us.

"Your dinner, Madam."

Madam?

She might have noticed my look of incredulity, but her gaze was respectfully—and abnormally—lowered to the serving platters she quickly set out on the table. I shifted uncomfortably.

First came a plate of roasted potatoes drizzled with a fragrant sauce, followed by a dish of salted pork (Sami had been practically gleeful when the hedge allowed a pig through a month earlier), a tureen of vegetable stew, a slab of fresh, crusty bread that still steamed—the delicious scent wafting toward me, making my stomach growl in response—and finally a pitcher of fresh water from the well.

I stared at the largesse with wide eyes. Mahsami must have emptied the larder to prepare a meal this size. What would we eat after this night's waste? For there was no possible way we could consume everything she'd prepared and put before us. She'd used a week's worth of food on this one dinner.

"That will be all. Thank you." Mother nodded imperiously at Mahsami, who curtsied in response and backed away, taking the now empty cart with her. One wheel squeaked, the only sound in the entire salon.

Mother had been desperate to make Halvor leave only a few hours ago but now she seemed to be doing everything in her power to present him with the appearance of a life in the citadel that didn't truly exist. The life of a noblewoman.

"Shall we say a blessing over this food?"

Mother clasped her hands and bowed her head without waiting for a response.

Attempting to mask my disbelief, I followed suit. Apparently she was a *pious* noblewoman. An interesting turn for someone who had often told me she couldn't believe in a god that would allow her to be trapped here.

"Oh, Gracious God, we give thanks for the food we are about to eat. And also for our unexpected but welcome guest. May he be blessed in his endeavors and for the duration of his stay."

I couldn't help but open my eyes at that even more surprising sentiment. When I lifted my gaze Halvor was also looking up, his forehead creased. *What? You didn't think yourself a welcome guest after she tried to physically drag you away from here?* I had to smother a sudden urge to giggle as I quickly bowed my head again.

"We pray for thy blessings. Amen."

"Amen," we echoed simultaneously. When I looked up, I caught Halvor watching me, but he quickly glanced away, toward the food.

"So, Mr. Roskery, where do you call home?" The clang of the silver serving spoons against the china Sami usually only used for birthdays was a tinkling counterpoint to Mother's pointed question.

"Please, call me Halvor." He reached for a piece of bread. "Originally, I was from Segara. But Master Barloc and I traveled here from the Libraries of Mercarum."

"All the way from Mercarum, *Mr.* Roskery? That is quite a distance, indeed."

I took a bite of my food, but barely tasted it. My attention was wholly riveted on the boy across from me.

"What could have possibly induced you to leave such a grand city for this dismal place?"

Halvor paused with a spoon of stew partway to his mouth. "Are you familiar with Mercarum, Madam?"

"Both cities, actually. But we are not discussing me," Mother pushed, ignoring my noise of surprise. She'd never told me where she lived before Gateskeep and the citadel, and Sami didn't know. Only that they'd traveled quite a distance, mostly at night, to get to the citadel. "What has brought you from the warm, bustling coast to our rain-soaked mountains?"

"It hasn't rained yet . . ."

"A rarity, I assure you." Mother's friendly tone turned cool, her attempt at polite conversation barbed heavily with intent. If Halvor didn't respond to her directly soon, I was afraid he would be witness to her wrath. A prospect that could possibly induce him to take his chances with the poisonous hedge.

"Lucky for us, then." He finally took the bite of stew and after chewing and swallowing, the sound of it easily audible as we both waited for his response, he said, "I have been an apprentice to Master Barloc for three years. In truth, he's also my uncle. After my parents died, I was sent to live with him. He's dedicated his life to studying the Paladin, often at great cost to his professional advancement among his peers. His dream has always been to travel to the Citadel of the Paladin—and when I came of age and received my inheritance, I agreed to help fund his expedition."

"An inheritance?" Mother's pointed look at me was hard to miss, and I flushed. "Hopefully you didn't spend it all on such a foolish journey."

"I hardly think it foolish—we're here, aren't we? I'm *in* the Citadel of the Paladin, *eating dinner* where the Paladin ate, no less. I believe my monies have been well spent."

"It's gone then." Mother's hopeful expression turned dour.

"I didn't say *that*." For the first time, Halvor's words were almost as frosty as hers.

I shifted uneasily on my seat. I had very little experience with polite society, but even *I* knew her frank discussion of his finances was not appropriate. "Why was studying the Paladin costly to Master Barloc's professional career?" It was the first question I could come up with, and once it was out, I could only hope it was at least slightly less impertinent than my mother's.

The relief that washed over Halvor's face warmed my belly in a way that the stew and crusty bread I'd managed to eat hadn't accomplished. "Well, between the fear and mistrust, and the former king's edict to—"

"It's a complicated matter." Mother's eyes sliced toward me, a clear warning to drop this subject.

But for the first time in my life *someone* was willing to answer my questions—someone who had studied the Paladin for years. Bravery burned hot and heady beneath my skin, pushing out the cold clutches of fear, regardless of the consequences that were sure to come. I turned back to Halvor. "What edict?"

Halvor's eyebrows lifted. "You don't know what I'm referring to? But you live . . . *here*."

"This is not really a relevant—"

"There are many things of which I am probably unaware . . . even living here." I was the one to speak over Mother this time, chafing acutely from my lack of knowledge. The intensity of her answering glare was a physical thing; I could *feel* the anger emanating from the head of the table. It was like standing too close to a fire, the side of my body nearest her growing increasingly hot.

"You've truly never heard of the Treason and Death Decree from King Velfron?"

"A *death* decree?" I was too shocked to be embarrassed by the incredulity in his tone. "Who was he putting to death?"

"The Paladin. And anyone who supported them."

"*What?* But the Paladin saved—"

"That is enough," Mother cut in. Halvor didn't seem to hear her—or chose to ignore her.

"The former king charged the Paladin with attempting to over-throw the kingdom and rule over us with their superior abilities, and had as many as he could find—"

"I said *that's enough*," she repeated, her voice almost a shout.

Halvor's mouth snapped shut, leaving me shocked and confused.

Overthrowing the kingdom? A death decree? "I . . . I didn't real-ize . . . I didn't know . . ." My response was faint as I thought of my sister. What would the people of Vamala do to her if they could reach her, if their hatred had truly grown so strong—if there was a *death* decree? "But why would he do that? Why would anyone believe them to be the enemy? If their wish was to rule over us, why didn't they stay?" The Paladin had saved all of Vamala from the rakasa . . . hadn't they?

Halvor leaned forward. "You truly don't know any of this?"

I shook my head; Halvor's honey-brown eyes, the color of gin-gerbread, were unwavering on mine from across the table. The candlelight danced over his tanned face, sunburnt cheeks, and wavy hair. Something inside me danced too, but I wasn't sure if it was from getting answers *at last,* or the feeling of sitting across from a boy—almost a man—and having his focus trained entirely on *me.* It was simultaneously terrifying and exhilarating.

"I would be happy to tell you of what I know—what Master Barloc's studies have uncovered."

"I think that is quite enough of that topic for one night," Mother trilled, with a sudden wave of her hand. A strange, high-pitched noise followed her words; it took me a moment to realize it was an attempt at a laugh.

I turned to her. She would refuse to let him speak, and still truly think there was a chance of forcing this boy to marry me? For surely that's what all of this was—the candlelight, the dining sa-lon, the unnecessarily lavish supper, the use of the best china . . . it was an attempt to . . . what? Bewitch him so that he might pro-pose this very night and whisk me away in the morning, partially completed dowry and all?

"I, ah . . . I'm not entirely sure that is an appropriate discussion to have with a young lady," she continued. "The fact is that they are all gone, and there's no need to worry her about the specifics." Mother kept her gaze focused on her plate, where she methodically cut her roasted potatoes into halves, then halves again and again, until the pieces were so small she had to scoop them up with her spoon to eat them as if they were peas.

"We *thought* they were all gone, until today," Halvor pointed out with a meaningful glance toward the door, where, perhaps, he still hoped to see Inara come through.

"She is not what you think," Mother bit out.

My heart clenched beneath my rib cage. What would happen if the hedge *did* let him leave in the morning—if he spread word of not just humans, but a *Paladin* living in the citadel?

"And this is not an appropriate conversation to have with my daughter."

"Respectfully, I must disagree. I find that the female mind is perfectly capable of as much learning and lively discussion as the male's."

"Of course it is," Mother retorted sharply, while I nearly choked on my bite of vegetable stew I'd forced myself to take in an attempt to hide my fear, "but that doesn't make it appropriate for a young lady to converse about scandalous histories and theories that have little or nothing to do with her present or future life."

"Little or nothing?" Halvor echoed incredulously. I could practically *feel* the words he managed to swallow, even as his gaze traveled around the room as if to say, *You do realize you* live in their citadel, *right?*

"How old *are* you?" Mother set down her silverware, her attention now fully focused on him.

"Excuse me?"

"You said you received your inheritance when you came of age. Does that mean you are eighteen? Or did it take some time to put your 'expedition' together?"

"I don't see how that—"

"Zuhra just reached her maturity, a month ago. Despite our—*secluded*—existence here, she is well prepared to be mistress of her own home. I have seen to it personally."

"I am sure she—"

"Zuhra can play the pianoforte, she can sew and darn *and* do needlepoint. Her stitches are superb. She can read and write, making her a valuable asset to any young lord."

"Mother." I turned pleadingly toward her. My blood dredged through my veins, thick with the protests that I didn't dare voice.

"It is unfortunate that you . . ." She trailed off with a shake of her head. "Well, there's nothing to be done for it." And she suddenly stood, pushing her chair back, though we'd barely eaten a quarter of what Mahsami had brought out for us. "Your room is prepared for you. I will show the way."

Halvor stared at her for a beat, then hastily stood. He looked both bewildered and irritated as he sketched her a bow and then turned to me. It was Mother's special gift: to inspire multiple—often conflicting—emotions in a person at once.

I forced myself to rise to my feet and dropped into a curtsy, hoping Halvor could read the apology in my eyes. *She does not speak for me,* I shouted to him within the confines of my mind. *I am not her and her beliefs are not mine!*

But if he understood my silent messages, he gave no indication as he stiffly bowed without meeting my gaze and then followed after Mother, who had already turned for the door, the click of her heels on the stone floor the only sound in the cavernous room.

SIX

"What will we do with all of this?" I stared at the platters of food in dismay.

"I will store what I can in the larder, and the rest . . ." Sami sighed.

"Perhaps you could take it to a family in Gateskeep?" I didn't look up from the dishes I was drying when I made the suggestion.

Sami clucked disapprovingly. "The hedge would never let me out for something such as that. If we were in *need* of food, that is another matter. But to distribute excess? Not likely."

"How could it possibly know? Why does it *do* this to us? To *them*?"

"It's Paladin magic, love. There's no use worrying your head about it. 'Twill only make you madder than a rabbit in a thistle patch."

I'd only seen a rabbit a few times in my life. The hedge sometimes allowed animals through; when the first rabbit showed up, it was during a particularly terrible snowstorm when Inara had been sick, confined to her bed with a fever, and our supply of winter vegetables—only capable of being grown by her hand, through her power—had fallen alarmingly low. I'd been the first to notice the creature, hopping across the snowdrifts. I'd read about pets in my fairy-tale book and had foolishly asked to keep the rabbit as one. But Sami had quickly seized the chance to keep us alive, and instead made us rabbit stew. It was hard to imagine the poor creature being mad, when all I could summon was a memory of its big brown eyes . . . and then watching in fascinated horror as Sami skinned it later that night. The stew *was* good, though different—we rarely had meat. So though I didn't quite understand her warning, the intent was clear.

It was my turn to sigh, as I plunged my hands back into the sudsy water to retrieve another plate and wipe it clean. The kitchen was as warm and bright as always. The large fire where Mahsami boiled our water and cooked our food popped and hissed behind us, enthusiastically devouring the wood she'd fed it. The room was fragrant with the yeasty scent of dough, the sharp, wild tang of herbs, and even the lingering aroma of the bread, stew, and potatoes we'd had for supper. Sami stood next to me, working side by side to clean up the mess, as we always did. It was peaceful and comfortingly familiar.

I could almost pretend nothing had changed.

Almost.

"Sami," I began, my hands going still on the china dinner plate I held, "Halvor said something at dinner . . . about a . . . a *death* decree. He said the king thought the Paladin were trying to overthrow the kingdom."

She stiffened slightly next to me, but merely said, "Did he now?"

"I know you said many have come to fear them and the power they wielded, hoping they don't return. But why would anyone think they were trying to rule us—when they willingly left?" I forced myself to keep drying the plate, to set it gently on top of its gleaming sisters on the counter. "Why would he say that the king wanted to . . . to *kill* them?"

"I suspect because it's true."

I nearly dropped the knife I'd picked up to wash.

"Zuhra." Sami turned, waiting for me to stop and face her. When I did, her gray eyes were soft and sad in the firelight. "Your mother . . . she doesn't want us to discuss these things."

"You think I don't know that?" She flinched at the bitterness I couldn't conceal. "What *does* she want? She claims to wish me married, but the first chance I have of making a connection—no matter how remote it might be—she tries to throw him out and then humiliates me in front of him. And what if he *had* shown even a modicum of interest in me? What if I had somehow convinced him to propose and the hedge had miraculously let me pass? Mother would send me to his world unprepared—naïve and uninformed of even the most basic beliefs of the people I was to go live among? Ignorant of my own heritage—of my own *father*? Of the fact that even if we *could* leave here, we never *should* because Inara would be *killed* for what she is?"

Sami took both my hands in hers, a gesture she hadn't done since I was in knee skirts and braids. "Zuhra, your mother loves you." I nearly snorted at that, but Sami continued undeterred. "She has a hard time knowing how to show it. She's suffered in her life— she has experienced pain and loss that you can't fathom."

"Because she won't talk about it—she won't tell me!"

"Because she doesn't want to relive it," Sami admonished. "You were too young to remember, but she *was happy*. When she came here . . . with *him* . . . she was a different person back then. But even then, their life was never easy."

The flash of memory I'd had tonight at supper, of her in the meadow, hair down, a smile unlike I'd ever seen lighting her face, rose up once more. It stung, a prick of pain that burrowed into the buried bruises of my heart, to realize Sami was right. Mother *had* been a different person then, with him. And we—Inara and I— hadn't been enough. He'd broken her when he left us here, and we'd never been sufficient to put her back together.

"I remember the hedge was smaller before that night—that it grew when he left," I spoke quietly to our clasped hands. "Did he do it? Did he trap us here?"

Sami was silent a long time. I didn't dare look up.

"I don't know. But . . . I'm not sure what other explanation there could be."

A cold heaviness settled into my belly, upsetting the little bit I'd eaten at the disastrous dinner.

Sami squeezed my hands. "Your mother's choices have pushed you into a life that has given you very little choice or freedom. You've been locked out of too many doors. Perhaps this Halvor Roskery coming here is a window finally opening for you." Sami squeezed my hands once more then released me. "Here, love. Why don't you take this plate to Inara? She hasn't had supper yet. I helped her up to her room just before you came."

I took the proffered tray in one hand, a lit lantern in the other, and turned for the arched doorway to exit the kitchen.

"Oh, and Zuhra," Sami called out to me just before I walked underneath the stone archway that was etched in the language of the Paladin—swirls and lines that were as familiar to me as the wrinkles on Sami's face, but completely incomprehensible in their meaning. She hurried over to put a mug of fresh water on the tray. "I already took your mother her nightly tea. I think she will probably sleep quite well tonight."

I looked up sharply, eyebrows lifted. Sami's gray eyes were trained on mine, speaking words that her lips didn't.

"I don't know why the boy was let through, but I do know there must be a reason. And if he's worth anything, he'll look past your mother and really *see* you. Perhaps this may be your chance at finding happiness of your own. May he only be so lucky."

I blinked, a hope too painful to acknowledge rising in my chest. She reached up to cup my cheek briefly, the look on her face far more maternal than any I'd seen on my own mother's, and then stepped back.

"Hurry along now, before her food gets any colder."

I nodded and then turned and left Sami and the kitchen behind, her words echoing through my body, creating a want so intense, a desire for happiness—*true* happiness—that was so powerful it made my bones ache.

The door clicked shut softly behind me as I exited Inara's room, after making sure she ate at least some of her supper and then helped her into bed. I didn't *have* to help her anymore, not like when we were younger. But it still gave me comfort to tuck the covers around her shoulders, to see her in bed, before we shut the door and locked it for the night, knowing she was safe in her room. I hated having to lock her in, but it was better than lying awake for hours, worrying that she might be wandering the citadel and get hurt—or worse. She'd wandered into the kitchen once when she was four, during the night. The crash of pots and pans had woken Sami, who was closest to the kitchen. Luckily, she hadn't been hurt, but the fear of what *could* have happened forced us to make the heartbreaking decision to turn that key every night. As much as I hated doing it, I couldn't stop the worry any more than I could stop the Paladin power from holding her captive in her own body.

I stood outside her room, the circle of light from my lantern the only illumination in the dark hallway, my thoughts a jumble. Sami's cryptic hints could only mean she'd added a sleeping draught to Mother's nightly tea—her way of giving me the freedom to seize this chance with Halvor. To . . . what, exactly?

My gaze caught on the tapestry that hung across from Inara's bedroom door, depicting a scene of an entire battalion of Paladin soaring on their gryphons, toward a human village besieged by a herd of Chimera, one of the most fearsome rakasa that existed.

I'd always believed the Paladin had saved us, had made our world safe from the monsters that had once roamed across Vamala, bringing death and suffering in their wake—and were now eradicated, thanks to them. That was one of the few things Mother had told us, and the books I'd managed to sneak from the library about them written in our language seemed to corroborate her claim.

But then why didn't the rest of Vamala think so too?

You haven't heard of the Treason and Death Decree?

Had I been irrational to believe that even though my father had left us, trapping us within the hedge as his parting gift, that the rest of the Paladin were heroes—that their power had rescued the humans from destruction? The only two instances I'd seen of it in my life—the hedge and Inara—had given me no reason to believe them to be *good,* but I'd also never had a reason to second-guess what I assumed to be true. Until tonight. As much as Mother hated Adelric for leaving us, she'd never spoken negatively about the Paladin as a whole. Surely she would have been the first to proclaim their villainy if it were true. If a death decree had been warranted.

My breath came faster as I squinted into the darkness, straining to listen for any indication that Mother was awake. But as

Mahsami had promised, everything was silent, completely still and dark.

I didn't know what the morning would hold—if the hedge would open and let Halvor escape our prison, or if he would remain trapped with us. But I did know one thing: he was here now.

And he'd spent years studying the Paladin.

Though Mother would have claimed it indecent, I removed the slippers from my feet so that I only wore stockings, stowed them behind a large vase that stood in the alcove between my room and Inara's, and lowered the light on my lantern until it barely emitted a glow. I hurried on silent feet away from our rooms in the east quarters that overlooked the hedge and the mountains beyond, to the west wing rooms that pressed up against the sheer cliffs that continued to rise above the citadel. They'd been unused my entire life. I'd snuck into that wing a few times, when the sun was shining brightly enough through the interspersed windows to chase away a bit of the gloom of so many shut doors and abandoned rooms. I remembered opening those doors, catching glimpses of enormous beds and tall, proud dressers through swirling eddies of dust, stirred up by my unexpected arrival. But there had been an eerie sense of intrusion, like I was barging in on a scene I wasn't intended to see, and with a shiver, I'd shut the doors, leaving the rooms unexplored. Leaving them to await the masters that would never return. Earlier that night in the kitchen, Sami had confessed that Mother put Halvor there for the night—as far away from our rooms as possible. I could only imagine the state it must have been in and had to suppress a shudder at the thought of rodents, spiders, or worse nesting in the most likely ruined bedding and furniture.

Poor Halvor Roskery.

Thankful the dress I'd worn was dark, I slipped from shadow to shadow in the familiar corridors of our section of the citadel, toward the unused wings where I was forbidden to go. But despite not knowing this part of my home very well, I didn't dare increase the light of the lantern.

Sami hadn't known exactly which room he was in, only that it was in the west wing. Creeping forward, I strained to see any flicker of light beneath a door or for a hint of sound from any of the rooms. There was nothing except dust and silence.

And then I heard a creak. I froze, tilting my head to the side, trying to ascertain exactly where it had come from.

The doorknob had already begun to turn when I spotted the faint glow just ahead to my left. Inhaling a squeak of alarm, I simultaneously shuttered my lantern and flattened myself against the wall next to a tapestry, with a silent prayer that it was too dark for him to spot me.

Firelight flooded the hallway when the door opened, but was quickly doused again as Halvor hurried to shut it. I stood immobile, breath held. He looked left first, away from me, then right, his gaze sweeping past where I pressed against the wall. I nearly sighed in relief, but then he paused.

"Who's there?" Halvor lifted his left hand, gripping something that looked unsettlingly like a dagger, and stepped forward— directly toward me.

SEVEN

My lungs burned with the need for oxygen, but I didn't dare breathe, let alone move.

Halvor moved closer. "Reveal yourself or suffer the consequences!"

Left with no choice but to do as he said or possibly get stabbed, I threw the shade open on my lantern and stepped forward, lifting the sudden burst of light into his face. "Where are *you* going?" I demanded, inserting every ounce of bravery I didn't actually possess into my words.

Halvor blanched and hastily lowered the knife. Then he squinted. "It's *you*?"

"My name is Zuhra."

"I remember, I just—"

"And you'd best thank all the stars in heaven that it *is* me, and not my mother."

"Yes, of course, I—"

"She would have—I don't even know *what* she would have done if she'd caught you sneaking around, holding a dagger, trying to . . . um . . . what exactly *are* you doing?"

Halvor waited a moment this time before responding, and I flushed. Not that he could tell in the meager glow of the lantern. I hoped.

"I've dedicated three years of my life to studying the Paladin, and my Master much longer than that," he finally responded when

I didn't cut him off again. "If I truly am to be sent away in the morning, you couldn't expect me to waste my one night in their citadel *sleeping*?"

The note of desperation in his voice struck a responding chord deep within me. The darkness surrounding us was heavier now that he stood in it with me; somehow his presence made the lack of light that much more real—that much more dangerous. I was alone, in the forbidden section of the citadel, with a young man I didn't know, *talking* to him as if I did this all the time. I, who had only vague, dreamlike memories of the only man I'd ever known.

But I, too, was desperate. And I had come to find him for a reason.

"Mother might *try* to send you away, but it's not really up to her." I shuttered the lantern once more, until it barely emitted the faintest trickle of light. "Still, you have a point. If tonight is all we have, then let's not waste it."

His eyes widened and my neck heated as I realized too late how my words would sound. I didn't know much about the physical relationship between a man and a woman, but Mother had taken the time to explain the basics to me. And somehow I instinctually guessed his mind had gone *there*, because I was pretty sure that act was something couples engaged in at night.

"To learn about the Paladin," I rushed to add, flustered. *You're doing this all wrong!* "I was going to take you to the library."

"Really?" Halvor's entire face changed, lighting up with such anticipation that I could *feel* it radiating from him. "There's an entire *library*?"

The relief from his response was like having a weight you didn't even know was resting on your chest lifted; I could suddenly breathe deeper, my blood felt somehow lighter in my body. Maybe I wasn't quite as terrible at conversing with a strange boy in the dark as I'd first believed. "Yes, but we have to be quiet. Do exactly as I do, and if you hear someone coming . . . well, let's just hope that doesn't happen." I turned and beckoned him. "Follow me."

He didn't question my warning, though his eyebrows lifted as he fell into step behind me. I hurried back the way I'd come, my stockings stained brown from the dust when I glanced down at my feet. The air grew charged as we moved silently and swiftly through the citadel, as if it were coming alive somehow—unfurling from a slumber that my mother had placed it under with a lifetime of rules and restrictions that I was breaking.

I'd never dared spend more than a minute or two in the library, fearing her reprisal if she caught me. Most of the books were written in Paladin anyway and the few in my language I'd managed to sneak out had rarely been helpful, other than the one about the different kinds of rakasa—the monsters that the Paladin had fought and driven back into their world, saving ours. But the idea had come to me and I'd seized it. Surely a scholar could be plied to share what he knew with endless shelves of books—even if they were in a foreign language.

At the bottom of the stairs I paused, head cocked, before creeping the opposite direction from the dining salon, kitchen, and morning room. We passed the grand ballroom that was still draped and unused beyond massive double doors; they were heavy enough that I hadn't been able to push them open until I was nearly thirteen.

Our destination was the southernmost wing of the citadel where *all* of the rooms that fascinated me most—and were the highest on my mother's absolutely forbidden list—resided. The room with the massive circular table and chairs of varying sizes and shapes. The room with yellowed maps tacked on the walls, their edges curling like a witch's nails, and rows of desks with dozens of locked drawers. The library full of shelves, heavy with books coated in dust and grime, parchments that hadn't been moved in over a decade, and brocade drapes that were pockmarked with moth holes. And finally the mystery room that comprised the farthest corner of the citadel.

The citadel had been constructed all the way at the very edge of the cliff it sat on, so that the southern wall hovered directly above the steep drop-off and the waterfall that crashed to the valley floor far, far below, as if the mountain had been spliced, part of it ripped away and destroyed. The doors to the hall were even heavier than those to the ballroom. I'd tried to open them many times with no luck. Until last year, when I'd finally managed to get one to *start* moving, and discovered the doors were not only heavy, they were also *loud,* scraping and groaning open, like a great beast waking. Loud enough to alert my mother to what I'd done. I only caught a brief glimpse of soaring ceilings and a wall made of windows through the crack I'd managed to create before the sound of boots clacking against the stone hallway preceded Mother's shout: *Don't open those—whatever you do, leave those doors shut!* I'd expected her fury, but that came later; first, there was only her sheet-white face drained of blood and her winter wind–chilled hands grabbing mine, yanking them from the door handle, and the bone-deep groan of effort it took for her to push it back, throwing her entire body against the thick wood until the narrow band of discovery I'd managed to procure shut off again with a resounding *thunk.* She was silent the entire awful march to my room, and only once *that* door was safely shut behind us did the color return to her cheeks, simultaneous with her wrath spewing from her mouth in the form of nearly unintelligible screaming, while I cowered on my bed. I was locked in my room and given only one meal a day for four days to prove her point of how *dangerous,* how *wrong* I'd been to try and open that door. Worse than the lack of food was the separation from Inara. I'd been forced to watch her work in her garden from my window, my cheeks damp and my heart hot with anger, with my own fury. But her methods, though harsh, were effective. I'd only dared return to the mysterious doors once, during a thunderstorm at night, when she was asleep and I could mask the echoing groan of their movement with the rumble of thunder.

But instead of trying to pry them open once more, I'd only stood there in the dark, my hand splayed on the door. The storm had been so close I'd felt the thunder rumbling through the wood beneath my fingers. Stronger than my curiosity was the memory of watching Inara from my room, unable to speak to her, to explain why I had suddenly disappeared. Eventually, I'd returned to my room, defeated by my mother even in her sleep.

With every door we passed as we hurried toward the southern wing, Halvor's curiosity grew stronger, until it hummed through the space between us, a thread of energy that made my own heart ache with all that I didn't know, all that I *wished* to know. My need for that knowledge was my only claim to fire; not visible in my eyes like Inara's, the flame of my desperation was known to no one but me. But, oh—how it *burned,* turning my blood hot as we finally reached the library and I stopped.

Halvor wasn't looking at the entrance to the library, though; his gaze was fixed on the double doors at the end of long corridor— or more specifically, the plaque *above* the doors.

"Hall of Miracles . . ." he muttered, so low I barely caught the words, but they turned the fire in my veins to an inferno.

"You can read that?" I hadn't even realized I'd grabbed his arm until he startled. He looked down at my fingers clutched around his wrist and I immediately released him.

He whispered back, "Of course . . . can't you?"

I shook my head.

Halvor seemed about to say more when the citadel groaned around us. His mouth snapped shut as he glanced up in alarm. The noises the slumbering beast made at night—when the wind pushed at its stone walls and scraped at the glass windows, making it rattle and moan—were still unnerving for *me,* and I'd lived there my whole life. Halvor paled, the bump in his throat moving when he swallowed.

Motioning for silence, I handed him the lantern. I quickly worked to open the door, then ushered him into the library before following and closing it behind us.

Whatever fear he may have felt moments earlier must have fled in the presence of the grandeur before him. When I faced him, his mouth was hanging slightly open, his hands slack at his side, barely managing to keep hold of the lantern that had slipped dangerously low on his fingertips. I snagged it moments before it would have fallen to the ground, possibly shattering and setting the room ablaze.

"Oh." He shook himself as if coming up from a dream. "I apologize, it's only . . . this *place* . . ."

"I know," I agreed, because truly, I did.

Moonlight filtered in through the two-story-high windows that flanked shelves even taller than Halvor, illuminating the hundreds of books that stood like small sentinels in rows upon rows upon rows all round us, guardians of knowledge—right there, *so close*—and yet impossibly distant because I couldn't read most of them.

But Halvor—perhaps *he* could. Somehow he had read the plaque.

"How did you know what it said?"

Halvor glanced over his shoulder as if his vision could pierce through the door now separating us from the unfamiliar markings that I had spent hours staring at above the other, larger doors.

"I told you my Master and I studied the Paladin . . . that included learning their language. At least, to the best of our ability with our limited resources."

"*You* can read *their* language?" I breathed.

Halvor's brow creased. "Can you not?"

I looked down at the lantern I clutched. "No." That one word contained a world of shame and desperation. Another mark against me in his book.

"Zuhra, I have to be honest with you. I don't understand *anything* that has happened today. I keep trying to figure what all of this means"—he lifted his arms in a circle, encompassing the library, the citadel beyond, most likely even me and my family in their rooms far away—"but every time I think I've started to put a few pieces together, they change on me and I find myself more confused than before."

I was silent.

"What *is* this?" he pressed. "Why do you live here—and how do you control the hedge? Is it Inara? Does she choose who stays or who goes? How can she be your sister when she is a Paladin—when she even has an accent—and you . . . do not?" I flushed, but he continued before I could respond. "Why can't you read their language when you live in their home? Why am I here and Master Barloc out there somewhere, suffering . . . perhaps even . . ."

"I'm certain he survived," I assured him when he trailed off.

Halvor half choked on a noise that resembled a laugh but that lacked all humor. "You're 'certain he survived,'" he repeated when I stared at him, bewildered. "Do you not understand the absurdity of such a statement? We're *scholars*, not explorers or . . . or . . .

warriors or some nonsense like that. There was never supposed to be a question of *survival*!"

As he spoke, his words grew not only in pitch, but also in volume.

"Ssh." I pressed my finger to my lips and waved him away from the door. Though Sami had assured me Mother would sleep soundly through the night, part of me still feared the creak of her footsteps outside the shut door. It was difficult to believe a woman as indomitable as she could be susceptible to something so mundane as a sleeping draught slipped into her nightly tea.

Halvor sighed, but followed me deeper into the room, toward the windows that overlooked the last of Inara's gardens and the hedge beyond. From this vantage point, we could see where it ended—abutting the southern edge of the citadel that jutted out above the cliffside.

The Paladin had built the edifice so that the south wall was flush with the edge of the cliff it sat upon. I thought of the glimpse I'd had of the "Hall of Miracles"—if Halvor had read the plaque correctly—through that cracked door last year. I'd also seen it depicted in a large painting in the hallway near the morning room, but the scene was from the outside, as if the painter had been a bird, hovering above the cliff, looking in through the two-story windows—or a Paladin riding a gryphon. I'd often stood in that hallway, imagining I stood *inside* the painting, behind those windows, staring down at the abyss directly below me, my head swimming with fear and a sudden surge of adrenaline. It had been exhilarating and horrifying to imagine; all too easy to picture the pane of glass shattering beneath my hands and falling, falling, *falling* to smash on the rocks at the bottom of the waterfall that were obscured by mist in the painting. But here, in the library, if the hedge hadn't been there, rather than the terrifying drop-off, we would have been able to see the trail winding down the mountainside to the valley below and Gateskeep nestled there at the base of the mountain.

We both looked silently out at the grounds for several long moments, washed milk-white by the moon, and when I finally spoke it was to our reflections in the window.

"My father was a Paladin. And I didn't realize . . . I didn't know how *dangerous* it must have been for them . . . But my mother . . . she really did love Adelric. I *know* she did—she loved him fiercely." Once the words began, I couldn't stop them; the secrets and memories flowing out of me faster and faster with each one shared. Yet another dam inside me broke, torn down by the upheaval of Halvor Roskery showing up in our garden—and my life. "She loved him enough to marry him, to leave her family, and follow him here. We were both born here. But the night Inara . . . the night my mother began to labor . . . he left us. He disappeared when Mother needed him most.

"And then Inara was born with her burning eyes, and that hedge trapped us here, and my mother *hates* him now—hates *all* the Paladin and anything to do with them. I'm forbidden to come here, to come in any of these rooms. But all I want is to *understand*. I want to know who they were—what that makes *me*. What it makes Inara. I want to know . . . I . . . I . . ." And suddenly I was sobbing, choking and empty, and all my secrets and my loneliness and my hopelessness strangled me, frost-coated fingers of desperation clenching tighter and tighter, squeezing the air from my lungs until I was gasping. And Halvor—poor, unsuspecting Halvor—he stared at me, bewildered. This was not what he'd expected when I'd offered to bring him to the library. He'd expected books, answers, knowledge.

I needed to stop—*had* to stop—before I frightened him irreparably. But I couldn't breathe—couldn't see through the tears that I'd held in for months, *years*—

"Zuhra." His voice was quiet, a low note to the noise of my despair. "It's all right." I barely even realized he'd moved toward me until his arms hesitantly came round my body. I stiffened immediately, my sobs shocked into stillness. He froze—but didn't let go.

A hug. He was *hugging* me.

I started crying again, but this time it was the soft rain after the violence of a lightning storm, a gentle washing away of the tumult that had seized me before. Slowly, gradually, I let myself breathe, let myself relax into the comfort of *touch*—of arms that tightened slightly, gathering me closer. This veritable stranger, who had unwittingly been trapped here with me, was offering something

I had no recollection of having been given before. At least, not since the night Inara was born.

When I had finally regained control of myself, I pulled away and he quickly released me to take a step back, his eyes shadowed in the moonlight as he studied my face.

"I'm sorry," I managed to croak. My neck and cheeks were warm with embarrassment, but the rest of my body felt hollowed out, drained to the point of being chilled.

"There is no need for your apology." He shook his head, ringing his hands in front of him as if he wasn't sure what to do with them now that we'd broken apart. "It is I who should ask your forgiveness. I shouldn't have pried . . . I had no idea . . ."

"You couldn't have known. And you have every right to ask questions."

"So . . . the hedge . . . none of you can control it?"

"No." I stared out at our hulking captor. "I know it sounds ludicrous, but somehow it's . . . *alive*. Not the way other plants are, but the way you and I are. You saw what it did today—how it closed off, how it attacked your master. Whenever any of us have tried to leave, that's what it does. Except for Sami. She's been allowed to leave before."

"She has?"

I nodded.

"But then . . . she came back?"

"I don't know why. If I could leave, I would never return. But yes, she's always come back."

"Even if the hedge only let *you* leave and kept Inara here? Would you go?"

His question was a sharpened blade, carving through my certainty; my silence was answer enough. He was right—the only way I'd truly leave was if Inara was with me. And now, after what he'd told me tonight, I didn't know if I'd even dare go *then*—to risk her life for freedom.

After a long, uncomfortable pause, Halvor looked down at his hands and said, "I'm sorry he left you. And I'm sorry you've been trapped here your whole life. If there is anything I can do . . ."

"You believed yourself to be our hostage moments ago, and now you are offering to help me escape?"

"Well . . . yes?" He shrugged sheepishly.

An unexpected burble of mirth rose within me, escaping my lips with a lightness that carried away some of my sorrow, especially when Halvor's responding chuckle joined my own. Within moments, we were both laughing uncontrollably, until my stomach ached, and my lips hurt from smiling, and the empty, cold space within me shrank slightly, the chill receding in the wake of the warmth of burgeoning friendship.

That's what this was—wasn't it? Smiling, talking together—laughing together? He was my first real chance in eighteen years at having a friend.

I was pitiful.

The laughter trailed off as I shook my head ruefully. "Honestly, I don't know how you could help, though I appreciate the offer."

"Perhaps we can find an answer here—together. There is nothing like it in the rest of Vamala, so the hedge must have been planted by the Paladin. There has to be a way to escape . . . or destroy it."

"If there is, I haven't been able to discover how—and neither has anyone else who has tried."

Halvor stared out the window, as if hoping for the beastly plant to reveal its secrets to him by sheer will power alone. "Your sister . . . Inara . . . she has Paladin power," he mused haltingly. "That's the only explanation for her glowing eyes. Perhaps she is the answer."

"Inara obviously inherited some of my father's power, but I honestly have no idea what she is truly capable of . . . or what *he* was capable of doing either, for that matter."

Halvor glanced out the window, to the grounds below. "Did they fly here?"

His question took me off guard and it took me a moment to realize he meant my parents. "I . . . I don't know. I don't think so." I'd often stared at the depictions of Paladin on their gryphons and wondered if my father had been one of them . . . if my mother had ever ridden on one. But it was a question I'd never dared ask. And

I'd certainly never seen any evidence of a gryphon living in the citadel during my lifetime. The stables were in total disrepair, full of rodents and cobwebs.

"He had to have been a Rider," Halvor pressed. "All the Paladin who came to Vamala were, you know. That's how they tracked down the rakasa. It was far too slow on foot—Vamala is too large. It took us months to get here from Mercarum. But on a gryphon . . . it probably only would have been weeks. Maybe even less."

I nodded as if I did know, too embarrassed to admit that *no,* I *hadn't* known that—and that I didn't know if my father had a gryphon or what had happened to it if he did. But I'd definitely *wondered,* and had even let myself imagine it once or twice—what it would have been like to ride on one, to soar up into the sky, the citadel dropping away below me, far from the reach of the hedge, the world opening up before me . . .

When the silence drew out long enough to be uncomfortable, he turned back to me and asked, "I hope you don't find this question impertinent, but what happened to Inara today? I was eager to see her at dinner—to make certain she was all right."

It was my turn to stare out the window, at the night-shadowed grounds that were Inara's domain during the day. I thought of her lying in bed, locked in her room on the opposite side of the citadel from us, hopefully sleeping. I'd never had to explain my sister to someone before—had never spoken to anyone who didn't already know her, or at least *of* her. A handful of times some of the villagers had come to the gates, shouting at us through the hedge. Mostly curses, blaming us for some misfortune that had struck the village. Though none of them had actually seen Inara, they called her words I'd never heard before and demanded she pay for their suffering.

They quickly learned—like all the others who had come—that although the hedge was our captor, it was also our protector and attacked if threatened.

"What you saw 'happen' to her this afternoon—that's how she is the majority of the time. To have met Inara when she was lucid was . . . rare." I spoke to the moon hanging full and ripe in the velvet sky, afraid to see repulsion or worse on his face—afraid of what I would do if I did.

I'd claimed my mother had loved Adelric fiercely, and I was certain she had, because only a powerful love could have engendered such hatred in its wake. But the love I had for Inara went beyond fierce, it was . . . *everything*. My entire life—my every waking moment—was spent thinking of her, taking care of her, wishing I was with her, or trying to come up with a way to help her tap into her power so I could steal a few precious minutes of conversation with her. Even my fascination with the Paladin and my efforts to learn more about them were mostly in hopes of discovering anything useful that might help keep my sister with me longer.

"She said 'it's coming' before she . . ." He trailed off, but though he seemed uncertain of how to describe her condition, he didn't sound disgusted or put off by it. I hazarded a glance at his reflection in the window and saw only concern on his face. "What did she mean by that? What was coming?"

"She calls it 'the roar,'" I began, hesitant, unsure, knowing my response would only bring more questions—questions I didn't want to answer. What I wanted was for *him* to answer *mine*. But perhaps if I told him everything, he would be willing to help me—to help *her*. "She has tried to explain it to me before, during her lucid times. She said it fills her body, so loud and so heavy it drowns everything—and everyone—else out. She can't control it and she can't focus because of it. Trying to communicate with her is nearly impossible. She doesn't have an accent—she speaks like that because she's had to learn to talk in short spurts of lucidity throughout her life, and the rest of the time, she can barely hear or understand any of us."

"What causes it?"

I shrugged, watching my shoulders rise and fall in the window, my reflection ghostlike in the moonlit glass pane. "I think it has something to do with the Paladin power, but I don't know for certain. She can . . . do things. That's her garden down there—that's where she spends almost all of her time during the good-weather months. If I can get her to help her plants, sometimes the glow in her eyes . . . it . . . um . . ."

"Spreads?" he suggested.

"Yes," I agreed, turning to him in surprise.

"That's how their power works," he explained. "From what I've learned in my studies, when a Paladin suppresses their power, the glow of it is only visible in their eyes. But when they use it, the power travels from the internal source of it somewhere inside them, through their blood and out of their hands, making their veins glow the same way as their eyes. Is that what you've seen?"

"*Yes*," I answered breathlessly. He truly *did* know about them; he knew precisely what I was talking about—and even *why* it happened. My heart quivered hopefully beneath the cage of my ribs as I stared at him in wonder. "That's *exactly* what it looks like. And if I can get her to do that—to use her power, as you said—the 'roar' goes away for a few minutes."

"And you get your sister back." Understanding dawned on his face.

I nodded.

"Zuhra . . ." He paused, lifting his hand as if he'd reach out to me, but then thought better of it and let it drop once more. "I'm very sorry. I had no idea when I approached you this afternoon that she . . . that I was using up your valuable time with her because of my intrusion."

"You couldn't have known," I murmured, but his apology—his understanding—meant more than I was able to express to him in that moment.

"All the same, I *am* sorry." Halvor stared down at the gardens below us, eyebrows pulled together in an expression I was beginning to learn meant he was concentrating, trying to work something out in his mind. "How often are you able to get Inara to use her power and help her mind clear?"

"Not nearly enough. Maybe once every week or so."

"That's all? And the lucidity . . . it only lasts for . . ."

"A few minutes usually in the summer. In the winter, when she has to keep her vegetable plants alive inside, without sunshine, it seems to take much more of her power, and sometimes we get a couple of hours together, if we're very lucky."

Halvor shook his head, turning away from the window to pace

toward the nearest bookshelves. "So little time . . ." he murmured, more to himself than me it seemed.

"Do you see why I need you to tell me everything you possibly can about them? If tonight is all we have—if the hedge lets you leave tomorrow—I need to know *anything* you can think of from your studies that might help her." I still clutched the lantern in my hands; the metal handle bit into my skin from gripping it so tightly. *"Please."*

Halvor reached up to touch the spine of one of the books, running his fingers down it as I imagined one would stroke a lover's jawbone. It was an intimate, almost reverent, touch. Even from where I stood, I could make out the familiar but undecipherable characters of the Paladin language. "Yes . . . yes, of course," he whispered, and I wasn't quite sure if he was responding to me or to some unspoken thought in his own mind.

"What does it say?" I asked when he didn't say anything else for several moments. "Can you truly read it?"

Halvor shook himself and glanced over at me, then back at the shelf where his hand still rested on the books in front of him. "Oh, the book?" He bent closer, studying it, and then, "It's called *Plants of Visimperum*—which might prove useful, actually. Perhaps it will have something about this hedge of yours in here." He pulled the book out, his face glowing with something akin to veneration as he gazed down at the tome in his hands.

"Visimperum?" I repeated, baffled.

He glanced up, forehead creased and eyes wide. Apparently "Visimperum" was something else that should have been familiar to me that wasn't. Before I could ask, he hurried to explain: "That's the name of the world where the Paladin and rakasa came from."

"Oh."

"Your mother really has kept you ignorant of . . . many things."

I flushed. "Maybe that's why the hedge let you in. Perhaps it's time I learned."

Halvor's eyes met mine. His fingers tightened around the book he held when he nodded. "We'd better get started then."

EIGHT

"So you believe her power has been trapped without an outlet for too long, and that is why it has this effect on her?"

Halvor nodded, his honey-brown eyes warm in the lantern light, even though it was nearing dawn and neither of us had slept. His wavy hair was askew from the countless times he'd pushed his hands through it during the night. Books were strewn around where we sat side by side on the floor, our backs resting against the cold windowpane. I'd been nervous to lean against it at first, but Halvor had studied the windows for several long minutes, his eyes wide and fingers pressed experimentally against the pane, before turning to me and assuring me that it was no ordinary window—that it was Paladin glass, created in Visimperum and imbued with Paladin magic making it clearer than any glass manufactured in Vamala, but twice as strong. He'd looked almost as excited about the glass as he'd been about the library.

"It's the only explanation that makes sense. She uses that power to help her plants grow, and in so doing, it releases the 'pressure,' so to speak, just enough for the roar to recede—albeit only briefly."

"That's the part I don't understand. If it *is* a buildup of power, why doesn't releasing it help longer?" I looked down at the books Halvor had eagerly skimmed, longing to be able to understand them as he did. We'd spent hours there; he scanned the pages silently while I watched and impatiently waited for him to explain what he'd read, trying to wrap my mind around the reality that I was sitting next to a *boy*, in the library, reading *Paladin* books together. *Talking.* I was *talking to a boy* . . . and hopefully didn't sound like a complete fool.

"Well . . . I do have *one* theory."

"Yes?" I prompted when he didn't immediately expound.

"What if . . ." He cleared his throat, keeping his gaze down. "Perhaps your sister is far more powerful than you realize. If that were the case, it would stand to reason such a small release of power—encouraging a plant to grow—would barely be enough to clear her mind and only for a few minutes, as you've seen."

Could it truly be so simple? After all these years of trying and failing to help her . . . all I'd needed to do was find a larger outlet for her power? "But . . . *what*?"

Halvor had already gone back to his book, flipping pages eagerly, until my question made him pause and look up.

I clarified, "What else could I do to help her use a greater portion of her power?"

He placed his finger in the book before closing it to hold his spot. "I'm not sure. What else has worked?"

I rubbed at my eyes, trying to ignore the sensation of grit beneath my eyelids, as though I'd been standing in a sandstorm for hours instead of a library. "Not much," I admitted. The burned curtains came to mind, but if she had regained lucidity after accidentally starting the fire, I hadn't seen it, because Sami had rushed her away while I'd tried to calm Mother down and put out the fire.

"There must be *something* more than growing fruits and vegetables."

"Is it possible that her power only works on plants?" I shifted on the hard floor. My back ached from sitting for so long, leaning against the night-chilled windowpane. Outside, the moon and stars had slowly been blotted out by clouds of onyx and slate slithering over the distant peaks and creeping across the sky toward the valley.

Rather than responding, Halvor began rifling through the stacks of books he'd pulled from various shelves. I forced myself to wait, having already learned in the few hours we'd spent together that he often seemed to be ignoring a question or like he'd forgotten to answer me, but in reality was searching for the very answer I awaited. He was so very methodical, from the way he moved, to the things he said, even the care with which he held the books and turned their pages with his long, tapered fingers. A scholar's fingers, with residual ink stains still on a few knuckles, despite his months of travel from Mercarum to Gateskeep and the citadel. I had to resist lifting my own fingers to compare them to his.

Finally, he chose one—a beautiful tome bound in black leather with lettering that looked to be gold leaf embossed on the cover. He scooted slightly closer to show it to me until his arm brushed my arm. Halvor seemed oblivious to the contact as he tapped the words on the cover exuberantly, but I couldn't ignore the proximity of his body to mine—the warmth and solidity of a living person pressed against my side compared to the lifeless chill of the glass at my back.

"This word here"—he underlined it with his finger—"means 'power' in the Paladin language. With any luck, we might find some answers in this book."

"Do you really—"

The door across the library suddenly banged open and Sami rushed in, her nightcap askew and a robe haphazardly tied over her sleeping gown. Her age-worn cheeks were blotchy and her hairline was damp as if she'd run the entire length of the citadel. I launched to my feet, my heart lurching up to my throat.

"*She's up*," Sami gestured wildly, her eyes frantic. "She already summoned me for some tea. Come! *Hurry!*"

Panic seized me and I rushed for the door, the books forgotten in my alarm. I still wore my dress from the night before and my hair was untouched. If Mother found me in the forbidden wing of the citadel—with Halvor—and deduced that we'd spent the entire night there . . . I didn't dare guess what punishment she would dole out. She'd preferred a wooden spoon when I was younger, but the days of isolation after trying to open the door to the Hall of Miracles last year came immediately to mind—and that small act of defiance was nothing compared to *this*.

The pain, the hunger . . . those I could handle. But being sepa-

rated from Inara *now,* when I'd finally summoned the smallest ray
of hope that I might be able to find a way to bring her back to us for
longer periods of time—that would be nothing short of torture.

I glanced over my shoulder to see Halvor following after me,
but his speed was hindered by having scooped up as many books
as possible to take out with him. Behind him the windows revealed
the first blush of dawn limning the cliffs to the east in a smudge
of light, barely enough to separate the craggy peaks from the inky
sky. But it meant sunrise—and my mother—were coming swiftly.

"Leave them!" I cried. The thought of abandoning so much
knowledge—so many possible answers—was a pain as keen as the
crack of a wooden spoon across my knuckles that was sure to come
in mere moments when Mother discovered none of us were in our
rooms. I hadn't even thought to muss my bed to make it appear as
though I had spent at least a portion of the night there. And if
Halvor came dashing through the citadel clutching an armful of
Paladin books . . .

His eyebrows sank over his crestfallen eyes, but did as I said
and dropped the books onto the nearest shelf—all except one,
which he stuffed into a pocket of his jacket. It bulged slightly, but
didn't warrant too much notice, especially on a scholar. I hoped.

As soon as he hurried past me, I remorsefully heaved the door
shut, unsure when I'd be back. If Mother somehow discovered
what we'd done, it wouldn't be surprising if she devised a way to
ensure that I was never able to visit this wing of the citadel again.

"Both of you go to your rooms. I'll try to find a way to divert
her, but she's sure to wonder why I disappeared for so long after
her summons as it is," Sami panted as we hurried through the hallways still enshrouded in the darkness of night, though every window we passed revealed the sable sky ever-lightening to rich indigo
shot through with streaks of tangerine.

In the space of a minute or two that felt like hours, as if we
were running through molasses—sticky and thick, sucking at our
feet and slowing us down—we reached the cavernous main hall.
The sound of our footsteps echoed back to us from the domed ceiling that soared far above us, impossibly heavy with the intricate
carvings of rakasa and Paladin locked in battle over our heads as

a solemn reminder of what Vamala had once suffered—how the Paladin had done what we couldn't have done for ourselves, no matter what the king came to believe.

"Do you remember the way to your rooms?" I paused to point Halvor in the right direction.

"I believe so—"

"What is the meaning of this?"

My mother's cold voice shot ice through my veins, freezing me in place, too terrified to turn. Halvor's eyes flashed to mine and then past me. My mother's presence loomed behind us, every bit as foreboding as the hedge outside.

"Madam, please forgive them. I was lost and called out for help—they were kind enough to—"

"Spare me your lies," she snarled.

The slap of her heels on stone stamped over the harsh throbbing of my heartbeat. She paused to grab my sleeve, yanking me to face her. "Slept in your clothes, did you, Zuhra?"

I kept my eyes on the ground, my guilt bitter and sharp on the back of my tongue.

Mother released me and faced Halvor. "What *exactly* were you doing with my daughter?"

"Nothing dishonorable, Madam. I swear it."

"Nothing dishonorable," she repeated. "Did you or did you not spend the entire night with her—*unchaperoned*?"

"No . . . that is, not like *that* . . ."

I barely swallowed my whimper of dismay. He'd as good as doomed us.

"Like *that*?" It was practically a shriek. "Like *what*, exactly? Like a young man and an unwed girl alone for the heavens only know how long in the middle of the night? The only proper recourse is to wed her immediately."

"Mother!" My face was so hot it must have been vermillion.

"We were merely *reading*!" Halvor interjected and my stomach turned to lead. He probably thought himself helping, but he couldn't possibly know that trespassing into the library was probably a much higher sin than fornicating on my mother's list.

"Reading?" Her voice dropped to a frosty whisper.

I still stared at the stone floor that leeched the heat from my body, trying to restrain the trembling in my knees. I'd gone too long without sleep, without food; I was woozy with exhaustion and the ashes of my dying hopes.

Mother spun to face me. "You took him to the library, didn't you." It wasn't a question. *"Didn't you!"*

Finally I looked up, meeting her hazel eyes that I knew were mirror images of my own. The angrier she got the greener they were—and right now they flashed jade with only a thin rim of amber still visible around her irises.

"He could help, Mother," I began, knowing my argument was lost before I even started. But I had to at least *try*. "He knows so much about them—he can read their language. If he had some time, he might even find some answers for—"

"It is *forbidden*!" She flung the words at me like they were knives, intended to cut me down, to slice through my defense. "Zuhra, you *know* that and yet you continually defy me!"

"I know, Mother. And . . . I'm sorry." My throat was thick, words and air getting jumbled and caught and tangled. My head pounded with the force of a lifetime trapped in this place. "It's just that *Inara*—"

"I don't want to hear it." Mother cut one hand through the air and turned her back on me. "If you won't wed her, then you must leave."

I didn't dare look at him, didn't want my last memory of Halvor Roskery to be a look of panic—or worse—on his face at the prospect of marrying me; a face that had somehow come to mean so much to me in the space of a single night. A night that would burn like a dream in my memory: the hours of watching him read by the light of the lantern, learning the angle of his jaw and the brush of his dusky lashes on his sunburnt cheeks when he blinked at my questions, always so careful to think before answering.

His silence spoke more loudly than anything he could have said.

"Then go. *Now*," Mother barked.

No. Let him stay.

The words burned in my mouth, aching to be loosed, but I swallowed them, scorching my throat.

Mother stormed past me, a force of nature trapped in a cage of flesh, and snatched Halvor by the arm. She was already outfitted for the day, in her most severe dress of charcoal and black lace trim, her hair scraped into a hasty bun. I shrank back instinctively, though I hated myself for it. This night's work was going to result in worse than bloodied knuckles and a hungry belly. Anger emanated from her like the spark in the air an instant before lightning struck.

"Madam, I am capable of walking on my own. I insist you unhand me." Halvor's voice was laced with steel as he yanked his arm free.

"You will leave my home at once!" Mother's shrill command reverberated around us.

There was a pause, when Halvor's eyes finally met mine for the space of a mere intake of breath. I stared back, fighting a sudden sensation of falling, as if the glass in the Hall of Miracles truly had disappeared beneath my hands, sending me plummeting to a sudden end that I wasn't ready to accept.

"If that is your wish" was his stiff response.

I shook my head mutely. He couldn't go, not yet. Not when I'd hardly even nicked the surface of what he knew, had dredged up the tiniest particle of hope that he might be the key to helping Inara. The book he'd managed to take was a telltale bulge in his coat pocket, a concealed reminder that he possibly held the answer *right there,* mere inches from his hands. But Mother had already turned on her heel and stormed to the door, dragging it open and gesturing for him to precede her outside into the gray dawn.

Halvor didn't look back when he exited the citadel.

I stood rooted to the spot, my limbs leaden and unwieldy, but nothing heavier than the painful thump of my heart beneath my ribs.

"Don't let him walk away," Sami murmured, startling me. I'd forgotten she was there. "This is your window opening. Don't let her shut it, too."

I turned to her, my throat tight with the wishes and dreams I still hadn't let fully form.

Sami raised a hand to my cheek and then nodded. *"Go."*

I lifted my skirts and ran.

NINE

Ashen mist skulked across the courtyard, coiling around Inara's carefully tended bushes and trees. Mother stood like a specter outside the door, caught between the fog at her feet and charcoal sky above, arms crossed over her chest as she watched Halvor march resolutely toward the hedge and the gate it concealed.

The damp soil soaked my stockings as I darted out the door. If he reached the gate before me, the hedge might let him through—he might disappear into that mist and never return.

I tried to bolt past my mother, but she reached out and snatched my arm, yanking me to a stop.

"Halvor!" His name ripped out of my throat and he paused, but didn't turn.

"Don't you *dare* go after him," Mother hissed, her grip so tight her nails bit into my skin even through my sleeves.

"I thought you wished for me to marry someday—to at least have the chance!"

Her eyes were fevered when they met mine. "Not someone obsessed with *them*."

Was it a trick of the uncertain light or had some of the vines fluttered—a sign of the hedge beginning to part? I squinted, but couldn't be certain.

"*Please,* Mother."

"*No.*" She stepped back, toward the citadel, tugging me with her.

Urgency beat in time with my blood. "He can help," I insisted and then I jerked my arm free with the sound of my sleeve ripping, leaving Mother with a handful of fabric and nothing more.

A sudden gust of wind tore through the courtyard, clawing at my hair and dress, stinging my eyes as I sprinted for Halvor and the gate. The hedge rippled, the leaves undulating. *Don't open, don't open,* I prayed silently, the dewy ground slippery and uncertain beneath my feet. Did he *wish* to leave? Why hadn't he stopped when I called out for him?

"Halvor!" Only a few strides separated us, and the hedge hadn't parted yet. Relief poured through me, hot and heady, when he spun at the sound of my voice coming from so much closer to him. It wouldn't open now—not with me by his side. Not with the chance that I could escape with him.

"You don't have to go. She can't force you to."

"Zuhra . . ." My name sounded like regret, like an apology.

"If we stood up to her—*together*—"

He shifted, glancing over my shoulder to where my mother stood on the stairs, shouting my name, demanding I come back so the hedge would open for him. "I apologize if I, in any way, led you to believe that my intentions were"—he cleared his throat—"dishonorable . . . or of a matrimonial nature—"

"*No.*" My answer was too fast, too abrupt. "No," I tried again, forcing calm into my voice though my blood was a frantic hum beneath my skin. "My mother—she—you must excuse her. She won't force you to marry me. She *can't.*" To the east, the first true sunrays had just broken free of their nightly cage, streaking the clouds above us currant, setting fire to the sky. "I'm asking— *pleading*—with you to stay. To help me help Inara." In the fiery light of dawn, his eyes glowed cinnamon.

I felt his indecision in the way he still remained half-turned toward the hedge, saw it in the uncertain flicker of his gaze back to the citadel before settling somewhere just above my nose, refusing to meet my eyes.

Everything in me sank.

"If the hedge will let me, I must go. Master Barloc needs me . . ."

"*Inara* needs you," I asserted. He was intrigued by her, I knew. I'd seen it yesterday, had heard it in his voice when he'd asked about her. I wasn't enough to induce him to stay, I knew that now in his uncertainty . . . but perhaps *she* was.

Before he could answer, Mother was there. "You will regret this, Zuhra." The threat was so quiet, I was certain only I heard her. She latched onto my arm again, and I knew this time, I would not be escaping. "Let me give you a word of advice, young man." She turned to Halvor. "Abandon this fascination with the Paladin. Help your master return to his library and then leave him. Study something else—*anything* else. Trust me, only misery and suffering will come of an interest in those . . . those monsters."

I stared at her, too shocked by her words, by the sudden sheen of tears in her eyes to try to pull free. When she turned on her heel to lead me back to the citadel, I didn't fight her. *Monsters.*

She'd called them monsters.

"We will go in and shut the door," she called back to Halvor. "The hedge should open if we aren't out here."

I looked back at him one last time. His mouth moved and I thought he might have said "I'm sorry," but the wind tore his words away from me.

Mahsami still stood in the same place, her expression expectant when I walked back in. But when Mother followed immediately behind and shut the door firmly after us, Sami's expression fell.

It wasn't my window. That's what I would tell her tonight, when we were in the kitchen doing dishes together, as we always did.

All traces of emotion were erased from Mother's face, but the unmasked suffering that she'd exposed—however briefly—moments before had struck me more deeply than any of her barbed threats or bursts of temper.

"It's better this way," she said matter-of-factly. "He was not the one we'd hoped for."

I nodded, morose—resigned.

"I will deal with you in a moment, but first . . ." Mother moved to the window.

I couldn't bear to watch, to see the hedge part and then swallow him whole. Instead, I looked up. Buttery-yellow daylight touched the dome above us, turning the carvings of the Paladin and rakasas into gold. I stared up at them, at the excruciatingly beautiful faces of the army of Paladin men and women, seated upon their gryphons in the air, weapons raised, some with hands wielding balls of fire, all bearing eyes that glowed blue with lapis lazuli. In contrast, the rakasas were terrifying, all teeth and claws, some monstrous in size and others in the viciousness depicted in the scene.

The light spread slowly but surely, the dawning of a new day. Inara would be waking soon. For a brief moment, I thought of alerting Mother to the fact that Halvor still had one of the Paladin books, but then decided against it. I'd never be able to read it, so he might as well keep it, to take back to their library with his master.

"Sami, take Zuhra to her room and lock her there." Mother's sudden order pulled my attention away from the ceiling to where she stood by the window, still staring out at the courtyard.

"Mother!"

"You've proven yourself unworthy of my trust." She spoke to the window, her knuckles white where she gripped her skirt. "You will remain in your room until I deem you capable of resisting the temptations of this place *properly*."

"But *Inara*—"

"Perhaps you will think of her next time *before* making the decision to disobey me."

Ice-sharp desolation scraped beneath my skin. "Please, don't do this—I was only trying to help her!"

"Sami! Take her up to her room *immediately*."

Mahsami murmured an apology before gently tugging me toward the staircase that would lead us up past Terence, the Paladin statue, then on to our rooms.

I allowed her to guide me away, knowing if I didn't obey, she, too, would suffer the brunt of my mother's wrath, though my legs grew heavier and heavier with each step.

When we reached the landing and turned down the hallway toward our rooms, Sami slowed her pace. "I'm sorry." Her apology was so quiet, I barely heard it. "I was certain I had made the draught strong enough for her to sleep well past dawn."

"You don't need to apologize. You were only trying to help."

We both fell silent, resigned to our own fates.

When we reached my door, I paused before opening it. Inara's room was next to mine, but there were no sounds from within yet. I didn't know when I would be allowed to see her again. Though I longed to, I couldn't bring myself to wake her up and force her to leave the release of sleep.

Rather than helping her, my actions had caused me to unintentionally abandon her instead.

"I'm sorry, Zuhra, but she'll be waiting for me, to make sure I did as she asked."

"I know."

The door creaked when I turned the knob, but then I paused again, this time to look into Sami's familiar gray eyes.

"Mahsami . . . I have to know. Why did you stay?"

A flash of sorrow skimmed across Sami's face. In all the years together, I'd never dared ask her that question. But suddenly, I *had* to know.

"Oh, Zuhra . . . You know why."

"No. I don't."

I'd never been whole, I knew that. I'd aged all wrong; my body had lengthened and grown tall while I'd steadily broken apart inside. Day after day after week after month of my mother's rebuttals and rules, of Inara's distance and suffering, of the shadows of a father I barely remembered but couldn't forget around every corner, of living in a mausoleum of the heritage I was forbidden to discover but hungered to know . . . Pieces of me lay scattered across the stone hallways of this citadel, shards of a child's heart that yearned only for love and slivers of a soul that ached for understanding—belonging, even.

But I'd been careful to keep tiny bits of myself safe, protected behind a carefully hardened wall of disillusionment.

Until Halvor had shown up yesterday, until I'd spent an entire night beside him and stupidly, *foolishly* let that wall crack, allowed tiny fissures of hope to weaken it. And now he'd left the citadel—had left me—as everyone did eventually. Physically or mentally, whether by choice or not, it didn't matter. The result was the same. I was alone. Always utterly alone.

Except for Mahsami.

And so I had to know now, finally, after fifteen years, why she had stayed then—and why she stayed now. Why I should let myself believe that she wasn't going to disappear one day too.

"Please, Sami." She wavered in front of me, like someone had spilled water on a painting, smudging the details of her face.

Only when she reached up and tenderly wiped the moisture from my cheek did I realize I was crying. "My dear girl . . . I stayed because I saw a chance to right an old wrong. And because even though I was never able to have any children of my own, something inside me knew you and Inara might be in need of a mother."

"We already had a mother." I didn't say or mean it unkindly— it was a question. A terrible question, but one that I felt I deserved an answer to.

"In body, yes. But you didn't just lose your father the night your sister was born" was all she said back, with a look of such tenderness that I couldn't respond except to nod. She patted my cheek and then let her hand drop.

Every moment that she remained, talking to me, she risked my mother's fury being turned on her. No matter how badly I wished for her to stay, I forced myself to open the door the rest of the way and walk into my room.

"Thank you, Sami," I whispered, even as she took out her key ring to lock me in.

She wiped her cheek on her sleeve without looking up, thumbing through the keys until she found the right one.

I couldn't bear to close myself in, so instead I turned my back, letting Sami do it herself. The door clicked shut softly and I exhaled. Sami's voice was muffled by the heavy wood separating us, but as the lock slid into place and her key scraped back out, it sounded like she'd murmured "I'm sorry" one last time.

My room glowed honey-gold as the sun crested the peaks visible through the single window across from where I stood. I always left my curtains open; I loved waking to the sunrise warm on my face, my walls shimmering with the light of a new day. But I felt no joy from this dawn, only a bone-deep exhaustion and the knifing pain of new loss—something I'd believed myself impervious to, until today.

Though I knew Halvor was gone by now, and I wanted nothing more than to crawl underneath my covers and give myself over to the oblivion of sleep, part of me had to see the evidence to make it true. I crossed the room slowly, telling myself that last crumb of hope I clung to—that he would still be standing there, waiting for the gate to appear—was completely futile.

The hedge was so tall, it rose even with the top of my window, blocking my view of Gateskeep, the trail leading down to it from the citadel, or any of the valley between the cliff we lived on and the rest of the mountain range to the east.

I did, however, have an excellent view of the courtyard below. The *empty* courtyard . . . and the wrought-iron gate, completely clear of vines, gleaming ebony in the morning light.

He, too, had truly left then.

As abruptly as he'd come, Halvor Roskery was gone.

TEN

"Inara!"

Inara, Inara, *Inara*. A shout, a buzz, a curse. Through the roar, through the dark, through the light—

That is who I am.

Is who I am.

Who I am.

Who am I?

Who am I?

Flesh made pain, pain made flesh. Roaring and howling. Inside me—crawling, creeping, crying.

Skin stretched tight, too, too tight. Light too deep, too heavy, too *loud*. Roaring and roaring and ROARING.

A new voice, a deep voice. Sounds that bang and bump and I try, try, *try* to focus, but the light is blinding and the roar is deafening and she's gone. Why is she gone? Why doesn't she come?

Who am I?

Where is she?

Where am I?

The roar is worse and I *need* her. I feel blindly, I see but don't; I hear but can't understand . . . and the roaring is worse, worse, worse . . .

And then pain. Shooting, blinding, breaking. Screaming—the screaming is mine, it's me, I am hurt. Am I hurt?

A deep voice, an image that swims through the blinding light, through the roaring dark, eyes of umber, of richest soil between my fingers, of edges of leaves curling and burning and I must heal them, must *help* them . . .

But it's not her.

It's roaring, blinding, deafening.

Who I am.

Who am I?

ELEVEN

Mother allowed Sami to bring me a large pitcher of water, one loaf of bread that first morning, and then . . . nothing. I'd expected her or Mother to come later that night with a meal, as she'd done when I'd been locked in my room for trying to enter the Hall of Miracles, but no other meal arrived. After dinnertime came and went without a knock at the door, I began to regret consuming the bread and water so hastily earlier in the day.

I crawled into bed shortly after the last of the sunlight was absorbed into the cloaking darkness of the coming night. Sleep was slow in coming, partially because of my unsatisfied belly and partially because of the onslaught of thoughts careening through my mind. Halvor, the Paladin, the hedge, Inara's unknown powers . . . too many questions and not nearly enough answers to allow me rest.

Still, I eventually drifted into an unsettled sleep, tossing and waking repeatedly until I sat up to a bleary dawn, subdued by clouds heavy and low with rain. Muffled noises came from the room next to mine, where Inara was probably waking, waiting for me to unlock her door and come in to help her change and braid her hair.

The sharp clench of pain that spasmed through my empty stomach had nothing to do with hunger. I rolled over to bury my sudden tears in my pillow, soaking it with my guilt and remorse. I'd known it was a risk . . . but I'd been so *desperate*—so willing to do whatever it took to get the answers that had been kept from me for so long. And now she was suffering alongside me from the consequences. But . . . I told myself it *had* been worth it: Halvor had given me a possible key to unlocking my sister's mind, a tiny serving of hope that I could free her from the roar for longer periods of time. Even with the punishment, even being forced away from Inara . . . I couldn't regret what I'd done. Mother wouldn't leave me in my room forever, and once I got out, I would start experimenting—I would find a way to help my sister.

No one came for hours. We'd had rough winters with little food, especially when I was very young and Inara wasn't good at helping grow our food all through those dismal months yet, but I'd never gone this long without *anything* before. I was hungry in a way that went beyond my stomach, leeching through my entire body, a burning, aching need to eat that was *painful* in its intensity.

Finally late in the morning the lock scraped back and the door eeked open. I lowered the book of fairy tales that I'd read hundreds, if not thousands of times, and glanced up. Mother slipped through the small opening (did she think I was standing there waiting to knock her over and try to escape?) and set a tray down on the dresser nearest the door. Her eyes flickered to me then away, to the cup of water and plate with sliced fruit on it.

"Should I expect anything else later or had I better ration that for the day?" A strange, heady anger seized me, filling the aching hole in my belly with anger—with *fury*. A fury to match Mother's. Inara was out there somewhere, still lost in the roar, and I was locked away, holding a possible key to her freedom and unable to use it.

I was ready for her to snap back or ignore me and shut the door, slamming the lock back in place. Instead, she stared at the meager food she'd brought me silently and when she finally lifted her chin and met my defiant gaze, it wasn't anger, or even irritation on her face . . . it was something else, something . . . *worse*. It was a look that, until then, I'd only seen in memory. The expression shadowing her features as she stood across my room melded with her face from the night Inara was born, separated by years' worth of wrinkles and scowls, but it was the same. It was . . . *fear*?

"You *have* to learn, Zuhra," she finally spoke, quiet but fervent. "Do you think I *want* to do this to you? Do you think it makes me *happy*?"

I stared, stunned speechless.

There was a pregnant pause, heavy with so many things unsaid, unknown . . . but then she sucked in a breath and, as if the air she drew in had reinflated her flagging strength, her shoulders rose back into her normal domineering posture. It was only after she straightened that I realized she'd been hunched in on herself slightly before. "Like that hedge out there, some things are better left alone." She reached out to touch the edge of the tray, but she didn't glance back down at the food again. "This is all you will get for the day. You have to learn," she repeated, the normal steel returning to her voice, and then she turned on her heel and left, shutting the door behind her, the lock slamming back into place with a resounding *snick*.

By afternoon, when the fruit and water had both been gone for hours, I called out a few times, but then resolutely closed my mouth, refusing to give my mother the satisfaction. I'd tried to control myself, to leave some for later, but the hunger and thirst were insatiable and before I knew it, both were gone.

I sat by my window and stared outside, longing to be anywhere but there. It started raining in the morning and continued unabated throughout the day, a steady drizzle coating my window in droplets that ran rivulets down the glass to pool at the base. Gray and green, sky and plant—my only views. My vision blurred from looking so long at the damp earth, the puddles of water dotting the courtyard and soaking the bases of the grove of trees I could just see the edge of if I pressed the side of my face to the glass . . . and of course the hedge. Always, always, the hedge.

Mother was wrong. She *had* to be. Looking for answers, trying to figure out who my father was, who his people were—and what that made me and Inara—wasn't like touching the hedge. Books didn't attack with poisonous thorns. The citadel didn't pose any threat. Even the hedge had never hurt any of *us*, only those trying to get past it. Knowledge wasn't dangerous . . . it *couldn't* be.

I watched for Inara, hoped to see her wander through her gardens at some point, perhaps with Sami at her side, despite the rain. But if she ever did exit the citadel, it wasn't anywhere within my view.

When night came once more I silently climbed back into my bed, even though my belly ached and staring at the drizzle all day had only made my thirst that much worse. I lay beneath the cool, smooth sheets, listening for any bit of sound, any hint of Inara in the room next to me . . . but the citadel was so quiet that my ears began to throb from the weight of the silence.

It took hours for me to fall into an unsettled sleep, only to jerk awake what felt like moments later. A door slamming—that's what had woken me. *But which one?*

Inara.

The vestiges of sleep still had claws of disorientation embedded in my mind, muddling my thoughts as I flung off my covers. I tried to shake it off and rushed to the door, grabbing for the handle, only to find it immobile in my hand. Locked.

Muffled sounds came from outside the door I couldn't open, a jumble of voices, barely audible over the thundering of my blood in my ears. Clarity slammed back in a rush of memory. I was locked in my room. I couldn't get out to make sure it wasn't—

"Inara!"

That shout from the hallway—all terror and urgency—was like having a fist shove past my skin and bone and grab my heart. The shriek and *crash, thud, thud* that followed crushed it entirely.

"Inara!" I screamed, grabbing the handle and yanking on it again and again, though I knew it was locked, knew I couldn't open the door. "Someone let me out! Please, *let me out*! *Nara!*"

I'd never been so frantic—so helpless—in my life. Had she fallen? Was it the stairs? *Oh, please, don't let it be the stairs!*

The voices were far away now, little more than a low, urgent hum, underscored by a soft, distant sound that might have been crying.

"*Someone!* Please! Is she all right? *Please!*" I slammed my hands against the door, over and over. I shouted until my throat was raw, until I tasted blood and my voice flayed itself out of use.

But no one came.

No one answered.

And all too soon, the low murmur of voices was gone, leaving only silence.

A door opening. A shout. Inara. The stairs. That scream . . . that thud.

I sank to the hard, cold floor, pressing the heels of my bruised hands to my eyes, my entire body shaking. Minutes bled into hours, until I was as chilled as the stones beneath me, my body rigid with stillness—from a terror so all-encompassing, so heavy, I'd curled into a ball beneath it, hadn't moved again, my cheek on the ground, my arm outstretched so that my fingers were pressed as far as they could go beneath the tiny crack of space below my door. At one point I thought I heard footsteps in the hallway and weakly rasped out, "Is she all right? Is Nara okay?" But if someone was there, they didn't respond, neither did the footsteps sound again, leaving me to wonder if it had been my imagination to begin with. My need for someone to come was so intense, it conjured the sounds of deliverance from nothing.

Somehow, I drifted off at some point. When I startled awake again, still curled into a ball on the frigid stone floor, morning had dawned, even darker than the previous, the sky a tumult of charcoal clouds tumbling through a sea of ink. The rain had stopped for the time being, but in its place distant thunder growled across the heavens and the window whined beneath a barrage of wind that whipped the orchard branches into a frenzied dance below.

I forced myself to sit up, my body frozen and muscles rigid. The ache in my belly had grown teeth, becoming a serrated, constant pain. I'd never realized it was possible to feel so hollowed out, my insides shredded, *burning* with the need for both answers and sustenance.

What had happened to Inara?

I made myself crawl back to my bed, and curled back up in my sheets, shivering violently from my night on the floor. The heat snap had broken with the onslaught of storms, and the citadel had soaked up the rain greedily, the stones cooling and the air turning humid and chilled, feeling even colder than normal after the intense heat wave.

Sleep was my only escape from the hunger and terror; but at first it eluded me, and the rare times I did drift off, I startled awake from sweat-soaked nightmares, my sheets twisted around my damp body. As the morning slowly passed without a sound outside my door, I drifted from dark dream to dark awakening back to dark dreams once more. By the time my walls were washed honey-gold by the afternoon sun, my tongue was swollen in my mouth, dry as bone. My head throbbed, but the vein at the base of my throat fluttered thinly against my fingers; my heart was a panicked butterfly caged within my chest.

Nara. Nara. Nara. Each desperate pulse beat out her name beneath my skin.

I tried to shove my panic away, rejecting it, but the only other thing to grasp onto instead was a growing anger. The emptiness within me, carved out from fear and hunger, was ample room for my fury to unfurl, for it to take the teeth in my belly and the fire in my throat and claim them, turning them from Mother's tools of penitence into my weapons of defiance.

To leave me locked in my room when Inara had somehow gotten out and been hurt was extreme, even for her. I'd known it was a huge risk to spend the night alone in the library with Halvor, when she'd meted out severe punishments in the past for minor crimes in comparison—sneaking a book to my room, trying to open a forbidden door. But if her goal was to break my will . . . she would soon learn just what a terrible mistake she had made. As the hunger pains turned to spasms, and my mind replayed scenario after possible scenario of what had happened to Inara in horrifying detail, I stared up at the swimming white canopy of my bed and let the fury build within me.

Never again would she have the power to lock me away, to keep me from my sister.

Never again.

It became my mantra, it became the lifeblood the rage within me fed upon, a beast that I had no desire to tether or tame. And as soon as this punishment ended—as soon as I could devise a way—I would unleash it on her and escape this place. And I would take Inara with me. Somehow—some way, despite the king's edict. We could hide, we would find a way to survive. This couldn't be all that my life was destined for; these walls and this room and that hedge, always the hedge.

Inara *had* to be all right; whatever had happened last night, she would recover and I would be released from my room eventually, and together, we would find a way to escape.

Halvor's words rang in my ears, a distant and uncertain promise. Perhaps Inara had far more power than I'd thought. Maybe if I could get her to tap into it her mind would clear—for good.

And I knew just the plant to try it out on.

The sound of the lock moving snapped me from my half-conscious delirium to full awareness in less than a pulse of my heart. I flung myself to my feet in one swift movement as the door opened, but was hit by a wave of dizziness and had to sink back down on my bed.

"Zuhra! Good heavens, child, what's wrong?"

Sami rushed in the room, haphazardly plunking a tray of food down on her way, then hurrying to my side. She brushed her soft, cool hand across my forehead.

Her eyes widened. "You're burning up! I can go make you some tea—and here, there's—"

I grabbed her arm when she turned to bustle away again and *yanked,* forcing her back to my side. "Where's Inara? What happened to my sister?" The questions came out a snarl and she flinched back, but I couldn't bring myself to care. Something had happened to her, and Sami was one of the ones who hadn't let me out to be with her—to *help* her.

"Oh dear, did you hear that last night? I told your mother we had best check on you, but we—"

"What. *Happened*," I bit out, my fingers tightening around her fleshy arm.

"She's fine, Zuhra. She got hurt, but now she's just—"

My brain turned off after the words "she got hurt"; I released Sami and jumped to my feet, only to be hit by a wave of dizziness again and stumble forward.

"You need to sit down, Zuhra. Your sister is *fine*. I promise. But *you* have a fever—you need to rest." Sami was the one to grab my arm this time and push me gently—but firmly—back to my bed. I was shocked to find myself so weak that she was able to do it; I couldn't fight back even though I wanted nothing more than to shove past her and rush to Inara's room. A wave of cold crashed over me; suddenly I was shivering so violently she was able to press me back to sitting on my bed and pull some of my blankets over me.

A *fever*?

No. I couldn't be sick. I had to get to Inara. I had to get to my sister.

I must have spoken out loud because Sami responded softly, lifting my legs back onto the bed and tucking my sheets around me as I continued to shake, "I told you, she is fine now. I will bring her to you. Will that help? Then you can see for yourself."

I nodded, my vision swimming. "Yes," I whispered. "Please let me see her."

"I'll go get her, but then you must eat something and you *must* stay in bed."

I nodded again, as Sami hurried over to the tray that teetered half on, half off the table where she'd set it so haphazardly to retrieve a piece of toasted bread, muttering to herself under her breath. "I told her this was a bad idea . . . I warned her not to do this . . ."

When she reached my side again with the toasted bread, she handed it to me. "Here, nibble on this, but go slowly."

I took the rare treat with trembling fingers, still fighting off the chills that I realized now were from the fever. "Please, go get Inara. I'll stay in bed, I promise." I took a nibble to prove to her that I meant it.

When she left I lifted the bread to my mouth to take another bite. Though my hunger was barely satiated, I forced myself to go slower than my mind wished, all too aware of how unsettled my stomach still felt. As I slowly chewed and swallowed, a hundred different scenarios played out in my mind of what had happened to Inara. No matter how I tried to repeat the words "she's fine" to myself, I couldn't stop the fear that quickened my heartbeat—and an even greater increase of anger at Mother. *It can't have been that bad, if Sami can bring her to me.*

But the attempt to reassure myself fell flat. *Any* injury to Inara was unacceptable. How had they forgotten to make sure she was safe? The shouts from last night—the crash and the crying—scraped through my memory like claws on stone. Had she tried to get outside by herself and hurt herself in some way? Surely if I hadn't been locked in here, no harm would have come to her.

Another dark mark to lay at my mother's feet, to fuel the monster of fury within me, to assuage any guilt I might have still harbored from my hope to somehow escape this place and leave Mother behind us. There *had* to be a way. And I wouldn't stop searching, not even if it took months . . . or years. Though Halvor's revelation about the death decree complicated things, I knew I could protect my sister somehow—especially if I wasn't worried about being locked in my room.

I'd spent a lifetime telling myself that Mother loved me, that she even loved Inara in her own troubled way . . . that she struggled to show it, to express it, because of the constant reminder we represented of the hurt inflicted on her by Adelric all those years ago.

But as I lifted the crisped bread to my mouth, shaken that such a ridiculously small movement had become difficult, I realized perhaps I'd been wrong.

A soft knock came at the door, but when Sami didn't open it right away, I called out, "Enter!" wondering why she didn't just do so on her own. She knew I couldn't get out of bed—had forced me to stay there, in fact—and that I was desperately eager to see Inara.

But then the door opened and the bread I held dropped to my lap.

"Hullo, Zuhra," Halvor Roskery said, his hands shoved into the pockets of his trousers. "Are you sure it's all right if I come in?"

TWELVE

I stared uncomprehendingly for a beat and then realized he'd asked a question. "Oh—yes. Of course, come in," I managed over the clamor of other questions in my mind: *How are you still here? Didn't the hedge let you out? Where have you been the last two days?*

Halvor shuffled forward, leaving the door ajar. He wouldn't quite meet my stunned gaze, looking instead at the bread I'd picked back up and clutched into crumbs in my hand. His hair was unkempt, sticking almost straight out on one side, and there were dark circles under his eyes. "I tried to convince her to let you out." He stared straight down at the ground now, his hair flopping forward to obstruct my view of his face. "But when she realized I'd taken the book out of the library . . . she said my punishment would be to know your suffering would last even longer. I—I'm sorry." Halvor's voice cracked and he stopped abruptly.

"This is *not* your fault," I immediately reassured him.

His shoulders lifted slightly then dropped again. "It's at least partially my fault. I was the one trying to sneak around the citadel that night—I was the one who took the book with me. And Inara . . . I know what she means to you, and I . . . I—"

"Sami said she's fine," I interjected at the same moment he admitted, "It's my fault she got hurt."

My mouth snapped shut audibly and I could only stare at the top of his head as he continued to study his boots.

Finally I managed, "*You* hurt her?"

"No!" Halvor finally looked up, shocked into lifting his eyes to mine. "I would never—not on purpose!" His denial was immediate and so vehement, I believed him. "I picked my lock and snuck out at night. I was going to help you—I intended to pick your lock and get you some food and water. But I got the door wrong."

I listened silently, horrified to realize my mother had locked him in his room as well. Was it just at night or this whole time? He didn't look starved . . . but sleep deprived, certainly.

"When I opened it, Inara was already there. She pushed past me—repeating your name over and over, like she had been all day before your mother made Sami lock her in her room. She was so loud, I was afraid she'd wake your mother . . . I tried to reach for her, tried to tell her to be quiet, but she was frightened of me. She ran away—right for the stairs. I yelled for her to stop, but she was staring back at me, her eyes so wide—so scared—and she didn't see the stairs—" His voice broke again and he cut himself off to clear his throat.

I shook my head, horror blooming like a wound in my chest. "Sami said she was *fine*. She said—she *promised*!" This time when I threw off my covers, there was no one to stop me.

"She *is*—Zuhra, it's all right—she—"

But I wasn't listening anymore. Ignoring the rush of wooziness when I stood, I stumbled forward, pushing past him. Sami had *lied* to me—she'd sent him here to tell me the truth, to tell me that while I'd been locked in here, half-delirious with a fever, Inara had fallen down the stairs and—

Then Sami was there, standing in the doorway. "Zuhra! Why are you out of bed?"

Sami's frustrated exclamation echoed dully through my brain. I only had eyes for my sister—for Inara, who stood directly behind Sami, well and whole.

I collapsed to my knees, dry sobs ripping through my chest.

"Zuhra, I'm sorry—you didn't let me finish." Halvor was there, crouching beside me, putting his arm around my shoulders, trying to help me to stand. But I just stared at Inara, my gaze roaming over her body, looking for injury—for bruises or cuts or any sign of what had befallen her.

"*Zuhra* . . . Zu Zu . . ." She tilted her head, looking *at* me, not through me.

"I'm here, Nara. I'm here." I clutched Halvor's proffered hand and clambered unsteadily to my feet. Sami guided her toward me until she was close enough that I could touch her. Though I risked spooking her, I lifted my hand to her face. Instead of yanking away as she often did, she merely gazed at me, her blue-fire eyes trained on mine.

"Zu Zu," she repeated softly, pressing her cheek into my hand, and I began to silently cry.

"I'm sorry, Nara. I'm so sorry," I whispered brokenly—for leaving her against my will, for allowing her to fall down those stairs, for whatever else had happened to her while I'd been locked away.

"Zuhra, there's more," Halvor spoke softly from beside me, his hand still encircling my arm to help hold me steady. "When she fell . . . she *did* get hurt. It was her left leg . . . it was bad. She couldn't stand up."

Even though she stood before me at that very moment, obviously fine, my heart still constricted as if his words were a vise squeezing it too tightly. "I—I don't—"

"She has more power than just helping plants grow," Halvor rushed on as I stared into her burning eyes. "Zuhra . . . your sister *healed herself.*"

"She was lucid for *eight hours*?"

Halvor nodded, somehow looking thrilled and miserable all at once, as if he knew how much it would pain me to know she'd been there—she'd been *herself*—for the longest period of time in her entire life and I'd been locked in here, completely unaware. "The rest of the night and most of this morning. She is still somewhat there, but it's slowly getting worse again."

That explained why she'd said my name, looked directly at me. But nothing more. I nodded, unable to speak over the thickness of gathering tears in my throat. I blinked hard, attempting to hold it back. My mind skipped over the surface of the thought that I could have had *eight hours* with Inara, unable to truly delve into that realization because it threatened to break me apart. What would we have talked about—what could we have done? I'd never had more than a couple of hours with her, and even that was so rare. Halvor—this virtual stranger—had probably been able to get to know her better in that one night than I had in our entire lifetime.

We sat at the small table near the window in my room, the door still open so we could hear if Mother approached. Inara had started getting agitated in the small space, and Sami had taken her back outside to her plants, promising to do all she could to keep Mother distracted for as long as possible so Halvor and I could talk uninterrupted about everything that had occurred. I was grateful for the time to prepare myself to face her—I still didn't know what I would say, what I would *do*.

"Are you sure she couldn't stand—that her leg was . . ."

"Broken," he finished. "Yes. I'm positive."

"I . . . I don't understand."

"Will it make you more upset to hear the details? Or would it help?"

I was quiet for a moment, looking down at the now empty mug sitting between us. "Why are you still here?" I asked instead, not sure if I *could* handle hearing about Inara's fall and what suffering she must have endured—even though it obviously had a happy resolution. A *miraculous* resolution. "I saw the gate—the hedge had receded—and you were gone. I watched from my window."

He blinked at my sudden change in topic. "The hedge seems to be toying with me. It recedes whenever I am too far away to reach the gate, but as soon as I come near enough to attempt leaving, it closes over again—so fast I have no hope of getting through in time," Halvor explained. "By the time you looked out your window, I must have already returned to the citadel."

"Oh."

"Do you wish I had gone? I was under the impression that you felt . . . otherwise."

He was right—I had made it very clear I'd wanted him to stay. But for some reason, I felt betrayed. Not because he was still there, but because I hadn't known. Because I had spent hours mourning his loss and missing my sister; when in reality, I should have been comforted by the fact that he would be there when I was finally released from my sentence and fearing for my sister's safety far more than I'd even realized.

And I was struggling to contain my irrational anger that *he'd* been the one to get all the time with Inara, instead of me.

"Of course not," I finally answered. "I'm glad you're still here . . . I'm having a hard time taking it all in, though."

Halvor nodded, looking down at his clasped hands resting on the polished wood of the table.

We were silent for a long moment, thoughts and questions darting through my mind one after another. And then I remembered what he said about Mother taking away the book.

"Did you get to read any of it—before she took it away?" Perhaps he'd been able to at least find out something useful. Perhaps there was a way to reach Inara—to help her stay with me longer— other than a potentially catastrophic injury.

Halvor shook his head. "No. She noticed it in my pocket when I had to return to the citadel. I'm sorry."

"Oh."

I tried to hide my disappointment by drumming my fingers on the table, the only sound as yet another uncomfortable silence descended.

"I won't tell you the details if you don't want to hear them," he finally blurted out, rushing to speak before I could protest, "but you should know she kept asking for you. She wished to see you desperately. At first we were too busy trying to help Inara to think of getting you, but then, once she healed . . . and was lucid . . . We begged your mother to let you out—to let you speak with your sister. But she refused. She said nothing would make you realize how serious she was than to make you miss that time with Inara." He cleared his throat, shifting uncomfortably on the chair, his face flushing as if *he'd* been the one to make such a cruel choice. "And I . . . I didn't know what to do. I'm sorry. For all of it."

I had to blink back tears again, but I nodded. "Thank you . . . for trying. And I'm sorry too. Sorry that you're trapped here with us . . . with *her.*"

Halvor hesitantly placed his hand on top of mine. The touch

was a jolt, a wave of sensation that started where his fingers brushed my fingers, and washed up my arm to the rest of my body. "We'll find a way—together. We'll figure out how to help Inara. Now that we know her power can be used for more than just growing plants, we can experiment, find other ways to help clear her mind."

"You're not suggesting that we *purposely* hurt her." I yanked my hand back, horrified.

"No!" Halvor blanched, jerking in his chair as if I'd slapped him. "I would *never* . . . You must know that I could no more intentionally cause Inara harm than I would willingly hurt myself. I meant only that we could try other things. Besides her plants. That's all."

I flushed at the almost reverential way he said her name, at the look of pure dismay that crossed his face at the mere thought of what I'd suggested he intended. My own stomach sank and I didn't put my hands back on the table.

He liked her.

And not just as an interesting specimen for a scholar to study.

"What did you talk about? Were you with her the whole time she was lucid? Did my mother stay and speak with her at all?"

Halvor looked relieved at the turn in conversation, at my nonchalant tone. If he only realized the amount of control I had to expend to maintain that nonchalance as he dove into story after story of what he and Inara and Sami had spoken of during the time her mind was clear. How she'd tried to explain to them, as she had to me, what it was like when her power took over. How he'd told her all about losing his parents and his subsequent life at the library. His long journey to come to the citadel. How Inara had thanked Sami for her years of service—that she was aware of it, even if she couldn't show it normally.

Halvor explained that even though she could finally speak with her daughter, my mother had only stayed for a brief time. He told me that Inara had begged Mother to let me out but had been refused and then when Inara had asked Mother to explain *why* this had happened to her—what the power meant—that my mother had looked stricken and immediately left. He told me how at first they hadn't understood why her mind had cleared, only that she couldn't move because of the terrible pain, but within minutes, the pain diminished and she slowly regained the use of her leg and they realized what was happening—how they'd all cried at first, and then laughed. They'd played games. *Games.* Halvor and my sister had talked and shared stories and played games for hours and hours and hours.

And I'd been here, in the room next to hers, completely un-aware.

I listened to him relay all of this to me, and I smiled and laughed at the appropriate places, even as I crumbled inside.

"She healed quite rapidly, but she said it felt like her leg was on fire at first," Halvor was saying when the sound of footsteps and voices in the hall made us both pause and turn.

"What does he think he's going to accomplish?"

"I'm not sure, but he refuses to go."

I looked to Halvor in confusion. They couldn't possibly be talking about him, could they? Before I could ask, Mother stormed into my room, her steely gaze skipping right past me to land on Halvor, Sami on her heels.

"That *man* is out there causing a ruckus again. He refuses to leave unless you come out and speak with him."

Halvor pushed back his chair to stand. "Master Barloc?"

I stood as well, a blanket around my shoulders to ward off any lingering chills, my legs slightly less wobbly after the additional toast and tea that Sami had brought me. In fact, now that the initial nausea had passed, I was ravenous and fairly certain my fever had broken.

"Please go explain to him *again* that *we* are not holding you here captive." She gestured at the open doorway, clearly expecting him to obey.

"Of course." Halvor pushed a hand through his unruly hair, tossing an apologetic look back as he quickly did as she bade.

Once he'd gone, I sucked in a deep breath, a tumult of words and anger that had been banked for hours having risen the moment I heard her voice coming toward us in the hallway. But all that came out was a strangled "How *could* you?"

She wouldn't meet my gaze; instead, she stood stiffly by the door, her chin lifted slightly, the tendons in her neck flexing when she swallowed once, her teeth visibly clenched. Sami's gaze swiveled between us, blanching as the silence drew out, growing heavier by the second.

"*How could you?*" I shouted.

Mother finally turned to me, her eyes blazing, but her lips bloodless. "I hope you have *finally* learned to leave all of that alone" was all she said, and then without another word—but what had I expected, an *apology?*—she spun on her heel to leave.

And all that fury, all those teeth in my belly, born of anger, born of desperation, born of a shout, and a *thud*, and a scream, and a locked door, reared up within me, and lashed out before I could swallow it back down. "I hate you," I spat, just before she made it through the open door.

I actually *saw* the impact of my words, her whole body flinched as if I truly had ripped into her with teeth and nails, and not just vitriol. But she didn't pause, didn't turn, didn't respond. She merely marched away, the *clack clack clack* of her shoes on the stones the only sound beyond the wild pounding in my ears.

As quickly as the rage had come, with her departure it drained out of me, leaving me empty and shaken . . . and ashamed.

Did I hate my mother? Hot tears burned in my eyes and acidic guilt burned in my gut. Despite everything, the truth was *no*. I didn't. But it didn't matter, because now she *believed* that I did. And I didn't know how to fix it—or if I even *should*.

A squeak of a shoe on stone reminded me that Sami still stood there, that she'd witnessed my viciousness, a cruelness I hadn't even realized I was capable of.

"I'm sorry," I whispered at last, swiping at my cheeks.

There was a pause when I feared she would reprimand me—a verbal lashing that I certainly deserved. But instead, she merely said, "I know."

I turned, her familiar face wavering in front of me. "I didn't mean it."

"I know," she repeated, and then with a soft sigh said, "Zuhra . . . your mother has made mistakes in her life, and you have borne the brunt of some of them. But she does love you. Though she handles it in ways we disagree with, she does these things because she's *afraid*. She's hurting—and has been for a long time. She believes she's trying to protect you."

I couldn't hold her gaze and instead looked down to the ground where my toes peeked out from underneath my dress—the one I'd worn for the duration of my punishment. How could I be so miserable and yet still so angry all at once? I hadn't meant to say that to her—but I was still mad about what she'd done. About what had happened to Inara.

"Why don't I help you get cleaned up," Sami offered when I didn't respond. She stepped close enough to press the back of her hand to my forehead again. "Thankfully the fever has broken," she announced. "I think a warm bath will do the trick nicely. I always feel like a new person after bathing."

"Thank you," I said softly, still looking down.

She bustled over to my dresser and then clucked disapprovingly. "That man doesn't know when to quit."

I glanced up to see her looking toward the window as she pulled out one of my dresses—a dark green one I had spent hours trimming with black lace that she'd brought back from one of the rare times she'd left the citadel for the village—and then walked over to where I stood.

"Who?"

"It's his master. He's been coming and shouting at us until young Master Roskery goes out to speak with him through the hedge."

"Master Barloc?"

Sami nodded as she helped unbutton my dress and pull it off. My arms were still a bit shaky when I tried to do it on my own. The dress was stale and crumpled from all the time I'd spent in bed. Her nose wrinkled. "Why don't you wrap up in this clean blanket while I go fetch some water for you to bathe?"

My face heated to think that Halvor had been sitting so near to me as I took the proffered blanket from Sami and wrapped it around my body. She gingerly lifted my dress and then stripped my bed as well. "I'll just wash these right up for you. It will be lovely to sleep in clean sheets tonight, wouldn't you agree?"

"You don't have to do that—I can come help you—"

"I'm happy to. It's the least I can do after . . ." She trailed off, her arms tightening around the bundle of sheets. "You just stay here and I'll be back soon."

I wanted to argue with her, but I couldn't very well go traipsing about the citadel in my undergarments and a blanket with Halvor there. And besides, much as I hated to admit it, I still felt unnaturally weak, though I wasn't sure how much was from the effects of the fever, or what was from the lingering guilt over what I'd said to my mother. My legs trembled as I moved over to stand by the window, gripping the blanket around my shoulders to ward off the chill that rose from the glass pane. Halvor already stood by the hedge, gesturing emphatically though Master Barloc couldn't see him through the thick greenery.

Mother stood halfway across the courtyard, watching, her arms wrapped over each other across her waist, as though trying to hold herself together. The wind whipped at her skirts and her bun, pulling a few wisps of dark hair free. She looked even smaller than normal with the hedge rising beyond her and the vast peaks cleaving the slate clouds tumbling toward us in the distance.

A tiny, immovable mountain given flesh.

But for just a moment, as I looked down at her, I thought that she looked almost . . . lost. The burning in my eyes and belly returned with a vengeance as I watched her. The memory I'd had when I'd first walked into the dining salon the first night Halvor had come—of her smiling and laughing, her hair long and loose down her back—rose unbidden and something clenched within me. Inara and I had never been enough, had never been able to make her happy again . . . but what would it do to her if—*when*—I found a way and we left her here truly alone? Was it possible to escape? Should I even try? Halvor's warning about the king's edict had changed things—would Inara be safer out there, or here, behind the hedge? Even with Mother?

She turned and looked up at the citadel, her eyes going to my window, as if she could sense my gaze on her. I quickly drew back, hoping she didn't see me.

It didn't matter, I told myself, forcing the barbed pangs of guilt away and thinking of Inara hurt—asking for me and being refused again and again. Mother had gone too far this time.

And I wasn't going to let it happen again. Even if it meant facing the world beyond the hedge.

THIRTEEN

I didn't see Mother again until dinner that night. But when I began to walk toward her, intending to apologize, she turned her back to me, her spine stiffening, and I'd stumbled to a confused and guilty halt. She hadn't said a word to me during the entire miserable meal. Inara was lost to the roar once more, and Halvor had only focused on his food, silently eating without ever looking up. I'd managed to eat a little, then excused myself to go to bed early, claiming I felt weak—which was true but still felt like a coward's move.

By the next morning, I'd regained my strength and we bumbled our way into a semblance of our normal routine, though having Halvor there added an element of the surreal to our lives. I did my best to act penitent in my mother's presence in the morning room, to try and mend what I'd broken, and to allay any suspicion of what I intended to do. But she barely spoke to me—or anyone, for that matter. She'd retreated into a weighted silence that was almost more terrible than her normal domineering demands. I wondered if what I'd said had finally made her realize she'd gone too far this time.

As much as I told myself it didn't matter, twin needles of guilt and pity pricked at me, puncturing holes in my certainty that leaving was my only option.

And to make matters worse, it rained all morning, trapping us inside, not stopping until long after breakfast finished. As soon as the deluge paused, I stood.

"May I take Inara outside?" I asked, readying myself for her refusal.

Mother just continued to ply her needle, ignoring me entirely. I glanced to Sami, who shook her head slightly. But if she wasn't going to explicitly tell me no, then I wasn't about to willingly stay in the morning room with her awful silence pressing in on me. The suspense of her reprisal for my meanness was almost worse than whatever was to come.

Halvor accompanied us outside. I knew he wished to spend more time with Inara, but as the morning went on, we found that she was unpredictable around him. At times she hardly seemed aware he was there, but then she'd unexpectedly grow so agitated she'd begin pulling at her hair and I'd have to send him away to try and calm her.

"You have a soothing effect on her," he observed just before lunch.

"It's being outside," I disagreed, though secretly I was pleased he thought so.

"No, I noticed it this morning, as well. When you would sit with her."

The rain that had trapped us inside longer than normal had made Inara tense, but there was little we could do besides going out in the downpour. I'd tried everything I could think of, but her mumbling and counting had grown louder and louder and she'd begun to pull at her hair and ears, leaving angry red marks on her skin from her nails. However, she'd quickly calmed afterward as the marks had faded and then disappeared altogether.

"No . . . it wasn't me," I spoke slowly, realization dawning. "It's because her body is healing itself. She scratched her ears but now the marks are gone."

Halvor's eyebrows lifted. "Maybe it wasn't enough to clear her mind—but it helped calm her down?"

"I think so."

Inara stood between us, pushing her fingers into the soil around some of her bean plants. I snuck a glance toward the morning room windows, wondering if Mother ever paused in her useless work to look out at us. If she ever wished to join us. I still couldn't make sense of her continued stubborn silence—and that she'd let me come outside with no argument. I could only attribute it to being unable to stand remaining trapped in a room for hours with Inara.

Or because of the three words that still sat between us, a poisonous hedge of my own making.

"I wish there was something else we could find for her to use her power on. Besides plants and healing." Halvor's gaze was on my sister, but I watched him—the way he looked at her, the way he bent his body toward her.

"If only we could get that book back. Maybe it would explain it better. I wonder what my mother did with it."

Halvor finally looked away from Inara to me. "Do you think she would have put it back or kept it?"

"I have no idea. We could ask Sami if she's noticed any books in her room." Even as I said it, I knew it was a futile hope. Mother would have made certain to hide the book—I wouldn't have put it past her to even destroy it. The thought of all that knowledge gone forever tore at me. I could only hope she wasn't *that* spiteful.

Lightning flashed in the distance, illuminating the charcoal clouds momentarily with a jagged pitchfork of brilliant white light. Within moments thunder growled, a long, low bellow, like a thousand hellhounds charging through the blackened sky. Inara shuddered beside me, mumbling something unintelligible. The respite hadn't lasted long.

"We're going to have to go back in." Halvor sounded as disappointed as I felt.

"Maybe we can go to the kitchen and help Sami make luncheon. Come on, Nara." I gently reached for her hand, turning her from her plants. She startled and looked up, her eyes burning as bright a blue as I'd ever seen. "It's all right. It's me. It's Zuhra."

"Zuhra . . . Zuhra," she repeated softly, my name a thick noise that was barely intelligible. She shook her head, but allowed me to pull her back to the citadel.

"Yes, come on. Let's go find some food," I coaxed.

Slowly, we made our way to the kitchen, where Sami was kneading dough, little puffs of flour accentuating each push of her fists. Her cheek and hair were streaked with it, as if she'd forgotten it coated her hands and had pushed an errant strand back in place before remembering. I inhaled deeply, a bit of the tension that tightened the muscles between my shoulder blades loosening as the scents of herbs and fresh bread wafted over us, along with the heat of the fire from the hearth. Of all the places I was "allowed" to go in the citadel, this was my favorite.

"Come to make trouble?" Sami teased as she finished with the dough and put it in a bowl to rest and rise. Flour was a rare delicacy for us, something she'd procured on her last trip to the village last winter when supplies had run dangerously low, despite Inara's plant-growing skills. Sami rationed it religiously. Making bread must have been her way of a peace offering for her part in keeping me locked away—or for what had happened to Inara.

"Never." I snatched a fat strawberry, the last of the spoils from Inara's magic that first day Halvor showed up, and plopped it in my mouth before she could stop me. "We thought we'd help you."

Sami came to Inara's side and helped guide her to a chair near the prepping table.

"Your help is always welcome. Just so you know, your mother had a headache. She went to lie down."

"Then can we eat in here, with you?" I asked, eager to stay where it was cozy and warm—and free of my mother's anger and my guilt.

"I don't mean to pry, but couldn't you eat all your meals with us at the table in the other room?" Halvor asked. "Not that I'm complaining—I like it here, too."

"Sami can eat anywhere she wants." I bristled at the unspoken accusation.

"I *choose* not to eat anywhere except my kitchen. If I wished to eat with Mistress Cinnia, I'm sure she would allow it." It was startling to hear Sami use my mother's actual name as she ladled out some vegetable soup into three bowls and passed one to each of us. I retrieved a knife and cut a few pieces off one of the steaming loaves of bread sitting on the counter, the crusty bread easily giving way beneath the sharpened blade. Paladin steel—it never dulled.

We ate in quiet for a moment. I savored every bite of the rare treat. Even Inara ceased her mumbling to take a few bites of the bread that I placed in her hand, closing her fingers around it.

"Again, forgive me for my impertinence," Halvor suddenly spoke up, "but if I'm to live here now . . . for the foreseeable future . . . I wish to understand your situations better, if you don't mind answering some questions."

Thunder grumbled once more, but there in the kitchen, deep in the belly of the citadel, it seemed distant and almost unreal. The rain came down with such force it pinged off the single window in the room, but it was a mere counterpoint to the cheerful crackle of the fire and the clang of silverware and dishes as we ate. We were cocooned in the safety and warmth of Sami's domain, where every inch of space was filled with evidences of her love and care. The pots and pans were well worn but polished until they gleamed where they hung above the cast-iron stove. The counters were tidy—every carefully collected herb and spice and ingredient had a place, filling the kitchen with scents and colors of a dizzying array, making it feel full but not cluttered. She was an excellent cook, capable of turning our meager supplies into masterpieces, and I had spent many, many hours with her there, not only cleaning up after meals, but learning to make them as well.

"You may ask, but I can't guarantee we'll have all the answers you seek."

Halvor nodded at Sami's warning, tearing his slice of bread into smaller pieces as he deliberated. Finally, he asked, "How did you come to be here? I understand that Zuhra and Inara are her daughters—they didn't have a choice. But how do you fit . . . that is to say, are you . . ."

"Their servant?" Mahsami rescued him.

No, I thought immediately, but my stomach clenched in anticipation of her answer. Is that how she saw herself—how she thought my mother saw her?

"I suppose I am, of a sort."

"No, Sami—"

She continued over my protest, "They arrived in the middle of the night all those years ago. Adelric showed up in Gateskeep the next morning and begged us not to turn them in to the garrisons that regularly came to our village, checking to see if there had been any activity in the citadel. The army relied on us townsfolk to tell them if we'd noticed anything; they didn't like searching it themselves. When the Paladin rebuilt this place, protections were put in place to guard it, including the hedge, just before the gateway shut for good. Though it was smaller back then, it was still dangerous enough to make even the king's most formidable warriors afraid of trying to get past it to the citadel. However, if word got out that a *Paladin* was living there . . . who knew what the garrisons would have attempted to do. Adelric made promises of peace, to leave us alone, and even bribed those who were hesitant to do as he asked. Eventually, we all agreed to pretend they weren't there, as long as they kept to themselves. He was only one Paladin, after all—with a *human* bride . . . and though we were nervous, we weren't a bloodthirsty lot."

I listened silently, hardly even remembering to eat. I'd heard bits of this story before, but she'd never told me *this* much. A part of me bristled that she was willing to share this story—what should have been *my* story—with Halvor, when I had asked her so many times over the years to tell me more. But I swallowed my hurt, far more eager to hear more than to voice my discontent.

"They kept their word," she continued, "and we didn't see them, other than the few times they braved coming into town for supplies—though it was usually just Cinnia. Adelric rarely left the citadel from what we could tell."

"But wouldn't you have at least seen him on his gryphon?" Halvor broke in. "They all had them, and from what I understand they require quite a bit of exercise. So where was his magical beast during all of this?"

I leaned forward, breath caught somewhere between my chest and my throat.

There was a long pause, a pendulum swinging between Sami's previous refusal to share and whatever had induced her to change her mind today, for Halvor. Finally, she slowly responded, "No, we never saw his." She glanced out the window, toward the stables visible through the rain. "I asked Cinnia about it—once. We'd never seen a Paladin *without* a gryphon and we were all wondering if he was somehow hiding his. But she told me they were attacked by a garrison on their way to the citadel, and barely escaped with their lives. His gryphon wasn't as lucky. She made it sound like the creature sacrificed itself in some way to protect them and allow them to escape."

Halvor grimaced as he took another bite of soup. I, on the other hand, could only stare at Sami, reeling from her unexpected admission.

I'd occasionally been brave enough to wander through the abandoned stables, wondering about the gryphons that had lived there, dreaming of what it would be like to see one—to *ride* one. Wondering how it would have felt to run my hands over the feathers on its head and neck; imagining the sound as it swished its leonine tail; picturing myself sitting upon its back, soaring into the sky. It was a different thing altogether to hear Sami speak of it, to admit *out loud* that my father had a gryphon; that my father *and* mother had ridden on one—until it lost its life protecting them.

Why had she kept so much of this from me until now? Almost as if she could feel the hurt building within me, she glanced my way as she hurried to continue—perhaps in an effort to keep me from speaking and asking her that very question.

"I knew them better than anyone, because I was the village midwife, but sadly, it still wasn't much. When Cinnia and Adelric found out they were expecting their first baby, she risked coming to Gateskeep to call on me for help. Which I'm ashamed to admit I was reluctant to give." She paused, her eyes sad, and when she tried to smile it was a small, rueful upturn of her lips. "Zuhra was a healthy, beautiful baby girl. The birth was easy and I wasn't needed afterward, so I didn't see any of them again for months, until the day Cinnia brought you to the village. For some reason, having a baby made her loneliness and seclusion at the citadel that much harder to bear. Despite the risk, she made efforts to reach out, to be my friend, but I rebuffed them all. Everyone did."

My soup sat forgotten in front of me, turning cold as my cheeks grew warm from these details I'd never known. Only Inara kept eating, her spoon clanking against her bowl, all her concentration needed to focus on eating. But I couldn't take another bite.

"Why?"

I was grateful Halvor was the one asking the questions so that Sami hopefully didn't notice my shock—and dismay.

She gazed steadily at him but I could see the flush creeping up her neck. "Because of Adelric, her husband. Because we all knew what he was."

"Even here—so close to their citadel—you'd come to fear and dislike the Paladin." He shook his head. "They'd *protected* you. They saved Vamala from the rakasa. Surely those who lived at their feet wouldn't have forgotten that as easily."

"The king's edict made it hard to know what to believe," Sami said softly.

The death decree that Halvor had mentioned the first night he came to us—the one that made me nervous to still try and escape with Inara. With everything that had happened after that night in the library, I'd never questioned him further about it. I looked to Halvor, hoping for more information, but he was fully focused on Sami. She swept some errant flour off the counter into her hand and then wiped it on her apron. Did he notice the way her fingers trembled? Part of me wanted to go to her, to hug her and tell her it was all right, that she didn't need to share any more. But I stayed unmoving in my chair, trapped by my own bewilderment and curiosity.

"Even here, in Gateskeep," she continued, "the rumors reached us—the stories that perhaps the Paladin weren't as noble as we'd believed. That perhaps they let the rakasa loose on Vamala on purpose, so that they could swoop in on their beasts and save us with their magic, and lord themselves as gods over us. And of course the king's orders only solidified that fear."

Halvor nodded, a flash of wistful understanding crossing his face. Understanding I wished I possessed.

"I'd hoped to discover otherwise," he admitted, "that perhaps the village at the base of their citadel wouldn't have believed King Velfron's propaganda."

I had to gulp down the words *Who is King Velfron* before I humiliated myself again by revealing a further lack of knowledge about any of this.

"Most of the village didn't know what to believe, and he was very kind and kept to himself, which was why none of us reported him to the authorities," Sami said. "But Adelric bringing Cinnia here . . . raising a *family* at the citadel . . . it left many of us wondering what he was hoping to accomplish. The Paladin had never done anything to purposely hurt us or rule over us in Gateskeep . . . but being this close to the gateway meant that we suffered a great number of rakasa attacks, and the Paladin weren't always careful in their attempts to capture or kill them. There were casualties."

Finally, I could bear it no longer, my desperation superseding my pride. "King who? And what gateway?" I forced myself to speak, over the thrumming of my heart. "Why have you never told me any of this?"

Sami blinked and looked to me, almost as if she'd forgotten I was there. "I couldn't risk telling you and having you say something and accidentally reveal the very knowledge your mother made me swear to keep from you. But now . . . with him here . . . things are changing. I always knew we couldn't keep the history of your heritage from you forever. I think your mother has begun to realize that as well."

"The gateway," Halvor added, "is here somewhere. Most scholars agree that the citadel was originally built on this cliff eons ago to hide and protect it. They rebuilt it to enable the Paladin to keep their warriors as close to the gateway as possible in case anything else got through."

"What kind of gateway? Where does it go?"

"*The* gateway—the one that the rakasa came through to Vamala in the first place?" The way he said it made it sound like a question—or a test. I shook my head, my neck hot with embarrassment.

Halvor and Sami exchanged a look, his one of disbelief and hers one of guilt.

"A thousand generations ago," he explained, "our worlds were connected, magical and nonmagical people and creatures living side by side, traveling easily from realm to realm. It was a time of slavery and suffering, for all but the most powerful beings. But after a massive war, a group of Paladin who had come to care for the nonmagical humans combined their power to sever the worlds completely, leaving only one possible link. The gateway hidden here is the connection to Visimperum—the realm where the rakasa and Paladin live. We remained separate for so long that the creatures and beings from the other worlds, including the Paladin and rakasa, fell into myth and legend, a tale used to frighten children into staying in bed. Until the day when it was reopened somehow, and rakasa escaped from Visimperum through the gateway and began terrorizing Vamala once more."

I could only stare as he relayed such earth-shaking information as if it were common, everyday knowledge. Which, apparently, it was to everyone in the world, besides me. "And that gateway is *here* somewhere? Why is there even a gateway at all? When did it get opened—and how? Is it closed now?" Questions rose faster than I could speak them, one on top of another, filling my mind and mouth.

"Those are the questions that the people of Vamala asked," Sami said. "Perhaps you can understand why some of the villagers were suspicious of the Paladin. That's why I allowed myself to look past the evidences of a loving, happy couple—of a good-hearted, kind man gifted with extraordinary abilities and a young wife who had left her family, her home, *everything*, to follow him—and turned a cold shoulder on them."

"What changed?" Halvor asked when I continued to look at her mutely, trying to absorb all of this information while reconciling the cold, unfeeling story version of Sami with the warm, loving one I'd always known.

"Inara. She changed everything." Sami's eyes were on my sister, her expression soft, almost mournful. "When your mother found out she was with child a second time, she called on me again. And once more, I begrudgingly agreed to tend to her pregnancy and birth. My fear and prejudices aside, I wasn't so unfeeling as to refuse to help a laboring woman. The night Inara was born, Adelric came to Gateskeep to get me. Once we returned here, I couldn't shake the sensation that something was off. I'd only been there a few times, but it was different that night. And Adelric seemed . . . *troubled*. He asked me to go immediately to their room to tend to Cinnia while he checked on something else in the citadel. I didn't question him—I thought perhaps he was going to find you." She paused and then: "We never saw him again. And the next morning the hedge had tripled in size, covering the gate, trapping me in the citadel with you three. I was furious . . . and frightened. But my presence was probably the only reason you and Inara survived that first year. Your mother was . . ."

"Broken," I supplied softly.

Sami nodded, her gaze still on Inara. My memories of that night rushed forward—Mother refusing to take the baby, calling out for Adelric, Inara's burning eyes, her tiny cry . . .

Halvor was quiet for a long moment before he pressed. "Zuhra told me the hedge has let you out before—when things are desperate and you must go to the village for supplies. If you were so upset at being trapped here, why did you come back?"

Sami's eyes darkened to slate and she blinked hard. "Because the girls needed me."

Oh, Sami. Something inside me crumpled but I tried to keep my voice steady when I asked, "But what of love—a family of your own?"

She brushed at an errant streak of moisture on her flour-dusted cheek. "I've known great love here, love for both of you girls. And even Cinnia, though you may find it hard to believe. If you'd only known her before—if you'd been able to see what his leaving did to her . . ." Sami shook her head and reached out to help guide Inara's hand to her bread on the table. "And . . . I didn't feel worthy to have a family of my own. I was too afraid of the curse in my own blood, too afraid of myself. So I missed my chance."

Halvor glanced at me questioningly, but I shook my head minutely. I had no idea what she was referring to. She'd never brought any of this up to me before.

"Sami, how could you say such a thing?"

She turned to me and I nearly reeled back at the sudden hardness in her eyes. "You think you know me, but you know only what I've chosen to show you—what I've chosen to share."

I flinched, my heart slamming against my ribs. She'd never spoken to me in such a cold, cruel way before. "What do you mean?"

"I had a sister too, once. She wasn't part Paladin, like yours, but she was . . . not right in the mind. And I wasn't like you, Zuhra. I was ashamed of her. We all were." A muscle in Sami's jaw ticked. "She suffered for it."

I opened my mouth to speak but then closed it again, not knowing what I could possibly say to ease the grief that seemed to age her right before my eyes.

"Hasanni could manage small, menial tasks. The wife of the innkeeper took pity on her when she was older and let her wash dishes in the kitchen for a bit of money. I was younger than Hasanni; at that time I'd just come of age. I had a beau, a boy from a nearby village who sold his father's wares to Gateskeep. We had spoken of courting—even marriage someday. And then, one winter night, when I was supposed to get Hasanni from the inn to walk her home, I was with him and I forgot. I completely *forgot* about her—my own sister." Sami bit the words out.

My blood throbbed unbearably hot in my suddenly cold limbs. I didn't want to know anymore, I didn't want to hear the rest. But I could no more stop her than I could will away the storm outside that still lashed the citadel with rain and lightning, the thunder making the walls shudder around us as she continued.

"She waited there, like she was supposed to. For an hour, she stood in the snow, waiting for me while I danced and laughed and tried to make myself forget she even existed. A traveler showed up late that night, and mistook her for a stable hand. She'd always been fond of animals and he had a beautiful roan stallion . . ." Sami's voice cracked, her cheeks damp while the suffering she'd held within her for so long—decades—came tumbling out.

I perched like a statue on the stool, my earlier curiosity turned to horror at realizing that I'd lived with Sami my entire life—for eighteen years—and had never truly known her. It had taken a stranger coming and questioning her to find out about her life before the one she'd led here.

"Hasanni tried to do what the man asked, but her movements were jerky under the best of circumstances, and there was a blizzard that night and the horse spooked. The gentleman tried to control his mount but . . . Hasanni was trampled. By the time I remembered my sister and rushed to the inn, it was too late." Sami stared down at her hands, her voice choked. "*I* was too late. She was gone."

"Oh, *Sami.*" I ached for her, for the burden she'd obviously carried for so long. "It wasn't your fault—"

"*Yes,* it was," she bit out, her heart-shattering grief transformed into bitter anger in the blink of an eye. "It was my duty to take care of her, and I was so absorbed in my dreams of leaving Gateskeep—of getting away from this place, from the shadow of the citadel, from *her*—that I failed her. I never spoke to the boy again. I wouldn't even consider courting anyone. Hasanni's madness ran in our family, and I had proven I wasn't capable—wasn't *worthy* of such a charge. I didn't dare seek out marriage or have children of my own. Instead, I apprenticed myself to Gabi, the village healer, and learned to deliver other people's babies."

The kitchen was silent for a long moment. I couldn't even move to scrub at the wetness on my own cheeks. I wanted to comfort her, wanted to take away her pain and guilt, I wanted her to know the gift she'd been in my life, in Inara's. But I was immobilized by disbelief, my mouth as dry as sand as I thought of a girl—a girl like Nara—being trampled to death in the snow while Sami danced with some faceless boy, safe and warm and wanted.

"It quickly became apparent that Inara wasn't learning to speak or communicate normally—that she had some . . . difficulties," Sami continued, caught up in her confessions, unaware of my turmoil. "As she grew I realized perhaps the hedge trapping me here was the Great God's way of giving me a second chance. I had failed my sister, but I wouldn't fail her. I wouldn't fail *you*: the kind of sister to Inara that I should have been to Hasanni." Sami reached up to lovingly tuck a strand of hair behind Inara's ear. The entire time, she'd methodically been eating her lunch, oblivious to us and the shattering truths Sami had revealed. "So I stayed."

Inara finally looked up, right at that moment, directly at Sami. And then she smiled. A real, genuine smile—so rare, a gift I held more precious than just about anything in my life.

"I stayed," Sami repeated, so softly it was almost to herself.

FOURTEEN

Mother didn't emerge from her room all afternoon. After her confession, Sami excused herself, leaving us alone in the kitchens. I was so shocked by everything she'd shared, I had wished to retire to my room as well, to try and process it all. But I couldn't leave Inara alone—or with Halvor. Instead, we took Inara outside when the rain let up again for a couple of hours. We walked around the muddy grounds together, letting her linger by her gardens, but there were no plants in need of attention, and so she merely let her fingers trail over the green leaves and growing berries, herbs, and vegetables one by one, her mumbling soft and incoherent, before moving on to the next one.

"So the hedge tripled in size overnight—the night your father, the Paladin, disappeared. And it rarely allows anyone in or out," Halvor mused as Inara made her way toward her grove of trees, the hedge rising far above their branches. "It's never allowed any of you three out, but Sami has been able to come and go at times—when things are desperate enough."

"Yes."

Halvor's eyebrows drew together, his forehead creasing. "It almost seems as though . . . perhaps it is somewhat sentient? It's almost as if it is trying to . . . protect you somehow?"

The sky overhead was a sea of graphite, dark and ominous, threatening more rain to come, though it continued to hold off for the moment. After such a long hot spell the previous week, it was unseasonably cold; the wind bit through my shawl, past my clothes and even my skin, chilling me to the bone. I shivered. Or perhaps it was Halvor's words that made me tremble and pull the shawl closer around my shoulders.

"I don't understand how it's possible, but yes, I think you're right."

How else could one account for the hedge's behavior? Even to think of it having *behavior* made me realize it *had* to be sentient, at least to some degree. There was no other word that came to mind that described what it did, that monstrous warden that had been as much a part of my life as Sami, Nara, or my mother.

"It's Paladin; it's not of this world," Halvor said as if that explained everything. And maybe for him, it did.

But that wasn't enough for me.

Before I could express that, I blinked and realized that in my distraction talking to Halvor, I'd lost track of Inara. With Sami's story still ringing in my mind, I quickly scanned the courtyard for her.

"Inara!" I called out when I spotted her far past the grove of trees, almost to the hedge. She usually stayed away from the thick green leaves that hid the poisonous barbs beneath. Why had she picked today to press doggedly toward it? She either ignored my cry or couldn't hear me.

"Inara!" I lifted my skirts and ran. The wind tore her name from my mouth. If she reached for the hedge, would it strike her? Was her ability to heal strong enough to defeat the poison the concealed barbs held? My heart raced my feet as I flew toward her. I didn't want to find out.

I was still too far away to stop her when she reached out and ran her hand along the rain-drenched leaves. The hedge shuddered slightly, but otherwise didn't move, keeping the poisonous thorns safely hidden behind the thick, heavy leaves hanging low from the rainwater still clinging to them.

"Inara!" I finally reached her side and grabbed her arm.

She startled with a screech, batting at me and stumbling backward into the hedge. This time it unmistakably moved, curving around her body, almost as if embracing her—or swallowing her. She would be pierced at any moment.

"Nara—"

I reached for her again and this time when I took hold of her hand, she allowed me to pull her free from the vines that still slithered behind and around her like jade snakes.

Halvor halted at my side, his eyes wide as Inara broke free and the vines fluttered to a stop.

"What was it doing?"

"I have no idea," I responded, quickly guiding my sister away from the hedge. I ran my eyes over her, looking for any signs of scratches or wounds. None were visible—thankfully. "Let's go back inside. It's starting to rain again."

Sure enough, tiny rings formed in the puddles still dotting the grounds as rain began to drip from the sky. Such a light sprinkling wasn't normally enough to make me take Inara in and face the confines of the citadel, but after everything that had happened and been revealed that day, I was spooked. Discomfort itched beneath my skin, a creeping sense that things were changing, just as Sami had said, and the rules of the citadel and its grounds were changing with it.

"Already?" Halvor trailed behind us, but I ignored the reluctance in his voice and marched resolutely toward the door, Nara's hand still gripped in mine. Luckily she came willingly. There were days when I had to cajole her into coming inside; and on her worst days, Sami and I would have to work together to literally drag her back in. But she was docile at my side, her gaze on the ground as she allowed me to tug her forward.

I heard Halvor sigh behind us, but I ignored him, my only thought to get Nara as far away from the hedge as possible.

Mother came to dinner that night, much to my dismay. It was a strained meal, with Halvor attempting to make small talk despite her continued curt remarks in return. I remained silent, barely looking up from my plate, more conscious than ever of Sami serving the food rather than joining us to enjoy it. Nara sat beside me, mumbling and pulling at her skirt rather than eating, no matter how many times I tried to offer her the food. Perhaps she could sense the tension in the room, even through the roar.

Guilt slithered in my belly, compounded by what I'd learned of my mother from Sami, making eating difficult for me as well. She'd given up her family, moved to a remote, abandoned citadel for Adelric, had been rejected by the townspeople, and then he'd left her, with only her two young daughters and Sami. And yesterday, I had told her I hated her.

Only after Sami had cleared our plates did I summon the courage to attempt a foray into conversation with her. "Mother, I—"

Before I could finish, Mother pushed her chair away from the table and stood. "I'm certain you said quite enough yesterday." Her eyes met mine, for the first time since she left my room, and I reeled back from the anger—the *hurt*—swimming in hers. My mouth snapped shut. "I can't shake this headache, so I believe I will retire for my nightly tea. I imagine you are tired after so much time outside today—I expect you all to retire to your rooms for the night immediately as well." I didn't miss the flash of warning on her face, the unspoken command that we *stay* in our rooms—*or else*.

Halvor belatedly stood as well, but I remained in my seat, my lips pursed tightly together, afraid of what would burst out of me if I tried to speak again. An apology—a question—more anger. I couldn't have hazarded a guess; I was a cataclysm of emotions, all crowding each other inside the too-small confines of my mind.

Though I *did* feel guilty for what I'd said, and what she'd been through, I hadn't even begun to forget the burning hunger, the hollowness of body and spirit she'd inflicted on me—the helplessness of knowing something had happened to Inara but being unable to go to her. And for what? Visiting a library that might give me answers about my father—about Inara? I lifted my chin, all the anger I'd spent days suppressing swirling back up, the beast she'd created within me woken by the challenge in her eyes.

"Would you like me to escort you to your room?" Halvor suddenly offered, standing and holding out his arm as if he were a gentleman and she a grand lady.

Mother blinked and turned to him, breaking the silent battle between us. "That won't be necessary."

"I will make you some more tea," Sami offered, stepping forward from where she'd been waiting by the door. "And perhaps a poultice to try for your headache?"

"Thank you, Mahsami. I would appreciate that." She inclined her head toward the older woman and I had to look away, ashamed to see the imperiousness on my mother's face. She *did* treat Sami like a servant . . . but their relationship was more complicated than I'd realized. Again that twinge of pity resurfaced when I thought of my mother living here all alone, save for my father, trying to reach out and make a friend, only to be rebuffed. But I still wanted to shout at her to stop it, to stop *all* of it—the ridiculous charade of gentility, the adherence to societal rules that made no difference in our tiny little world, the refusal to let us search the citadel for any and all clues about my heritage—and about the Paladin who had built it.

I waited for the sound of her footfalls in the hall to fade and then disappear entirely, before standing and hurrying to Sami's side. "You have to do it again."

Sami's eyebrows lifted.

"Stronger this time," I added, and understanding dawned on her face. "Make sure she'll be out for the *whole* night."

Sami's gaze flickered past me to Inara and Halvor then back again. A muscle ticked in her cheek; I could almost feel the refusal building within her, rising up her throat to crush my impulsive plan.

"Please, Sami," I pleaded before she could tell me no. "I can't take this anymore. I have to find a way to help Inara."

"But after last time . . ."

I hated myself for it, but I was desperate. "We have to do *something*, Sami. Please . . . help me help Nara. *Please.*"

Her eyes flickered to Inara again, and I knew I'd won. "All right. I'll make it stronger this time. But you must promise to hurry and be back in your rooms well before sunrise."

Impulsively I embraced her, holding on tightly, almost as tight as the constriction in my chest. "Thank you." My voice was muffled but I knew she heard me when she hesitantly hugged me back. I only hoped she knew I meant for far more than just the tea.

FIFTEEN

I waited long past the time when Sami took Mother her tea before daring to emerge from my room. I'd helped Inara get to bed at least an hour earlier, and there were no sounds from her room when I slipped past her door. I carried no lantern, and I'd dressed in all black—a black blouse and skirt that I usually saved for cleaning days, and black slippers that were soft enough to silence my footfalls.

The citadel was always a hulking monster at night; as a child I'd imagined I could hear it breathing, taking great rattling inhales and gusty, creaking exhales all around me, watching through the paintings and statues that decorated its halls, and the jeweled eyes of the Paladin on the ceilings above us. But tonight it felt alive in a way I hadn't experienced in years. That sensation of awareness crawled beneath my skin, a thousand tiny insects of paranoia scuttling through my body and making me want to simultaneously scratch my arms and continually glance over my shoulder.

Perhaps it knew I was determined in a way I'd never been before; my breath came like fire through my lungs, my blood burned through my veins. The darkness seethed thicker and thicker as I hurried through the hallways to Halvor's room, pressing in on me, heavy with expectation. The hedge was full of Paladin magic— what about the citadel itself? Did it know I moved within its belly, did it suspect what I intended to do? The walls were too close, the shadows played tricks on my mind. Twice I thought I heard a whisper of a voice from somewhere far away, a hint of words that I couldn't quite understand. I strained toward it even as a shiver scraped down my spine.

"*Stop it*," I scolded myself as I increased my pace, hoping the sound of my own voice would chase the specters out of my mind. Because surely that's all it was—fear, adrenaline, anxiety creating something out of nothing, making monsters and cognizance where there was nothing but stone and wood and fabric. Empty, lifeless objects that weren't watching me, tracing my progress through their domain.

When I reached Halvor's door I softly tapped on it twice, just enough to make the barest hint of noise. It immediately opened; he'd been waiting. The moment I saw him, the tension between my shoulders relaxed by half and my frenzied mind calmed. We were only two people, a boy and a girl, standing in an unremarkable hallway, the unfeeling stones beneath our feet cold and the air surrounding us sticky from the chilled humidity but nothing more.

"What is your plan?" Halvor glanced down the hall, his voice hushed, even though my mother was far from where we stood and completely incoherent to the world by this point.

The darkness swirled around us, a silken cloak of concealment that held us in its cocoon. "I want to find out how to help Inara escape the roar and then I'm going to find the way out of this place."

Halvor's eyes widened, so that the whites around the umber irises were visible. "But you said the hedge never let you leave."

I started to walk, knowing he would follow. Sami had assured me she increased the dose of the sleeping herbs in Mother's tea, but there was no time to waste. "It won't. So that's why I'm not going to try and go through the hedge. There must be another way."

"Another way? Such as . . ."

"I don't know. How strong did you say Paladin glass was?"

"I'm not sure I want to answer that question until I know the reason why you're asking."

I didn't respond, just continued moving through the citadel with Halvor on my heels. Through the grand entrance hall, with the Paladin carvings high above us, their jeweled eyes gleaming, even at night. Past door after door after door—including the door that opened into the library. I finally halted below the carved sign that Halvor had claimed said "Hall of Miracles" in Paladin, my heart thundering in my chest.

"You think the way to escape is in *there*?" Halvor's words were part strained hesitation and part breathless excitement.

"You said it's the Hall of Miracles. There are only two miracles I'm interested in—healing Nara permanently and escaping this place. So yes, I think if there *is* a way to help her or to get out of here, it must be in there."

He looked steadily at me, his expression unreadable. In the shadows his sandy hair darkened to soot and his cheekbones sharpened into distinct edges cutting across his face. Though the hallway was wide enough for a gryphon and its rider to walk through it, we stood close enough for me to feel the warmth of his body, even though we didn't touch. I'd never allowed myself to think of being touched by a boy, of hands searching and finding, of lips meeting and breath mingling like the couples in the fairy-tale book—those were things far beyond my reach, even in dreams. But as I stared up at him I suddenly found that my determination to escape, even to heal Inara, slipped and suddenly all I could think about was the curve of Halvor's lips, the hint of stubble that smudged his jaw and how it might feel against my own softer skin.

My neck heated at my own daring, even though I hadn't so much as stirred, let alone acted on my scandalous thoughts. Could he tell what I was thinking, what I was wishing? I had no experience with this . . . this *wanting*. Did it show on someone's face? Could he see it in my eyes? I'd noticed the way he watched Inara, the softness in his gaze and the protective bend to his body when she was near—something he didn't even seem aware of, acting out of some deeper instinct. He'd had an entire night and part of a morning to speak with her, to learn to want her, despite how untouchable she was—body and mind—before and after that accident.

I remembered all too clearly his desperation to escape the citadel when my mother had threatened to force him to marry me for spending a night with me unchaperoned.

And yet . . . he hadn't looked away, hadn't stepped back to widen the gap between our bodies. The chill from the stone floor seeped through my thin slippers but warmth swelled within me, tumbling in a heady rush through my torso out to my limbs. Air felt scarce again, much as it had when I was so frightened only a few minutes before. But where the fear had spiked my anxiety, urging me to flee or freeze, *this* made me want to move—but only enough to close what little space remained between us and melt into him.

When Halvor's eyes flickered down to my mouth and then back up again it ignited the heat within me, making me burn for his touch—aching to learn the feel of his lips on mine. It took every ounce of courage I still possessed to take that last step so that our faces were mere inches apart. We were so close my breasts skimmed his chest when we breathed.

I stared into his hooded eyes, willing him to truly *see* me—to want *me*. His breath was warm on my lips. For a moment it seemed as though he swayed toward me—I thought I felt his hands brush my hips—but then he hastily stepped back. Once, twice, until he bumped into the wall behind him.

The cold rushed back in all at once, chilling my blood into ice and my bones into stone, all except for the humiliation I could feel blossoming on my neck and cheeks.

"Zuhra." Halvor didn't look at me when he spoke, his voice rough as if he'd rubbed his throat with sandpaper. "I must apologize most profoundly if I led you to believe that I, ah, harbored certain . . . feelings for you . . . beyond those of a friendly nature."

My misery grew acutely worse with each bumbling word. And yet I couldn't keep myself from asking, "Is it Nara?"

Halvor didn't respond, but his silence was more than enough confirmation.

"I know you're obsessed with the Paladin—but she's my *sister*, she's a *real person*. Not a . . . a *subject* for you to study." I turned to the door, gripped the cold iron handles until my knuckles turned to white. "Help me open these doors."

"Zuhra, please—"

"*Help me open the doors,*" I repeated more forcefully and he fell silent. Without waiting to see what he did or didn't do, I yanked back as hard as I could. The doors groaned but didn't budge. I suddenly remembered why my mother had been able to get all the way across the citadel to stop me the last time I'd attempted to open them—they were massive, heavy . . . and they were stuck fast.

"Let me try," he offered quietly and I stepped away, gesturing for him to take my place. My blood thundered through my veins, somehow hot with shame and anger yet cold with dismay and grief all at once.

Halvor pulled, the lean, sinewy muscles of his arms straining as he tried to force the door open. It shuddered loudly and gave way a few inches with a terrible grinding noise as it scraped against the stone.

"You were right about the noise," he commented when he paused for a moment, his hairline growing damp with sweat from the effort. "It's a good thing Sami gave your mother that tonic."

Why do you think I asked her to? I thought, but remained stubbornly silent, my arms crossed over my chest.

Halvor turned to face me. "Please don't do this. Don't make things terrible between us. You are my friend, Zuhra. One of the only friends I've had in years."

Despite my better judgment, something inside me softened at the pleading tone in his voice, the sincerity in his face that had grown more and more dear to me every day. "You already know that you are my only friend. Besides Inara and Sami."

"Then can we remain friends? Can you forgive me for, uh . . . for not . . ."

"Not wanting me?" I supplied without thinking and immediately clapped my hand over my mouth.

Halvor cringed. "Zuhra . . ."

"I'm sorry. I'm sorry that I said that and that I tried to . . . that I thought . . ." I was the one bumbling through my words now. But I had to say it. In the cover of darkness, in the dead of this strange night, I had summoned the courage to try to find an escape, to have Sami drug my mother. I could be brave enough to speak my heart once. And then never, *ever* again. "I don't know how to be something that you will miss once I'm gone. I wish that I did."

There was a short beat of silence and then he hesitantly reached out and touched my arm. I flinched away.

"If I leave, if I never saw you again, of *course* I would miss you."

"No, you wouldn't. Not like *that*, not in the way I mean."

We both fell silent, the unresolvable truth a sudden, horrible blockade between us. One I'd erected with my attempt to get him to kiss me and cemented into place with my foolish admission. We could never go back to the easy friendship we'd had these last few days now, not after this night. I knew it the way I knew that I had to leave this place and take Inara with me. Sami, too. And Halvor . . . well, he could escape with us, but then he would return to his Master Barloc and continue on with his life.

And we would find our new one somewhere else, away from this place and the shadow of the Paladin and their citadel that seemed to stretch far further than just the mountainside it perched upon.

"Maybe if we do it together," I suggested, turning back to the door, miserably aware of the uncomfortable strain between us now.

"Yes, of course."

We awkwardly attempted to both get a grip on the handles without touching each other.

"I can see why you weren't able to get in here before now." He glanced over at me once we were in position.

"Not for lack of trying."

"I believe that." Halvor attempted a smile and I attempted to smile back.

It was almost worse than going three days without food.

"On three?" I asked.

He nodded.

"One . . . two . . . *three!*"

We both strained, pulling as hard as we could. With a thunderous groan followed by a horrific screech that shuddered through the citadel, the door finally, slowly scraped open. Halvor whooped softly in triumph. But when we saw the massive room beyond, he fell silent, his mouth slightly ajar. I could only stare, my heart in my throat.

We stood on the threshold of the one room in this entire massive place that I hoped and prayed held the answers I sought.

I took a deep breath and stepped into the Hall of Miracles for the first time in my life.

SIXTEEN

The ceiling soared so far above us, painted with the sun and clouds, the stars and moon, the details so beautifully wrought one could almost believe it *was* the sky, the unimaginable scope of it, day and night, magically condensed into this one room. The hall was much longer than it was wide, and the walls were covered in an assortment of weapons, huge, heavy, brutal things that sent a shiver over my skin. But nothing could compare to the wall made almost entirely of windows directly across from us. They were two stories high, like the ones in the library, but rather than a view of the gardens and the hedge, these windows looked down on nothing—and everything. I knew from the view in the library, and the painting I'd found, that the hall abutted the sheerest cliff imaginable, with a waterfall flowing directly beneath it from the underground river that our well tapped into, tumbling several hundred—maybe even a thousand—feet to the valley floor below, the bottom of it lost in a bed of mist.

And in the middle of the windows was a short staircase that led up to a single, massive door.

Something went through me, a thrill that danced up my spine. A call that spoke to me beyond the narrow confines of sound, beckoning to me.

"Please tell me you're not planning on trying to open *that* door."

I swallowed an unexpected laugh. "I wasn't expecting to find a door. It can't be *that* easy, can it?"

"But where would it go?"

"I don't know. Maybe there's a staircase below it to a secret cavern or something?" Though the painting hadn't shown anything like that, so I doubted it. "The door to nowhere," I whispered.

"What?" Halvor glanced at me.

"'The door to nowhere' because even if it *could* be opened, what would you do that for? To jump?"

There was a pause, and then: "Or what if . . . what if that's the gateway?" Halvor's voice, though hushed, still echoed through the empty room, reverberating back to us from the motionless weapons hanging on the walls on either side of us. We moved steadily toward the staircase, passing through the massive room, my eyes roaming over the ornate workmanship that had carved the thick wood and iron into whorls and swirls; the designs reminiscent of the beautiful ironwork of the gate outside, when the hedge peeled back enough to reveal it.

"The gateway," I repeated, so soft it was barely audible, and yet a shudder went through me. Was it my imagination or had the trembling originated from the stones beneath me, as though the citadel itself shivered in—what? Anticipation? Fear?

I shook my head. The night was getting to me. It was just a building—stone and mortar and nothing more.

But, then again, the hedge was just leaves and thorns and vines.

"It can't be the gateway. Why would it be on the edge of a cliff—and surrounded by glass windows? The rakasa would never have made it to Vamala, they would have been trapped here," I pointed out, forcing away the strange trepidation.

"Well, it wasn't like this when the gateway first opened again," Halvor explained. We reached the base of the staircase and stopped, both of us staring up at the strange, useless door. "The original citadel was in ruins when the rakasa came back. The Paladin who came through to defend Vamala rebuilt it like this—intentionally, I would guess, because that is no ordinary glass." He paused, then turned to me. "Zuhra, why did you ask me how strong Paladin glass was?"

I made myself turn away from the door—though it was a struggle to do so for some reason—and looked to the glass on either side of it. "I can't stay here forever," I began slowly. "I have to escape. *We* have to escape. I thought . . . maybe we could break the glass."

"And then what—jump?" he echoed my earlier question.

"No, of course not. I don't want to die." I turned to him. "I've thought about it a lot. There's a waterfall somewhere below this room, right? So that means there has to be a tunnel or something where the river is flowing. If we break the window, we could attach a rope in here and climb down to wherever that waterfall is coming from. If we have to," I continued when he looked about ready to object, "we can climb all the way down the whole damn mountain. But I can't live here for the rest of my life, locked up with my mother and all of . . ." I waved my hand around to encompass the room, the citadel, the hedge—my entire tiny world.

Halvor was quiet for a long moment. "And where would you find rope strong enough and long enough to accomplish this?"

I tried not to let myself grin. "Sami and I found a bunch of it in the stables a couple of years ago. We've never had any use for it, so it should still be there."

"Heavy rope? Strong enough for full-grown adults to climb down?" He stepped toward the windows, pressing his hand against the glass as if testing the thickness.

"No, it's some old twine. You don't think that would work?"

Halvor spun around in disbelief—until he noticed my pursed lips and cocked eyebrow. "Oh. You're mocking me."

"No, I'm teasing you. *You* insulted *me* by asking such a question. Of course it's thick, strong rope. I wouldn't have considered this plan otherwise."

"Right. Of course." He had the grace to look chastised. "Since you have obviously thought this through quite a bit already, how do you intend to break the window? Paladin glass *is* extremely strong. Honestly, I'm not sure what it would take to shatter it."

"I don't know." Then my gaze focused on the wall behind him. I gestured to the side of the room. "Would one of those do the trick?"

His eyes widened. "I should hope so."

I wasn't exactly familiar with weaponry, but the ones hanging on the walls appeared to be pretty terrifying—and hefty—in my opinion. I wasn't even sure I would be able to lift some of the larger ones on my own, but with Halvor's help . . .

"Which one do you think will work best?" I headed toward a massive ball with spikes all over the surface, attached to a long, thick piece of wood. "This one looks promising."

"That mace probably weighs as much as you do," Halvor commented.

"Then come help me."

"You want to do this *now*?" He came up beside me.

"Of course. Sami can't keep drugging my mother, night after night. This is our chance." I reached out toward the mace, as Halvor had called it, but right at that moment I thought I heard something and paused with my hand outstretched. "Did you hear—"

"*Zuhra!*"

My name echoed through the citadel, a little louder this time, accompanied by the slapping of feet against the stone floors. Halvor and I shared an alarmed glance and then I sprinted back across the room, toward Sami, who was still shouting my name. Something horrible must have happened for her to be so reckless, even with my mother having taken a sleeping draught.

"Sami, I'm here!"

She was already halfway down the hallway when I burst out of the Hall of Miracles, my heart in my throat.

Sami reached for me as if she could will me to her side; her face was mottled red and sweat slipped down her cheeks, dampening her gray hairline. "Zuhra—it's Inara—she's *missing*!"

SEVENTEEN

Everything inside me went cold. "No . . . that's not possible."

"I went to check on your mother—to make sure she was still fast asleep—but Inara's door was open. I've been searching and searching but I can't find her."

"*No*," I repeated, "I got her in bed, I locked her door . . ."

But a sudden nausea seized my stomach. *Had* I locked it? I'd been so eager to get out into the citadel tonight—to get to Halvor and the Hall of Miracles—what if *I'd* forgotten? The only reason I was trying to do *any* of this was to help her, to *protect* her, and instead—

"Where have you looked?" Halvor asked, his voice as calm as mine was frantic. If I hadn't suspected he harbored feelings for my sister, I would have thought he didn't even care she was missing.

"All the main rooms. I even checked the doors that lead outside, but they're all still locked."

At least I didn't have to worry about her being outside. But I couldn't keep from thinking about her falling down the stairs only a couple nights ago, when I'd been locked up. She'd been lucky to only suffer a broken leg. What if she fell again?

"If we split up, we will be able to cover more ground. Let's each take a section of the citadel," Halvor suggested.

"But she's frightened of you," Sami pointed out. "She may just run away from you again."

He grimaced. "Then I will go with you or Zuhra."

"I don't care who goes with who. There's no time for this!" I turned on my heel and rushed back the way we'd come only a few minutes ago, calling out her name. I didn't even care if I woke my mother—the only thing that mattered was finding Inara and making sure she was safe.

The darkness that had been heavy before was oppressive now, a thick, menacing blanket of concealment that turned my skin to ice as I dashed from room to room, calling Inara's name. Terror beat alongside my blood with every empty space I searched, every abandoned hallway I raced down, every empty echo of my voice returning back to me with no sight or sound of my sister.

Halvor was at my side, searching the rooms opposite the ones I went in, but I was hardly even aware of him. Somehow Inara had been swallowed up by the citadel. Panic fluttered in my chest, raced through my veins. I looked in the rooms for her even as images of finding her broken at the base of a staircase flashed through my mind.

When we'd gone through nearly every door in the wing where all the rooms we used were Halvor finally grabbed my arm and pulled me to a stop. "We've searched everywhere in this part of the citadel more than once." His calm mien had slowly crumbled until he sounded as panicked as I felt. "Where else could she be?"

"I don't know!" I snapped, even though I knew this wasn't his fault. *I* was the one who had left her room unlocked. If something happened to her, I would only have myself to blame. "Maybe she got past us somehow."

We stood outside my mother's door. None of us had dared open it, but if there was any chance she'd somehow gone in there . . .

I took a deep breath and turned the handle.

The room was dark and silent, except for the soft murmur of my mother's breathing. I swept the shadowed corners and empty chairs quickly. Nothing. Despite the rush, my gaze landed on my mother. Her hair was unbound, a dark pillow beneath her head, and her mouth slightly parted. In sleep her face was relaxed, all of the tension, the imperiousness, smoothed away by whatever her dreams held. As I watched, her eyes fluttered and she mumbled something, her hand flexing against the sheet she held near her cheek. Unexpectedly I had to blink hard a few times to clear my vision. She looked a decade younger asleep. She looked like a mother I could have loved, could have counted as one of my dearest friends.

Steeling my heart against the sidling remorse, I spun on my heel and marched back out, shutting the door firmly behind me.

Halvor opened his mouth to ask, but took one look at my face and shut it again.

"Should we go back to the south wing?" he finally ventured. "Has she ever gone there?"

An icy fist of panic seized my stomach and clenched. "Yes," I whispered. Then I took off at a dead run. As a child, we'd found her standing in front of the doors to the Hall of Miracles more than once. Doors that had remained firmly shut our entire lives—until tonight. A door that, in our haste, we'd left open because it was too heavy to take the time to shut.

We rushed back across the citadel, calling for her the entire way, without a response. Every empty hallway urged me to go faster, every darkened staircase tightened that cold grip on my stomach. Soon we were shouting Inara's name as loud as we could, heedless of my mother. If we hadn't woken her yet, I had no doubt she would continue to sleep for many hours yet to come.

"Inara!" Halvor called out, the timber of his voice a deep counterpoint to my higher one.

"Nara! Please, where are you?"

When we turned the corner the door to the Hall of Miracles was ajar at the end of the hallway, just as I feared.

And we were just in time to see a slip of white disappear around it. My heart lurched beneath the cage of my ribs.

We sprinted for the room full of weapons, any number of which could be fatal if mishandled.

"Inara!"

"Nara!"

Halvor's boots thudded down the hallway, his longer legs outdistancing mine even though I was pushing myself as hard as I could. The hard stones jarred my body with each step, my blood a roar in my ears, nearly drowning out our panicked shouts.

"*Nara!*"

We ran as fast as we could, but no matter how quickly I pumped my arms and forced my legs to move, the hallway felt interminable.

Halvor made it through the open doors moments before I did. I was in such a rush I misjudged the opening and slammed one of my shoulders into the heavy wood. With a cry of pain, I stumbled into the Hall of Miracles to see Halvor racing toward Inara. She had ignored the weapons in favor of the staircase—and the doorway beyond.

"Inara—*don't!*"

I didn't even understand my terror—but something inside me simultaneously urged me to get closer to the door while screaming to keep Inara away from there.

Halvor hit the bottom step, his arm outstretched, just as Inara reached for the handle.

The moment she touched it, her veins exploded with light, glowing as brightly as I'd ever seen them, the blue fire rushing from her eyes, down her throat, across her arms to her hands. But rather than stopping there, it continued out of her body, bleeding across the massive door, spreading through the carvings faster and faster, until every whorl and swirl had lit up, glowing as brightly as Inara's eyes.

I froze in the center of the room, staring.

The gateway.

And then she flung her head back and screamed—a noise of such agony it ripped through me as if she'd hurled one of the weapons surrounding us through my chest.

Halvor was ignited back into motion as her body curled backward. She looked as if she were in the throes of passion—or such extreme torment her spine couldn't hold her upright.

All other thoughts receded, leaving only an innate, almost guttural response: I ran to my sister.

I had no idea what I could do—I had no idea what was happening—I only knew my sister was suffering and I had to stop it somehow. Halvor reached her first and grabbed her arm to try to pull her hand free. A spark of blue flame exploded between them and he was flung backward so far he cleared the stairs entirely and slammed to the ground on his back, the crack of his skull echoing over the thudding of my heart in my ears.

He didn't move again.

I sprinted past, not daring to stop, even as my heart staggered within my chest.

Terror ran thick and hot in my blood as I dashed up the stairs.

With visible effort Inara turned her head toward me, every muscle in her neck straining, the blue fire rushing through her body, her eyes nearly blinding.

"No—Zuhra—*no*—" Each word tore through her throat, a half-panted, half-screamed warning. Past the unimaginably bright glow of her eyes and the veins in her skin, there was lucidity in her face. Lucidity and unadulterated terror.

I paused on the top stair. "Let go!"

"I—*can't*—"

The door almost looked alive from where I stood, the blue fire racing over and *through* it. Inara's power somehow flowed within the wood—so much, I couldn't even comprehend it.

I glanced over my shoulder at where Halvor still lay on the ground. I couldn't even tell if his chest was moving. Helpless tears burned in my eyes. Her power had done that to him—could do that to me.

"Try, Nara. Try to let go," I urged as tears spilled out onto my cheeks.

The muscles in her arms strained beneath the blue glow of her power, but nothing happened.

"I—I—*can't*—" she panted again, her own cheeks wet with shimmering cerulean tears that left iridescent trails on her skin.

Suddenly the door shuddered, as if an earthquake had gone through the citadel, but the floor was still beneath my feet.

Inara's sudden scream tore through me. Her head flung backward as a fresh wave of even brighter blue rushed through her body and into the door.

It was killing her.

I didn't care what it would do to me, I didn't care about anything except my sister. All hesitation erased by her agony, I stretched out and grabbed her free arm, clutching her with every ounce of strength I had, tensed for the blow to come.

A shock went through my body, stunning me, but unlike Halvor I wasn't flung away from my sister. Rather, whatever force held her captive to the door latched onto me as well. Instead of wrenching her free as I'd intended, I was now trapped beside her, my hand frozen to her arm. Something rushed through my body, hot and heady, like blood, only . . . *more*. With it came a roar, like the crash of thunder and the pounding of hooves and the clamoring of a thousand heartbeats all at once, filling me, consuming me, *drowning* me.

Inara's power.

This was what she lived with every moment of every day?

Fresh tears tracked down my cheeks as Inara strained to turn her head toward me again.

"I'm—sorry—" I tried to force my mouth to form the words, but everything hurt. I was being torn apart from the inside, scorched into pieces. Ravaged by the Paladin fire that her body could contain and wield, but mine couldn't.

The door shuddered once more. But this time, the glowing carvings wavered as if they were little more than a mirage; what had been solid wood and iron melted into *nothing*—air and light and power and nothing more.

And then, with a sudden surge that ripped through Inara into me, something burst *through* the glowing doorway. It was massive, so large it slammed into both of us, knocking both me and Inara backward, finally cleaving us away from the gateway's hold.

My head cracked on the edge of the stairs. I lay sprawled on my back, breathless for one long moment.

"Zuhra! *Move!*"

Dimly, I recognized Halvor's deeper voice shouting at me.

I blinked. Once. Then again.

"Zuhra!"

A muted panic pulsed within me, a distant memory of fear beneath the sharp throb of pain in my skull. Something was wrong and I needed to move. But I hurt. Everywhere. I tried to roll over to my knees. My head swam sickeningly, hot warmth running down my neck. *Blood,* I realized, my vision narrowing in on the crimson puddle of it below me. *My blood.*

And then an inhuman roar tore through the air, so loud it made the stones beneath me vibrate, followed by a scream that turned my veins to ice.

Blinking the blood out of my eyes, I lifted my head to see a Scylla—a creature straight from my most terrifying nightmares made flesh—flapping its massive, leathery wings to hover just above Halvor with Inara crouched behind him.

"*No!*" I screamed, my panic rushing back up in full force as the last of the haze from hitting my head receded.

Halvor flung his arms out in front of Inara, trying to protect her. The beast had a body like a horse, except it was covered in scales, its front legs ended in claws instead of hooves, and its head was abnormally round, more than half of it comprised of a mouth full of row after row of jagged, flesh-tearing teeth.

A *rakasa*. There was a *rakasa in the citadel.*

I shoved off of my hands to clamber to my feet, my gaze going to the weapons on the wall—they were our only hope—

Something wrapped around my ankle and yanked, slamming me back to the ground, my chest hitting first, then my jaw with a horrific crunch.

"*Zuhra!*"

Inara's scream was a dull echo over the roar of the beast, just as whatever had my ankle pulled again—dragging me *through* the door.

"*Nara!*"

My last glimpse of my sister was of her head turned to me, her mouth forming my name, her eyes wide with terror, just as the rakasa dove toward Halvor, its jaws opened wide.

And then Inara, Halvor, the beast, and the citadel were gone.

PART 2

SISTER OF LIGHT

EIGHTEEN

INARA

Silence.

The constant roar was gone entirely.

And so was Zuhra.

I stared at the door, now gone dark.

A bone-scraping scream split the sudden quiet behind me, followed by a roar—unlike any I'd heard before—so loud the stones shuddered beneath my feet. I whirled just in time to see the horrifying monster that had burst through the doorway drop the boy out of its bloody maw. His body slapped against the stones like little more than a discarded plaything.

Halvor. The memory of his name surged through me alongside the burn of my desperation. I was immobilized by horror, staring at his lifeless body, his shoulder and torso torn into fleshy shreds. *Go to him. Go to him, now!* But my feet wouldn't obey.

And then the beast turned eyes made of darkness and endless night on me. Terror, thick and heavy as ice, froze my limbs in place. My heart raced beneath my rib cage, pumping blood hot with panic as fast as it was capable to counteract the cold fear, but it wasn't enough. I trembled uselessly, a feeble mouse caught in the snare of its own weakness, unable to move as the beast dove toward me. I squeezed my eyes shut and turned my head, bracing for the agony that was surely coming.

But instead of a death blow from the monster's mouth, its claws seared through my skin as it snatched me and dragged me off the ground.

A scream rent the air and it took me a moment to realize it had come from me. Massive leathery wings beat above me, carrying us toward the two-story-high glass windows. Blistering panic finally beat out the icy terror as I realized the monster intended to break *through* the windows, carrying me out of the citadel. I twisted and writhed, desperate to free myself, but the creature's claws only dug in, slicing through flesh and even bone. A deluge of agony crashed over me, but I loosed an almost inhuman roar of my own and thrashed even harder. I couldn't give up—if I did, I was lost—

But even as I ripped free of one claw, the others embedded themselves even further in my body. Too many—I couldn't escape—

We crashed into the window. The beast's body took the brunt of the impact, but my head cracked into the hard, unbroken surface a split second after. The collision ricocheted the monster backward with an ear-shattering howl. Its claws suddenly retracted and I slammed into the ground with a dull crunch.

Everything went black.

Sound returned first.

A low thud—faint but fierce—that I belatedly realized was my heart.

A distant crash, followed by a crackle like the sound frost spreading across a window pane would make if it actually made a noise.

Heavy, unnaturally loud breathing that was half growl, half trembling roar came close—too close—before quickly moving further away.

And then a flood of agony broke over me, so intense I wanted nothing more than for it to end—for *me* to end if necessary—accompanied by swells of heat racing through my broken body; heat that was usually only present with the roar in my head. But, amid all the other noise assaulting me, *that* roar was still absent.

A susurration of air washed over me, and then there was another thud, but this time it was much closer—and louder—followed immediately by a rippling crunch like a thousand glasses cracking at once.

Realizing at last what it all meant, my eyes flew open just in time to see the monster fling its body against the spider-webbed window one last time.

It blasted apart.

Instinctively, I curled into a ball as the broken glass rained down. The creature loosed a roar that echoed across the entire mountain range, a triumphant threat as it stretched its bloodied wings wide and soared away.

I could do nothing but stare, silent tears leaking out of my eyes, my body too broken to even tremble as the monster banked sharply and winged its way out of view. Pain and fire raced over my skin, under my skin, through my bones and veins, and I wanted to scream and I needed to get up and I just lay there.

Zuhra. She would know what the monster was—why it was here. She would know what to do. Whenever I emerged from the roar she was there, she always had the answers. She kept the fear of not knowing where I was or who I was or *why* I was from swallowing me whole.

But . . .

Gone.

Zuhra was gone.

Her body hitting the ground . . . getting yanked through the door that wasn't a door . . . the glowing, sucking *thing* that had held me trapped, draining everything out of me until she took my other hand, until the monster exploded out of it, until—

Zuhra was gone.

I'd done something and she was gone and the monster was here and I was *burning,* and Halvor was—

Somehow, through the scorching fire that consumed me—*I was fire . . . was I fire?*—I forced my head to turn. There. His crumpled, bloody, lifeless body, within crawling distance. If only I could crawl. If only I could do *anything.*

But the flames licked my skin, they consumed my muscles, and melted my bones, and they were in me. They *were* me.

I was fire and it was burning me away until there was nothing left. Nothing, nothing, *nothing* . . .

I inhaled sharply. Exhaled slowly. Again. And again. And suddenly, *finally*, there truly was nothing.

The flames ebbed out of me, the heat leeched into the stones beneath me, taking my pain with it. *All* of it.

I was left lying on my back on the cold, damp ground; chilled, spent, terrified—but completely, utterly healed.

I knew it, somehow, even before I lifted my hands, to stare at my gore-covered but unmarred arms, to pat my blood-drenched belly and find no more than a wet, shredded nightgown. Not even a scratch remained.

I'd become fire, and then it had left me, and I was healed . . . and the roar . . . the roar that had been my constant companion, was still gone.

A low moan, so soft I barely heard it, jerked me back to my surroundings. Newly invigorated heart in my throat, I rolled onto my knees and crawled to Halvor, who had, unbelievably, made the noise.

"H-halvor," I croaked, my throat still raw from my screams. *I thought you were dead.* The words didn't leave my mouth, partially from fear that I had imagined his moan and he really was gone, and partially because speaking was too much effort. The sheer amount of blood surrounding him seemed more than it should have taken to fill his thin body. The skirt of my nightgown dredged through the puddle, sopping it up like one of Sami's sponges. It would have taken a dozen skirts to absorb it all. His skin was clammy and cold when I brushed my fingers across his forehead, leaving a streak of crimson. He didn't move, his eyes not even fluttering beneath his dusky eyelashes.

He'd been kind to me, this strange boy who had never been there when I'd awoken in the past and then suddenly was. I pressed my hand to his chest, hoping for the telltale throb of a heartbeat. I remembered that the hedge had let him through—the hedge that I could sense, like the brush of butterfly wings against my mind, always there, always there.

"Halvor," I whispered, trying out his name, letting it slide around my mouth and slip off my tongue. It felt forbidden, though I'd spoken to him for hours that one miraculous night. More time together than I'd had with Zuhra in many of my awake times combined. He'd told me it was because I'd healed myself and it had used enough of my power to clear my mind for longer than normal. Or what we'd *thought* was normal. When the roar had begun to build within me once more, I'd considered hurting myself again—on purpose this time—if only to make my body heal itself and keep the roar from claiming me again.

But I'd been too afraid.

And now he was dying—dead?—and I had healed myself again and the roar was gone and Zuhra was gone and the monster was out there somewhere and everything was *wrong*.

"Inara!"

My name was a distant sound, a concern-laden echo from somewhere deep within the citadel.

You healed yourself, Inara. The power inside you—the roar, as you call it—has the power to heal. Another echo, but this time the memory of what he'd told me, his eyes warm and bright, like sun-baked soil in my garden, his face lit with excitement. I didn't know him but I'd known that's what it was, the way his mouth had stretched a smile around his words and his hands had gestured, as if conjuring magic from the very air we breathed—that's what he'd called it, what I could do. *It's magic—this power inside you. You have Paladin magic.*

But Zuhra hadn't been there, and instead of joy I'd felt heavy with the fear of what it meant, and I'd wanted her to come to me and explain it, to tell me this boy wasn't lying to me.

Paladin magic. The power to heal. *Fire,* beneath my skin, in my veins.

I'd healed myself from wounds that should have killed me—I knew so little but I knew that to be true, somehow. That monster's claws had ripped through my body, shredding me apart. But here I was. It had torn into Halvor first and his once smiling lips were bloodless and I didn't know what to do, but I had to *try*.

"Inara!"

Closer now, and I should have answered, but he was almost out of time and I had to focus.

I exhaled slowly. Beneath my hands, his chest was still. So very, very still. But then—there. His ribs shifted. It was a shallow wisp of a breath, but he wasn't gone yet. Not entirely.

What do I do?

There was no one to tell me. The roar was still gone . . . What if my power was gone too? What if healing myself had used it all up?

He'd tried to explain what he knew of Paladin magic to me—that day when Zuhra had been locked away and Mother had refused to get her. To distract me, he'd told me how the Paladin were all born with power, but different Paladin had different gifts, and healing was apparently mine. He'd said it was something in the core of me. He'd said I had so much that healing my plants didn't use enough to clear my mind for long.

The intensity of the heat I'd felt while it healed me today had been almost worse than the pain it eventually erased.

Was there any left for Halvor?

I closed my eyes and tried to find it—to feel for a core of power inside me somewhere. My heartbeat sounded in my ears, too loud, too useless. A rain-scented wind rushed through the shattered window, whipping my hair across my face. I shivered, chilled, devoid of any flicker of heat—any hope of saving him.

My fingers curled around his ruined tunic and I let my head drop so that my forehead rested against his sternum, heedless of the gore and torn flesh and exposed bone. Zuhra was gone and it was my fault. I didn't understand *how*, only that it was because of me—that my power had given that door the ability to let that *thing* in and take Zuhra out. I couldn't bear to let this boy die because of me too.

Please. Please heal him! I dug my fingers into his flesh, which grew icier by the moment. There had to be more. There just *had* to be.

Heal him NOW!

And then—finally—a flicker of warmth prickled beneath my ribs, just below my heart. Relief washed over me, heady and exultant. I exhaled and the warmth fanned itself into a fire once more, building in intensity in my chest until it shot up my spine to my head and then exploded out from there, racing across my skin, rushing through my muscles and nerves, painful and exquisite at the same time. And finally down my arms, to my hands and out of my fingers, into his ruined body.

As my power flowed out of me and into Halvor, I sensed him—*felt* him—in a way I'd never thought to feel another person: the way his flesh had become more clay than living entity; how dangerously close what should have been the brilliant light of his living soul was to being snuffed out entirely. It barely even trembled, a ghost of a shadow left tethering him to this world. That was where I sent my fire first, to banish the darkness that held him in its grasp, nearly dragging him under. My light shot through the sucking black, a sun bursting through the grasping fingers of eternal night, and coaxed his to flicker in response. With it came a barrage of images and emotions—flashes of his life: on a boat under a brilliant sun with his parents, emerald green water spreading out as far as the eye could see around them; lying on his back stargazing with his father; the day he found out his father had died; holding his mother's hand in a small, dark room, her face gaunt and her eyes shut; the all-consuming grief that had nearly induced him to do something to join them after she was gone; the peace of being tucked into a corner of a massive library, surrounded by piles of books, his uncle sitting at his desk nearby; his first view of the citadel and the joy he'd felt to have finally reached his goal . . . All within the space of one heartbeat, pieces of who he was became imprinted on me.

Once he was no longer on the precipice of slipping away, I sent the flames of my power surging through his veins—out to his flayed muscles, to his serrated bones and shredded flesh. His pain became mine, and only through sheer willpower did I manage to keep my fingers clenched onto his chest, even as my head flung back, my mouth opening in a silent scream as his agony crashed over me, attempting to pull *me* into the waiting abyss.

I battled back, pushing my fire forward, sensing his body mending itself—skin knitting together, muscles and bones shifting and solidifying; until little by little what had been broken became whole again . . . as slowly, *slowly*, the pain ebbed and Halvor's light burned brighter and then brighter still.

Reassured that I had done it, that I had brought him back, I began to withdraw.

I forced my eyes open to see the veins in my arms and hands glowing bright blue, except where my knuckles were bright white, my fingers still digging into his now healed skin. As the last of my power uncoiled from his body and receded back to me, I had to forcibly release him. My hands were still curled into claws that I couldn't straighten after working so hard to maintain my grip on him despite the sheer agony that had threatened to rip us apart.

Halvor suddenly gasped, a loud, wet inhalation—his body's first triumphant return to full life. His eyes flashed open, going immediately to mine, but the fire had sputtered and gone out. I was the one in darkness, I was the one slipping away. I saw his lips form my name, saw his hand lifting toward me, but the ever-greedy eternal night reached me first and I succumbed to its velvet embrace.

NINETEEN

ZUHRA

I landed on my stomach on a patch of grass.

When I lifted my head, a blast of pain shot through both my jaw and the back of my skull. I saw only a massive archway among a few crumbling ruins.

The citadel, the Hall of Miracles, Halvor, the monster—*my sister*—they were all gone.

Then whatever had pulled me through the doorway—the gateway to Visimperum—yanked again, dragging me across the grass, away from the archway. Away from my only way back home.

I grabbed at the grass, digging my nails into the soil beneath, and bucked my body, trying to free myself. An angry hiss preceded claws slicing into the tender skin of my ankle, threatening to hobble me permanently if they cut much deeper. With a sudden jerk, the thing flipped me over, so that I was face-to-face with a rakasa, smaller than the one in the citadel, but no less terrifying. It had a long, flat body with six legs, each ending in four claws, one of which was clamped around my leg. Its short neck supported a head that reminded me of a boar's, with jagged fangs hanging outside its black lips. Drool a very concerning shade of greenish gray gathered on the tips of the fangs.

I'd only ever been able to sneak the one book on rakasa into my room, but I'd read it enough that dozens of competing facts about the different kinds of monsters rushed through my mind at once, flooding my body with hot panic. Predators, all of them,

some pack hunters, some solitary. Some poisonous, some devouring their prey . . . others taking their time, inflicting maximum
pain upon their victims . . . I racked my memory for an image
matching the beast that continued to drag me toward the copse of
trees at the other end of the clearing from where the gateway stood.
Nothing came—my mind couldn't seem to process that I was *seeing* a creature I'd only read about until now.

A shriek from above us sent a tremor through the monster. Its
short legs redoubled in speed, rushing for the cover of the trees,
but not before a massive creature that I instantly recognized as a
gryphon—with the head and wings of an eagle and the body and
tail of a lion—dove out of the sky to land directly in front of it,
forcing the monster to skid to a halt with a yowl of frustration. I
caught a glimpse of a man with glowing blue eyes vaulting from
the gryphon's back, one hand gripping a sword and the other lifted,
a ball of blue fire hovering above his open palm.

The monster hissed, recoiling away from the man—the
Paladin—trying to drag me back the way it had come. But more
shrieks sounded above; I had to blink multiple times to convince myself that I was seeing truly. An entire *battalion* of gryphons soared toward us, the first three also tucking their wings
and diving for the earth, landing in a circle around the monster,
trapping it. It would have been completely overwhelming if it
weren't such a relief.

"Help! Help me!"

The beast scuttled backward, its jaws clacking. A horrible
growl whined from its throat, as its claws tightened yet again
around my leg, yanking me below its belly. For the first time, I
noticed the smell of the thing—a mix between putrid meat and
decaying flesh.

One of the Paladin shouted something in their language. I
squeezed my eyes shut and prayed.

Another shout and then a cacophony of shrieks blasted through
the air. The monster bellowed; its claws spasmed against my leg,
then abruptly released me. It began to drop, its belly pressing me
into the ground, threatening to crush me. A loud crack sent a shudder through me and dimly I realized it was my arm bone snapping—

And then suddenly the creature was gone, lifted straight up off the earth. I scrambled away as quickly as possible, using my one good arm and dragging my destroyed foot behind me toward the first pair of legs closest to me.

Once I was sure I was no longer underneath the monster, I flipped over to see three gryphons dragging it through the sky, away from us, the monster's head hanging limply, a tendril of brackish smoke rising from a hole in its chest.

I let my eyes close and my head dropped back on the earth, all of my adrenaline draining away with the removal of the threat, leaving me trembling and overcome with pain. My jaw and arm were definitely both broken, and I didn't even dare look at my leg. I'd never experienced anything like the agony that swelled up from where the monster had most likely severed muscle, tendon—even bone.

The group of Paladin—*a group of Paladin*, standing *right there*, more people surrounding me than I'd met in my entire life— murmured quietly above me in the unfamiliar but melodic language of theirs, until a male voice cut over the rest.

"*Zuhra*," he said in my language, his voice hesitant and thick. "Is it truly you?"

My eyes flew open to see a man I would have recognized anywhere, even after fifteen years apart, on his knees next to me, glowing blue eyes glistening with the sheen of withheld tears.

It was Adelric—*it was my father.*

INARA

I'd never felt more at peace than in those moments of pure darkness, in the minutes when I nearly lost myself. But something inside, something stronger than peace, or rest, or release, whispered to me, urged me to turn back, to *fight* back. It was a voice I knew, a voice that had called me from the darkness of my own mind so many, many times.

Come back to me, Nara. Come back . . .

Over and over she'd asked and I'd tried, oh, how I'd tried. And no matter how many times I'd failed, she'd stayed, she'd whispered, she'd urged.

Come back to me, Nara. Come back to me . . .

And so I turned from the velvet night and fought toward the small, distant light and all that accompanied it: pain, exhaustion, fear . . . guilt. I couldn't remember *why*, only that it *was*—that *all* those things awaited me if I forced my way back out of the dark. And still, I climbed, I grasped, I reached.

Come back to me, Nara. Come back . . .

To Zuhra, to my sister, to my home. It was she who called me, who had always been there, calling for me. It was she who I stretched out to reach. And, finally, at long last, I surged up, up, up, back into myself, and woke with a gasp.

My eyes opened to a broken, empty room, and my body crumpled with the memory of it all.

"*Inara!* Oh, praise the Great God!"

I turned to see Sami kneeling beside me, her wrinkled cheeks glistening with wetness. Tears. Tears for me?

Beside her, Halvor crouched, watching me solemnly. A strange *awareness* filled the space between us—I could sense his trepidation and relief, almost as if they were my own emotions.

I couldn't meet his gaze. My eyes dropped as I forced myself to sit up. I cocked my head, waiting for the roar, but there was . . . nothing. The sound of my own breath, the muffled noise of Sami's sobbing, the groan of the citadel—as if it knew of the assault it had undergone—and the muted murmur of the wind, exploring this new space through the shattered window.

"She's gone," I said.

Sami's quiet crying cut off with a sharp intake of breath.

"I lost her."

"We can get her back." She reached out to pat my hand, but I jerked away. I never jerked away from touch—I felt it, *knew* it, so rarely—but I had let in a monster . . . I *was* a monster . . . and I didn't want her comfort.

"*I* lost her," I repeated. "I did this." I gestured to the room, encompassing the whole of my awful deeds.

"You healed me." Halvor's whisper drew out a flicker of fire deep in my core—a tiny flare of the thing within me that had woven him back to life. "I should have died."

I stared at my hands in my lap—my bloodstained, perfectly unmarred hands.

I didn't know what to say, I didn't know what to *do*.

I'd done enough . . . I'd never be able to do enough.

Zuhra was gone.

My skin was whole, my body was healed, but no power in the world could mend the serrated edges of the unseen wound within me, the hole that was so big I didn't know how I could function with it inside me, how I could ever live with her missing from my life.

How did a body hold all of that inside? How did it contain blood and bone and muscle and power and fear and guilt and a gaping hole wider than the broken window that let the chilled breeze steal in the citadel and brush the wetness on my cheek, like a cruel lover relishing my pain, sending a shiver down my spine?

You did this, the wind whispered as it fingered my hair, as it scraped cold nails down my skin.

I closed my eyes and lifted my chin, accepting its truth, accepting my fault. And wishing I had ignored her voice and remained in the dark.

Perhaps I had gone the wrong way. Perhaps she had been calling to me from *within* it, not *out* of it. Perhaps I had lost her far beyond any hope of ever reaching her again, until the darkness came for me once more.

"What do you mean, Master Roskery?" Sami's voice was an alien thing, her question so far removed from where I wished to be that I winced. "In the citadel, I heard . . . I *thought* I heard . . . What *happened* in here?"

I felt his hesitation, his concern, as he paused and gathered an attempt at a response.

What, indeed.

"A monster." I spoke before he could.

"A monster," Sami repeated slowly.

I pointed at the wound the citadel bore. I'd healed Halvor. I couldn't heal *that*.

"She . . . she touched the door—the gateway," Halvor began

quietly. "It absorbed her power and opened. A rakasa came here and . . . and something else dragged Zuhra through it."

Sami made a noise that was part terror and part gut-twisting anguish. "A *rakasa*? Here? *Now*? And Zuhra . . . she's . . . she's . . ."

"In Visimperum. She *must* be," Halvor insisted.

I didn't know what that was. I didn't know what rakasa meant or gateway or anything he said other than: *I* had touched the door. *I* had done this.

A monster had come, yes, but a monster had already been within the whole time.

"That's not possible. It's closed. It was supposed to be *closed*!" Sami's voice rose until it was nearly a shout.

The silence after was crushing.

Halvor didn't respond. He didn't have to.

"We have to *do* something. We have to warn them—we have to—"

"How? How can *we* do anything? We're *trapped* here!" For the first time, Halvor's voice rose too, a sharp bite that cut off Sami's hysteria.

"I did this." I forced myself to stand on legs that trembled and threatened to buckle.

"Inara?"

I forced myself to walk across broken glass, tiny pricks of pain cutting and tiny bursts of flame healing. Not gone, then. Little embers of power still flickered through me. *Good, good*, I thought as I climbed the stairs, *come to me, fire. Come back to me, Zuhra.*

"What is she doing? What are you *doing*?"

"Inara, stop! Don't do this!"

I heard him behind me, I felt his terror coating my tongue—or perhaps it was my own—but I was closer, faster.

"Going to get her," I said and then, ignoring his shout right behind me, I grabbed the handle.

TWENTY

ZUHRA

"How do you know me?" Speaking was agony, but I couldn't keep the question from blurting out.

He stared at me, his glowing blue eyes glistening. "I would know *my daughter* anywhere. You—you look just like—"

In all the scenarios I'd dreamt of seeing my father again someday, none of them had involved him saving my life, being unable to finish his sentence because of the emotion thick in his throat, and then grabbing me in a bone-crushing hug, holding me as if he were just as desperate to have had me in his life for the last fifteen years as I'd pretended I *wasn't* to have him in mine.

And the *last* thing I'd ever imagined in all of these made-up scenarios was how badly I'd needed to have my father *want* to hug me, for him to cry when he finally saw me again.

"Oh, Zuhra . . ." he mumbled against my hair, his body shaking. "My sweet, baby girl."

Not even the pain from his shoulder pushing into my broken jaw or his tight grip on my broken arm could have induced me to pull away in that moment. My father had called me his *sweet, baby girl*. He was in Visimperum, not out in Vamala somewhere, as my mother had assumed. But . . . how? And *why?*

"The girl is gravely injured. She's losing blood rapidly," someone else finally observed in my language—another male, but this one sounded younger.

My father immediately let go and though I tried to conceal my wince, his eyebrows drew together in concern as he quickly ran his eyes over my injuries—pausing on my ravaged leg that was in fact surrounded by a growing puddle of blood. Ignoring the fresh waves of agony and the lightheadedness starting to overtake me, I stared up at him, drinking in his features. Strong jaw, long straw-yellow hair tied back off his face. Squint lines at the corners of his glowing blue eyes—or perhaps laugh lines. Though his expression was grave at that moment, I could easily imagine him smiling, laughing—I could imagine him as a loving and devoted husband and father, not the monster my mother had painted him to be.

That maybe she'd had to *force* him to become in her mind, to survive his disappearance.

"Raidyn, do you have enough left to heal her? I used too much on the Bahal for wounds of this magnitude." I hardly knew him, but even I could recognize the change in his voice—the tightness, the alarm—as he glanced over his shoulder. My gaze followed his to a Paladin standing a few paces back, watching us with his arms folded across his chest, his gryphon sitting back on its haunches beside him. I realized he was the Paladin who had spoken of the magnitude of the injuries I'd been trying to ignore.

Raidyn was . . . stunning. I couldn't think of any other word to describe the young man, whose expression was completely unreadable as his brilliant azure-blue eyes traveled over my body in a cold, clinical manner. His hair was the color of sunshine, and though he wore it shorter than my father's, it still fell forward across his tanned face, forcing him to brush it back out of his eyes. His white tunic was pushed up to his elbows, the supple leather of the vest he wore doing little to conceal the breadth of his shoulders and chest. "Her injuries are quite severe," he said quietly.

Something unspoken passed between them, an unnamable emotion flashing through Raidyn's eyes. A strange tension built around us; I could sense the other Paladin standing nearby shifting or exchanging glances.

"Are you asking or issuing a command?" the younger Paladin finally asked.

After a moment, my father simply responded, "She is my

daughter, Raidyn. My daughter who I thought I would never see again."

There was a long silence, heavy enough to make even *me* want to squirm. I would have been overpoweringly intimidated to have not one but *two* men talking about me—*hovering* over me—except with each passing moment, a growing weakness had begun to spread through my body alongside the pain. The men's features swam before my eyes. I didn't understand what was happening, what was being asked of him—only that it was obviously not something to be taken lightly.

"I should be capable of doing enough," Raidyn said at last.

My father sighed, an exhale redolent with relief, and shifted away from me. My concern must have shown on my face because he immediately took my good hand in his and squeezed. "Don't be nervous. Raidyn is very talented for one so young. He will do a fine job, I assure you."

"A fine job of what?" Speaking was excruciating, my words were garbled, and I was afraid of exposing my ignorance. But I had no idea what he'd just agreed to do to me. The younger Paladin closed the gap between us and knelt at my side, his eyes narrowing when I spoke.

"Her jaw is broken as well."

Ignoring Raidyn's pronouncement, my father answered, "He is going to heal you."

Heal me? As in . . . entirely? It hurt too much to question his claim, but I supposed it shouldn't have been too shocking. If what Halvor had told me about Inara was true—about her healing herself—perhaps it was possible for the Paladin to do the same thing for others. My father's hand tightened around mine, a surprisingly reassuring gesture from the man I'd been pretty sure had ruined all our lives up until a few minutes ago.

Raidyn looked at me for a moment longer, directly into my eyes. He was so beautiful, it was almost painful to hold my own gaze steady, especially as it felt as though he were looking *through* me, not *at* me. It was all I could do to keep from shivering beneath the intensity of his blue-fire scrutiny. But then, mercifully, he closed his eyes, and the blue fire raced down through his veins, lighting up his skin as he placed both of his hands on my body: one on my broken jaw—his fingertips brushing as softly against my skin as a butterfly's wing—and the other on my thigh, pressing more firmly into the muscles just above the mangled mess of my leg the Bahal had torn to shreds.

A heat that was both delicious and excruciating suddenly entered my body from both points of contact with his hands and quickly raced through my veins and muscles and tissue, flaring even hotter at every point of injury it encountered. I wanted to watch him use his power, but as the agony of the magic surging through me escalated, my spine arched backward and my eyes shut as if they had a will of their own. Dimly, as though he were suddenly a great distance away, I heard my father urge me to hold still.

And then there was nothing except for fire and pain. I wanted to cry and scream and thrash and make it *stop*, but somehow, beneath it all, a gentle, soothing murmur deep within my mind assured me it would all be over soon. It was a wordless promise, a touchless caress, a deep thrumming presence that I knew wasn't me and yet felt as if it were threaded into my very being.

Raidyn. Somehow I knew it was him. His power had infiltrated every part of my body, even my mind—my *soul*. But instead of feeling violated or upset, the sensation of his steady, calming presence within me was the only thing that kept the inferno beneath my skin from overwhelming me.

It was the single most intimate and painful and beautiful experience of my entire life.

And then, suddenly, it was over.

The fire ebbed away, the comfort of his presence withdrawing alongside it, receding from my body as quickly as water draining from the sink in the citadel's kitchen, leaving me completely drained—empty in a way I'd never experienced before . . . as if having him *there* and then *gone* left me hollowed out.

It took a few beats of my heart for awareness to seep back in— the soft itch of grass beneath my arms and legs, the pressure of my father's hand on mine, the balmy breeze brushing my damp hair from my face . . . and the realization that my pain was gone. *All* of it.

"Take a deep breath, my sweet girl. It might take a few moments to regain your equilibrium after such an intense healing."

My father's suggestion still sounded further away than it should have for someone kneeling beside me, and I did as he suggested, keeping my eyes shut and inhaling slowly. I was afraid of opening them—of looking at Raidyn, the veritable stranger who had somehow become *part* of me for a space of time. At least, that's what it had felt like. My neck and face warmed at the thought.

"Are you able to speak and move freely now?" The sound of Raidyn's voice outside my mind was almost foreign, even though I hadn't truly heard him speak to me during the healing. I'd . . . *felt* the words he'd been sending to me as his power had infiltrated my body. But somehow, that wordless, soul-baring communication had seared his voice into my memory. "Is there any remaining pain?"

Raidyn's questions induced me to finally crack my eyes open. He crouched beside me, watching me with hooded eyes that barely glowed, dulled to indigo, as if the light within him had almost burned out. What had it cost him to do that for me? I flushed even hotter as I tested my jaw, hesitantly lifted my arm and then my head. Nothing remained, not even a twinge or lingering stiffness.

"The pain's gone. I feel . . . fine. *Better* than fine, I feel *perfect*," I hurried to add in case "fine" was insulting after what he'd done for me, and then had to suppress a groan of embarrassment as I pushed myself to sit up. I was on the verge of babbling. I had spent my entire life trapped with three women until last week. I had no idea how to go about interacting with a male who had woven himself into my very being within minutes of meeting me, and healed injuries that could very well have been life-threatening.

Raidyn nodded once, a brief dip of his square jaw, and then he silently stood and walked away to his gryphon, who hadn't moved from where it sat, watching me with its sharp eagle eyes. When Raidyn reached the creature's side, it clacked its beak and pushed its head into his chest, a soft bump in what seemed a gesture of concern.

It was all so . . . *much*. Though I was no longer losing blood, a strange lightheadedness still lingered. I was sitting on the grass in a *different world,* with my *father* next to me, surrounded by *gry-phons* . . . and *Paladin*—had just been *healed* by one of them—

"Zuhra—*how* did you get here?"

My father's question was a dose of icy reality.

"Inara," I breathed and scrambled to my feet.

"Zuhra?"

I ignored his alarmed cry and ran back toward the gateway. It stood partially up a small hill, surrounded by crumbled ruins of what might have once been a building mostly buried under earth and grass and weeds. Normally, I would have been awed to be looking at something other than the confines of the citadel and its grounds, but instead there was only panic. The stone archway was cold, nothing more than stone—the glow of Inara's power was gone.

Which meant I was trapped here . . . and she and Halvor were trapped in the Hall of Miracles with the monstrous rakasa.

"Inara!" I shouted, rushing up to the gateway and slamming my hands into its cold, hard surface.

"Zuhra! What are you *doing*?"

I spun to face my father, who had dashed after me, the rest of his battalion staring at me like I'd lost my mind. I had to ignore the overwhelming sight of so many gathered in one spot to focus on my father—on what truly mattered.

"We have to open it! I have to go back! She's stuck there—with the monster! She'll die—they'll *all* die!"

My father halted at my side, his eyes wide. "Slow down, Zuhra. What are you talking about? *You* opened this gateway?"

"No." I couldn't calm the racing of my heart, the panic that sped through my veins like bee stings. "Inara did—my sister! And a rakasa came through and they're trapped there—"

"Your sister," he repeated, stunned. "She opened it *by herself*?"

"That monster is in there with her—with Halvor and Sami and . . ." The word "mother" died on my lips but he recoiled, stricken, as though I had said it after all.

"*Cinnia,*" he whispered, turning to face the gateway.

"We *have* to open it—we have to go back!"

My father lifted his hand and pressed it to the cold stone, his head falling forward in defeat, a shadow of such utter sorrow cross-ing his face it turned my stomach to lead. "I can't. *We* can't. I've tried . . . for years. It takes an inordinate amount of concentrated power and the council won't . . . I don't know how one Paladin opened it on her own—if I could have done it on my own I would have come back. I would have come back," he repeated, a haunted whisper.

I shook my head, unable to comprehend what he was saying. "But . . . *Inara*. That rakasa . . ."

A female Paladin shouted something in their language, and my father whirled.

"We have to go," he said, grabbing my arm and tugging.

I yanked back. "No! We can't leave—we have to find a way back!"

"If there was one, I would have done it!" He grabbed my arm again, more firmly this time. "I know how upset you are—believe me, I do. We'll go straight to the council—we'll make them let us open the gateway. But right now we *have* to go."

"General!" The female shouted in my language this time. "The rakasa are nearly here!"

"Zuhra, if we stay here, we could die."

I still resisted, everything in me screaming to get back to Inara—to Halvor, Sami, even my mother. I had been trying to find a way to escape, but I'd never wanted to leave her trapped in the citadel with a *monster*—I'd never wanted her to *die*.

"We'll come back—I promise! But we *have* to go!" My father looked as panicked as I felt and finally, with tears burning in my eyes, I let him pull me from the gateway toward his gryphon, who had closed the distance between us and waited only a few feet away.

He made a gesture, and all the Paladin swung onto the backs of their gryphons.

"You're small enough to ride behind me," my father said, lead-ing me to the side of his mount. "Hurry!"

"To ride . . . on that? On, um, her? Him? It?" I eyed the crea-ture with newfound trepidation. It was one thing to stare in awe at the murals and carvings of Paladin riding on the backs of their magical creatures, and quite another to find myself being helped onto a small saddle attached to the back of a living, breathing gryphon, just behind its massive wings.

"Him," my father supplied as the creature craned his neck to look at me, and snapped his beak in a show of either aggression or welcome—I wasn't sure which. "His name is Taavi. He's plenty strong enough to carry us both back to Soluselis. Give me your leg!"

This was really happening. After a lifetime of imagining myself climbing onto the back of a gryphon, I was actually doing it. There was a lot more trembling and fear involved than I'd expected.

One of the other gryphons who had remained airborne the entire time, circling above us, swooped down and the Paladin riding it whistled, two sharp bursts of sound.

"Grab on!" My father shouted over his shoulder. "That's the signal—more rakasa have been spotted. We must go—*now*!"

I wrapped my shaky arms around his torso and buried my head into his back as the gryphon took two bounds forward and then spread his wings and leapt into the air, leaving my stomach somewhere between the earth below us and the gryphon's beating wings on either side of my body.

"We'll come back," Adelric shouted over his shoulder as we rose higher and higher and the ground dropped further and further away. "I promise!"

"Where are we going?" I yelled back, unsure if he could hear my words before the wind ripped them away.

"To the High Council," he shouted over the whistling wind and the beating of Taavi's wings. "To petition your grandmother to open the gateway!"

TWENTY-ONE

INARA

I gripped the door handle for several moments before I was forced
to admit that nothing was going to happen. It remained cold, dark,
nothing more than a round knob of steel beneath my hand.

"It wasn't your fault."

Halvor's quiet voice startled me and I spun to face him, standing two steps below the frustratingly lifeless door. It took all my
strength to remain on my feet, to not crumple to the ground in
defeat.

"It didn't work."

"No," he agreed. "It didn't. Maybe you used too much of your
power to open it the first time and then healing me."

And myself, I added silently. It was true, I was tired in a way I
couldn't remember ever feeling before—a bone-deep exhaustion
that weighed me down so heavily I could barely force myself to
move, to go back down the stairs and walk to where Sami stood
in the center of the room, watching us with solemn, shadowed eyes.
Not even the honeyed glow of the dawning sunrise could warm
the sallow shade of her skin.

"Here," she suddenly said, shrugging out of her robe and wrapping it around my shoulders. "Your nightgown is ruined."

I glanced down at the bloody shreds of the garment I'd worn to
bed for so many years, at my exposed belly and legs beneath the
rips—drenched with half-dried blood but not even a scratch visible

on my skin. With a shiver, I pulled the robe tight around my body, concealing the evidence of what I'd done beneath it.

"Where's my mother?" It was the question I usually asked Zuhra when I surfaced from the roar, when my mind cleared and I could speak and hear and see. It had taken me far longer this time to get to it, but at long last there it was—the world had been ripped apart around us, and my mother still hadn't come.

Sami shifted on her feet, her eyes dropping to the ground. "She's asleep."

"*Still?* How?" When the roar ensnared me, I could barely think, could barely function. It *might* have drowned out what had happened here. But I knew that Mother didn't suffer from the same problem—no one did. It was just me.

So how did she sleep through such a horrible—and loud— ordeal?

"I . . . I gave her a sleeping draught," Sami admitted softly.

"Draught?" I repeated, glancing at Halvor to see if this announcement meant something to him. But he looked as uncomfortable— and guilty—as Sami.

"Special herbs that made her sleep. Heavily."

"Oh." I glanced between the two of them, hoping I didn't look as confused as I felt. It was one of the worst parts of drowning and surfacing and drowning again and again—the confusion, the disorientation. "Why did you do that?"

"Because Zuhra—"

"It doesn't really matter now," Halvor spoke at the same time, overriding Sami.

A distant roar, so far away it was barely audible, echoed over the mountains, carried on the wind that still blew through the broken window. All three of us whirled to face it. The first edge of sunlight had crested the distant, jagged horizon of the eastern mountains, and silhouetted against those brilliant, hopeful rays was a shadow that sent a scrape of dread down my spine.

The monster that had almost killed me and Halvor was coming back.

"We have to warn Gateskeep," Sami breathed.

"*Warn* them? Did you forget we're *trapped* here?" Halvor turned away from the window and the shadow that was winging its way back across the canyons, slowly but steadily growing larger.

"Of course I haven't forgotten that! You have only been trapped here for a week. I have spent years and years in this place."

Halvor's shoulders sloped inward slightly at her sharp retort.

"There's a bell in the top floor of the east wing," she continued. "The Paladin used to ring it to warn the villagers."

"A *bell*," Halvor repeated. "So we ring it and then what? Wait and watch as that *thing* destroys their homes—kills them?"

"Do you have a better idea? At least they'll have a warning—a chance to hide or escape."

Their words—their tension-ridden bickering—hurt my head, almost like the roar. Though I wanted nothing more than to curl up on the floor and sleep for hours, days, *forever* . . . instead, I turned away from them and slowly moved toward the windows, staring not at the beast winging its way back toward us, but at the hedge below—the reason Halvor and Sami believed us to be trapped.

Always there, always in the back of my mind—the breathing, living soul of the looming captor surrounding us. All things—wood, glass, air . . . *everything*—had at least a tiny flicker of life within. Even the stones beneath my feet held a whisper of it. And plants were second only to animals and humans. But no plants in my garden or trees in my orchard could compare to the might of the beating life force within that hedge. Its call had always been there, though for some reason it had always terrified me.

But today . . . today, I would go to it, at last.

"Inara! Get back from there!"

I stood on the edge of the broken glass, looking down, shards of it piercing my toes where they curled over the ledge. A hairs-breadth from falling. We were so high up that the top of the hedge was far below where I stood. It called to me, in a voice without words, a tendril of sensation that reached out to me through the earth, the stones, the very air that connected us to one another. I knew Zuhra's fear of it, remembered Sami's stories of it being dangerous—poisonous. But it would listen to me. As all my plants did.

It would listen.

"We're not trapped."

When Halvor grabbed my arm, it startled me, and only his quick jerk, yanking backward, kept me from losing my footing and falling. "What are you *doing*?"

I cocked my head, confused by the panic on his face—the fear I could feel through the strange new connection between us.

"We're not trapped," I repeated. "It will listen to me."

Halvor stared at me for a long moment, his warm hand still wrapped around the space between my shoulder and elbow, his grip solid, reassuring. In the warm morning light, his eyes were changed to honey, something I'd only seen once but had never forgotten because it had been so beautiful and sticky and sweet. "Do you mean . . ."

I nodded. "Take me down there. It will listen to me."

Halvor looked past me, meeting Sami's lifted eyebrows with an uncertain expression of his own.

"It's too risky . . . If Zuhra were here . . ."

I winced. *But she's not.*

"It's their only chance," Halvor argued. "There's no time to spare on the bell—and then hope that someone knows what it even means. If she thinks she can do it . . ."

"I can," I insisted, staring at the door that had stolen my sister. "I *can*."

Another roar trembled across the cool morning breeze—closer, louder. Time was running out.

"Follow me," Halvor said and released my arm, but only momentarily before grabbing my hand in his and dashing for the door, dragging me alongside him. He paused only to lift a wicked-looking weapon off the wall, and then we entered the belly of the citadel, our bare feet slapping across the stones in time with the pounding of my heart, Sami a step behind us.

All around us, Paladin watched our progress, their jeweled eyes unmoving, their mounts frozen in the air, captured by thread or paint or plaster. My father had been one of them. My father had given me his power—my ever-present captor, but also my savior.

It had driven my mother away.

It had lost Zuhra forever.

It had healed Halvor.

And now, I would have to find a way to use it to protect the village that had always feared me.

The soil was dew-damp beneath my feet; the morning air raked misty fingers through my sweaty hair. I was unaccustomed to running, unaccustomed to panic that wasn't carried away by the rushing roar of my power returning. But there was no time to dwell on the burn of lungs that had never needed to work so hard before, or to take note of the trembling exhaustion in my legs. I released Halvor's hand to dash forward, though he lengthened his stride and easily kept pace with me, leaving me to wonder if he'd been holding back for me through the entire headlong dash through the citadel.

We halted a few feet from the living wall. The hedge soared above us, magnificent and thrumming with an ancient, otherworldly omniscience.

"How do you know it will, um, listen to you?" Sami panted behind us.

"Because it knows me—what's *inside* me."

I didn't have to glance back to see the disbelief on her face—even after all she'd witnessed in this place—I could feel it rising between us, a barrier invisible to the eye but as tangible as the one in front of us made of vines, thorns, and leaves. "This hedge is different than all my other plants. It thinks, it listens."

"It can hear what we're saying?" Halvor's hair fell away from his forehead as he tilted his head to look all the way up to the top of the hedge, rising far out of our reach in the ever-brightening sky.

"Not the same way I can hear you right now. But . . . in a certain sense of the word, yes. I can feel it straining toward us—trying to decide if we are a threat or not. And when it senses *me* . . ." I took a step forward, disregarding Sami sucking in a sharp breath through her teeth, and stretched my hand toward the heavy green leaves, still slick with morning condensation.

I'd done my best to convince *them* I could do this . . . now I just had to convince *myself*. It was true I'd felt the hedge's presence, I'd felt its awareness, but to try and bend its will to mine? I stretched out a trembling hand to it. A ripple shuddered through the hedge when my fingers brushed one of the leaves, and a simultaneous thrill ran up my arm. A flicker of heat sparked within me. Magic calling to magic.

You know me, you know what I bear within me. I stared up at the vines, the leaves, the many parts that combined to make a mere plant into an impenetrable wall. Always on alert, always stretching, sensing, protecting. I felt the strain within the plant, the will to maim, entrap, gauge any threats.

You know me. As I ran my hand gently over its leaves, the initial tension within the massive entity waned. My power was depleted, the core of heat deep within little more than an ember. Was it enough?

You have done your job, and protected us well. But we must leave— you must open for us. I urged the tiny flame within me to slip into my veins, through my arm, out to the hedge. Not to heal, not to nourish, but to make it *move*. Somehow, an instinctual knowledge rose from deep within me—just as when I touched a dying or injured plant and knew how to coax it back to life. I closed my eyes, feeling only the earth beneath my toes, the air on my cheeks, and the hedge beneath my hands. A trickle of my power slipped out of me into its waiting embrace, and, as I bent all my thoughts on the need for it to part, to let us through, it began to move.

The vines uncoiled, slipping apart like a den of snakes dispersing; the thick, heavy leaves retreated, revealing the iron gate hidden behind them.

I stepped back, letting my hand drop to my side, as Halvor rushed forward and grabbed it, wrenching it open as if he were afraid it would disappear again before he made it through.

"You did it," Sami whispered. "All these years . . . all that time . . . and *you* had the power to free us. You could have . . ." She trailed off with a sharp glance my direction, perhaps having forgotten that I could hear her perfectly—that I was no longer lost in the roar of the power that had held us *all* captive here, not just me after all.

A terrible, burning heat coalesced inside my chest—a different kind than my power, that twisted my innards and made it feel as though the air had suddenly grown thin.

Shame.

A low ripple of sound trembled across the sky, not so different from thunder—except there were no clouds, no storm. Only the looming threat of the beast beating its way back toward the citadel—toward Gateskeep.

Halvor had already disappeared from sight, sprinting down the trail toward the village. But even though my heart thudded a determined beat, my body wouldn't respond. I stood on the precipice of the small world I had known, a ledge as terrifying as the broken window I'd balanced on to peer down at the hedge earlier.

Sami's warm hand on my arm was little more than a brush of her fingers across my skin as she passed, but it jerked me out of the sudden stupor that had seized me. Perhaps she understood, or perhaps she meant to urge me into motion.

Before my lips could part to speak, she'd hurried past the open gate—the hedge's leaves fluttered in a phantom breeze, as if unable to keep from fidgeting as it allowed her to pass by—and then she, too, was gone, her age-stooped body moving faster down the trail than I would have thought possible. Desperation did that to people, I supposed—made them move faster, speak words they'd held inside too long . . . or, in my case, held them captive as surely as if the hedge still blocked my path.

I stared at the trail, frozen, trapped, *useless,* as the shadow of the beast passed over me.

It had reached us, but instead of the citadel, it soared straight for Halvor. For Sami.

For Gateskeep.

TWENTY-TWO

ZUHRA

I was surrounded by a battalion of gryphons and Paladin, soaring up into the sky, a world I'd never seen before dropping away below me—and I had never been so overwhelmed and terrified in my life. After a lifetime of dreaming of an existence beyond the citadel and the hedge, I was suddenly, unexpectedly *far* beyond it— but this wasn't how it was supposed to happen.

I'd never been swimming before, but I'd read about it in one of the few books Mother had willingly let me read. A story of a sailor who thought himself strong enough to battle the tides of the ocean—and had been wrong. The description of his drowning haunted me for months.

For the first time, I felt I could relate to what he had gone through, except that I was being dragged *up* to the merciless sky, rather than down to the deep, silent bottom of the ocean floor. With every beat of Taavi's wings we were carried further away from the gateway—from my only hope of getting back to Inara and Halvor and the rakasa—and I'd never felt more helpless. My last sight of them had been the Scylla diving toward Halvor . . . Was there any possible outcome where Halvor survived an attack like that? My stomach twisted as I pictured his long, narrow body ripped apart, blood dripping into his rich, earthen eyes. And Inara . . . *What if she was already gone—what if the beast had already killed her and I was too late?* The question was too terrible to consider, but the memory of all those teeth serrated my hope until it lay in ribbons deep within me, an internal wound far worse than any I'd sustained from the Bahal—and a kind that no amount of Paladin magic infiltrating my body or mind could heal.

Her chances of fighting off such a beast and surviving were . . . *none*.

Was there any remote possibility she could have survived being trapped in there with that beast? Or was Inara . . . *dead*? My lungs capsized; it felt as though my rib cage were caving in, crushing my heart; I could barely breathe.

The icy wind buffeted my face and whipped the tears from my eyes. For some reason I'd assumed the closer we got to the sun, the warmer it would be, but I couldn't have been more wrong. As the world below grew smaller—an *entire new world*, massive in its breadth and *so different* from the tiny corner of the previous one I'd known, all rolling hills and thick copses of trees instead of peaks and hedges—the air turned colder and colder, until I wasn't sure how much of my increasingly violent trembling was from grief and panic and how much from my muscles freezing and rebelling.

The terror of the Bahal attack, the shock of my father rescuing me, the healing from Raidyn . . . those had all succeeded in distracting me from the horror of what had occurred in the citadel for a moment, but the gateway refusing to open, the horde of rakasa rushing toward us and forcing us to flee, the narrow escape had quickly brought it all back. We were safely airborne now—thankfully none of the rakasa had been the flying type—but my relative safety meant nothing. Though I clenched my eyes shut and buried my face in my father's back, nothing could stop the tightness in my lungs—the racing of my heart.

I'd failed her. The shaking grew even worse. I was gasping, desperately unable to suck in enough air.

A lifetime spent protecting my sister wiped away in one horrible moment.

I'd failed her.

I'd failed.

"Zuhra!"

Dimly, my father's shout penetrated the dizzying rush of blood in my head. His hands had enclosed mine, which were only loosely draped across his stomach now.

"Zuhra, you have to hold on!"

I heard his warning, despite the roar of the wind in my ears, and some small part of me knew he was right, but all I could see was Inara lying bloodied and broken on the ground of the Hall of Miracles, all I could focus on was an echo of the screams that must have reverberated from those walls, all I could do was curl in on myself as sobs of pure desolation wrenched me apart.

I'd failed her.

An especially strong flap of Taavi's wings was all it took. I wasn't prepared and the force of the gryphon's body moving to keep us airborne sent me tumbling off his left side. A sudden wrench on my arm—nearly ripping it from my body—and then I was dangling in the air, with only my father's hand around my wrist keeping me from plummeting to the earth below.

"Zuhra!"

My legs swung beneath me, my mouth opened in a scream that sheer terror and the wind ripped away before it fully formed. Taavi's wings beat valiantly, but his feathered flanks tilted, the weight of my body dangling below him too much to combat entirely. My father cried out, his grip slipping as he tried to keep *himself* seated on the struggling gryphon.

I reached for him with my free hand, attempting to grab on to his sleeve, but my hands were slicked by sweat and my fingers slid off. The extra movement made my body jerk and my father's grip slipped a little more. The veins in his arms and face stood out as he strained to hold on.

I tried one last time, lurching my body upward—toward him, toward safety and life and *not* falling to my death—but I wasn't strong enough and the wild twisting of my body was too much—my father's fingers turned to claws, but he couldn't do anything as my wrist slid through his hand and then—

I fell.

I'd spent so many hours imagining myself standing at the windows in the Hall of Miracles from that painting, staring down at the unfathomable drop to the earth far, far below, simultaneously thrilled and terrified at the thought of the glass shattering beneath my hands and plummeting through all that air to my death on the rocks at the base of the cliff. But no amount of fearing or dreaming of such a fall could have prepared me for the actual sensation of dropping from the sky, my arms and legs flailing, begging for purchase, for something—*anything*—to grab onto and finding nothing but wind and cloud and earth rushing up to meet me far too quickly. Though some small part of me knew it did nothing to help, I couldn't keep from screaming until my voice gave out.

How much would it hurt?

Would I lie there broken but alive as the life seeped out of my crushed body—or would it be instantaneous?

Should I keep my eyes open to catch my first and last glimpse of the world I'd longed to see and know when my time was up or squeeze them shut?

Hot tears were slashed off my face as soon as they formed by the punishing wind.

And then a large shadow whistled past, wings tucked and rider flattened against the feathered neck. The gryphon continued its nosedive for several seconds before opening its wings and catching the updraft, leveling out directly below me, obscuring my view of my oncoming death. I barely had time to register what was happening before the rider—a flash of sunshine hair and brilliant blue eyes—managed to throw himself at me without losing his legs' grip on the saddle, and literally snatched me out of the air, knocking the wind from my lungs, bruising my ribs, and somehow dragging me in front of him to land safely on his gryphon's back.

The reality that I was safe—that I was no longer plummeting to my imminent death—took several frantic thumps of my beleaguered heart to sink in. The Paladin's arms were like a vice around my waist, trapping me against his body so ferociously I could barely draw breath. But I was glad for it. I had no strength of my own to hold on to either him or the gryphon; my trembling was so violent I would have been humiliated had I not been so steeped in desperate relief. A little bruising and rough handling was a far better alternative to what I'd been prepared for when I'd reached the earth again.

"What *happened*?"

I knew that voice—I knew my rescuer now.

Before I could respond, another shout came from above and Taavi swooped beside us, beating his wings just enough to tread air the way some animals tread water. "Zuhra!" My father's face was ashen, his knuckles white on his gryphon's reins.

More of the battalion quickly encircled us, all the different gryphons flapping their wings similarly to remain airborne but no longer moving forward.

"I-I'm s-sorry . . ." My teeth clacked together, making the words nearly unintelligible.

"Do you have her?" My father's eyes moved past me to the Paladin whose arms still squeezed my ribs tight enough to hurt—and I found that I didn't care. In fact, I relished the discomfort, as long as it meant I wouldn't fall from the flying beast again.

"Yes, sir."

My father's gaze flicked back to me then away again before he jerked on Taavi's reins, lifted a fist into the air, and spun it around once. As one, the entire battalion of gryphons fell into what was obviously a formation and within seconds we were all rushing through the air once more, presumably toward Soluselis. Only this time, my father rode in the front of what appeared to be an arrowhead shape, with the gryphon carrying me and Raidyn in the center of it, his strong arms encircling me. The entire length of my back was pressed against his chest and abdomen; each flick of his wrist on the reins inadvertently brushed his hands against my belly. It was an entirely different experience than riding behind my father.

"Was it on purpose?"

His low voice in my ear sent a warm shiver down my spine, until his accusation sank in and I stiffened so fast my head whacked his nose. He jerked back with a grunt of pain, but his arms didn't even loosen around me—he was concerned for my safety no matter what, apparently.

"No," I shouted to be heard over the wind. "I . . . panicked." Embarrassment warmed my cold skin, turning my neck hot.

He leaned closer again, his mouth so near to my ear I could feel his warm breath on my jaw. "Many are quite nervous on their first flight after months of training." His voice was deep, almost melodic, but it had a slight husky quality to it that sent a shiver down my neck to my belly. "There is no shame in being scared. But you must hold on."

"I was—I *am*—n-nervous. But it w-wasn't that," I insisted, my trembling slowly ebbing away the more we spoke. His gryphon's wings beat on either side of us, and for some reason, the steady thrumming had become somewhat comforting. "It was *so* much space . . . and so many p-people . . . and leaving the g-gateway . . . it was leaving my s-sister to her . . . to her death." I could barely force the words out, but once I spoke them, it was as though I'd inhaled the frigid air straight into my abdomen, where it lodged, an icy chunk of despair twisting my insides.

It made it real.

Raidyn was quiet for a handful of wing beats, but his arms tautened almost imperceptibly around me, somehow easing my discomfort, leaving a small thrum of solace from the tightness of his hold on my body. "You are very close to your sister."

A statement, but I nodded anyway. Taavi had dark feathers, almost the color of the night sky, but this gryphon had tawny feathers that blurred into a haze of gold as fresh tears filled my eyes.

"Did you *feel* her loss—*truly* feel it deep in your heart?" He still spoke close enough to my ear that I could easily hear him. "Has a part of you gone missing, a hole that suddenly tore open within you that could only be her spirit departing this life?"

His response took me off guard, but I found myself searching for the feelings he was describing and finding only fear and a desperate, unsure kind of grief. "I . . . I don't know."

"When someone that close to you dies, you feel it—you *know* it. No matter how far apart you may be." It was difficult to know for sure with the wind battering us, but I thought I heard his voice catch briefly. "If she were truly gone, there would be no question. If you are unsure, then I believe your sister still lives."

Like the first brush of dawn, his fervent words coaxed the tiniest ray of hope, limning the edges of my dark despair with a hint of light.

"And I promise, we will do everything we can to convince your grandmother and the council to let us go through and make certain."

"My *grandmother*," I repeated. In the rush of leaving the gateway, my father's words hadn't really sunk in until Raidyn repeated them.

I'd never even *thought* about grandparents before . . . let alone *meeting* them. They'd seemed as unreal to me as life outside the citadel. And why did *she* need convincing? Before I could properly formulate a question, Raidyn released me—with just one arm, but it still made my stomach lurch and I seized his one remaining arm with both hands. A vibration went through his chest that seemed suspiciously like laughter against my back.

"I'm not letting go," his already familiar voice in my ear assured me. "Look." He pointed and I followed with my gaze. "This is my favorite part of coming home."

We'd been flying over rolling hills, thick with shrubbery and trees, but Raidyn had succeeded in distracting me so well I hadn't noticed how the hills had grown bigger and taller—turning into lush mountains surging toward the sky in ever-higher crests, culminating in two massive peaks directly ahead of us. They were so close together, at first glance I thought it was one giant summit, until the gryphons in front of us—including Taavi with my father on his back—began banking, swooping a bit lower and then angling their bodies nearly sideways, their riders flattening themselves against the beasts' necks and then disappearing between the narrow gap.

"No. No, no, *no*." I shook my head, instinctually pressing backward, away from the looming towers of death, but there was nowhere to go except to push harder into Raidyn's unmoving body.

"Good, lean back just like that." He ignored my protests as he shortened his grip on the gryphon's reins around me. "I will hold on to you and her and it'll be over before you know it. I won't drop you," he promised and leaned forward, forcing me to do the same, until I was pressed against the gryphon's neck and he was pressed into me. "But promise to keep your eyes open—you don't want to miss this."

I was half tempted to ignore him and keep my eyes safely shut—

how had he known?—but there was something in his voice that made me obey, even as the gryphon soared toward the two peaks that were almost close enough to touch now. Or splat against like a bug against a windowpane. Instead the gryphon dipped her left flank, angling her body so that her wings were parallel with the cliff face. My stomach plummeted as my heart leapt to my throat when I began to slip sideways off her back, but before the scream rushing up my throat could escape, Raidyn had wrapped both arms around the gryphon's neck and pressed his legs over mine, effectively trapping us against the gryphon's body as she glided through the narrow passageway. I inhaled the scent of earth and stone, tree and cloud, and felt the coolness of the rock faces we slipped between on my exposed skin, and then we were through, bursting free of what I'd been sure had been our imminent death, and—

My mouth fell open. I hardly even noticed the gryphon straightening out and gliding forward as Raidyn gently pulled me back to sitting; I could only stare. Admittedly, I had seen very little in my life—not even the town that I knew was sequestered at the base of the mountain below our citadel—but I knew that even if I *had* visited all the towns and cities of Vamala, I still would have been awed by the site of Soluselis.

The city gleamed white and gold, spreading in concentric rings across the valley, a sea of beauty surrounding a hill dwarfed by the cliffs that protected us on all sides, and yet my eyes were drawn to that hill, not to the peaks slashing the azure sky—to the stunning castle perched atop it. The magnificent structure blazed in the sunlight, shards of light refracting off its impossibly high walls and spires, making it appear to glitter as the gryphon soared over the roofs of the outlying buildings, heading straight for it.

"I told you it was worth it." I could feel Raidyn's deep chuckle where he still held me against him, even though my fear was erased by the grandeur of this city—far more stunning than any I'd seen in any book—of this *world* . . . of his home.

I merely nodded, at a complete loss for words. I couldn't even fathom having grown up in a small village somewhere, with neighbors and friends and maybe even family other than my mother, Inara, and Sami. What would it have been like to grow up *here*? It was impossible to take it all in at once. I wanted the gryphon to slow down, to allow me to swivel my head and commit the details of every alabaster building and cobblestone street to memory. The closer we got, the more details flashed by us: lines strung up with brightly colored clothes fluttering in the breeze, pottery on porches filled with overflowing flowers of all sizes and colors, and the people—the Paladin, I realized suddenly, as they glanced overhead at the battalion soaring toward the castle and I glimpsed flashes of their glowing blue eyes.

An entire city of Paladin. Men, women, *children*.

I'd known that's where we were going, but to see it—to see *them*—right there, below us, was overwhelming.

Far too soon, the entire group of gryphons had crossed over the city and begun landing in a huge field within the wall surrounding the castle—a wall made of vines and leaves, I realized with a lurch.

"The *hedge*," I breathed. It was exactly like the one at home—except even *bigger*. If I'd thought our citadel and the gardens had been large, they were to this castle and grounds what I imagined Gateskeep was to Soluselis.

"Hold on, the landing can be a bit jarring," Raidyn warned as our gryphon tucked her wings slightly. We coasted for the ground where the rest of the battalion waited, including my father, who stared up at us, crease marks etched into his forehead.

I squeezed my legs tighter against the gryphon's flanks, but needn't have worried. Compared to everything else I'd been through, the slight jolt when the creature touched down with her back paws first and then her front talons was nothing.

Raidyn hadn't even completely released me before my father vaulted from Taavi's back and sprinted to our side.

"Zuhra—are you—did you—I am so, *so* sorry—"

"Breathe, General," Raidyn said. He easily dismounted while still keeping one hand on my hip to steady me as I tried to sort out how to unhook my leg and slide off the animal who had saved my life. "She is just fine. In fact, I daresay she has already grown a little bit fond of flying. Don't you agree, Naiki?"

The gryphon tossed her head and made a soft hooting noise as my father grabbed me under the arms, helped me to the ground, and then turned me around and enfolded me in a hug so tight I could hardly draw breath.

"I'm all right," I assured him.

"I'm *so sorry*." Somehow, his arms tightened even more.

"You're going to crush her, General. I'm too drained to heal her again." Raidyn's wry observation was finally enough inducement for my father to release me and step back—but he kept his hands on my shoulders.

"Are you certain you're all right? You're not hurt? What *happened*?"

"I'm not hurt. I just . . . I, uh . . ."

"General Adelric, what is the meaning of this?"

A woman's voice rose above the din of the battalion's voices in the field. They all fell silent simultaneously.

A muscle in my father's jaw tightened and he exhaled. "I hoped to have more time to explain a few things to you . . ."

"General Adelric!"

I turned to look, but my father's grip on my shoulders tightened, pulling my focus back to him.

"Know this—she most likely will not be as happy that you are here as I am. But don't let her fool you. Her gruffness is all bravado."

My confusion and alarm must have been evident because as we both turned to face the source of the shouts, Raidyn leaned over and whispered, "She's your grandmother, Zuhra. Get ready to meet Ederra, the leader of the High Council of the Paladin."

TWENTY-THREE

INARA

I stood immobilized as the monster tucked its wings and dove out of sight, straight for the village hidden below the mountainside full of trees. *Zuhra wouldn't just stand here . . . Zuhra would go help fight.* But I had no weapons—no way to defend or protect—and worse . . . I had no courage. The miserable truth was simply that I wasn't Zuhra. I needed *Zuhra*.

But she was gone and I wasn't. A distant scream, so far away it seemed little more than a higher-pitched whistle on the breeze than normal, brought the memory of a flash of claws, bloodied fangs, and unimaginable pain . . . and I realized at last what I *could* do.

I could heal.

If there was any last drop of power within me, I would use it to heal the villagers who survived the attack. Surely the monster with a body of a horse but the head of a demon wouldn't massacre *everyone*.

Though the hedge had receded and the gate stood open, it still felt like a barrier existed that I had to push past as I forced one foot to lift, then the other, carrying me toward then through, passing underneath the safety, the *security*, of the hedge that had protected and watched over us for so long. I sensed the shudder go through it that made its dark green leaves flutter.

"Inara!"

The sound of my name was an unexpected jolt that made me stumble just outside the hedge. At first I'd almost thought it *was* the hedge—who else was left?—then I remembered.

I spun and saw my mother, standing on the steps of the citadel, her hair askew, her dress blowing around her ankles, revealing her bare feet. She stared at the open gate. I'd never seen her in such disarray.

I'd never heard her call for me.

And yet, I couldn't stay. Another roar was carried to us on the wind from below, spiraling up from the village where unimaginable horror was visiting them *because of me*. Because I touched that door and lost my sister and let the beast in.

"Inara! How did you—"

But the rest of her question was swept away by the wind as I turned my back on the woman who had long ago turned hers to me, and resolutely marched away from the only home I'd known toward the massacre surely taking place below us.

The path slashed through the mountainside, still frighteningly steep even though it switched back and forth through the dense trees and foliage in an attempt to make it more traversable. My nails bit into my palms as I picked my way down the trail, legs stiff and my lower back aching. I hoped I was at least halfway to the village, but it was impossible to tell; I could only see soil, foliage, and sky.

The entire time I kept expecting the familiar roar to begin at some point, for the noise to start to build within me, swelling until it drowned everything else out—as it always had before—but it never came. The silence inside was simultaneously a massive relief and unsettling. What if I made it to the village only to find I had nothing left to give? It always came back . . . but how long did it take after how much I'd used already today?

Was it possible to have used it all up—for it to be . . . gone?

I wondered if Zuhra would know. I faltered when I remembered that she, too, was gone and not ahead of me on the trail. How long would it continue to take me by surprise that my sister was never coming back?

Hot tears burned down my cheeks as I forced myself to go faster, despite my toes catching on roots and little flares of pain spiking all over my feet from pine needles and rocks. The only small comfort was the answering flickers of heat—sparks of my power healing every small wound from the trail on my unprotected skin.

Another roar reverberated from below, but this time it was much closer, so loud I skidded to a stop, throwing my hands over my head instinctually.

Be brave, Inara. Zuhra would want you to be brave. She would be running down this trail to help the villagers.

My vision was still hazy and my cheeks were still wet, but I straightened and forced myself to pick up my speed. I still didn't dare run, but it didn't take much longer before I started to glimpse thatched roofs and other signs of the village between branches and leaves up ahead.

And hovering in the air above them all, the beast that had nearly killed me and Halvor before breaking out of the citadel.

A shudder as heavy as ice coating a window went through me. Not only from the monster, but from all those *homes* . . . all those *people*. I'd never liked the stories Zuhra read to me during awake hours about large villages or cities. I preferred the tales of sisters, or small families, living in the woods, secluded, *alone*. Like us. Safely ensconced behind the protection of the hedge—the protection I'd left behind. My heart raced, my blood throbbed, my mind roared.

Go back go back go back . . .

But now that I was close enough, I could hear the wailing— the cries and screams—and that finally spurred me forward. I had no clue what to say, or what I could do, only that I had to do *something*.

This was my fault.

I burst out of the trail and then skidded to a terrified halt near a clump of buildings.

Monster—Paladin witch—murderer—

Words shouted, flung, stabbed at us—at *me*—from beyond the hedge that I'd only heard once but it was enough to make my legs halt once more, fear choking the air from my throat. There were dirt pathways between the homes but they were abandoned. Cries sounded from further in the village. My gaze went to the sky, but the beast had momentarily disappeared.

More screams sounded, followed by a roar so thunderous it vibrated through me—something I not only heard but *felt*, all the way into my bones.

Be brave—like Zuhra.

I forced my feet to move, to dash between the homes, keeping to the shadows, eyes darting for signs of wounded that I could attend to. But there was no one . . . no sign of life. Where were all the villagers?

It wasn't until I passed a window and happened to glance in that I realized where they were—hiding within their homes, huddled in groups, the whites of their eyes visible when their gazes met mine.

Don't be afraid of me. I will help. I will do what I can.

I rushed by home after home, small cottages nestled together like the hens Sami kept in our courtyard.

And then—suddenly—the homes ended and I stumbled to a halt in a large open square, where a group of men and women stood in some sort of formation with their backs to each other, wielding bows, arrows, and long, deadly-looking spears. The monster was airborne again but its wings were even more shredded, and two arrows protruded from its chest. Its legs kicked in agony, its claws where hooves should have been opening and closing.

A terrible keening caught my focus and I whirled to see an older woman kneeling over the bloodied body of a much younger woman near another pathway between more homes, a sword covered in gore lying a foot from her prone body.

This was what I'd come for—this was what I could do. I could help her. If she had life remaining within her, I would find it and I would bring her back.

I rushed over and dropped to my knees next to the crying woman.

"I can help," I said, reaching my hand out to place it on the girl's still chest.

The woman looked up into my face and then screamed, "*No!*" and shoved me in the shoulder so hard it knocked me back onto my bottom on the hard ground, near the bloody sword. "Don't you touch her, Paladin witch!"

An icy wave of disbelief was almost immediately overtaken by a rush of burning shame. "B-but I can help . . ." My voice broke and I cleared my throat roughly, humiliated to realize I was near tears.

"Get away from her!" The woman's cheeks had mottled red. When she lunged at me I scrambled back until I collided with the wall of the home behind us with a painful thud.

Another roar exploded across the village, a long sound that shook the very ground beneath us. I looked up to see the beast snapping its jaws at a spear buried halfway into its chest. Taking advantage of the distraction, the villagers with bows loosed a volley of arrows, shredding the monster's wings in a matter of moments. It tried to flap harder but the arrows had done their work; it careened sickly to the side, then tried to correct but instead plummeted toward the group of would-be protectors.

They screamed and scattered, moments before the monster's body crashed to the earth, crushing several of the villagers not quick enough and skidding into a nearby cottage that crumbled at the impact, burying the beast in stone, mortar, and a cloud of dust.

"Inara!"

Halvor. He was alive—he was *here*—

Something cold and sharp pressed against my throat and I froze.

"Don't move a muscle, or I will slit you open right now." The woman who had called me a witch and refused to let me touch the dying girl pressed the bloody sword against my skin. "I have her!" she raised her voice. "I caught the witch responsible! She's a Paladin! She did this!"

Spittle splattered against my cheek and I flinched. But I didn't argue. My stomach turned to lead. I'd been foolish to come, to leave the safety of the hedge, to hope to help. I *was* responsible, and apparently I was to pay for it—and soon.

"It's dead . . ."

"Was the king's garrison summoned?"

"How did this happen? I thought they were all gone!"

"Jesper! No—*Jesper!*"

All across the square townspeople began to emerge, rushing to bodies lying strewn on the ground, staring at the now unmoving beast half-buried across the way . . . or turning to stare at me as my captor continued to shout.

"Let her go. *Now*." Halvor's cold command took us both by surprise and the woman jerked. The sword slipped, just enough to slice into my skin.

I sucked in a breath at the sharp pain and the immediate flair of heat within me as my power rushed to heal the wound she'd inadvertently inflicted.

"She did this! She killed my Toma!" The woman clutched the sword more tightly, but her arms trembled from the effort.

Halvor, disheveled and dirt-streaked, grabbed her arms and pulled her backward so fast she couldn't harm me again. "*She* didn't do this—she didn't kill your daughter. If you would have let her try, she might have been able to *save* your daughter. She has the power to heal!"

"No." The woman shook her head, her eyes going round and filling with tears. "No no no *no!*" Her entire body began to tremble, so violently that Halvor went from restraining her to supporting her. The sword fell from her grip, landing with a clatter on the rock-strewn earth in front of where I still knelt, prepared for the furious woman to dole out her version of justice. When Halvor gently released her, she crumpled to the ground and crawled to where her daughter lay, eyes open and unseeing, pressing her forehead to the girl's chest, heedless of the blood, sobs wracking her body.

"Who is she?"

"Is she a *Paladin*?"

"Did she do this?"

Halvor reached out but I shook my head, wrapping my arms around myself. "I won't let them hurt you," he murmured, and tried again, bending over to slip his hand through mine and tugging me to my feet. My legs shook as though the reverberations from the beast crashing to the earth were still quaking the ground beneath me. Halvor squeezed my hand and turned, angling his body to cover most of mine, but not releasing my hand. The villagers not busy attending to the wounded or dying began to encircle us, closing in, their fear quickly transmuting into fury now that the immediate danger was gone.

I tried to disentangle our hands, but Halvor held on tight. "They're going to think you're with me," I protested.

"I *am* with you," he said, glancing over his shoulder at me briefly, his eyes flashing warm honey-gold in the sunlight that seemed at complete odds with the horrific morning. It should have been a crimson sunrise, sunlight slashing through ebony clouds, dismal rain pelting the blood-soaked earth; instead the breeze had blown the sky a clear, endless azure, the sun blazing above us as cheery and bright as ever.

But nothing warmed me more than Halvor's words and the firm grip of his hand on mine.

I am *with you.*

"Get away from her!"

"That witch killed my Jesper!"

"Stop it, all of you!" Halvor bellowed—more loudly than I thought him capable of; he'd always seemed so quiet, a man driven by intellect and the pursuit of information and learning. But he was formidable enough to make the villagers pause. "She is not the enemy!"

Another man pushed his way through the gathering crowd, an older man, with Sami following in his wake. Her hair and hands were streaked with blood. My lungs tightened, I suddenly couldn't draw enough breath, but Sami must have read the panic rising on my face because she called out, "It's not mine! I'm fine!"

"Step away from the Paladin girl." Another voice spoke up, this one deep and authoritative.

Rather than obey what sounded like an order to me, Halvor took a half step backward, *closer* to me. "She did not do this to you. She wouldn't hurt anyone—she's a *healer.* She saved my life from wounds inflicted by that beast this morning!"

I peeked over his shoulder to see a very large man marching toward us, one hand holding a bow and the other gripping a short sword. His dark beard and clothes were speckled with dust and debris—he must have been very close to the cottage that had collapsed on top of the beast's dead body.

"Only a Paladin could have allowed a rakasa back into Vamala." The man's voice was like rocks grinding together, raspy and low and utterly terrifying. "And the only Paladin I see is that girl. So, I will ask you one more time. Step away from her. *Now*."

"I will not. She did nothing wrong!"

The man lifted his sword. The crowd gasped. The older man by Sami jumped forward with a protest. But before anyone could do anything, I slipped out from behind Halvor and faced the bearded man with the sword and the rest of the village.

"Inara, what are you *doing*?"

I ignored Halvor's protest, his desperate tug on my arm.

Be brave, Inara. Be brave like Zuhra. "I did save his life this morning." I tried to keep my voice from shaking, but it was impossible when my entire body trembled like the last leaf on a dying branch being buffeted by a storm. "But you are right, it is my fault the rakasa came."

"Inara—*no!*"

A burst of sound erupted from the gathered crowd and the bearded man's lips pursed together into a line so tight, all color was erased from them.

"I didn't mean to—it was an accident! And I lost my sister because of it! I came here to try and help your wounded!" But no one was listening to anything else I had to say.

"You see? She admits it!"

"Paladin *witch*!"

"Kill her now!"

"No, she wouldn't hurt a spider! Please—you don't understand!" This last was from Sami, who bustled to my side, her eyes wide, pupils dilated with fear.

"Silence!" the bearded man roared, and the square fell quiet. Sami grabbed my other hand, so that I stood sequestered between her and Halvor, facing the entire town. "You admit that you brought the monster to Vamala?" He lifted his sword, not to threaten but to point at me, his surprisingly light eyes narrowing.

"I didn't mean to—I didn't know—" I stammered. Somehow my face and neck were hot while the rest of me felt as cold as the ice that coated my gardens in the midst of winter. "I came here to help. I wanted to help," I finally offered lamely.

Something flickered across the bearded man's face—a hint of

pity or perhaps sadness—but he merely shook his head and proclaimed, "Then, as the constable of Gateskeep, I hereby place you under arrest, charged with the crime of using Paladin magic to bring harm to the peoples of Vamala, to await the arrival of the king's guards and thence receive your just punishment."

"No! You can't do this! She's just a child!" Sami pushed me behind her.

"Mahsami, I suggest you remove yourself, or else I will be forced to place you under arrest as well." The bearded man stepped toward us.

"Don't do this, Javan. She's like Hasanni. She didn't know—she doesn't know what she's doing right now!"

That same flicker crossed Javan's face again, but he clenched his jaw and lifted his sword to point it at Sami this time. "Move aside. This is your last warning."

The gathered crowd surged closer, pressing in on the four of us.

"Just kill her now—before she can hurt any more of us!"

"You can't trust a Paladin!"

I'd been scared many times in my life, but I'd never felt more terrified than the moment that Sami released my hand and stepped away, with a whispered, "It's going to be okay, Inara. I won't let them do this to you. I promise."

But her words were swallowed up by the jeers and shouts as Javan grabbed my arm and quickly yanked me around, ripping my other hand from Halvor's grip, and twisting my arms behind my back.

"I believe that you might not have known what you were doing," Javan bent forward to murmur in my ear, a low rumble of sound, "but that doesn't change your guilt. I'm sorry, but the law demands justice."

"What is the punishment?" I somehow managed the words past my quivering lips.

There was a pause, and then, "Death."

And with that, he roughly shoved me forward, toward the sea of dusty, bloody, angry faces demanding their form of justice.

Demanding my death.

TWENTY-FOUR

ZUHRA

The woman marching toward us seemed ageless—and more than a little terrifying. My father's warning that her gruffness was just bravado did little to reassure me as her piercing blue eyes landed on me and widened momentarily before narrowing. Her hair was the color of fire, brilliant shades of red and orange, streaked through with strands of white ash, and her skin was an even darker olive than my father's. Her glowing blue eyes stood out starkly as she stormed up to where I tried not to cower next to my father and Raidyn.

Rather than attempting to escape what appeared to be the building fury in the Paladin woman descending on us, the rest of the battalion subtly drew closer to their leader and to me—though that was more by default, I assumed, than by a desire to protect someone they didn't even know.

"Adelric, that is a *human*," Ederra bit out by way of greeting when she halted a few feet from where we stood, her eyes flashing in a way that made me want to duck and cover my head.

"Yes. And she is also your granddaughter" was his succinct response.

A strangled noise came from my throat and I flushed. I attempted to smile—but my lips twisted, only one half even lifting, as I flinched back from the fury on her face. *Great first impression, Zuhra.*

"Hello," I tried again and then snapped my mouth shut when

my grandmother's eyebrows lifted, her burning eyes raking over me. Raidyn coughed next to me, but I had a sneaking suspicion he was really attempting to hide a laugh. I'd never had the urge to elbow someone in the stomach before in my life, until that moment. *Focus,* I coached myself. *You have to impress her. This woman holds the power to get you back to Inara.*

I opened my mouth to try once more, but before I could speak, Ederra curtly announced, "I don't have a granddaughter," and turned her back on me.

It took me a heartbeat to snap my mouth shut and try to erase the devastation surely evident on my face. The sunshine on my cheeks was warm, the light breeze balmy, but I wrapped my arms tightly around my waist, suppressing a sudden shiver.

I don't have a granddaughter.

It only took two more heartbeats for me to make a decision.

"Zuhra—"

I couldn't tell if it was Adelric or Raidyn who spoke over the thundering of my heartbeat and the rush of blood in my ears, but I ignored the troubled tone and rushed after my grandmother.

"Wait!" I shouted.

She paused halfway across the field and glanced over her shoulder at me, her eyes wide but her lips downturned.

"You don't have to want me," I panted when I finally reached her side. "Just help me get home, please. Help me get back to Inara—to my sister. The rakasa got through and if she's not dead yet then she will be s—"

"What?" Ederra's hissed question cut through my pleadings. "What rakasa? What is the meaning of this?" Her voice rose as she looked over my head. If I'd thought my mother had mastered the glare, she had nothing on this woman. I was almost afraid the blue fire glowing in her eyes was about to erupt out and burn us all on the spot.

"I would have told you if you'd given me a second to do so." Adelric's reply from directly behind me was much calmer than mine would have been. How was he not shaking in his boots?

"I'm giving you *half* a second to explain what she's talking about *right now.*" My grandmother—could I call her that if she refused to accept me as her granddaughter?"—Ederra pointed at me as though I had single-handedly caused the entire catastrophe.

"Her sister has immense Paladin power, just as I suspected," my father began. "Power that has been suppressed—unused—for fifteen years, ever since the night she was born and I was sucked through the gateway by the surge from her birth. And today, she finally touched the gateway in the citadel."

A muscle clenched in Ederra's cheek, her lips pursed into a thin line. My father's words echoed in my mind: He was *sucked* through the gateway—by *a surge from Inara's birth*? He hadn't abandoned us at all then . . . he hadn't left us willingly. And I already knew he'd spent fifteen years trying to reopen it with no success to come back. Everything my mother had believed . . . everything she'd tried to ingrain in us . . . was *wrong*.

"Please, let them open the gateway so I can get back," I pleaded. "The rakasa that got through was huge. I have to help my sister and Sam—"

"How is it that you came to be here?" She cut me off again, her voice as cold as ever, brushing away my terror for my sister and everyone else trapped in the citadel with that monster as if it were meaningless.

"Something grabbed my ankle and pulled me through. But my *sister*—"

"Was it still open?" Ederra addressed Adelric, ignoring my plea yet again.

"No, it closed shortly after Zuhra was pulled through."

"This girl opened the gateway by *herself*? Just by touching it?"

I nodded, jumping in before Adelric. "Yes, my sister did. And I have to get back to her as soon as—"

"Your *sister* is a danger to herself and to both of our worlds. She has already caused irreparable harm."

"So you'll help me get back to her?"

Ederra's eyes burned cold. "No. I won't."

"But . . ."

She turned on her heel and strode away.

This time I stood unmoving, my hands trembling. Hot anger boiled through my veins, but beside it beat a desperate grief that pricked my eyes. Was I stuck here—forever? If Raidyn somehow was right, and Inara hadn't died yet, every hour that we wasted not rushing straight back to the gateway was another hour closer to the possibility that I wouldn't ever see her again. Had Halvor survived the attack? Could he have been able to get one of the weapons and stop the beast?

"Don't worry, I'll talk to her." My father hurried past me, following in his mother's footsteps, heading for the castle that no longer looked as beautiful as it had to me at first. I wasn't sure how meeting my grandmother and having her be so gruff could change the appearance of a building, but somehow it had. Now the glittering walls and golden turrets seemed as cold and unfeeling as she.

I stood in the center of that field, staring at the massive structure, surrounded by Paladin and gryphons—more living beings near me than I'd ever experienced—and had never felt so alone in my life. All the fear and grief Raidyn's assurances had managed to assuage for a time came tumbling back up. It didn't matter how beautiful this place was, or how many unknown family members might live within those walls, or if potential friends could have been standing within talking distance right now . . . I only wanted my sister. My quiet, secluded citadel. Sami. Halvor. Even my mother.

All I'd wanted to do for so long was to escape, and now all I wanted was to go back.

If only there was some way to return to the moment when I'd left Inara's door unlocked and redo that brief second of distraction that had led to all of this. The Paladin had unimaginable power, but even *I* knew none of them possessed the ability to change time.

"Don't lose hope yet," a female voice said in my language.

I swiped at my cheeks furiously before turning to face a young woman with deep auburn hair and alabaster skin brightened by a splash of freckles across her narrow nose standing beside Raidyn. "Who said I've lost hope?" I snapped. "And why do you all speak my language?" It was irrational to be angry about *that*, I knew, but I couldn't help it.

They exchanged a glance, a look that spoke far more than their words, and revealed a closeness that only served to remind me how alone I was here.

"She can be very intimidating," the girl said.

"Sharmaine is right. It would be difficult to find someone who isn't at least a little bit afraid of your grandmother. But that doesn't mean things can't change."

I exhaled and added, with a bit more control, "I just have to get back there—as soon as possible."

"General Adelric is doing what he can, I'm sure of it. And though she is the leader of the council, Ederra isn't the only say. Perhaps the rest of the council will side with him—with you," Raidyn offered. "My mother used to say 'as long as you're breathing, there's always hope.'"

Sharmaine put one hand on Raidyn's arm, a gesture that was so instinctive she almost didn't seem to realize she'd done it. A strange flare of heat went through me to see her touch him, to witness the softness in her gaze when she glanced up at him. I swatted it down, baffled and disconcerted at my immediate reaction that I had no right to feel.

"I still think it's true," she said, almost too low for me to hear, and then turned to me. "Zuhra, I know you're worried about your sister, but what's done is done, and—"

"It is *not* done!"

Sharmaine startled at the vehemence in my tone and I hurried to continue.

"It can't be *done* . . . because that would mean we can't change anything. And that might mean she's dead and she can't be. She *can't* be! Because . . . b-because . . ." *That would mean it's my fault.* The words stuck in my throat, serrating my last strands of control. I buried my face in my hands, the only thing I could think to do to at least try and hide the sobs that unexpectedly overwhelmed me. I'd seen the monster diving toward Halvor. Surely he was gone. No one could have survived that. He'd only been a part of my life a short while, but I'd come to care for him—even though he hadn't reciprocated the depth of my feelings. The thought of his death ripped through me. And Inara would have been next. Raidyn was wrong about knowing. He was *wrong.*

There was no way my sister would have been able to fight off that rakasa by herself, trapped in the Hall of Miracles. Not unless a true miracle had occurred. Unless . . .

Unless her power to heal herself was strong enough to keep her from dying.

I inhaled sharply and let my hands drop. Raidyn had folded his arms across his chest, watching me with hooded eyes, but Sharmaine had stepped closer. Her hand hung in the air as though I'd caught her mid-attempt to pat me on the shoulder.

"As long as you're breathing, there's always hope," I repeated with a hesitant smile, despite my tear-streaked face.

Raidyn lifted one eyebrow, baffled at my sudden change of countenance.

"I have to talk to the council right away. Can you help me do that?"

"Um . . ." Sharmaine glanced over her shoulder to Raidyn.

"We can try," he offered. "But"—he continued before I could thank him—"even *if* we are able to get them to convene, though you will surely find some allies there, you had best be prepared for the fact that some of them won't be thrilled that you're here."

"It doesn't matter. I can convince them. I'm sure of it. I *have* to."

Because Raidyn and his mother were right—there was always hope. There had to be. It was the only way I could continue on—the only way I could find the courage and strength to face a grandmother who didn't want me, a council of Paladin who held my future in their hands, and a world full of monsters and men with more power in their eyes than my entire body.

If my sister had enough power to open a gateway my father hadn't been able to get back through for fifteen years just by touching it, surely she had the power to heal herself from a rakasa attack.

And I wouldn't stop until I made it back to her.

TWENTY-FIVE

INARA

The tiny jail cell was dank, musty, and smelled of feces, urine, and worse—the decay of things long dead. I sat in the center of the cell, my arms wrapped around my knees, reciting the few nursery rhymes I could remember that Zuhra used to sing to me at night to help me get to sleep. I knew she thought I couldn't hear her through the roar, and usually that was true. But sometimes, especially at night when I was close to sleep, her voice would burrow through the constant growl of power in my mind.

Rest your eyes and rest your tiny toes,
Go to sleep, and I'll bring you a rose.

Silly, nonsensical rhymes but they'd brought me comfort then. I squeezed my eyes shut and tried to summon the memory of her voice to sooth me now . . . and found only silence. The absence of my sister, the absence of the only home I'd ever known, and the absence of the power that had always consumed me. For so long I had wished for it to go, had longed for the rare moments of silence when I could actually communicate with Zuhra to last . . . but now they were both gone, and all I wanted was for them to come back. I wanted the numb, oblivious peace the roar allowed me. I'd never recognized it as such before now—but being alert for this long had finally made me realize there were times being *unaware* of what was happening around you was more of a gift than a curse.

At least when what was happening around you was being trapped in a jail cell smaller than your closet at home, all alone, awaiting your execution.

And as much as I tried to convince myself otherwise, my deepest fear—even more than my own death looming over me—was that I had lost Zuhra forever. That she had been sucked through that doorway to *her* death.

Halvor had tried to protect me, but Javan and the villagers knew the truth and their demand for justice was . . . well, justified. I had brought death to my family, and to theirs. I'd touched the door, my power had summoned the monster somehow.

My power.

A groan came from the cell next to me, as it had occasionally all night. "The town drunkard," Sami had whispered before she left. Whoever it was sounded miserable. And the smell coming from his cell was even worse than mine.

Sami and Halvor had both pleaded with Javan, begging him to release me, claiming they'd take me back to the citadel, that no more harm would come—that it had been a fluke and wouldn't happen again. But he'd refused and eventually they'd both been forced to leave.

My mother had never come.

Not that I truly had expected her to, but I couldn't keep from hoping that perhaps word would have reached her—that my impending death would be enough to induce her to perhaps *try* to help me. Or, at the very least, come speak to me before my "trial" the next day. The meeting where I was to be judged and then executed.

Sami had cried when Javan dragged her away from my cell.

Halvor had merely stared at me for several long moments, then left without a word.

And my mother never came.

And Zuhra was gone.

For the third time since I'd been left there in the cold, damp dark, Sami's robe got soaked from the tears I tried to press back by digging my knees into my eyes.

Zuhra, if you're already gone, will you help me be brave for the trial and execution? Will you be there when I die?

"Inara!" The low whisper made me jump and I scrambled to my feet, almost expecting to see her ghost.

Except the voice had been distinctly male.

"*Halvor?*" I whispered back, when I realized he was crouching on the ground outside my door, dressed entirely in black; only his dusty brown hair revealed his identity. That, and his familiar voice. "What are you doing?"

"I'm helping you escape."

There was an odd jangling sound.

"Escape?" I repeated, baffled.

"They're going to kill you, Inara. But if we can get you back to the citadel, the hedge will protect you. They won't be able to hurt you."

"What about the trial? Where's Javan?"

"Shh!" He glanced over his shoulder and after a moment of silence resumed his work. It was hard to tell in the darkness, but his hands seemed to be trembling. The lock rattled against the metal bars of the door. "You have to be quiet or they'll catch us."

"What you're doing . . . It's wrong. Isn't it?"

He was silent for a long moment and then with a snick the lock popped open. "What's wrong is to murder an innocent young girl for a mistake she had no control over." He stood and swung the door open, triumph lighting his eyes.

Young girl. For some reason those two words rang in my ears, making me flush, though I wasn't sure why.

"Let's go—*hurry.* Before we get—"

Halvor turned right into the man who had emerged from the shadows behind him.

"Beat me to it, boy."

I didn't recognize the man's voice, but Halvor must have because instead of reacting in anger or fear, he threw his arms around the man. I recognized him as the one who had stared at me in the crowd—but not with anger or fear. With something akin to . . . awe.

"Barloc, we have to get her to the citadel. The hedge will protect her—it will—"

"No," Barloc answered, his voice similarly pitched low and

quiet. "There is a family that came to me and asked if it was true that Paladin can heal. Their son was injured in the attack and has taken a turn for the worse. They wish for her to come before the trial."

"And then what? Thank her for saving their child's life and wave as the executioner takes her to the town square to be strung up?"

"*Halvor.*" Barloc's gaze snapped to mine then back again. "Watch your mouth."

"I'm sorry, but I don't see how sneaking her into one family's home to heal their child is a good idea. We need to get her away from here, as soon as possible. She already offered to help heal their wounded and they imprisoned her!"

I stared at the two men as they discussed my fate, wondering if I should speak up or allow them to choose for me. I knew so little, and by healing Halvor somehow I'd come to know him intimately—his mind, his heart. Even now, I could sense his emotions—anxious but earnest. I could trust him. And if he trusted Barloc, then I did too. So I stood still and waited as they argued over my fate.

"If she heals their child, they have agreed to testify on her behalf—to argue for her release. Having someone on her side from within this town could only help her cause." Barloc paused and then added, "If what you've claimed her capable of is true, that is."

Halvor looked to me this time; our eyes met and a flash of memory rose within me at the look in his gaze. The feel of his body beneath my hand, the flicker of life within him almost gone, the beautiful light of his soul returning in full force as my power infiltrated his wounds and made him whole once more. "She can" was all he said.

"I want to help," I offered quietly. "I don't want anyone else to die because of me."

"It was *never* because of you," Halvor protested, "and you need to stop saying that!"

"But I—"

"This is not the time to argue about this," Barloc interjected, glancing over his tense shoulder to the shadows that swam through the mostly empty building. The prisoner next to me had begun snoring sometime during the whispered conversation. "She said she wants to do it, so let's go."

Halvor sighed—a sound heavy with displeasure—but gestured for me to follow after Barloc. I stepped out of the cell silently, the stone floor cold on the pads of my feet as I hurried after the older man, Halvor close behind. I wished he'd thought to get Sami. Her presence would have gone a long way to soothe the sudden trembling in my knees as we rushed past other dark cells and then out into the cool night.

The sky was a rich canvas of velvet black dotted with silver pinpricks of starlight above us. No moon had risen, offering us the cover of darkness, and the stars' light was too distant to do much more than flicker as they watched us rush between a handful of cottages. The ever-present breeze was gentle that night, caressing my face, tangling its wild fingers in my hair and sweetly lifting the lightest strands from my neck and cheeks.

But for all the peace surrounding us, my heart was wild within my chest, thundering blood through my shaky legs. Every doorway and window loomed menacingly, every undulating shadow twisted into snarling faces, ready to spit epithets at my glowing blue eyes. Barloc was quick, almost too quick, and I stumbled more than once trying to keep up with his pace. The third time I went down with a swallowed cry as my knee slammed into the rocky pathway and cut open.

"Quiet!" Barloc hissed a warning, pausing to glance back as I clambered back to my feet.

Halvor was there in an instant, gripping my elbow, helping me up, and even once I was standing he didn't let go, sliding his hand down my arm to enfold my cold fingers in his warm ones.

"Are you all right?" he murmured, so low I barely heard him, let alone Barloc.

I nodded, too nervous to speak. *Young girl* rang through my mind again, but he didn't *look* at me like I was nothing more than a young girl when I glanced up at him and our eyes met beneath the stars. His hand tightened over mine and something responded in my chest, hitching my breath somewhere between my lungs and throat.

Barloc made a small noise of impatience, and as one we both turned to face him.

"It's right there." He pointed to a house that stood across a larger pathway dividing two rows of homes. The house he indicated was encased in darkness, but burned with light from within, every window glowing, eerie shadows moving across them as the inhabitants rushed from room to room. Even from where we stood across the way, I could sense the panic, the desperation—it seeped out through cracks in the house's mortar and slithered toward us, calling to me.

A flicker of fire awoke in my chest, reaching toward that home—to that injured person within.

I hadn't even realized I'd begun walking until Halvor's tug on my arm pulled me back to a halt. He quickly spun to place himself in front of me, our bodies mere inches apart. I'd never stood so close to anyone—let alone someone . . . *male*. It was . . . flustering. I could smell him—oak and ink and salt and a vague hint of something citrusy. I could *feel* the heat of him. His lips moved. "Someone's coming." His voice was barely audible, but it was enough. I stiffened, a rush of cold dousing the flicker of power urging me toward that home.

"Bit late to be out, Master Barloc."

I didn't recognize the female voice, but she didn't sound accusatory.

"I was worried about the Dunlox boy. Came to see if there was any change."

There was a clucking noise, followed by a sigh. "It doesn't look good, not good at all. And she just lost the baby last year, too."

"That poor woman."

She'd lost her baby already and now her son was dying? No wonder she was willing to risk the punishment of stealing me from my cell to try and heal her boy. I *had* to get to her—to *him*—before it was too late for this one as well. Halvor must have sensed the urgency surging through my body, because he moved in even closer, holding me back, so that his thighs brushed mine, and my breasts pressed against his chest. He squeezed the hand he still held once—a warning. I had no choice but to wait for this woman to pass.

"What are *you* doing out so late?" Barloc queried, turning the focus from himself masterfully.

"Long night at the pub. There were a lot of upset townsfolk needing a drink before bed."

"Ah, I see. Do you wish for me to accompany you home—make sure you arrive safely?"

"You're too kind, Master Barloc, but these old bones know the way just fine. Thank you all the same."

"Well, I will bid you goodnight then, Madam."

There was the sound of shuffling feet, a returned farewell from the woman, and then silence. My heart beat so hard I was certain Halvor could feel it—partially from my desperation to get to the injured person in time, and partially because I had never stood like this with a boy before—with a *man*. And some strange, unknown corner of my heart not focused on the imminent healing urged me to ignore everything else and to inhale the scent of his skin more deeply, to tilt my chin up and look into his eyes once more, to let the curious cacophony of sensation in my belly grow and expand and encompass my entire body—

"She's gone." Barloc's muttered announcement startled me. Halvor moved back so suddenly I stumbled forward a step at the loss of his body. I hadn't even realized I was leaning into him. "Come on."

I wasn't sure if the note of irritation I heard in Barloc's voice was real or only imagined because of my embarrassment, but regardless, I hurried after him without another glance at Halvor.

Instead of going to the front door, Barloc led us around the side to a door at the back. I followed, but each step that carried me closer to that door—to more strangers, more people, *not* my home—grew heavier, my feet slower. I was eager to help, I *needed* to help . . . there was just so much fear inside me, chewing through any courage I might have possessed, tearing away my foolish confidence that I could do this. What if I couldn't save the son?

It was too late to turn back now.

The home bordered the forest, so there were no neighbors to witness him rapping softly twice and the door swinging open moments later to reveal a woman with wide eyes, a tear-streaked face, and a half-falling-out bun.

It was still a shock to see another face—too many new, different faces—than the only three I'd ever seen for fifteen years.

"She came?" The woman gasped, her eyes immediately moving past Barloc to find me, awkwardly hovering a few steps away.

"She wants to help," Barloc answered before either Halvor or I could.

"Come in. Hurry. He's not . . ." She broke off, her voice catching, and instead gestured while opening the door wider.

Barloc moved aside so I could precede him into the house. After a deep, fortifying breath, I stepped through the doorway into a kitchen where a fire burned. The overly hot air smelled of yeast and herbs and something else beneath it all, something putrid.

That panic—the *desperation* I'd felt seeping out toward me earlier festered within the home, filling it with a dread far greater than my paltry fears about facing strangers, entering a home I didn't know, or even my concern that I might not be able to save him. My conviction to help—to at least *try*—returned tenfold, swelling within me, leaving no room for anything else.

"He's in here."

I followed her out into a small hallway, the scent of herbs fading and the putrid undertone taking precedence, toward another doorway, where a tall, thin man hovered. The woman brushed past him with a touch of her hand on his lower back, and he moved so I could follow. I felt his gaze trained on me but kept my focus on the woman, preparing myself, trying to summon that flicker of fire once more.

"He was one of the spearsmen," the mother explained. "He hit the monster, but the monster swiped him with its claws and—"

Her words stopped computing when instead of the boy on the bed, my gaze landed on the man standing at the footboard, his arms folded across his chest, his dark eyes trained on mine.

Javan.

TWENTY-SIX

ZUHRA

My father opened the door to the castle and gestured to the opening with a flourish. I stood a few feet away, unmoving. I'd never set foot in any building besides the citadel in my life—unless the dilapidated stables counted. But beyond that doorway was so much more than just another threshold. It was the line between the life I'd lost and the new one here—in Soluselis, with the Paladin. Without Inara.

"Zuhra?"

I summoned a smile, tremulous but hopefully convincing, and forced my feet to carry me forward, to where my father waited, his own smile faltering a bit at my hesitation.

If I'd believed the grand entrance to the citadel to be large and ornate, it barely held a candle to this one. Everything there was stone, somewhat dark and imposing. Here, everything was so open, so *bright*.

"It's pretty remarkable," my father commented quietly from beside me.

I merely nodded, not sure what to think—or say. It was breathtaking and amazing and . . . not my home.

After a pause, he continued, "It might take a little getting used to."

I followed him silently, attempting to take it all in. The walls and floor of the castle were made of polished white stones that gleamed like untouched snow. Pools of sunlight shimmered in perfectly spaced intervals from the skylights overhead.

"They've given you a room just up here."

"I don't need a room." The same refrain I'd already repeated multiple times. Giving me a room implied my stay was anticipated to be long enough to require a bed. "We have to leave *today*—we have to go back."

"We will," Adelric assured me, as *he* had multiple times. "But you can at least get washed up and rest for a moment, while the council convenes. I was told there are clean clothes and a bath already drawn up for you."

I bit back a reply that I didn't have time for a bath or rest. The urgency of the situation didn't matter; when word of my arrival with Adelric's battalion—and *how* my arrival had happened in the first place—reached the right ears, they'd agreed the council needed to assemble to decide what to do next. But it took time to gather them all.

How much time, no one would tell me.

The one thing that had been made clear was that no decisions of this magnitude—choosing to open the gateway—were made without the *entire* council. And they were not all at the castle at that exact moment.

So I took step after step in my father's wake, each press of the cool stone against my bare feet a reminder that I was walking *away* from my sister instead of toward her. He paused at a door, gave it a light rap, and then pushed it open.

"Here you go. I'll be back for you as soon as I hear anything." But he didn't retreat, instead shifting his weight side to side, his gaze moving from my face to the ground to the empty room and back again.

My father.

In all the turmoil of the last several hours, that truth hadn't had a chance to do more than skim the surface of cognizance. He'd saved me, hugged me, claimed to love and want me, brought me here, and was fighting to get his mother—and the council—to hear our plea to let us reopen the gateway. All these things I'd seen, felt, been a part of . . . and yet, in that moment, as we stood there in that beautiful hallway, just the two of us, it truly *hit* me.

This was *my father*. This man—this living, breathing *Paladin*—had once loved my mother. He'd once loved *me*. *He*'d given me my olive skin and Inara her burning eyes. He'd been a hissed curse in our home, the unseen ghost that dodged all our steps, and the aftermath of his supposed betrayal had obstructed every doomed attempt to learn more about who—and what—he was.

But Adelric was none of those things—not a curse, not a ghost, not even an aftermath. He was *real* and he had crinkles at the corners of his brilliant blue eyes from laughter and lines at the corners of his mouth from heartache, and a habit of talking too fast when he was nervous, and a scar near his left ear, and he'd cried when he realized who I was. He'd *cried*.

"What *happened* that night?"

The whispered question was out before I could think better of it; but I knew the events surrounding Inara's birth, nearly sixteen years ago, were what had kept him standing near the door, his hands shoved into the pockets of his trousers, rather than immediately leaving me to my proffered bath and rest.

"Why were you even near the gateway and not with Mother?"

His eyes snapped to mine and the Paladin fire that made them burn guttered, smoky anguish and haze-smeared regret clouding the brilliant blue to smudged ink. "That night was . . . I *never* would have gone up there if I'd *known*—" His stumbling starts and stops only reinforced the realization that what my mother had assumed happened had been so very, very wrong. "Your sister . . . what is she like?"

"Inara is . . ." How to describe her? How to put into a few unworthy words all that made her who she was? "She's . . . she's *everything*."

It would have to be enough, because my throat closed off and there were no more words. *Inara*. Her back arching, the blue fire racing through her veins, out of her hand, and into that door, opening a gateway and ripping our tiny world apart.

My father—*our* father—nodded and swallowed. "Inara," he repeated, rolling her name over his tongue, the lilt of his accent turning the single word into music. He shut his eyes and tilted his face up to the edge of sunlight from the skylight above. But not before I saw the sheen of tears—for her, this time. For Inara. "I felt it that night—I felt her coming. I'd heard stories of such occurrences, but . . ." He paused, then restarted. "I was so young when the Five Banished found the gateway and reopened it, thrusting us into your world. I was very knowledgeable about some things, but sadly, not others. So when that swelling of imminent power gathered near your mother as her labor began—when I sensed the hedge responding, I wasn't entirely certain what it meant, but I had my suspicions."

Question after question piled upon the last as he spoke, until there were so many they filled my mouth entirely and I could do nothing except listen, silently choking on my lack of understanding. The Five Banished? The hedge *responded*—to Inara's birth?

"My greatest fear was that if the birth sent that surge of power out into the world, as I'd vaguely remembered hearing was possible, that it would be enough to reopen the gateway again, since it was in such close proximity to us. I'd thought the citadel the only safe place to bring your mother when she decided she wished to marry me. It was . . . a dangerous time in Vamala for a Paladin. But there were many safeguards prepared by the Paladin who built the citadel that would protect our family from any of the king's garrison if they were needed . . .

"I'd never thought until that moment that I might have actually put us in even greater danger from what could be lying in wait on the other side of that gateway in Visimperum.

"So I kissed your mother and told her I had to see to something and went to the Hall of Miracles. I had to protect my family. I only intended to create a barrier of some sort, to slow or stop whatever might come if the gateway was opened, and return immediately to the birthing room—but the baby came too fast. I felt the moment of her birth; the shock wave of her power entering the world hit just as I was climbing the stairs. It was like an explosion had gone off from behind me, knocking me into the door just as the wave of her power hit it. It did just as I feared and opened the gateway. But instead of something coming through into our world,

I fell through it back into mine . . . and it shut behind me, trapping me here."

"You . . . you were trying to protect us?"

My father rubbed a hand over his face, deep lines etched into his forehead revealing themselves when his brows drew together. "I have fought and pleaded for fifteen years to have the gateway reopened—even just for a moment—so that I could go back. And I have been refused every time. I never got to see Cinnia again . . . I missed watching you grow up . . . I never even met Inara . . . I—" His voice shattered, the shards of his grief impaling me, crushing every last preconceived notion I'd had forced on me, and when he lifted trembling, hesitant, terrified arms, I willingly and gratefully stepped into his embrace. "*Zuhra*," he said, and my name was a shudder that started with him and ended with me. "Oh, my little girl. *My little girl.*"

The deep timbre of his voice, the sunshine and soap smell, the strength of his embrace—so unknown and yet achingly familiar all at once—brought a surge of memory that I had lost long ago. The name I had learned back then, back before Inara and the surge and his disappearance. This man—this Paladin—this father. He wasn't just *Father* to me. "Papa," I whispered, and his arms tightened even more as my own tears—of anger at the injustice of it all, the grief at the years stolen from us, and the hurt spread across us all—joined his.

The room they'd given me (who "they" were, I wasn't sure—I just knew it couldn't possibly have been Ederra, who I hadn't seen again) was smaller than my room in the citadel, but it was warm and bright, with the same glowing white walls and floors as the rest of the castle. Two large windows let in gobs of sunlight, making the cream and yellow curtains and bedding practically glow. A freestanding copper tub had been dragged in and set up in the corner near the armoire. The water was no longer hot, but it was clean and smelled of lavender and mint. Despite myself, I couldn't pull my clothes off fast enough to sink into the fragrant bath. I didn't sit in it long, as it was barely even warm to begin with and only continued to cool. I quickly scrubbed the dirt and blood from my skin, wishing the guilt and grief were as easy to remove.

As I passed the washcloth they'd provided me over each part of my body that had been ripped apart or shattered by the attack, the only physical reminder of what had happened was a shiver of memory, a blurry, smudged recollection of the pain I'd endured. I propped my foot up on the edge of the tub and inspected it—the skin was flawless, no bruising, no marks, not even a hint of scarring. Completely healed . . . because of Raidyn. The memory of his presence *inside* me sent a wave of gooseflesh over my skin. I'd never experienced anything like it. And then when he'd saved me from falling to my death . . . the way he'd held me, calmed me . . .

I shivered in the cool water and forced myself to stand, grabbing the towel folded neatly on the chair set next to the tub, and quickly rubbed myself dry. The clothes they'd left on the bed were softer than anything I'd ever owned—and they were obviously brand-new. I lifted the delicate white underclothes and fingered them reverently. They felt like clouds slipping over my body, silky and smooth and so *clean*. No matter how hard I tried, none of my clothes at the citadel were ever this fresh and spotless . . . years and years of wear were impossible to erase, no matter how much care I took with my washing and darning and attempts at embellishments.

The blouse and skirt were also unbelievably soft, and fit like a dream. Fitted enough to show the form of my body, but with enough room and flow to allow easy movement. They'd also left me a pair of trousers, but I'd opted for the skirt. I'd never worn pants before and I didn't dare try them for the first time now, when I was planning on going before an entire council of powerful Paladin to plead with them to do something they'd refused to do for fifteen years.

I sat at the armoire to brush out the tangles in my hair but instead found myself staring out the window at the busy courtyard below, the roofs of the city visible past the hedge spreading down the hillside like melted butter, and the sky-scraping mountains beyond. The enormity of being in a *different world* washed over me again, vastly terrifying and exhilarating all at once. There was too much to take in, too much to worry over, too much to fear. The temptation of a nap—of letting my frantic mind shut down for at least a little while—sounded much more appealing than I'd originally thought.

Ignoring the call of the bed, I set down the brush, quickly braided my hair back, then thought better of it and took it down again and headed for the door.

I was done waiting.

The hallway was empty, and I had no idea where to go or what I even intended to do. I just knew I had to do *something*—I had to find a way back to my sister. And the fear that I refused to fully acknowledge was that the council would tell me no, as they apparently had my father.

So I walked and I tried to come up with a plan, though I knew, deep down, that I had no control here. I had no way of getting back to my sister unless this council said *yes*.

I passed doors and hallways and Paladin who paused and glanced or halted and outright stared, but I ignored them all and kept walking, moving, *doing something* . . . even if it was just . . . wandering. The castle was a marvel; golden ceilings soared overhead, deliciously bright paintings adorned the clean white walls, and nearly everywhere I looked diamonds decorated and adorned furniture, tables, vases, statues—I even wondered if they were embedded in the flooring, if that's what made it shimmer in the squares of sunshine from the skylights.

The castle seemed to be built as though it were encircling something; every hallway curved. The closer to the center of the building, the more dramatic the curve. I was hopelessly lost and couldn't have found my way back to my room even if I'd wanted to, but there was a pulse within me, separate from my heartbeat, something *different*, but still a part of me somehow . . . and it urged me inward, deeper into the castle. I let it pull me toward the middle—toward whatever this castle had been built around. The closer I got to the center, the stronger that strange pulse became and the more I wanted to follow it.

Finally, I found a connecting hallway that cut straight to the center of the castle. The entire place was full of skylights, letting in plenty of daylight and illuminating the hallways. But the light at the end of this hallway was different. It came from *within* the castle, not outside, and it . . . *glowed*. I could almost feel the warmth of it, even from where I stood, staring—but not *on* my skin, underneath it somehow, *inside* me.

Everything within me urged me closer, yet my steps slowed, expecting someone or something to block me from passing through the arched opening into whatever room lay beyond.

But nothing and no one ever came.

I stepped through the archway into a room that surpassed any ability I possessed to ever describe. The domed ceiling soared high above where I stood, made entirely of glass so that at first glance it appeared as though there were no ceiling at all, only a vast expanse of endless blue sky. The floor I stood on only continued forward the length of five or six strides and then came to a balustrade—the entirety of which was made of diamond—which in and of itself was beyond comprehension. And beyond that, there was nothing. Nothing except pure, brilliant *light*.

It filled the entire room, refracting through the massive diamond railing, shattering into a million more dazzling shards that danced on the walls, the floor, my arms, and in my eyes.

"Remarkable, isn't it?"

I choked on a half-emitted squeak of shock and whirled to see a tall male Paladin standing a few feet away. He was quite a bit older than my father, he had deep lines etched in the grooves of his mouth and near his eyes, and yet he exuded a vitality and energy that took me by surprise. He also looked a lot like—

"I'm sorry if I startled you, Zuhra, but I had to meet you." His burning blue eyes were somehow gentle when they met mine, gentle and . . . full of wonder. "I couldn't believe it when Ederra first told me, and yet, here you are.

"After eighteen years, I finally get to meet my granddaughter."

TWENTY-SEVEN

INARA

At the sight of the man who had locked me up only a few hours prior, I froze so fast Halvor crashed into me from behind, making me stumble forward farther into the room. Halvor whirled on Barloc.

"What is *this*?" he thundered—the loudest and angriest I'd ever heard him.

"I didn't know! They promised they only wanted her to help . . ." Barloc had blanched, going nearly as white as the streaks in the hair he wore long and pulled back from his face.

I still hadn't moved; a mouse caught in the sights of a cat.

"You get one chance," Javan said, his dark eyes trained on mine. "Heal him and I will let you go. Fail and . . ." He didn't have to finish his sentence. I already knew what awaited me with the sunrise.

Death.

I nodded, my tongue too thick in my mouth for a response.

His cold gaze followed me as I moved forward on numb feet, my blood spinning through my body in a dizzying rush. This was all still so foreign to me; I knew I had the ability to heal him . . . but what if it didn't work this time? What if I failed—in front of Javan and the boy's family?

The skin between my nose and my lip grew damp and I swallowed as I stopped by the side of the bed, staring down at the boy's face. His dark hair was plastered to his head, his skin sheened with sweat, but he was as gray as ash. His chest lifted and fell with great sucking sounds and the smell of rot hovered over his body. Infection had grabbed him and far too quickly. He looked Zuhra's age, maybe a little older. But the violent tear through his abdomen was quickly stealing any future of unknown promise from him.

I can do this. I can do this.

"Do you need anything?" His mother hovered so close, the added heat from her body in the already too hot room was almost more than I could stand. There were so many people pressing toward me—watching me. "Water? Cloths? Herbs?"

I shook my head. "No." I forced the word out, but said no more when even that one word came out a tremulous whisper.

"She needs space," Halvor announced suddenly. "She can't do this with all of us crowding her."

"She bloody well better hurry," someone growled, but I couldn't tell who it was over the thundering of my own heartbeat in my ears.

Finally, I took a deep breath, reached out shaking hands, and pressed them onto the boy's exposed rib cage. His skin burned to the touch, but beneath the raging, angry fever, a terrible, endless cold had already begun to take its place deep within him, unfurling within his bones and seeping out to the rest of his body. He was minutes from death.

Vague sounds of the others talking faded from my awareness, becoming little more than a distant, low rumble as my focus turned inward, to the flicker of power that awakened in me the moment I put my hands on the dying boy's chest. The relief that my power responded so quickly this time was almost as intense as my fear had been. Either I was getting better at summoning and using it, or the forced break from accessing it in the jail cell had been what I needed for it to respond faster; it didn't matter which, only that it was there, that I could use it to save this boy.

As before, the burning heat of it grew within me, hotter and hotter, until it exploded out through my veins, down my arms, to my hands, and into the boy's body. Distant gasps were little more than wisps on the periphery of my hearing. There was only me and the boy and the need to chase away death before it claimed him as its victim.

It almost felt familiar this time as I sent my power through his skin, muscles, veins, and bones, as I insinuated myself into his body, seeking out the injuries, the infection, the pain that held him deep beneath the surface of consciousness. And as I worked, as I healed, as I burned and shuddered with his pain, I also learned—I felt his desperation to impress his father, his love for his mother, his guilt at wanting to leave this place, his fear of hurting her when he did. I saw flashes of his life. Just as I had with Halvor, I felt . . . *him*.

I had no way of knowing how long it took, but finally, the boy began to stir and, with a gasp as the connection broke, I reeled my power in and pulled my hands free of his body. The force of the separation sent me stumbling back a couple of steps until strong arms encircled me, halting my fall. I recognized the feel of his hands and the smell of his skin even before Halvor murmured, "You did it. You truly are a marvel," in my ear, his arms tightening briefly before he released me.

"Malim!" The mother's cry sent a wave of warmth through me, despite the exhaustion that made it hard to even remain standing, as she rushed to her son's side. His eyes fluttered and opened just as she threw her arms over his now perfect skin. *Malim*. It struck me then—the oddness of realizing I'd just healed him—had learned some of his deepest feelings and thoughts in the process—without even knowing his name.

"She did it. She actually did it." Barloc's whisper drew my attention as I slowly came back to myself. He'd spoken so quietly, almost as if it had only been to himself—an internal thought he hadn't quite realized came out of his mouth. But his eyes were on me. He was visibly awed, lit up by a fervency that bordered on . . . *worshipful*. It was a little . . . unsettling.

I sought out Javan as the family surged forward, surrounding the boy's bed. The bearded man leaned against the wall, his eyes wide and his hands hanging beside his large body. When my gaze met his he merely gave me a brief nod, but I didn't miss the moisture gleaming in his dark eyes.

"We should go," Halvor said from behind me.

"Where are you going to take her?" Javan moved toward us, his voice pitched low to keep from disturbing the tearful reunion at Malim's bedside. "A runner has already been dispatched to summon King Varick's garrison—they will know of your existence within the next day or two, if not sooner."

"King Varick?" I repeated, not understanding the reason for the tightness in Javan's voice or the quick, darting looks he kept shooting out the darkened window, as if he expected this garrison to show up for me here and now, right in the middle of the night.

"Let's talk out here." Halvor gestured for us to go out in the hallway, leaving the family with their son.

Once Javan had exited and shut the door behind him, he turned to face me, Halvor, and Barloc. In the small space he loomed, like the mountains towering over the citadel. The darkness curled over him, wrapping around him like a familiar cloak.

"You did as you said, and for that I . . . thank you," Javan spoke haltingly, as if the words scraped on their way out. "But though I will keep my word and allow you to leave this night, I must warn you that I can't stop the garrison. They will hunt you down and if they find you, they *will* kill you. No matter what you may or may not be able to do."

My shoulders caved forward and a shudder snaked down my spine. "But . . . *why?*" I was weak from the effort of healing the boy; my power was banked, only embers flickered deep within. But the effects seeped out of the rest of my body, leaving me chilled and barely able to remain standing. Yet his words still sent a rush of adrenaline through me; my legs trembled with the instinctual need to flee. "Why does everyone want me dead?"

"His father, King Velfron, had a . . . complicated history with the Paladin," Halvor haltingly explained, a new tightness at the corners of his mouth following Javan's announcement. "After the rakasa were eliminated from our lands, King Velfron issued the 'Treason and Death Decree.' The garrisons that had worked side by side with the Paladin to keep our people safe were suddenly ordered to turn on all their former friends who hadn't immediately returned to Visimperum. Many of the remaining Paladin were accused of crimes, many without any basis whatsoever. They were hunted down and murdered for those 'crimes.'"

My eyes widened and I swallowed hard to push the lump in my throat down. "Didn't they help everyone? I thought they *saved* Vamala. I thought they . . ."

"They did. There are rumors about what made the king choose to turn on them, but now's not the time to go into all of that," Barloc interjected. "We need to get her away from this place, especially if the garrison has already been summoned."

"I hope you two have a plan." Javan looked over my head to the men hovering behind me.

"We do," Halvor said, curt now for some reason. "And we'd better be going."

His hand brushed my lower spine, a slight pressure pushing me back the way we'd come, past Javan to the kitchen and the door.

I gulped down the terror from the image in my mind of row after row of men like Javan, all hunting for *me*, all intent on killing me, and forced my legs to move, carrying me past the now silent jailer. His dark gaze followed me; I could feel the keen focus of it even when he was behind me.

We'd almost reached the kitchen when I heard the bedroom door open and a female voice ask, "Did she already go?"

"Almost" was Javan's reply, and I turned just in time to see the mother hurrying toward us, with her arms outstretched.

She grabbed me into a hug, burying her tear-streaked cheeks in my dirty hair. I stood stiffly for a moment, shocked into stillness. But then I hesitantly lifted my own arms, putting them loosely around her, unsure whether or not I was supposed to reciprocate. I had very little experience with touch, sometimes from Zuhra and, rarely, Sami. This woman was a stranger, and yet there we were, in the crammed hallway, hugging.

"Thank you," she whispered brokenly. "I will never be able to thank you enough for saving my Malim." Impossibly, her arms tightened even more, every ounce of her body humming with emotions stretched so thin it was a wonder *she* was still standing. But where before it was sheer desperation and panic, it was now a gratitude so all-encompassing even I could feel the depths of it.

When she finally released me, I had to blink a few times. At least I'd done *something* good . . . something remarkable, even. I'd brought death to this town, but now I had also sent death away. I only hoped it would be enough to enable me to sleep . . . if sleep was even in Halvor's plan.

With a final thank-you, the mother hurried back to the bedroom and her son, and we exited the house into the relief of the dark, cool night. I'd never experienced the kind of exhaustion that struck me now, as I numbly forced my feet to follow Halvor's chosen path, toward the woods, rather than back toward the town. Every part of my body felt as though I were under water, every movement required extra effort, my muscles and mind rebelled as we silently trekked through the trees, winding our way to the path that led up the mountainside—back to the citadel.

"You think to hide her in plain sight? The first place the garrison will look after they find out she's escaped the jail is the citadel," Barloc protested.

"They can try, but like the others before them, they'll never make it through that hedge" was Halvor's confident response, and I exhaled in relief. I'd been afraid he would suggest we flee somewhere far from here—but the citadel was my *home*. And, no matter how often she'd ignored or mistreated me, my mother was still up there. I couldn't just leave her. Not with Zuhra gone and Sami—

"Wait," I called out, my legs woodenly jamming to a stop. "We have to go back—we have to get Sami."

"She's busy." Barloc paused and glanced over his shoulder. "She once trained to be a healer, you know. Her services are in high demand at the moment."

"But . . . her home is with us. With *me*." My protest was as weak as my trembling muscles.

Halvor came even with me, his eyes roaming over my face. Where Barloc struggled to hide his obvious irritation, Halvor's initial frustration quickly gave way to a softness in his eyes that loosened the sudden knot in my chest. "Then we'll go tell her where we're going and give her the chance to decide."

"You want to take the girl back to the village? We barely got away as it is." The wind tugged at Barloc's tunic, as if agreeing with him, pushing him up the mountain, away from potential danger. "If you let those townspeople find her walking about, free as a bird, you can guarantee they'll have her locked up—or worse—before you can blink."

Halvor was quiet. "Sami is family to her," he said at last, his eyes still on me. "We have to at least give her the chance to come back with us."

Barloc grumbled angrily about the faults of youthful inexperience, but he followed us as we hurried back the way we came. It was a surprise to me, the way my exhaustion ebbed away at the newfound urgency in its place. I couldn't forget Sami, I couldn't just leave her there. Once that place had been her home, but it was no longer. Her home was the citadel, her home was with me.

It was still full dark, no sign of dawn on the horizon. I had no idea what time it was, but I hoped the town would still be asleep.

At the first line of homes Barloc crossed his lips with one finger. "Why don't you two wait here? I'll go find her," he whispered.

Halvor looked about to protest, but then lifted and dropped his shoulders. "Don't return unless you find her—and make sure she knows Inara wishes for her to come back with her."

Barloc nodded, then turned and quietly walked forward, toward the slumbering town. Surely Sami must have been attending a family somewhere, another injured person. She wouldn't have abandoned me . . . would she?

"I could help," I whispered to Halvor. "If there are more injured . . . I could heal them."

"You're barely capable of standing on your own two feet. What you need is to rest." He gently took my elbow in his hand and guided me toward a fallen tree stump back a little ways from the path, mostly stripped clean of branches and leaves, creating the perfect spot to sit and do as he instructed.

Only once I'd sat down did the final dregs of energy seep out of me, as if the very act of choosing to rest signaled to my body that it no longer had to push through the exhaustion. I could barely stay upright; the temptation to curl up on the pine- and leaf-strewn dirt at my feet was so strong I nearly crumpled forward to do exactly that.

When Halvor took a seat beside me, I swayed toward him, to the warmth and solidity of his body next to mine. Wordlessly, he lifted his arm and wrapped it around my shoulders, drawing me in closer. I had few solid memories from my childhood—most were wrapped up in the haze of the roar, warped by the power that had consumed me—but one was of Sami drawing me into her lap one afternoon, of the warmth and comfort her soft arms had given me during one of my alert times. I didn't remember why Zuhra wasn't there, or what had caused my need for comfort. The memory only held the actual comforting—the peace her tenderness had given me.

This moment with Halvor reminded me of that . . . except, even though his touch *did* calm and comfort, it also made my heart thump in my chest and brought heat to my cheeks—and deep in my belly.

"You can close your eyes if you wish," he murmured, his voice close and low. "I can't imagine how tired you must be. It's been almost two days since you've slept."

Had it been that long? I slowly lowered my head, inch by inch, until my cheek rested on the bony ridge of his shoulder. He shifted, moving just enough to adjust my position so that I was curled into his body, my face finding a more comfortable groove somewhere between his shoulder and his neck. My skin sparked everywhere he touched me, little flickers of heat that were something entirely different than the flames of my power. And yet, my eyes drifted shut and almost immediately, drowsiness overtook me. I inhaled the scent of his skin, now so close, mingled with the piney forest surrounding us.

It was a singularly inexplicable experience: to be so close to sleep and yet so badly wanting *not* to fall asleep, wishing to relish this moment of touch, this moment with *him*.

A moment I hardly deserved, after all that I had done in those two days of sleeplessness.

"Halvor . . ." I whispered, my heart pounding so hard I wondered if he could hear it, "do you think Zuhra is . . . gone?" I couldn't bring myself to say the word I meant. *Dead. Do you think she is dead?*

His arm tightened around me, his hand curling over my arm and softly stroking the bare skin. The lick of Halvor-induced fire where he touched me was at complete odds with the pit of dread in my stomach. How could I experience so many different feelings at once? How could I be terrified of his answer and yet wanting his touch to continue, to move up my body, at the same time?

"You opened the gateway to Visimperum with your power," he began slowly. "That's where the rakasa came from. It looked as though your sister was pulled through that gateway by a different rakasa. She was already badly injured, so I'm afraid . . ." He trailed off and I nodded, not needing to hear him say it. All warmth from his touch dissolved at the confirmation of what I'd been afraid to be true.

Zuhra most likely had died.

Because of me.

I sat up abruptly, pushing him away.

"Inara, *don't*." Halvor reached for my hand when I jumped to my feet, but I twisted out of his grip and took a few stumbling steps toward the trees, away from the town where others had also died because of me—because of the monster I'd let through.

Tears burned trails of guilt down my chilled cheeks.

"It wasn't your fault—you didn't—"

"*Not my fault?*" I whirled on him. His eyes widened at my vehemence. Even *I* was shocked at the anger in my voice. "*I* did this. You *just* admitted that—you said it yourself. *I* opened that gateway—*I* brought the monster here. My sister got dragged through it into that other place because of *me*. It's my fault that she's—that she's *dead*." The word ripped out of my throat and I dropped to my knees on the ground, the pine needles and bits of wood and rocks biting into my skin through the thin material of Sami's robe and my ruined nightgown beneath. But it was so much less than I deserved, those inconsequential pricks of pain.

"Inara." Halvor's voice was quiet, a soft *whoosh* of sound carried on the breeze, and then he was there, crouched beside me. When he reached for me, this time I didn't shy away. He turned his hand and gently brushed the tears from my cheeks, first one side, then the other. His own eyes glistened in the darkness. "I can't pretend to know how much losing your sister must hurt. But . . . I did lose both of my parents not too long ago. I understand the grief and rage you are experiencing, at least to a degree. And though I did say you opened that gateway, I never once meant for you to think that means that any of this was your fault."

I stared at him, more tears leaking out, but he brushed each one away, even as his voice thickened, heavy with his own grief. Grief I knew intimately, having experienced a portion of it while healing him.

"You didn't know what you were doing. You didn't intend for any of this to happen." His thumb rested against my jaw, softly rubbing back and forth. "And I know, if Zuhra *is* gone, she would be heartbroken to see you blaming yourself like this—to see you hurting."

I swallowed the clump of anguish in my throat that seemed to grow larger every time I let myself truly think about everything that had happened—and my role in it.

"Inara." He put his finger underneath my chin and tilted my face up to look into his, soft but insistent. "You saved more than one life today. Without you and your power, I would have died. That boy would have died."

"The only reason either of you *needed* healing was because of me—because of my power," I insisted, my eyelashes damp when I blinked to see him more clearly in the shadow-strewn forest.

Halvor opened his mouth, about to say something more, when I cut him off.

"How did your parents die?"

It was an insensitive question, and I knew it. But he'd claimed to understand my pain; he'd lost his family too. And for some reason, it became imperative that I found out how.

He let his hand drop away from my face, but I didn't turn away. A muscle near where his jaw met his cheekbone ticked once, twice. "My father was a fisherman by trade—a fairly successful one. His ship was quite large, big enough for my mother and me to accompany him on all of his sails. They truly loved each other, and despised being apart. I spent half my life at sea." As he spoke, though his eyes were on my face, his gaze was somewhere far away. I'd never seen the ocean in person, but now I knew what it looked like through his memories—the vast expanse of water, as wide as our mountains and as deep as they were tall. I wondered how much he missed it; for there was no doubt that he did. "By the time I was fifteen, Father had already been training me to work alongside him and his crew for years. But my mother was concerned about my lack of formal education. They agreed that I would be able to come on every other voyage until my tutor at home had assured them of his satisfaction with my learning.

"It was one of the voyages when I was left home. He was caught in a hurricane—a horrific storm," he added at my blank look, "and the ship barely made it through. But all their stores were lost, as well as a few members of their crew. They survived the storm, but without clean water and no food, when sickness hit the ship, they couldn't survive that, too. They somehow made it to port, but my father was too far gone. He died that night. My mother took me to Mercarum then, to the libraries where her family worked. But a few months after my father's death, she also grew sick and died."

I'd asked him to tell me, I'd wanted to know, thinking perhaps hearing about his pain would assuage my own. Instead, it only added to it, dredging up the memory of feeling his deeply buried anguish when I'd healed him—the brief flashes of his parents and their deaths. "Halvor . . . I'm so sorry."

They were useless words, and we both knew it.

"At least I was able to say goodbye to both of them."

I sat motionless, paralyzed by my own ineptitude—by my own lack of knowing what to do . . . how to comfort. Sami had pulled me into her lap when I was a child, Zuhra had hugged me when we were grown, even Halvor had put his arm around me moments earlier. But . . . was that what I should do for *him*? I lifted my hand, unsure. It was halfway to where his rested on his knee when a loud call startled us both and I jumped away, yanking my hand safely back to my side.

"Hal! Where are you, Hal?"

Halvor jumped to his feet and turned toward Barloc's shout.

"Here—we're over here!" He strode forward, and added, "Why are you shou—"

"They're coming!" Sami's familiar voice joined the older man's, and not even the alarm in her tone could temper my relief that she had come. "The garrison is already on its way here!"

Halvor spun to face me, the whites of his eyes flashing in the darkness. "We have to go back to the citadel—now!"

More voices sounded behind Barloc's and Sami's—villagers shouting, calling to one another. Yelling to find the Paladin witch before she got away.

My short-lived relief crumbled beneath a surge of panic.

"Go, Inara!" Sami came into view through the trees, waving her hands and arms at me. *"Run!"*

I stared at her for half a second. Then I lifted the skirts of my nightgown and the robe she'd loaned me and did as she instructed. I turned toward the trail and ran as if my life depended on it.

Because it did.

TWENTY-EIGHT

ZUHRA

I slid my hands along the smooth, hard surface of the balustrade. Grandfather told me it had been created by the force of a hundred fire-gifted Paladin at once on melded limestone. He'd commented to me about how valuable such a structure would have been in my world, but I had no care for that. The true value in this room was the fact that he'd *sought* me out—that he'd *wanted* to meet me. *My grandfather.*

Well, that, and the *luxem magnam*: the name of the light that the room—and the entire castle—was built around.

"It has burned without dimming for millennia," he explained as we stood, staring into the undulating, mesmerizing beauty of it. "The first two Paladin were born out of the *luxem magnam*, a man and a woman, each with a portion of this light burning within them. It is the birthplace of our power, and our most sacred place, where we may come to be healed, to be uplifted, and to be strengthened."

And yet I had walked straight here without a single obstruction. "Why was it left completely unguarded? No one tried to stop me even once."

My grandfather laughed softly, a sound that reminded me of my father—his son. His eyes crinkled the same way, too, when he smiled. "No one could harm the *luxem magnam*. It can't be destroyed or stolen. We don't guard it because any Paladin who wishes to visit it is welcome to do so at any time."

"But . . ." I hesitated and then, "I'm not a Paladin."

He tilted his head to look at me. "Why would you say such a thing? Your mother may be human, but you are still your father's daughter as well. Paladin blood runs in your veins."

My fingers tightened on the diamond banister, the jeweled structure cool beneath my skin, despite the warmth I still felt from the *luxem magnam*. "You've seen my eyes; I have no power."

"My dear girl, do you think glowing eyes are the *only* indicator of power?" His own azure ones appraised me frankly.

"Yes?" My answer was half question.

"It is rare, I will admit, but there are Paladin whose eyes are not like this." He gestured to his face. "And it doesn't indicate a lack of power. Merely a different type."

His words ignited something in me—a flare deep within that I hadn't experienced in far too long. Hope. "So . . . you think . . ."

"Paladin power is passed down through families. Each family has their own special and unique gifts. Your grandmother is one of the most powerful Paladin who has ever lived—hence her position as head of the council. Your father inherited that strength from her, as well as my gift to heal." My grandfather paused and hesitantly lifted one hand, reaching it out toward where mine still gripped the balustrade. When I didn't flinch or pull away, he softly rested it on top of mine. "We already know that your sister also inherited an enormous amount of power—far greater than anyone I've ever known—to have been able to open the gateway by herself, for even just a moment. But I have no doubt that you have also inherited power of your own. You merely have to find it within yourself and learn how to use it."

I stared down at his hand on mine, his dark olive skin, the perfectly round nail beds and neatly trimmed nails. *I'm afraid you're wrong.* I couldn't force the words out. He sounded so certain. But surely, if I had even a *fraction* of the power he claimed ran in our family, I would have seen *some* sign of it by now.

"Why did you come here today?" His question was gentle but there was a purposefulness behind it. It gave me the peculiar feeling that he somehow knew my thoughts even though I hadn't spoken out loud.

And something else told me I couldn't lie—not to him, not about this. No matter how silly it might sound. "I felt . . . drawn here. Like something inside pulled me to this place."

His fingers curled over mine and squeezed. "Your power is there," he repeated, even more confidently. "You only need to find it."

I stared down at the undulating *luxem magnam*; it looked like a lake, but instead of water, it was waves and ripples of light moving below us. Was it *possible*—could *I* have Paladin power?

"Zeph told me I'd find you here, Alkimos."

At the imperious female voice, we both turned to face Ederra standing at the archway, her arms crossed over her chest. Her burning gaze glanced over me and came to a rest on her husband.

"Has the council all arrived?"

"No." Her retort was short but emphatic. The light from the *luxem magnam* pooled around her as if she were *made* from it, as if it somehow emanated from *within* her. But rather than softening her high cheekbones or warming her eyes, it only brought out the coldness in her expression. "Yemaya is out on patrol and it may take some time to track her down. However, I need you to attend to some . . . business."

"Business," he repeated, bemused. "I believe I have fairly important *business* I'm already attending to here. With our *grand-daughter*."

Ederra stiffened at the reprimand in his tone—as did I, terrified that she might lash out at one or both of us at his daring. But then again, he *was* her husband. He knew her far better than I, and he must not have believed himself to be putting us in any danger by subtly calling her on her continued attempt to ignore my existence. On the other hand, I had the sudden, very convincing urge to get as far away from her as possible, as quickly as possible.

Her gaze didn't even flicker toward me when she bit out, "You are needed elsewhere," and then turned on her heel and stormed off.

My shoulders sank forward the moment she disappeared from view, as if she'd somehow absorbed all the hope my grandfather had given me and the rapture from the *luxem magnam*, and ripped them both away with her departure.

"Zuhra, you may not believe this any more than you believe me about your slumbering power." Grandfather turned to me, his face as soft and warm as hers was distant and cold. "But your grandmother's anger is not directed at you."

I nearly laughed out loud at that, barely managing to swallow my incredulity enough to merely make a noncommittal noise in my throat.

"I said you might not believe me. But you'll have to trust that I know her and have known her for most of my life, and I promise you, while it may seem as though she can't stand you—it is not what it seems. What upsets her is what you represent. What you force her to remember."

"I don't understand," I admitted.

"And sadly, I don't have time to explain. I had best go see what she needs. Not even I dare ignore a direct 'request' from Ederra. But," he continued, "I promise to explain it as soon as I can. For now, know this. What the Five Banished did took a heavy toll on your world, but it took a toll here, too. On some families more than many others. Ederra has been forced to make some heartbreakingly hard choices and they still weigh heavily on her, even now, all these years later."

"Who are the Five Banished? What choices?"

I could feel him preparing to leave me, and though I knew I risked her wrath at him, I was desperate to make him stay—to make him keep talking, to keep offering me hope in bits and pieces.

"Soon, Zuhra," he assured me. "I will try to come to you and explain it all soon. But for now, stay here as long as you'd like. You might be surprised at what you find in this room."

He reached up and gently squeezed my shoulder, then turned and followed in his wife's footsteps, leaving me standing in the light but feeling very much in the dark.

I stayed there for quite some time, until the hunger in my stomach grew stronger than the fear of facing more Paladin and the quandary of searching for my quarters.

Despite what my grandfather had claimed, I didn't find anything else in the room, but as soon as I left the *luxem magnam*, I had to fight the urge to immediately turn around and go back. It called to me in a way that went beyond words or sound or even feeling. It just . . . *was*. And I wanted to *be* there, letting it bask over me, filling me with that intoxicating hope: that perhaps the reason I felt anything at all was because somewhere, deep within me, a piece of Paladin magic lay sleeping, hidden for eighteen years, finally ready to awaken and unfurl.

And if it did, perhaps *I* could make my own way back to my sister.

As I wandered through the castle once more, I couldn't help but think of how much Inara would have loved the *luxem magnam*— how her fire-blue eyes would have widened with wonder at the sight. I wondered what it would have felt like to her, if I, who held so little of the Paladin within me, was so drawn to it. What would someone like her experience?

I must have made a wrong turn somewhere, because eventually I found myself at one of the large doors that led outside to the grounds where the gryphons had landed earlier, rather than any hallway that looked like the one where my room had been.

The sun had nearly dropped below the western peaks, casting shadows that crept over the castle grounds like great, dark monsters stealing the light. Rather than turning back, however, I slipped out the heavy door and onto the grounds. Only a couple of gryphons remained in the large field, leaving me to wonder where the rest had gone, until I noticed a Paladin walking her gryphon toward three rows of massive buildings that must have been the stables.

I had so many questions, and I longed for more time with my father and my grandfather, but as I watched her disappear within the building, her gryphon following docilely behind, a sudden idea struck me.

My whole life had been spent in a building and courtyard smaller than this field, and the thought of attempting what I was considering was enough to send a wave of panic so strong over me that it made me dizzy, and yet I still found myself resolutely walking across the well-trod grasses toward the gryphons' buildings.

For Inara, I can do this. I can be brave. I can be fearless.

Because that's what it would take to steal a gryphon, somehow make it through that tiny crack in the mountain, and then find my way back to the gateway.

Fearlessness.

I wasn't even sure what I'd do when I got there—I only knew I couldn't wait here any longer, I had to at least *try*. My grandfather had assured me that I must have Paladin power hiding within me . . . I could only pray that if it was, it would be enough to open the gateway as my sister had so I could return to her.

The closer I got to the first building, the more noises I began to hear. Gryphons clicking their beaks and making sounds similar to the chickens—only a hundred times louder and more terrifying. When a chicken squawked, it didn't raise bumps on my arms and make me jump back a step, rethinking the foolishness of my idea.

For Inara. For Inara.

It became my mantra, the beat that I forced my feet to follow as they carried me toward the door the Paladin had gone through and then slipped past it.

Inside, the stable was clean and I could tell that in the full light of day it would have been well lit, but as evening threw her cloak over the remaining daylight, the interior was cast into shadow. I slid into one of those shadows, watching silently from within its concealment as Paladin moved about, between rows of large doors that must have opened into individual stalls where the gryphons slept. Some of them carried buckets of water, others armfuls of what appeared to be dead animals—some small rodents, but other larger ones as well. I swallowed once, hard.

For Inara. For Inara.

I didn't know how long it would be before the council finally all gathered, and based on my second encounter with Ederra, I was more afraid than ever that the council would deny my request to open the gateway. Inara needed me *now*. I knew it, as well as I knew anything. If she was still alive, then she needed me. She always had and she always would.

I inhaled deeply, filling my lungs with air and hopefully a good dose of courage, and then hurried toward the nearest door. With one hard yank, it pulled silently open and before I knew it, I had entered the stall, slammed the door shut, turned, and found myself face-to-face with a gryphon.

The creature cocked its head to the side, peering at me with one large, black eye and I sucked back a gasp. Its leonine tail swished back and forth on the fresh, sweet-smelling straw in the corner of the large stall. I had the sudden terrifying—and far too delayed—realization that perhaps a gryphon might think a random girl walking into its stall was a chance for a live meal, rather than one of those dead ones swinging from the Paladin's arms.

I flattened myself against the now shut door, my heart beating so hard I could feel it in my throat. But the gryphon didn't attack. It didn't even flinch. It just continued to watch me, looking more bemused than predatory.

I stared at the massive creature, too terrified to move, and then realized it didn't have the saddle or harness on its head that the ones we'd ridden on earlier had worn. Of course they didn't leave those on them at all times. Assuming I ever summoned enough courage to move, let alone *toward* the creature, how was I supposed to ride it without any of that?

This had been a *terrible* idea.

I had just begun to slide my hand across the door behind me, searching for the handle, when it opened, dumping me unceremoniously to the ground on my rump.

"Would you like to tell me what, exactly, it is you're doing?"

I exhaled and squeezed my eyes shut momentarily. It would have to have been *him*. Summoning a bright smile, I turned and looked up at Raidyn, ignoring the way his lips were pursed together as if he were trying not to laugh. "I just wanted to get to see a gryphon again. Up close. *Very* close," I added when he cocked one eyebrow.

"You don't have much experience lying, do you."

I huffed and clambered back to my feet, keeping one eye on the gryphon—concerned it might still think of me as fresh meat. "Fine. The truth is that I was going to try to fly a gryphon back to the gateway. I *have* to get back to my sister," I rushed on when his jaw literally fell open. "You don't understand how much she needs me—what happens to her. Her power, what it does to her . . . without me there—"

"Zuhra," he cut into my frantic rambling, "I know."

The way he said it, so gentle, so apologetic, so . . . *knowing*, made me pause. "I . . . I'm not sure . . ."

Raidyn stepped back and gestured for me to exit the gryphon's stall. I did, and let him close the sliding door, latching it shut before turning to face me. Lanterns I hadn't noticed before hung at equal intervals between the stalls and now glowed blue—much like the color of the Paladin's eyes—illuminating the stable in a soft cerulean light that was both beautiful and eerie. It cast a strange glow on Raidyn's sun-bronzed skin, and turned his golden hair almost ashen. "When I healed you . . ." he began, halting and unsure, pushing his hands into the pockets of his trousers, his powerful shoulders sloped slightly forward. "Healing requires me—or *any* Paladin who does it, not *just* me—to, well . . . it's difficult to explain."

"I felt you," I cut in quietly. "As if a part of you—your soul—was somehow speaking to mine." The admission made me flush, and I had to look away from his brilliant eyes that glowed even brighter in the dimness.

Raidyn exhaled, a quiet *whoosh* of relief. "A soul speaking to a soul," he repeated, his voice low.

"I know that's probably not what really happened . . . but it's how it felt," I added lamely, embarrassed.

"No, I like that way of thinking about it. We call it *sanaulus*, which literally means 'heal together as one' in your language. Not all healings require that, but when the wounds are life threatening, *sanaulus* is inevitable. It's the only way to do it." He paused, clearing his throat before continuing a bit more slowly. "*Sanaulus* requires me to . . . feel things, even see things. Hidden, secret things, deep inside that person. Like your feelings for your sister. Like what happens to Inara when her power consumes her."

It was my turn for my jaw to fall open. "You *saw* Inara? You felt *my* feelings for her?"

He nodded, silent.

"Anything else?" I couldn't help but ask, even as my cheeks burned from the realization of how much he—this *stranger*—knew about me and my life.

"I would never share what I learn about someone when I'm healing them—that is a sacred trust I've been given because of my gift, and it's not my place," he responded, a nonanswer that did little to assuage my alarm. Just how much did he really know about me—how much had he seen, felt, or heard?

"Have *you* told anyone else about her yet—about what happens when she doesn't use her power enough?" His question refocused me, reminded me of my true purpose here tonight. It didn't matter what he did or didn't know about me and my life. Soon I would never see him again.

"No, I haven't had an opportunity to."

"If you want the council to agree to open that gateway, your only chance is by convincing them how dangerous your sister is."

"*Dangerous?* She's not—"

"Which she *is*," he continued right on over me as though I hadn't even spoken. "An uncontrolled Paladin with that level of power is a huge danger to herself and anyone near her. You've been lucky, Zuhra, that nothing worse than opening the gateway and letting a rakasa in has happened before now. *Very* lucky."

I gaped at him, struck silent. Inara was many things, but *dangerous?* Mother had acted like she was, she'd been afraid of her. But Inara had never hurt anyone. "I don't care what you think you saw or heard or felt, if you believe Inara is dangerous, then you saw wrong." If I'd had any idea of where to go, I would have turned on my heel and stormed away from him. Instead, I could only fold my arms across my body, trying to hold back the scalding anger boiling up and threatening to spill out of my eyes or mouth.

"I know how much you love your sister—I know you would defend her with your dying breath. But—"

"*Stop* it. Stop saying you *know* these things. You don't know me. You don't know *her*."

"And you don't know what an untrained Paladin with that kind of power could be capable of." His voice rose to match the level of my own, but rather than the heat of anger, his was as cold as a wintry night, full of frost.

"Causing trouble again, Raid?"

The new, unexpected voice unraveled the rising tension, and not a second too soon. My fury and fear collapsed in on me, like bread taken out of the oven too soon, crumbling in on itself. At the same moment, the frustration on Raidyn's face smoothed into indifference. I hadn't even recognized frustration had been there until it was absent, making me realize that as much as I protested him not knowing me, *I* knew *him* even less. Some part of me had immediately thought of him as an ally, as a friend even, but I had to remind myself that he was neither. He'd saved my life—twice—and that had created a false sense of a bond between us.

I didn't even know if I could trust him.

"I don't cause trouble." Raidyn's flat response did little to indicate whether the person speaking behind me was someone to fear—or thank for the interruption.

"You must be Zuhra," the male continued, ignoring Raidyn.

I took a deep breath and turned. He was tall, at least as tall as Raidyn, with hair as dark as night and eyes that glowed green instead of blue, like moss turned to flame.

"I'm Loukas." He grinned. "And I can see that Raidyn is doing what he does best, so I thought I would come rescue you."

"That's enough, Louk." Raidyn's eyes flashed but Loukas seemed completely undeterred—in fact, if anything, Raidyn's discomfort only seemed to goad him on. "She doesn't know you're jesting."

"Who says I'm jesting? I'm entirely earnest. You excel at frustrating and annoying everyone you meet. It's a wonder you have any friends."

"I'm fairly certain I will soon have one less."

Loukas merely laughed, his grin even wider.

My gaze bounced between the two of them, unable to ascertain if they actually were friends or if Loukas was truly antagonizing Raidyn. I'd never heard an exchange like this before—I was simultaneously uncomfortable and fascinated.

"Do you have a purpose in interrupting us? Or were you just bored?"

"I noticed you two having a rather . . . emphatic . . . conversation, and I thought perhaps I might be able to help." Loukas leaned toward me, as though preparing to confide something, but his voice wasn't lowered one bit when he said, "Don't let him get to you. He really does mean well, even if his methods are proven to be ineffective."

"He healed me," I offered, which I only realized was completely inane the moment *after* the words left my lips, but there was no taking it back, so I scrambled to justify why I'd said it. "So he thinks he knows me—and my sister. But he's *wrong.*"

"He often is," Loukas agreed affably.

"I need the council to open the gateway—I need to get home to her. And he thinks the only way to do that is to convince them that she's dangerous."

Loukas nodded sympathetically, but I didn't miss the way his gaze flickered to Raidyn and then back to me—something passing between them that I didn't grasp.

"There has to be another way, right?" I pressed, ignoring the uncomfortable suspicion that *I* was truly the one at the receiving end of the joke, not Raidyn. "You said you wished to help—can you help me convince the council to open the gateway?"

"Well . . ." Loukas hedged, with another glance past me, but Raidyn merely gestured for him to proceed. This time Raidyn was the one who looked amused at Loukas's discomfort. "No," he admitted, the joviality draining from his face, leaving him as grave as Raidyn.

The tiny seed of hope that had momentarily unfurled withered again.

"I'm sorry, I wish I could," Loukas continued, "but in this case, you may be forced to listen to Raidyn after all."

My stomach plummeted, but my eyes went to Raidyn, who stood with his arms folded across his chest, his face a mask.

The main door to the stables opened and a young Paladin girl burst through it, heaving a sigh of relief when she saw the three of us.

"Master Raidyn, you must come immediately. The council has been summoned to meet."

"Thank you, Jeley." He flickered a brief hint of a smile toward the girl. "I'll come straight away."

She bobbed her head up and down and turned to dash out of the stables again. Raidyn shot Loukas another unreadable look and then nodded at me before following the young girl.

"Wait . . . If the council is finally all here, why did they ask for *him* and not *me?*" I moved to follow, but Loukas reached out and gently grabbed my arm, stopping me.

"He didn't tell you," Loukas said quietly, all traces of humor gone now.

"Tell me what?"

"Zuhra, Raidyn is *on* the council."

TWENTY-NINE

INARA

I *ran.*

Even when the stones and pine needles and weeds cut and bruised my feet. Little flares of power kept igniting and racing through my veins, but new wounds were inflicted again before the others could fully heal.

I ran.

Even when my legs caught fire beneath my skin, my muscles burning, ripping, searing in protest.

I ran.

Even when my throat tasted of blood and my lungs felt as though blades had been thrust into them, serrating and stealing my ability to breathe.

I ran.

Shouts followed me, refusing to let me slow or stop. The trees burned red behind us from the lit torches of the villagers racing in pursuit of the one they still blamed for the dead beast lying in their square. For the death of one of their own.

I ran.

Somewhere behind the villagers, I wasn't sure how close, my doom marched toward us—in the form of King Varick's garrison, who had been summoned because a Paladin had opened the gateway.

They were all coming for me.

And suddenly, the very thing that had held us captive my whole life was my only hope of escape and protection.

The trail arced sharply upward, carving its way through the tree-dense slope like a curved blade, slicing through the mountain's flesh. Dirt and rocks tumbled behind me as I tried to keep my footing and not fall. Halvor stayed beside me, occasionally reaching out as though he would grab my arm and pull me up, *faster*, but continued to drop his hand before doing it. Sami and Barloc tried to keep pace behind us, but they soon fell behind.

When I could no longer hear her labored breathing, I slowed, glancing over my shoulder. Almost immediately, my muscles seized, locking up.

"No—keep going!" Halvor shouted, and this time, his fingers did curl over my wrist, dragging me back to a run.

"Go—Inara—just *go*!" Sami echoed from behind, in between mucous-thick gasps of air.

"I . . . can't . . . leave . . . her!" Each word tore out of my already wounded throat, punctuated by the slaps of my feet on the earth as Halvor continued to drag me forward.

"They will *kill* you, Inara," he shouted back at me, yanking even harder, his grip surprisingly strong and painful as we struggled up the mountain. "Do you understand that? They don't want Sami or Barloc. They want *you*. No more trials, no more waiting. They want blood."

Hot tears burned trails of guilt down my cheeks as I allowed myself to be dragged toward the hedge—toward safety—leaving Sami and Barloc behind. But even with him pulling me, it was only a few moments before my left thigh seized and I stumbled to a limping halt. Halvor's grip tightened, but when he tried to yank me forward, my legs buckled and I crashed to my knees on the forest floor, my breath tearing through my throat in harsh gasps. I'd never run in my life, let alone *up* a mountain. And even with my death bearing down on me, I couldn't do it. I couldn't run one more step.

"Inara—you *have* to get up. We're so close. You can do this."

I shook my head, more tears leaking out, making tiny *plops* of moisture in the dirt between my shaking hands on the ground. "My leg . . . something's wrong . . ."

A bird cawed nearby, its cry transmuted into a cackle that mocked my uselessness, carried on a bruising wind that flung pine needles in my face, as though the very elements and earth itself were mocking my attempt at escape. Perhaps I wasn't meant to—perhaps I didn't *deserve* escape. Perhaps . . . I truly was the monster, as I feared. And monsters deserved to die. Didn't they?

"Then I'll carry you."

Halvor's quiet but resolute statement jarred me. I blinked the dirt from my eyes to see him crouch down, and before I knew it, he'd hooked one arm under my arms and the other under my knees and with a grunt, lifted me up against his body. He was thin, and studious, and red-faced, and somehow, he was *carrying* me up that mountain.

"Halvor—what *happened,* boy?"

The shout from his master came from behind us, but he didn't respond or slow. I clung to him, the muscle in my leg still wound as tight as my mother's yarn on a skein, and though my power flared again and again, it seemed unable to heal this pain—a muscle pushed to the brink but not truly injured. I longed to tell him to put me down, afraid he was going to hurt himself trying to bear my weight up the trail, but he resolutely gripped me and marched up, up, *up.* Sami's and Barloc's cries of concern drew closer and closer until, at long last, Halvor turned one last corner and the hedge rose before us, bursting out of the foliage to soar above our heads, and beyond that, the citadel hunkered against the cliffside it had been built on, a dark, hulking beast of a home. I'd never realized before how truly massive it was—I'd never seen it from this angle, the whole thing rising past the hedge.

"You . . . have . . . to . . . open it . . . again . . ." Halvor was the one gasping now, as he gently set me back on my feet. "Can . . . you . . . walk?"

"Where is she?"

"Stop her before she gets through that hedge!"

The villagers' shouts were echoes through the swaying, reaching, gnarled trees, far enough away to seem almost as if they were no more than cries carried on the wind, but close enough to be understood, which meant our time to escape was nearly gone.

"Yes." The scorching pain exploded through my leg with each limping step, but I grit my teeth together and stumbled up to the hedge, reaching out to its emerald leaves. It fluttered beneath my fingers, welcoming me home. My power flared within, but I didn't even have to ask; I'd barely even run my hands over it when the vines and leaves separated, rushing back from the gate, like it understood the impending danger—as if it were eager to gather me back inside its protected domain.

Just as I grabbed the gate handle and yanked it open, Sami and Barloc burst through the trees at the top of the trail, half stumbling, half jogging toward us, both red-faced, sweaty, and dirt-streaked.

"Go! Go now! They're coming—they're right behind us!"

"I'm not closing it without you!" I shouted back, waving my arm at Sami.

In the few moments it took for them to cross the distance between the start of the trail and where Halvor and I stood, the trees behind them glowed crimson, the fires of a dozen torches igniting the forest with wavering light.

"Hurry!" Halvor shouted unnecessarily; we all knew we were out of time.

He slammed the gate shut the moment they crossed through, missing Sami by inches. We caught a glimpse of the first few villagers' faces breaking through the trees, their anger and the firelight turning their expressions grotesque, before the hedge rushed forward, closing over the gate, blocking them out.

I sank to the ground next to the hedge, emitting a little noise that was half sob, half gasp. Sami bent forward to grab her knees, sucking in deep breaths of air; Barloc was little better off beside her, his cheeks and neck puce and his gray hairline nearly black with sweat.

"Come back out!"

"Burn it down!"

"Get the Paladin witch!"

The hedge could protect us from their hands and spears, but not their furious words. I sat in a puddle of my torn, dirt- and blood-encrusted nightgown and Sami's robe, my face wet, everything inside me flayed and raw.

"Don't touch it!" someone warned, but the others must not have listened, because the hedge moved once more, a mere flutter on our side, but it was met by a howl of pain on the other.

"It's alive!"

"It *attacked* him!"

I glanced over my shoulder in alarm at Halvor, Barloc, and Sami.

"Let's go in. There's nothing we can do for them," Sami suggested, her voice quiet and heavy. "The hedge will protect you now." She tilted her chin up, her eyes following the foliage to where it met the sky, a new respect on her face that had never existed before.

"But that person . . . the hedge is poisonous." I climbed painfully to my feet, whispering so as not to draw the angry villagers' attention.

"They knew that when they made whatever foolish attempt that was to get through it."

I still stared at the thick green leaves that hid barbs as long as one of my fingers, struggling against the urge to offer to heal the person who'd been hurt. *They want to kill you,* I reminded myself. *If you go out there, you will die.*

And still, the desire—the *need*—to heal that person, beat with every *thwump* of my heart.

A hand on my arm pulled my scattered thoughts back, homing in on the shouts, the yells, the fear that slicked my palms with sweat even now, behind the protection of the hedge. "Inara, come on. Let's go."

"Sami? *Inara?*"

I sucked in a breath. The names were spoken with a tremor; her voice achingly familiar for one I'd heard so little in my life. But I'd grasped onto the rare sound of it, treasured it, hid it away deep within me, beneath the roar and Zuhra's gentle refrain *She's inside* that we both knew was an evasion of the truth. The truth that *she* evaded *me*.

Until now.

I'd run away from her. I'd left her here, in this place, alone. Some part of me had thought—*hoped*—that she would follow; that I was enough to carry her past the walls she'd been bound by for so very long. The few things she'd spoken of to me had always been of escape, of leaving. But when the chance had come, she hadn't—she'd stayed. *Why?*

Nothing could have prepared me for what I saw when I turned to face my mother.

She stood barefoot, hair askew, in the same nightgown she'd been wearing when I'd left her behind the hedge, yelling for me. But now she was silent and the villagers were the ones yelling. Grooves I'd never seen before had been etched into her face, lines that creased the skin at the corners of her mouth and eyes, a map of . . . grief? Anger? Despair? Maybe all of those and more. There was a wildness in her eyes as they dashed among the four of us, bouncing from Sami to me to Halvor to me to Barloc and back again, that raked ragged nails down the ridges of my spine.

"*Cinnia?*" Sami breathed and it took a beat before I realized it was my mother's name she'd spoken in that fearful tone.

"Burn it down!"

"Cut it down!"

"You can't escape us this time, Paladin *witch*!"

The shouts still continued, but they were muffled now, dampened by the thunderous realization that my mother wasn't as immovable as the citadel, as I'd always believed. This broken version of her, trembling and pale and sunken, was proof of how wrong I'd been. Her eyes finally stilled on Sami, but then something even worse happened. They filled with tears.

"They left me, Sami. They *all* left me." The words were low, almost guttural, torn from the deepest recesses of her unfathomable heart; like the rare times I could remember eating chicken, how we'd tear the carcass apart, ripping the bones and tendons away to strip the very last vestiges of meat and then boiled the bones for days and days until they were completely sucked of all marrow and flavor . . . Somehow, though I'd spent the majority of my life buried in the roar, I still recognized that this admission—

this spectral version of my mother—was the days-old bones, stripped bare and boiled dry.

In the end, she was unable to leave the citadel, because everyone else had left her first.

Including me.

"Mother," I whispered as I—for the first time in my limited memory—crossed the distance between us and wrapped *my* arms around *her*, offering her the comfort she'd never given me. Comfort I still wasn't sure how to give. "I'm . . . sorry."

She stood in the circle of my attempted embrace, unmoving, except for the trembling in her shoulders. But I refused to let go. I'd needed her. All my life I'd needed my mother. What I'd been given was Zuhra . . . and now she was gone and we two were all that was left of our family. And I wasn't going to let go until she responded, until she acknowledged me, until she *saw* and *felt* and *heard* me. I was no longer lost in the roar and we only had—

Her hands fluttered at her side, an uncertain spasm of movement. And then, slowly, finally, she lifted her arms and loosely circled them around me.

"They all left me," she repeated, her voice muffled in my shoulder—I'd never realized how much taller I was than her, how *small* she was, until that moment.

I responded, "I'm not gone. I'm here. I'm right here."

She pulled back suddenly. "Where's Zuhra? Where is she?" Her eyes moved wildly again, darting and wide.

My guilt was a pit of vipers, but the vipers were the veins in my body and the venom was my blood, burning beneath my skin. "She's . . . she's gone. Through the gateway."

Mother's gaze flickered to the hedge and I shook my head. "No, not that one."

Mother shrank back, curving into herself with a violent shake of her head; her lips twisted, a muscle ticked in her cheek.

"About that." Barloc took a step toward us. "I have an idea on how we can find out if she's . . . if she survived."

I turned to the older man, a tiny ripple of uncertainty breaking over me. Could he be serious? He was Halvor's master—he was the true expert on Paladin.

"What do you mean?" Halvor flinched at a particularly vile epithet shouted through the hedge at the same moment as his question.

"I think I know a way for Inara to open the gateway again," his eyes locked onto me, "so that we can go after her sister and find out if she made it or not."

Hope, painful in its resurgence, clawed its way up from the depths of the despair that had been drowning me from the moment she'd been dragged through that glowing door. *Zuhra.* Was there any possibility that she had lived through whatever horrors had awaited her on the other side of the gateway? If there was any chance of finding her alive, no matter how remote, I had to take it.

"Tell me what I need to do."

THIRTY

ZUHRA

It was dark when I yanked the door back and slipped out of the stable, Loukas right behind me. Only a sliver of crimson limned the jagged western peaks; the rest of the sky was slick black velvet, dusted with stars that gleamed their cold light from so very far away.

"You can't just storm into a council meeting," Loukas warned as he followed me across the field toward the castle. It somehow glowed, as though the very walls emanated light, even at night.

"Watch me," I muttered, lengthening my stride. Raidyn was already nowhere to be seen, even though he'd only left a few moments before I'd spun on my heel and rushed after him—immediately following Loukas's revelation that his friend was actually *on* the council. *On it.* He'd been offering me no more than little cryptic "suggestions" on how to sway them when he could have just admitted he had the power to speak for me, to *fight* for me—and Inara—the *whole time*.

I'd been furious before in my life, mostly at my mother, but I'd never experienced anger like *this* before. It was hot blood rushing in my veins and my heart thumping with an alarming ferocity, but also icy hands and sweat-slicked palms and the most awful crushing sensation in my chest. Even though I'd tried to warn myself that he wasn't necessarily my friend or ally, I'd obviously still clung to the hope that perhaps Raidyn was . . . *something* like that, because now that his deception was laid bare, it was so painfully obvious that he *wasn't* and I . . . I didn't understand why it hurt so bad to now *know* what before I'd only feared to be true.

"Zuhra, wait." Loukas jogged past me and turned, so that he continued to move when I did, except he was now moving *backward*. I doggedly kept going, forcing him to keep jogging. "I admit I don't know you well, but if I had to guess, I would say you are quite mad at the moment."

"Goodness, what gave me away?" Mad was a much better guess than anything else he might have assumed about my reaction to his news. I liked mad. It was much better than the unsettling, creeping bleakness that had begun to worm its way through my anger, the closer we got to the castle and the council . . . and Raidyn.

"Listen, I know you are new here, and all of this"—he gestured to the castle, but I knew he meant more than just the luminous building—"is completely foreign to you. I wasn't lying when I said I wish to help you. And the first bit of help I'm going to offer is advice. Before you continue that eye roll"—he held up a finger—"let me finish. I meant what I said about Raidyn earlier, though not quite the way I made it sound. The first thing you told me about him was that he'd healed you . . . and that is exactly why you need this advice. There are many Paladin who have the ability to heal, but Raidyn is one of very few who are as powerful as he is. And when he has to heal someone with injuries as extensive as yours were—"

"He already told me about *sanaulus*," I cut in, a rash of heat rising up my neck.

"He might have tried," Loukas said, gentle but firm, "but I know him too well, and I'm sure he left out a few key details."

"Such as?" The heat crept higher, even as my stomach sank lower.

"Such as," Loukas continued, "the fact that *sanaulus* creates a, ah . . . bond . . . of sorts, between the healer and healed. One that is often felt far more strongly by the one who was healed than the healer. He has trained himself to withstand it, to recognize it for what it is, and reject it. But you . . . This is all new to you, and you have no such training, and I'm just concerned that, perhaps . . ."

I could barely swallow the sticky-thick lump in my throat before I interjected, "I'm fine. I don't feel a bond with Raidyn. I just want to get back to my sister—and he could have been helping me this whole time. *That's* why I'm so upset." But even as the declaration left my lips, the weight of Loukas's words pressed in on my beleaguered heart. A bond . . . because of the healing. Because of *sanaulus*. I was alive because of Raidyn, and miserable because of *that*. "I'm fine," I reiterated, realizing too late that repeating myself did nothing to convince Loukas of my *fineness*, and in fact probably only served to convince him otherwise.

"It does pass, with time. If that helps at all."

I glared at him. "It doesn't matter whether it passes or not, or whether he's rejected it or not—all that matters is getting back to Inara. So either do what you said you came to do and *help me*, or get out of my way."

"You don't even know where to go," he pointed out.

"I'll find it." *Eventually.* Even if I had to open every door in that massive place.

Loukas shook his head, but one corner of his mouth quirked as though he were trying to suppress a smile. "Has anyone ever told you you're a bit stubborn?"

"No," I answered honestly, because though I knew he was probably right, no one ever had.

Loukas's eyebrows lifted. "I find that hard to believe."

"And I'm done wasting time here." Attempting to hide the trembling in my hands from my daring—daring I didn't even know I possessed—I shoved past him, marching the last few steps to the massive doors I'd come out only a short time earlier on my ill-fated attempt to find a way to the gateway on my own. I had to yank on it with all my strength to get it to budge, slowly groaning open. "What is it with you people and your doors?" I muttered as I strained to make a space wide enough to slip through.

Loukas's hand closed over the handle directly above mine, and with one strong tug, he pulled the door open far enough for both of us to walk through.

"Heavy doors are harder for rakasa to break through," he said as he yanked it closed once more. "If they somehow made it past the *custovitan*, these doors are the next line of defense."

"The what?"

"That huge, living wall out there. It's a *custovitan*—very rare and very powerful. In your language it means Guardian of Life."

"Oh." I flushed and turned away, resisting the urge to chew on a finger, painfully aware of my lack of knowledge, yet again. Is that what surrounded the citadel? It had to be. But there was no time to wonder about it when my goal to get back to my sister hung in the balance. I deliberated which direction to start searching for the room where the elusive council was meeting.

Loukas started walking left, leaving me there. Or so I thought . . . until he paused with a glance over his shoulder.

"Well, do you want me to show you where they are or not?"

He strode away without looking back again, rightly assuming that I would follow. We hurried through the curving hallways, passing door after door, before he lightly jogged up a flight of stairs (pausing only briefly on the landing until he heard my footfalls behind him) and then continuing further into the castle. I was hopelessly lost once more, and the sensation of the *luxem magnam* beckoning to me grew stronger and stronger the closer we got to the center of the building. I began to wonder if that was actually our destination, picturing them standing in a circle, hands on the balustrade, their faces lit by the bluish-white light; until, at last, Loukas stopped.

"Here?" I whispered, with a jerk of my chin toward the simple wooden doors—no carvings, no embellishments, nothing to mark it as the entrance to a special room—the place where the council would decide my fate . . . and Inara's.

Loukas nodded and bent forward to murmur, "Just don't tell them I helped you. They won't punish you for doing this, but *me*, on the other hand . . ."

I drew back, alarmed. Loukas winked and then sauntered off, his hands pushed into the pockets of his pants, leaving me to wonder if he'd been serious or not. He was so hard to read—though not as hard as Raidyn. I wondered, if I'd been around more people in my life, whether I would have been able to deconstruct them more readily . . . or if they were just difficult no matter how much experience one had.

It didn't matter whether I understood him or not, so long as he'd led me true and I would find the council to plead my case to when I walked into that room. With a deep breath, I faced the doors, my hands resting on the double handles. Raidyn was in there. And my grandmother. And who knew how many other faceless Paladin who held the power to trap me here as they had my father.

Convince them she's dangerous . . . because she is. Though accepting Raidyn's advice still felt like swallowing a thistle, sharp thorns shredding me apart, I wondered if, perhaps, he truly *had* been trying to help me. There were only two reasons for him to give me advice—to help me, or to sabotage me. And while I wasn't sure if he was a friend or ally, I couldn't bring myself to think of him as a potential enemy, attempting to keep me from returning home. Especially with how loyal he seemed to be to my father, his commanding officer.

But then again . . . why was *he* on the council, but *not* my father?

Their relationship and dynamic was unfathomable and I had no time to parse it out. I could only inhale deeply once more, turn the handles, and pray I was making the right choice.

The room was much larger than I'd anticipated when I pushed the doors open and walked in, dominated by a massive circular table set in the dead center where the council all sat—and every single one of them turned to peer at me with varying degrees of reaction on their faces, from outright fury (my grandmother, Ederra, of course), to unreadable scrutiny (Raidyn), and a variance of the two extremes on the other ten Paladin. A number of other Paladin stood against the wall, including my father and grandfather, which only increased my frustration that I had been kept from this meeting. The weight of all those stares was crushing, a *physical* force that nearly pushed me back out of the room to the safety and silence of the hallway. Instead, I forced my leaden feet to shuffle forward one step, then two, away from escape.

"I-I have come," I began with a humiliating quaver that began in my knees and somehow worked its way out through my voice, "to plead with you to open the gateway so I can get back to my sister."

"That is precisely what we have convened to discuss." Ederra sat directly across from where I stood, her hands folded on the table in front of her, spine so straight I had the strange, fleeting thought that it was a shame she had never met my mother—they might have gotten on quite well, actually. "And, as you are *not* Paladin, and don't understand our proceedings, you were not invited to participate."

If the weight of their scrutiny weren't enough to cow me, her public denouncement would certainly have done the trick—had this meeting been about anything other than my sister.

You can do this for Inara. Be brave for her.

Ignoring the trembling that had graduated to full-on shaking, I lifted my chin and straightened my spine. Mother had spent hours teaching me to stand up tall, to bear myself like a lady, even if I'd only ever ruled over our empty citadel. But her lessons came in handy now as I met my grandmother's glare with one of my own, also trying to channel my mother—though she'd never purposely taught me *that* skill, only by example. "I am half-Paladin, and the only reason I remain ignorant of your traditions is because of your refusal to allow my father to return to his family for the last fifteen years."

Even untouchable Raidyn's eyes widened at that, and I almost lost my nerve. Ederra's mouth opened and then closed, struck silent—but only momentarily, I knew. I had a short window to speak my mind.

"But my sister—she has more Paladin power than most of you in this room. I've spent my life protecting her, keeping her calm, keeping her from hurting herself or others."

"That is enough—"

"She's *dangerous*," I practically shouted over Ederra's cold pronouncement, shocking all of them *and* myself. My father's head snapped back as though I'd physically struck him. "She opened a gateway *by herself,* just from touching it. And I was the only one who could control her and now she's there *alone.*"

"I said *enough,*" Ederra repeated, slamming her hand down on the table, a crackle of blue flame singeing the wood before evaporating into a tendril of ebony smoke that snaked toward the ceiling. "You are not permitted in these proceedings. You must leave—at once."

I fell silent at last, knowing I would get no more chances and hoping the little I'd said was enough—and that Raidyn's advice had been the right thing to follow.

My father broke away from my grandfather, moving quickly toward where I stood, hands hanging at my side, my shoulders slumped now that I had spoken my mind. I didn't dare look at my grandmother, or Raidyn, or any of the other unfamiliar faces still turned toward me.

"Come, Zuhra," my father murmured, gently taking me by the elbow. He steered me back out the doors, quietly closing them behind us.

I crossed my arms over my chest, shoving my shaking hands under the opposite arms. "I'm sorry," I whispered. "I had to at least *try*."

"I understand. But why did you call her dangerous? You've never claimed that before now."

I glanced up at him, into his blue-fire and crinkle-cornered eyes, and just shook my head. Did I dare tell him that Raidyn had told me to?

"They're going to be meeting for quite some time. Why don't you go back to your room and rest and I will come find you as soon as they decide anything."

No! Everything within me shouted, but I forced my chin to dip down, the barest semblance of a nod. "I don't know where it is," I admitted softly, defeated.

"Oh." My father glanced down the hallway, first left, then right, but it was empty. "I need to get back in there . . . but I suppose I could—"

"I'll just wait here," I volunteered. "I promise not to come in again, unless they invite me to. But I can't go to that room and lie on that bed and try to pretend that I can sleep right now." Without waiting for his approval, I took three steps and sat down on the ground, my back against the wall, directly across from the double doors.

"You're sure? It could be *quite* some time."

"Positive," I assured him, folding my arms again.

Adelric stood there for a moment longer, looking even larger standing while I was sitting on the ground, and a bit older than before with the shadows carving out deep grooves in his drawn face. "All right. If you insist."

I nodded and he sighed.

"Your mother was stubborn too. I loved that about her, but it drove me mad sometimes." He paused, and then added, "You remind me of her."

He didn't know how much that comment cut through me, how painful it was in my ears. But he'd known a different woman, I had to remind myself, thinking of the one memory I'd been gifted that night in the ballroom with Halvor, when I'd remembered her in a field, with loose hair and a smile as bright as sunshine on her face.

When I didn't respond, a flicker of confusion crossed his face, but he just nodded, and turned, pulled the door open and slipped through, shutting me out in the hallway by myself to begin my long vigil.

I sat in the hallway waiting for hours. The skylights above me were cloaked in darkness; the hallway was lit by the same ethereal lanterns as the stables, their blue light both comforting and disconcerting at once. It didn't take long for my back to begin to ache and my tailbone to alternate between going numb and coming back to life with spikes of pain shooting down my already cramped legs. I tried to adjust my position often enough to avoid the cycle, but as the time passed, I found myself nodding off, despite the hard ground and hard wall and the fear in my heart. I'd jerk back awake every so often, my neck seized by a cramp from my head lolling forward.

And then, finally, just as the skylights turned a muted gray, the doors opened.

I scrambled to my feet, ignoring the pinpricks of pain in my left foot as blood rushed back into it. Several Paladin I didn't know walked out first, the looks they gave me varying between curiosity and pity, but it wasn't until I saw the devastation etched into the grooves of my father's face that my heart sank.

His eyes met mine as he crossed the threshold and shook his head mutely.

No.

The impact of that minute movement was like running full speed with my head turned back to look over my shoulder and slamming into a wall.

They had decided not to open the gateway.

I was trapped here.

I was trapped.

And I'd never see Inara again.

THIRTY-ONE

Inara

The fire in the grate should have been unnecessary on a summer's morning, but it was unseasonably cold as the sun broke over the eastern mountains, visible out the window, past the top edge of the hedge that had fulfilled its purpose of protecting us magnificently—and continued to do so. If I strained, I could hear the lingering shouts through the mortar and glass that separated us from their cries. Even though I knew we were safe here, a shiver of dread still slithered down my spine. The hedge had withstood the garrison's attempts to break through or destroy it so far . . . but how long could it last? How long before they lost their desire for my blood?

If I followed through with Barloc's suggestion, the four of them would be left to defend the citadel and our lives without my help—because I would be lost once more. Consumed by the roar.

"How long do you think it will take for it to build up once more?"

"It's hard to say." Barloc answered Sami's question with his gray eyes on me, an eagerness in his expression that was a bit discomfiting, though I knew his intentions were good. Halvor had explained how, as a lifelong scholar studying the Paladin, meeting me and getting to see me use my power was such a thrill Barloc had a hard time tempering his excitement. "If she doesn't access her power at all, it could be a couple of days, or it might be closer to a week or more before it regenerates to that level. Only time will tell."

Halvor sat beside me on the couch, close enough for me to be acutely aware of his body, the weight of it dipping the cushions, the warmth of it hovering between us, but too far for contact—not like before in the woods. I wondered at his thoughts, at his opinions on all of this, but he had remained silent through much of the conversation, barely offering a nod here and there, his gaze on his hands clasped in his lap.

I wished he would tell me if he agreed with his master—if willingly choosing to let my power build up until I was lost to it again was the right thing to do. That peculiar sensation of connection stretched out once more in the space that hovered between our bodies, the fine, gossamer tether that grew stronger the closer we were and thinner, more fragile with distance. It was quite strong right now, less of a string and more of a cord, urging me to slide toward him—filling my already muddled mind with further feelings of confusion and concern. Mine or his? It was all a jumble and I didn't even know if it was *real* or merely imagined.

"It's just that . . . I'm not sure . . . that this is wise," Sami continued, her words stopping and starting in short bursts, as though it were taking all her control to hold back, but little leaks of worry kept bursting out.

I forced my focus away from Halvor and his disconcerting silence, pausing over my mother, who sat perched on the edge of her seat, her back ramrod straight out of sheer habit. She, too, hadn't spoken since we'd come to the drawing room to hear Barloc's idea away from the looming hedge and the screams it couldn't block. Her gaze remained turned to the window, her skin wan and her lips pressed into bloodless slashes against her drawn face. She wasn't the mother I'd known, that I'd heard in dreams and nightmares and sometimes in waking, but this wasn't the time to ponder the changes in her.

Instead I looked to Sami, whose eyes were already on me, her body tilted forward slightly, the force of all that weighed on her too heavy to bear upright.

"There is no cause for concern," Barloc assured her. He had settled in the chair opposite where I sat beside Halvor, next to Sami, so that they spoke to each other while both watching me.

"It will be no different than what she has experienced her entire life."

She is right here, and is perfectly capable of deciding this herself. The words died in my throat and I swallowed them down. While it grated, the way he said "she" as if he weren't looking right at me as he theorized on my future, it wasn't true that I could decide for myself. I had no clue what to do now. Zuhra had always been the one to guide me.

"But . . . you've never been lucid like this for so long," Sami pressed. "Are you certain you are willing to take the risk of going back to that . . . place?"

What if you don't come back this time?

The unspoken question swelled in the brief silence that followed, but before that fear could take hold and truly dig its tentacles into my already flagging courage, Barloc shook his head emphatically.

"I have studied the Paladin for most of my life and I assure you there is plenty of documentation on this very thing. It is well known among them that if they suppress their power it will build until it either requires an outlet for release, or overtakes the host, as you've all witnessed with Inara throughout her life. This same process will happen again, and just as before, she will be able to open the gateway—allowing us to go in search of her sister."

My mother jerked in her chair, a strange, unnatural movement; it took me a moment to realize she was shaking her head *no.*

"Cinnia?" Sami half stood, her arm outstretched toward my mother, a different—but no less powerful—sort of concern on her face.

"No," she finally rasped. "Not *there*—not *them*. No. Inara—*no.*"

I stared at my mother—stricken. She'd turned to me at last, limned by the window. The woman she'd been was stripped away, revealing a gaunt stranger so ravaged by grief as to almost make her unrecognizable.

"But . . . *Zuhra* . . ." My voice shook as badly as the hands I shoved beneath my legs to hide.

"Don't go, Inara. Don't leave me. *Don't go.*"

She didn't stand and take me in her arms, she didn't even *move,* but the pleading in her voice broke me apart, tearing me between my need to reach Zuhra and the first time my mother had ever needed *me*. I'd known her in snippets of memory, from brief interactions and absences that spoke louder than words, but those glimpses of an immovable, indomitable woman were indelibly seared onto my mind, coming in sleep when the roar couldn't keep dreams from rising over its tumultuous presence. And this woman, sitting by the window with shaky hands clasped in her lap and eyelashes spiked by looming tears, was completely unknown to me.

"I have to try and get Zuhra back," I whispered. The words felt like a betrayal, even though my only purpose in doing any of this was to bring my sister home—to *return* someone to her, not take *me* away.

"No one comes back. She's gone. She's *gone!*" My mother stood at last, her last words torn from her like a scream wrenched from the deepest recesses of a heart that I had no idea contained so much pain.

We all jumped to our feet as well—to stop her? Protect her? I didn't know . . . I didn't understand why the woman I had known had crumbled away, the hardened shell she'd presented my entire life shattered overnight. Zuhra had always felt that Mother didn't love either of us—that our father's disappearance had turned her heart cold, made her incapable of love. She'd felt that neither of us was enough to fill the hole he'd ripped apart inside her when he left us.

Apparently, she'd been wrong. Mother had been able to pull herself together enough to at least *function* after my father was gone. But losing Zuhra had broken her entirely.

Mother's eyes flashed over each of us in turn, and then she mumbled, "I'll be in my room," and rushed across the morning room and out the door, the echo of it shutting behind her loud enough to make me flinch.

Barloc sat back down, but the rest of us remained on our feet, torn with indecision—at least in my case. Before I could decide if I should follow after her or not, Sami spoke up.

"She shouldn't be alone right now," she murmured, with an apologetic glance in my direction. "I'd best . . ."

I nodded, hoping she could read the relief in my expression. I had no experience offering comfort; I had no idea if my presence would even *be* a comfort to my mother. Though she'd begged me not to go, I was still the daughter with the Paladin power in my veins, whose eyes burned with the unerasable memory of Adelric.

"I'm very sorry that this ordeal has had such a terrible effect on your mother," Barloc commented softly, watching Sami quietly close the door once more as she exited the room.

I didn't know what to say, so I didn't say anything. I merely sank back down on the couch, feeling acutely my own uselessness. Halvor sat down as well, perhaps a tiny bit closer to me this time. The cushion compressed under the weight of his body; I had to dig my fingers into it to keep from sliding toward him.

After a few seconds of silence that pressed in on those of us left in the room, Barloc ventured a hesitant "Are we decided then?" Before I could respond, he continued, "I know your mother is upset, but surely once the initial trauma of the recent events passes, she will see the wisdom in at least *trying* to go after Zuhra and bringing her home."

"If she survived." I stared down at my thin legs, their outline visible through my tattered, bloody nightgown and Sami's robe. I needed a bath and clean clothes and to go to sleep and wake up and find this was all just a dream.

Halvor hesitantly lifted his hand into the space between us, reaching forward slowly, jerkily, before coming to rest on top of mine. His fingers curled over my palm and he squeezed softly.

"I can't go the rest of my life not knowing." My gaze had moved to Halvor's hand over mine, the weight and warmth of his touch like water to a dying plant—like *my power* to a dying plant. I could heal everyone and everything else, but Halvor seemed to have the power to heal *me*. "I won't use my power."

"Are you sure?"

I looked to Halvor, meeting his honey-warm eyes in the morning light, and nodded.

"We have to at least *try*. I want to open the gateway again."

THIRTY-TWO

ZUHRA

I sat on a large boulder, one of many interspersed in the gardens east of the castle, letting the night-chill of the stone seep through the fabric of my clothes into my bones. The sun's rays set the sky ablaze over the ragged peaks it had to crest before it broke free entirely to fill the sky with its light. I had only vague memories of how I'd even found this place or got on that rock to stare, dry-eyed and hard-souled, at the dawning of a new day—the first of my forced residence there.

It was a stunning sunrise, a tumble of clouds shot through with crimson and sienna, bright sunbeams piercing the sky in a dazzling show of sublime power. And I *hated* it. I hated every last beautiful view that surrounded me on all sides. I wanted to scream and kick and tear the sun from the sky and pour darkness over the castle behind me and curl into a ball and never emerge, and instead I sat and I stared and I imagined myself turning to stone, just like the one I sat on. Immovable, unfeeling, cold.

"Zuhra?"

A strange sort of vindictive pride beat in my chest when my father's hesitant voice didn't so much as make me flinch. I *knew* this wasn't his fault, I knew he'd been fighting his own battle to return for fifteen years, but it didn't matter. In that moment, for the first time, I hated him entirely on my own, free of my mother's borrowed anger. I hated him for going to check on the gateway, for not staying by my mother's side and letting whatever happened at Inara's birth come, for being taken from us, for not being there to teach us, *help* us, help *Inara*—to keep her from opening that gateway unknowingly and ripping us apart.

I could see him in the periphery of my vision, a tall figure split into two halves—light brushed on the front and shadowed where the sun hadn't risen high enough to reach yet—but I didn't turn to him. I resolutely kept my eyes on that horizon and clamped my teeth together.

"I know how upset you are," he continued, quiet and heavy. "I just wanted you to know we won't give up. This time the *majority* of the council voted to open the gateway."

That made me turn at last, lingering spots of sunrays partially blocking his face from my view. "What do you mean *the majority* voted to open it? Then *why*—"

"It has to be unanimous," he supplied before I could even finish.

I exhaled and turned back to the horizon. Then it would never happen, I realized. Because Ederra would *never* agree to it.

"We aren't giving up," he repeated.

"They never agreed to let *you* go back; why would they do it for—" The words choked off by the rise of the emotion I'd been attempting to ignore from the moment he'd shaken his head and I'd turned and fled, somehow ending up here.

"I don't know." His honesty took me off guard. When I glanced at him, his arms were folded across his stomach, his gaze on the sunrise now too. "But I will never stop trying. I *can't*. And I imagine you probably feel the same way."

It took me a moment, but when I nodded, it was a hard jerk of my head. Of course I felt the same way; of course I couldn't just turn myself cold and give up. That's what I'd been contemplating, and my own weakness made me sick. But if my father had any inkling that I'd been ready to do just that, he didn't give any indication of it as he gestured to another boulder a few feet from mine, separated by a sea of flowers as tall as my knees and such a dark purple they were almost blue. "Do you mind if I join you?"

There was only a beat of hesitation before I said, "All right."

"I have to admit, I've never done this before," he said as all six feet, three inches of him climbed up that boulder like a massively overgrown child and folded himself into what looked like a fairly awkward sitting position.

"Sat on a rock?"

"No, sat on one of *these* rocks." He glanced at me, a wicked light gleaming in his burning eyes. "This is my mother's special garden, with all of her favorite flowers, and no one is allowed to walk off the paths or pick them. But I must admit, I quite enjoy the thought of making her upset right now."

An unexpected warble of laughter burbled up my throat; my father doing something to purposely annoy his mother—the most formidable person I'd ever met, and that was truly saying something—was too unexpectedly comical.

He smiled back, but it faded all too quickly. "I *am* sorry, Zuhra."

My laughter died before it even fully formed, the darkness inside, which no amount of sunlight could force away, consuming it once more. "There's a massive rakasa loose in Vamala. If Inara's unchecked power isn't enough to induce them to help, shouldn't *that* be?"

My father sighed. "It should be. It almost was . . . but some are more stubborn than others."

"Ederra," I supplied and my father shot me a shrewd glance. "If she's going to pretend I don't exist, I can't quite bring myself to call her 'grandmother.'"

"She's not pretending you don't exist—she's . . . complicated."

"I'm not sure the reasons *why* she's acting like this make it any easier for me to be fine with it."

"You might be surprised." He turned more fully toward me on the boulder, loosely circling his arms around his knees. "Did your mother ever mention my sister to you?"

"You have a *sister*?"

"Apparently not." A shadow crossed his face. "And yes, I *had* a sister."

It took less than a heartbeat for his meaning to sink in. "Oh."

"I was a battalion leader, but she was older than me, and one of three head generals who oversaw the efforts to eradicate the raka-sas in Vamala. We were assigned to different areas, so I rarely saw her." Though his eyes were still on me, his gaze was somewhere else, somewhere far from this garden. "Anael was . . . she was like the sun—bright and shining and powerful. She brought that light with her wherever she went. She and my mother were very close, and letting both of us go through the gateway to fight the rakasa was very hard on her. But she was a council member even back then, and she believed just as much as anyone that it was our duty to right the wrongs committed by the Five Banished."

"Who are they?" I broke in. "I don't know what that means." With everything else that had happened, I'd forgotten about hearing that phrase when I'd first come through the gateway and my confusion about what it meant.

"They are the ones responsible for reopening the gateway. The Paladin are generally a very peaceful people, but inevitably there will always be some who want more power or control and are willing to do whatever it takes to seize it. The Five were some of the worst criminals of their time—all imprisoned for such vile acts that they were sentenced to death. Before the punishments could be enacted, however, they broke out of the prison—something that had never been done before—and went deep into the lands inhabited by the rakasa. There they found the gateway that had fallen into myth and disuse ages ago when the connection between our worlds was severed. Using their combined power, they reopened it. And in their rush to escape without being recaptured, they *left* it open."

I stared at him, wide-eyed. "Oh," I finally said, too overwhelmed to say much more.

"That is why, once the horrific breach was discovered, we sent our battalions and armies to not only hunt down and stop the rakasa flooding into your unsuspecting world, but to also track down the Five and stop them from hurting your people.

"My mother believed it was our duty to help Vamala as much as anyone. She sent her only two children there, but she stayed behind with the council to protect the gateway and fight off any more rakasa from going through it into your world. They rebuilt the citadel to house those who were traveling between Vamala and Visimperum, and they would open and close the gateway at specific times, so Paladin could travel through—to either return home or join the fight. But the constant use of so much power at the gateway drew hordes of rakasa to it, making it necessary to keep Paladin there to fight them back. My mother was one of the ones who stayed the entire time—wanting to be there when her children returned. It took years to find all the rakasa in Vamala and to track down four of the Five. Despite our best efforts, one remained out of our grasp.

"The Five did terrible things in your world, things that built fear and animosity toward the Paladin in your people. As rumor of the heinous atrocities the Five enacted on the unsuspecting humans spread, where they had once looked to us as their salvation, they began to see us as their doom. By that time, Anael had become high general of all the armies, and she worked closely with King Velfron and his armies to try and finish what we'd come to do. His son, Varick, was acting as the king's general for the human armies and he and Anael . . . they fell in love." As his story turned back to his sister, his voice grew thick, as though his memories were closing in on him, clenching his throat too tight. Dread twisted my gut. "I met him, once, when I was able to go to the castle to report to Anael. She was so happy and he truly loved her, anyone could see it. But the king, unbeknownst to any of us, was keeping a secret.

"The last missing of the Five, Leander, had made his way to the castle and persuaded the king that the other Paladin had lied about why their armies were there. Leander convinced Velfron that we were intent on stealing his throne and making ourselves rulers over his powerless people—and he saw Anael's involvement with his son as proof. First, the king passed laws organizing whole garrisons whose entire purpose was to track down 'rogue' Paladin and put them to death."

"What would constitute a 'rogue' Paladin?" I wondered if I looked as dismayed as I felt.

"That was the question—and far too many Paladin couldn't quite figure it out until it was too late. The garrisons used almost any possible justification to arrest us. At first, we submitted to it peacefully, thinking it was a mistake. But when the first group was taken to the courtyard before the king, rather than pardoning them as they had expected, he had them executed. After that he didn't even try to hide his intentions—he published the Treason and Death Decree, and ordered any Paladin left in Vamala to be executed. The remaining Paladin fled for their lives and spread the word to others still in Vamala—get back to the gateway, get home, before the garrisons found and killed them all.

"Then Velfron and Leander snuck into Anael's quarters one night, and under Leander's abominable instruction, Velfron attacked her, performing a ritual that . . . that would have enabled him to steal her power . . . and . . ." He broke off, his voice choked. "Varick came in the room to find his father drinking Anael's blood and he attacked—he slayed his own father, but it was too late. Anael . . . was dead."

I stared, struck into horrified silence.

"Leander attempted to kill Varick, but Anael had taught Varick a few tricks to defend himself from a Paladin, and somehow through sheer adrenaline and grief, Varick fended off and slew Leander."

"Varick was always an ally to the Paladin, but when it was discovered he'd killed his father, the high judges took the opportunity to seize his power, and had Varick put on trial for the murder of the king. Lost in his grief, he did little to defend himself, and the judges had an easy time taking his throne from him. To have him put to death, the judgment had to be unanimous, and two of the eight judges found him not guilty—justifying his act as self-defense. Instead, Varick was imprisoned in his own castle, king only in name, as the judges took over ruling Vamala. They increased the attacks on the remaining Paladin, heedless of the fact that there were still rakasa we were trying to hunt down and protect the humans from."

"But . . . but they had so much power," I broke in, dazed at how much I'd truly been ignorant about. "How could the humans have hurt them—*killed* them?"

"One on one, a Paladin would almost always win. Against five, most likely. Maybe even ten. But a hundred? Two hundred? All intent on killing you? The humans beat us through sheer numbers and brute force. Oh, many Paladin were still able to escape, to hide, and try to make their way back to the citadel that had served as our home while we fought to protect Vamala. But the judges knew the citadel was our way of escape—that the gateway there would enable us to flee their 'justice' for our 'crimes.'"

I'd never heard my father's voice so cold, and it sent a shiver raking down my spine.

"Three different garrisons were sent to Gateskeep. They were told to kill any Paladin attempting to reach the citadel. But they couldn't stop the airborne battalions on their gryphons, so rather than just staying in the city, the garrison stormed the citadel and attempted to break *through* the gateway into Visimperum. My mother and the council were put in an impossible position and ultimately she made a choice to protect our people, rather than her own family. She'd already lost her daughter, and that had nearly destroyed her. But I was near Mercarum with my remaining battalion, too far away to warn: the council decided that in order to protect Visimperum they had to plant the *custovitan* hedge to shield the citadel from further intruders and then close the gateway, trapping all remaining Paladin and rakasa in Vamala . . . including me."

His icy rage was gone, replaced by a quiet, softer grief, but somehow *that* tore through me more violently than his anger had.

"So perhaps, while it may not make a difference, maybe it will at least explain why she has refused to open the gateway again for any reason, even to let me go back to my family—or for you to get back to your sister. After thinking she'd lost us both to help a world that had turned on us, and then miraculously having me return . . . it nearly destroyed her. What remains is the hardheaded, stubborn woman you've met. But somewhere inside her, there is still the mother I once knew, the one who willingly sent her two children to defend those who couldn't defend themselves. I can only hope to reach her again someday, to convince her that despite the terrible cost, it *was* worth it—and it still is."

The sun had broken free of the horizon, its warmth spreading across the sky, distilling down upon us and chasing away the chill of night. I closed my eyes and turned my face toward it, letting its rays wash over me alongside the revelations about Ederra—about so many things that I'd been blissfully ignorant of, that Sami had kept from me. And Halvor; even he hadn't revealed the whole truth to me, though he'd given me more than Sami. I had to inhale and exhale slowly twice before I could open my eyes without tears blurring them.

My father was looking down at the flowers, the ones he'd claimed to not mind trampling after the council's decision, but now the look on his face was one of utter desolation and it tore me apart. I couldn't imagine what he had been through—leaving his home to help the humans, only to have his sister murdered, his way back home shut to him, and then to eventually make it back to Visimperum and lose his wife and children in the process.

"How . . . how did you and Mother meet?"

He glanced up, his eyebrows lifting, taken off guard. "Hasn't she told you?"

"Erm . . . not as much as I'd have liked," I hedged, not wanting to add to his burdens by telling him just what his leaving had done to her . . . and us.

"Oh, well, it was actually shortly after the Treason and Death Decree. My battalion had been taken unawares, and only two of us escaped the ambush—"

"General, there you are!"

We both turned at the shout, to see a young boy running toward us on the gravel pathway, a note clutched in his fist.

"What is it?" My father jumped off the rock to his feet, deftly avoiding as many flowers as possible to reach the pathway once more, where the boy skidded to a halt, waving the note toward him.

"It's General Sachiel. She sent a message to you and said it was *urgent.*"

My father took the note, his gaze sliding to me and then back down to the white, slightly crumpled vellum in his hand.

"It's fine," I said before he could try to offer an apology. I couldn't expect him to spend the entire day with me, moping.

"Are you sure you'll be all right here . . . by yourself?"

Though I had *so* many questions and wanted nothing more than for him to stay, I swallowed all of them and only said, "Of course. I'll find . . . something to do."

Adelric's eyes narrowed slightly; his mouthed twitched. "I'll come back as soon as I can, I promise."

I nodded, making a shooing motion with my hands. "I'm eighteen, and apparently I'm stuck here. I'll figure something out. I'll be fine," I repeated, even if I wasn't so sure *I* even believed it.

"General, it is *urgent*!" The boy shot me a glare then did a double take when his gaze met mine—most likely because of my plain old hazel eyes, which were anything *but* plain here, where everyone's eyes glowed with Paladin power. I'd yet to see another human, and after what my father had told me, I doubted any lived here.

Besides me.

"All right, all right. I'll see you soon," he added in my direction before following the antsy child back the way they'd come, pulling the letter open and reading as he walked. I glimpsed one corner of his mouth turning down before he hurried beyond the castle wall and out of sight.

I stayed on my perch for a little while longer, absorbing what my father had told me, and despite myself, when I thought of Ederra, a pinch of pity had crept into my heart . . . maybe even sympathy. I couldn't imagine having my daughter murdered and then almost immediately having to close off my son, leaving him in the same place with no hope of ever seeing him again. What kind of strength must she have summoned to endure such heartache? And then, to have him suddenly show up again, all those years later . . . Though I was still furious with her, a tiny part of me understood why she would be so against opening the gateway, even knowing that he'd left a wife and two children behind. Our people had taken *both* of her children from her, and many, many other friends and comrades.

I was wandering the halls of the castle, still too lost to locate the room they'd given me, which I was now resigned to having to use much more than I'd originally hoped, when a familiar voice called out to me, stopping me in my tracks.

"Raidyn?" I turned to see him striding toward me, his lips stretched in what I think was *supposed* to be a smile, but it resembled more of a resigned grimace.

"I came to see if you'd want to come down to the training ring with me."

"A training ring?" I repeated with raised eyebrows, trying to decide if I was still mad at him, too, or not. "To do what?"

"To *train*." Raidyn stopped a few feet away, his hands shoved into the pockets of his breeches, his powerful shoulders hunched slightly forward. He didn't quite meet my eyes as he added, "To help you pass the time."

Because you're trapped here now. The unspoken words fell as heavily between us as if he had spoken them out loud.

"But I don't have any power to train *with*," I pointed out, feeling prickly, and annoyed that *this* was what my father had thought would help. It could only have been his orders that would have induced Raidyn to seek me out and offer to help me in any way.

"You are only half human, and your father is a powerful Paladin, from an extremely strong family. You have power inside you somewhere, we just have to draw it out. This might help." He still wouldn't meet my eyes, gazing at my shoulder, or the top of my head, or somewhere just past me altogether.

It made me want to slap him in his beautiful, frustrating face.

Maybe training *would* be a good idea. "Do you train how to fight in *other* ways, too? Not everyone has the same kind of power, right?"

"Yes, of course. Physical sparring is part of everyone's training, regardless of what kind of power they wield best."

I'd never been one to crave violence. I'd always preferred Inara's gentle spirit and Sami's soft, quiet stories, but I'd never felt more helpless in my life than in those moments in the Hall of Miracles and what had happened after, when I had no idea how to defend myself or anyone else. And I never wanted to feel that way again.

Plus, part of me just really wanted to hit Raidyn. And though I had no idea why such an idea appealed so much to me, I wasn't going to refuse the opportunity to do exactly that.

"Fine."

"Fine, you'll come?"

"Yes, that kind of fine."

"Excellent," he said, but somehow his tone seemed to imply the exact opposite. I would have felt bad for him, if I weren't so furious at him still.

He turned, obviously expecting me to follow, which I had no choice but to do, since I had no idea where the training ring was.

We walked in silence at first. I could practically feel the cloud of frustration surrounding him. That tenuous connection that I now knew was because of the *sanaulus* stretched taut in the space between my arm, hanging loosely at my side, and his, pressed against his body as if he were afraid of any accidental physical contact with me.

We walked out of the castle through a door I hadn't exited previously, into a different courtyard. The gryphons' field and stables were nowhere in sight. Instead, a second, much smaller building—though still quite large, only small in comparison to the castle—stood across another graveled walkway. It, too, was round, with a domed roof that glimmered in the full light of the sun high above us in the cobalt sky.

There was no one else outside, and I leapt upon the chance of not being overheard to blurt out, "Why didn't you tell me?"

Raidyn flinched as if I'd struck him, stopping halfway to the training building. "I'm not sure," he finally said, quiet, to the ground, still not looking at me.

"That's not an answer." I crossed my arms over my chest, my fingers digging into the opposite biceps.

"I was concerned that the decision wouldn't go in your favor, and . . ." He lifted his chin, staring at the door two dozen footsteps away from where we stood, a muscle in his jaw tightening. "I didn't want to get your hopes up that I could do anything about it."

"So you lied," I bit out.

"I never told you I *wasn't* on the council."

"You knew I had no idea you *were* on the council. You tried to give me advice with no context as to why I should listen to you—and then it didn't even end up mattering. I wasn't supposed to be there, and barging in and declaring my sister to be dangerous didn't help anyway!" Each word was kindling for the anger that had been crackling within me, until by the end of my tirade, I was shouting. Raidyn stiffened and finally turned to face me, his eyes burning as blue as the sky above us, as blue as the center of a flame.

As blue as Inara's eyes.

And then I was suddenly crying. Furious, hot, fat drops splashed onto my cheeks. I swiped at my face and turned my back on Raidyn.

"I tried, Zuhra." When he spoke, his voice was raspy, edged with razor-sharp regret. I felt it seeping out of him and winding around me, around my heart, softening my anger, turning it to something else . . . something far scarier than fury or even a desire to hit him. Curse that *sanaulus*. "We argued back and forth for hours . . . But I'm young, and Ederra . . . I really did try."

When his fingertips brushed the top of my spine, I flinched, but didn't pull away. Slowly, he curled his hand around my shoulder and with gentle pressure, turned me to face him once more. The heat of his touch burned through my thin blouse; I was aware of his entire body in a way I'd never experienced before, not even with Halvor. He'd been the only boy I'd ever met, and I thought what I'd felt around him must have been what it felt like to start to care for someone . . . in *that* way. But the pull I'd felt toward him had been nothing more than the fleeting warmth of a summer breeze compared to the conflagration of sensations Raidyn's touch kindled in me—what his *eyes* did to me, when he looked down at me, as he was now, the entirety of his burning gaze focused only on *me*.

"I am truly sorry, Zuhra," he said, and there was no part of me that could ignore his sincerity; not when I could hear it in his voice and see it in his eyes and feel it through his touch—through the connection that he'd been willing to create between us to save my life. The lingering vestiges of my anger withered to embers, doused by his earnestness.

"I . . . I am too," I stammered.

"You have nothing to apologize for," he protested, his fingers flexing against my back where his hand still lingered.

"Yes, I do." My arms dangled uselessly at my side. Every nerve in my body seemed attuned to each tiny movement he made—

especially his hand. "You . . . you've saved my life twice. You've done nothing but try to help me. And I've returned your . . . kindness"—a word that had never seemed so miserably inadequate before—"with . . . with . . ." I flung my hand up to indicate myself, but he caught it in his and shook his head.

"You have nothing to apologize for," he repeated, and I flushed—relieved, embarrassed, and on *fire*. His touch ignited something in me that made me tremble. Could he feel it? Did he know what—

"What are you two doing?" an amused voice called out and I sprang back from Raidyn, as though caught doing something wrong—though I had no clue why. "I thought you were bringing her to train, not giving her dance lessons."

All the heat Raidyn's touch had brought out in me rushed straight to my neck and face when I looked past him to see Loukas sauntering our way, one dark brow lifted.

"That *is* what you were doing, right? Some sort of new, very awkward dancing?"

Raidyn rolled his eyes—a gesture so wildly incongruous with the intensity of only a moment earlier, it forced an involuntary giggle out of me. *Both* of Loukas's eyebrows shot up at that.

I didn't think my cheeks could have been any hotter, but I'd been wrong.

"I hope you've realized by now that Loukas rarely has any idea what he's talking about."

"Oh, hoo! He finally retaliates—and we all realize why he so rarely does!" Loukas shot back, but his green eyes danced with mischief.

"You two are . . ."

"Devilishly handsome?" Loukas supplied when I was unable to come up with anything that appropriately matched their antics. "Wildly charming?"

"I was going to go with . . . alarmingly confusing?"

Loukas paused for a moment, as though considering. Then, with a shrug, "Ah, well, I'll take it. For now. Once you get to know us better, you'll revise your opinion. I'm sure of it."

Raidyn just shook his head, his hands back in his pockets again. It struck me in that moment how strong he was—how beautiful and tall and powerful—and yet, he held himself in such a diminished way sometimes. It made me ache for some reason, a buried yet sharp pain, small but impossible to ignore. Was it *his* pain I felt, or just something imagined?

Loukas reached us at last, and slapped Raidyn on the back. "He's fine at healing and riding gryphons and all that, but leave the dance lessons to me," he said with a lopsided grin that was impossible not to return. "I'm a *far* superior dance partner."

"I'll try to remember that."

"We should start her training" was all Raidyn said, with a small smile of his own.

"*Now* he wants to get down to business." Loukas threw his hands up in the air. "As soon as I come to join in on the fun. Of *course*."

Raidyn just shook his head. "Come on, Zuhra. The only way to get this one to close his mouth is to force it shut—something that *I* excel at."

Loukas's laughter washed over us as we turned for the training ring, and for the first time since I'd realized I was trapped in Visimperum for the unforeseen future, I felt a small root of possible happiness blossom within me.

THIRTY-THREE

INARA

"Have you started to hear it at all yet?"

Barloc's question, though well intended, bristled. He asked me multiple times from morning until we retired for bed, and after four days of his intense scrutiny I was weary of it—and him. I knew he only wanted to assist me and our family, to help us try and get Zuhra back, but I was beginning to feel like one of his books that he studied at all hours of the day and night. When he wasn't peering at me and asking if the roar had begun to manifest yet or not, he was deeply engrossed in one book or another. The citadel's library had nearly been enough to bring tears to his eyes when we'd first taken him there.

"No," I replied with a sigh, holding my frustration in check—or so I thought. Halvor, who sat in the chair next to mine, still glanced over at me, concerned.

"Soon, soon," Barloc said, almost more to himself than me, it seemed. "I'm sure of it. Just another day or two, maybe."

I nodded, partially to encourage him to get back to his books, and partially because he actually *was* right. Though I hadn't begun to hear the roar yet, it *was* coming; the buzz of its impending arrival pulsed in my veins, making me jumpy and on edge. I could feel my power building within me, pushing for release, pressing at my mind, my lungs, my *hands*. Now that I'd experienced what it was like to *truly* use it, to tap into it to such a degree as to completely clear my mind, it was a wonder I'd never realized before just how badly it wanted out—how much it *needed* to be used. Trying to hold it in was like trying to hold my breath: easy at first, but growing progressively more difficult, more *urgent*, until *not* using my power was almost all I could focus on. If it grew much more insistent, I didn't know how I would be able to keep from releasing at least a small portion of it, just for relief from the unbearable pressure inside me.

I jumped to my feet and announced, "I need to go for a walk," feeling like I would claw my own skin off if I didn't do something to distract myself from the urge to use my power on someone, something, *anything*.

Everyone in the room startled, even my mother, who sat by the window, her needlepoint lying unused in her lap, her face turned to the window—until that moment. Even she turned to look at me, but her eyes were bloodshot, her face gaunt; a mere ghost of who she was *before*.

Everything was broken into *before* and *after*. That one terrible night was the new focal point of our lives. *Before*, Mother had forced us all to eat together as if we were a grand family; *after*, Mother took all of her meals in her room, and Sami had confessed to me last night that every time she went to get her tray, it was almost always untouched. I'd gone to her room for breakfast, asking if I could join her to eat, but she'd turned me away, claiming she'd already eaten. *Maybe next time,* she'd said with a wan attempt at a smile that was more a contortion of her lips. I'd swallowed the hurt and chosen not to point out that I didn't have much time left.

Before, she might have commanded me to stay. Forced me to work on needlepoint as she'd once made Zuhra do every day.

After, as I turned and moved toward the door, it was no surprise that she didn't protest, but some small part of me still wished she would—that she would show at least a *trace* of the fire that she used to possess. How could one night have doused it so entirely, stripping her of all her strength and leaving her a broken husk that barely survived from day to day? If Zuhra and I had wondered why we weren't enough to make her happy after our father left us, that was nothing compared to knowing that I, alone, was not enough to even induce her to want to *live*. Because, as near as I could tell, that was exactly what losing Zuhra had done to her—stolen her will to even *try* to survive. She'd retreated inside herself, slowly starving, wasting away from a lifetime of grief finally breaking open within her.

Hot, angry tears burned at my eyes as I stormed down the hallway, toward the massive entryway. The painted Paladin soaring on their mounts that had watched over us our whole lives followed my progress across the marbled floor with their lapis lazuli eyes.

"Inara," a low voice called out from deeper within the citadel, a familiar, welcome voice, but I ignored him and yanked the door open, rushing out into the waiting embrace of the wind that whipped through the hedge and my fruit trees that I'd spent so many years healing, over and over again.

A healer, that's what I was. Barloc had spent two hours one night explaining it to me: how some Paladin had extra gifts, beyond the most common ability to wield fire, taking the burning blue flames within—visible in our eyes—and using it as a weapon. But my gift was healing. He said I could probably learn to wield the fire too, if his research was right, but healing was my true strength. It was what had kept us alive all those years, my ability to heal the plants in my gardens no matter what the weather did—rain or snow or unabated sunshine—always coaxing vegetables and fruits to grow and harvest, year round. Tiny, paltry uses for my *great power,* as Barloc called it, never enough to clear my mind for more than a few minutes.

My *great power*—that I had been so ignorant about, that had made my mother hate me, that had brought destruction and nearly death to the citadel, and lost my sister to me . . . possibly forever.

She's alive. She's alive. She has to be alive.

One pounding step on the ground for each word of the refrain that had almost become a prayer to me; little puffs of dirt to accentuate each syllable of my only hope at redemption.

"Inara—" Halvor drew up alongside me, slightly out of breath, his cheeks tinged pink from running to catch me. "Are you . . . That is to say, I'm worried that you . . . are not, ah . . ." He lapsed into miserable silence. With a slow exhale, I blinked back the tears I'd refused to let fall and turned to him.

"No," I admitted, my first honest answer in . . . a while. "I'm not all right."

Halvor's eyes roamed over me. The shadow that crossed his face had nothing to do with the thunderheads coalescing above us, racing across the sky with low, throaty growls to announce their impending arrival. "Is it Barloc's questions? I can tell him to stop. He just gets so eager and he doesn't always realize—"

"No," I interrupted him. "Well, *yes,* it's that, but it's not *only* that. It's . . . everything." I turned back to the rows of planter boxes full of thriving plants, bursting with all sorts of vegetables, heavy and ripe and glistening with the first few drops of rain that began to fall, landing on their jeweled skins and my face and upturned hands. I hadn't touched my plants in almost a week, hadn't so much as brushed a fruit with my fingertips. But the weather had been perfect, not too hot, not too cold, with a stray shower here and there to keep them watered, and they'd thrived, even without me.

"I never realized before just how much I *needed* to use this . . . this . . ."—I gestured at myself, from head to toe—"*thing* inside me. I didn't know how hard it would be to hold back, now that I've experienced what it's like to . . . to be . . . *free.*"

Halvor stood beside me, close enough for his arm to brush mine every time he inhaled, quiet but listening. He was so good at listening. He was the only one who truly did anymore. Barloc was too busy explaining—always eager to share his years of research with all of us. Sami tried, but she was distracted by Mother . . . and everything else. And who could blame her? It wasn't just my world that had been turned upside down by *before* and *after.*

The villagers had given up trying to break through the hedge after the garrison had shown up and also been unable to break through. But the threat that lay beyond its protection was enough to keep us in the citadel, that and my promise not to use my power—and the hedge only responded to me, it seemed.

"I can feel it coming," I admitted at last. "And . . . I'm scared."

"Oh, Inara." My name was a soft murmur of apology. "This is asking too much of you."

"No, it isn't," I insisted. "I just didn't realize how *hard* it would be. Something's different now that I did . . . everything that night.

It's like . . . I was merely scratching the surface my whole life and I was so *used* to it, that made the feeling—the *pain*—of holding all that power locked inside bearable. It just . . . *was*. It's what *I* was. But now . . . I'm *not* anymore. I know what it's like to be free of it, to do what I was *meant* to do with it, and now . . . trying to hold back from doing it is . . . It hurts, Halvor. It actually *hurts*. It's like trying to force something back into a place when there's no space for it anymore, because now *I'm* in that space—the *real* me, *this* me—and there's nowhere for all that power to go anymore, and it's pulling at me and stretching me and it . . . it *hurts*," I finally finished lamely, knowing I probably made no sense at all and sounded as weak as I secretly feared I might be.

Halvor put both of his hands on my shoulders and turned me to face him, his gaze as intense as I'd ever seen it. "Inara, you are the *strongest* person I've ever met in my entire life," he said, as if he somehow could hear even my unspoken words. "I know you can do this—for Zuhra. And as soon as you do, you'll *never* have to do this to yourself again. I *promise*."

"How can you make a promise like that? As much as you might want to protect me, you can't always be—"

He lifted one hand to press a finger over my lips, silencing me. "I will be right here, at your side, for as long as you wish me to be. I *can* promise that. And as long as I'm by your side, I will do what I can to make you happy—to keep you from having to hurt like this ever again."

The way he *said* it, the way he *looked* at me—it was as if he knew, *truly knew*, what I was feeling, what I was experiencing. Was it possible? Since I'd healed him, I'd felt as though I could sense him in new ways . . . *amazing* but somewhat alarming ways. The closer my proximity to him, the stronger it grew—that sensation that I could feel what he was feeling . . . that I was connected to him in some way. He stared down at me, his finger still on my mouth, and I wondered if he knew that a roar was building within me, rushing through my blood—but not from my power this time. A different, heady roar, made of heat . . . and *want* . . . and that *pull* thrumming in the small space between our bodies. I hardly knew *what* I wanted, only that I *did*, and that he was the cause of it.

"Inara." This time my name was not an apology, it sounded like a prayer . . . like a *plea*. His eyes were molten and it didn't take any Paladin power for them to burn through me as we stared at one another. His finger moved at last, but only to allow the rest of his hand to slide across my jaw, his thumb brushing my cheekbone, sending a ripple of heat through me. The power building within, that I'd held trapped for so long, leapt inside me, flames igniting everywhere—in my chest, in my belly, in my hands that burned to reach for him, in my skin where he touched me, in my lips that ached for him to touch *them* again—

"*Inara.*" This time my name was a low groan that somehow vibrated straight into the deepest part of my belly and then he *did* touch my lips, except he didn't use his finger this time. He bent and his mouth brushed mine and the flames exploded and everything was white-hot heat and I was *consumed*—

And Halvor was blasted off of his feet with a howl of pain, to land flat on his back.

I stood unmoving for one long, terrible moment, in petrified shock. Then I rushed forward.

"*Halvor!*"

I dropped to my knees at his side, terror pulsing through me. He hadn't moved, hadn't spoken—

He was staring up at the sky, touching his lips—lips that were bright white with thin ribbons of red—and when he saw me he *laughed*. He had the audacity *to laugh*.

"I . . . I don't know what you think is so funny," I mumbled, unsure if I should be concerned that whatever had just happened had affected his brain, or if I should be humiliated that he found it funny. That kiss—I knew that's what it was called from some of the stories Zuhra had read to me—had touched me to my core, had done something to me that I didn't even fully understand, but I did know it hadn't made me want to *laugh*.

"Apparently you *can* do more than just heal with your power," Halvor managed between great, gulping, shuddering gales of laughter. "And that will teach me to kiss you when you are trying to hold it all in."

"My power . . ." I hesitantly touched my own lips that still tingled—from his kiss or from the explosion of power that I'd had no control over, blasting him off of his feet? "Your mouth . . . I hurt you," I finally pointed out, a riotous mess of emotions swirling within me like the clouds above us. Somehow I'd failed to notice it had begun to rain in earnest until that moment. My hair dripped down my back, raindrops sluiced down my face and landed on his wounded lips.

"Yes," Halvor agreed, finally sitting up with a wince. "But you didn't mean to."

"That doesn't change the fact that I did!" I reached out toward his face. "Let me heal you."

"No." He jerked his face away, clambering to his feet. I quickly did the same, but he backed up. "You already used some of your power unwittingly just then—if you heal me, it will be too much. It will set you back *days*. Zuhra is more important. I'll heal on my own."

"But . . . your mouth . . ." I flushed even as I said it, as I thought of the delicious, heady heat of that kiss—for the instant it had lasted before I'd exploded and done *that*. His mouth was obviously injured—and no ordinary injury, either. How would he explain it, if he refused to let me heal him and hide the evidence of what we'd done?

"How bad does it look?"

Lightning carved through the tumult of clouds overhead, as white as the skin of his lips. "Pretty bad." I grimaced. "Does it . . . hurt?"

He paused a half second and then nodded. "I think you burned me," he admitted. "But luckily, I think it's just my lips. It didn't . . . go *inside* me or anything."

"I'm . . . I'm sorry," I mumbled, my cheeks the only part left in my body still hot. Everything else went cold with guilt, with shame. He'd touched me, offered to stay by my side for as long as I wished, had *kissed* me, and I . . . I'd *attacked* him—*hurt* him.

"Inara, don't." Halvor finally stepped toward me, reaching out and gently taking my hand in his. "You didn't mean to. And now we know—when you're holding in your power, that's not a good time to . . . do other things."

"Like kiss?"

Halvor blinked, then laughed again and I flushed even hotter. "Yes, like kiss," he agreed, pulling me toward him, until he could wrap his arms around me. "But I think *this* is safe."

Thunder crackled across the sky, and Halvor just held me, until the wild thrumming of my heart calmed and I relaxed into his arms—even hesitantly lifting my own to encircle his waist and hold him back. He'd been right. Even that one accidental expulsion of my power had been enough to release a bit of the pressure building within me . . . which meant it *would* take longer before the roar overcame me and I could try to open the gateway and get to Zuhra. As much as I wanted to heal the damage I'd done to him, his selflessness in choosing to deal with the pain so I could get to my sister sooner was only further evidence of . . . of what? How much he cared about her . . . or me?

I wasn't sure, but as I stood in the circle of his arms, with the memory of his hand on my face and his lips on my lips, my eyes closed and I let myself dream of a future . . . a future with him.

A future where I could use my power daily, and always be *me*, and kiss him again—and this time keep all that heat and power inside, where it belonged, so I could find out what happened *next*.

But first . . . I had to get to Zuhra. And that meant no more accidental slipups.

"We'd better get back inside." Halvor finally pulled back enough to look down at me, the sight of his lips—ghost-white and cracked—enough to make me wince. "We're getting soaked."

"What will you tell them?"

"Maybe I won't say anything and just let them guess."

This time *I* laughed as we turned, hand in hand, and ran back through the rain toward the safety of the citadel.

THIRTY-FOUR

"Inara . . ."

Inara, Inara, *Inara*. A shout, a buzz, a curse. Through the roar, through the dark, through the light—

That is who I am.

Is who I am.

Who I am.

Who am I?

Who am I?

Flesh made pain, pain made flesh. Roaring and howling. Inside me—crawling, creeping, crying.

Skin stretched tight, too, too tight. Light too deep, too heavy, too *loud*. Roaring and roaring and ROARING.

A familiar voice, a deep voice. A kiss in the rain. A monster in the night. Flashing teeth, tearing flesh.

I try, try, *try* to focus, but the light is blinding and the roar is deafening and she's gone. Why is she gone? Why doesn't she come?

Who am I?

Where is she?

Where am I?

The roar is worse and I *need* her. I feel blindly, I see but don't; I hear but can't understand . . . and the roaring is worse, worse, *worse* . . .

And *pain*. Shooting, blinding, breaking. Screaming—the

screaming is mine, it's me, but inside and I can't . . . *I can't* . . . I am hurt. Am I hurt?

That deep voice, an image that swims through the blinding light, through the roaring dark, eyes of umber, of richest soil between my fingers, of edges of leaves curling and burning, and I must heal them, must *help* them . . .

But it's not *her.*

It's roaring, blinding, deafening.

Who I am.

Who am I?

THIRTY-FIVE

ZUHRA

I jerked awake, my sheets sticking to my sweaty skin, my hair damp on my neck, and my breath trapped in my lungs from a half-swallowed scream. The dream had been so real. The thick gray fog so dense I could still feel its cold slickness on my skin, the terror of being lost within it, the sound of Inara calling for me but being unable to find her no matter how fast I ran, no matter how much I shouted back for her . . .

I threw off the bedsheets and hurried over to the washstand, where tepid water still sat in the basin from last night. The stone floor was cold on my feet as I leaned over to splash some of the water on my flushed cheeks. Outside my windows the sky was steel gray, a sheet of impenetrable clouds stretched from one side of the valley to the other, swallowing the peaks that encircled us entirely from view. A dismal dawn after another dismal night.

The nightmares were relentless, growing more frequent with every passing day, so that I now dreaded going to bed and did everything I could to avoid it as long as possible. The only thing that distracted me from the growing anxiety was training—sparring—pushing myself so hard physically that there was no room for thought, or fear, or panic. There was only sweat and pain and burning muscles and frustrating emptiness where my supposedly latent power was supposed to be. And so I spent nearly all my waking hours at the training ring—with Raidyn and Loukas, or without. I trained, and trained, and trained, until I was so sore, so tired, I could barely even move to drag myself back to my room and collapse into bed, hoping, pleading, praying for a dreamless sleep.

After I scrubbed the sweat of my nightmare from my body, I quickly braided my hair back and pulled on clean sparring clothes—a secure binding to hold my breasts in place, a loose blouse, fitted breeches with enough stretch to allow for kicking and jumping, soft, supple boots that Sharmaine had given me (it turned out we had the same size feet), and leather wraps to protect my bruised knuckles. My skin was cracked and mottled blue, black, and yellow, but I'd refused to let Raidyn heal them. The pain was welcome, it was *distraction*.

And I didn't want him in my head again.

Within a few minutes, I was already making my way out of the castle, forcing my stiff, sore legs into a light jog as I hurried toward the training ring. I already knew from experience that it took a little while to warm my muscles up, to stretch the soreness from the previous day's training out before I could begin in earnest on today's.

When I entered the ring, only one other Paladin was already there. His hands were also wrapped, but he had his shirt off. He was punching a bag filled with straw over and over again, sweat slipping down his spine, his muscles bunching and contracting as he moved: dodging, weaving, punching, punching, *punching*. Despite myself, I paused at the threshold, watching him. He had the grace of a dancer, but the strength and brutality of an assassin.

I wondered what nightmares stole his sleep and drove him here. Because no matter how early mine woke me, he was always there first.

Watching Raidyn fight his own demons, though I still had no idea what they were, made me ache. He was beautiful, he was fierce . . . he was a healer with the heart of a warrior. Hands that could be so gentle, so kind . . . or so brutal. With a cry that ripped its way out from the deepest part of his soul, he hit the bag so hard the leather split, spilling the straw onto the ground. He stopped, grabbing the broken bag with both hands to still its swinging, his head dropped forward, and even from where I stood I could see him trembling, his entire back glistening with sweat.

Not wanting him to catch me standing there watching, I retreated silently to the door, opened it, and let it fall shut loudly, as if I'd just walked in. He startled and glanced up. When he saw me, he wiped a hand over his face and walked over to where his shirt lay on the ground, pulling it over his head, but not before I caught sight of the sculpted planes of his stomach, the lean muscle that corded his arms and shoulders. My neck grew warm, the heat radiating from a strange, thrumming spot deep in my belly.

"Good morning," I said in Paladin. I'd spent an hour or two each day working on learning their language, and though I'd managed to memorize a few key phrases, I was still dismally terrible at it.

Raidyn nodded at me as he walked over to a basin of water and splashed it over his face and head, dousing the top of his shirt. "Couldn't sleep?"

"No." I paused a few feet away. "You?"

He shrugged. "I like getting up early."

I knew there was more to it than that. Thanks to the *sanaulus,* I could *feel* it in him—a pain that haunted him, buried so deep it only arose at night until he beat it out of himself in the mornings. But I didn't dare push him. "Oh."

There was a pause, and then:

"I'm going to take Naiki out for a flight today. She's getting restless."

"Oh," I repeated, embarrassed at the disappointment that immediately crashed down on me that he was leaving—that he wouldn't be sparring with me today.

Raidyn stared down at his hands and methodically began unwrapping them. "Would you . . . like to come with?"

"*Really?*" As quickly as my heart had sunk, it leapt inside me once more. "Yes—of course."

One side of his mouth quirked up at the corner, a hint of a smile. "All right. You can train for a few hours, and I'll come get you when I'm ready to go."

I bounced on the balls of my feet, swinging my arms back and forth to start loosening them up. "Thank you, Raidyn."

He nodded and, with a tip of his chin, strode away. "Good training," he said in Paladin, another phrase he knew I'd learned.

I watched him go, surprised that he'd even offered, surprised at the look in his eyes that had softened his burning blue-flame irises to azure. As the door shut behind him, I couldn't help the blossom of warmth that unfurled in my chest.

"Again, Zuhra! But this time, try to visualize that core of power within you igniting with every hit!"

Grandfather had taken a personal interest in my training once word of my dedication spread, and he'd come every day to shout out suggestions and generally make me incredibly nervous. My father tried to come when he could, but he had many more duties that kept him busy, something he apologized for every time he was able to come spend time with me or help me train.

Sharmaine was in the ring with me now, going easy on me, I knew, but I still felt as though I'd been battered with two rocks, not mere fists. We wore padding to protect our torsos and thighs, but every exposed part of my body was going to be black and blue tomorrow, I was certain.

Still, I refused to give up. I tried to remember the stance Loukas had spent an hour making me practice a few days ago, and nodded for Sharmaine to go again. She blew a strand of rich auburn hair that had come loose from her braid out of her eyes, and lifted her fists. Most Paladin only trained on physical combat an hour, maybe two at most, a couple of times a week. They spent much more time on honing their abilities with their power. I'd learned all sorts of ways they could use it. My father, for example, was able to draw enough power into one hand that it created a fireball that he could blast at any opponent, killing most rakasa, all except the largest. Some had additional gifts beyond the Paladin fire—like Sharmaine, who could force her power outside her body in an impenetrable dome, protecting their battalion from attacks. The healers, like Raidyn, my father, and Inara, of course. Sharmaine's mother was an artisan, she'd told me one afternoon—she was able to control her fire into such small, concentrated amounts she was able to sculpt statues and vases with it. It was rumored my grandmother could even shape her Paladin fire into a bolt, shooting it from her hands like lightning. So many variations and all useful in different ways.

So Sharmaine didn't *need* to spar with me—none of them did. But they did it because *I* wanted to, because it helped me, because it was all I *could* do. No matter how many different ways my grandfather or father tried to instruct me on how to access the power they were both sure I possessed, nothing ever happened.

At least Ederra never came to witness my failures—the one bright spot to her continued ignoring of my existence.

I'd passed her in the hallway only once since that council meeting, and though she'd misstepped when her eyes met mine, *almost* a stumble but not quite, she quickly averted her head and marched onward without a word. I'd tried to remind myself of the stories my father had shared with me, but none of it seemed to lessen the sting of her coldness to me—who had no part in any of the things that had hurt her so deeply.

So I took all of that and channeled it into my arms, my fists, my legs, and I *sparred*. I got hit, I got knocked down, but I always got back up and I hit back. I tried to remember to reach for my power at the same time, but there was a lot to think about already, to avoid getting knocked down yet again. Loukas and Raidyn were *strong* but Sharmaine was *fast*. She couldn't hit as hard, but that made her no less formidable as an opponent. She'd tried to explain it to me once—how she pictured a snake, the *quick-quick* lunge and recoil when they bit prey. But I'd never seen a snake attack, I'd only witnessed hers, and *that* was frightening enough.

After what felt like hours, someone whistled for the match to end, and though I'd clearly lost, Sharmaine held out her hand to shake as was the custom, and said, "You're really improving. I'm impressed." Where Raidyn's smiles were slow to coax into existence, and Loukas's were in overabundance, Sharmaine had an easygoing kind of cheerfulness about her—a genuine kindness that radiated from her face and her encouraging grins.

"You don't have to say that." I groaned and reached up to massage a particularly sore spot on my left shoulder as we both walked over to the side of the ring to get water and take off our sweaty pads. The training arena was built with one main ring in the center, open to viewing, and smaller rooms surrounding it for other types of training, separated by a wide walkway around the entire main ring, some with doors and walls so thick they blocked all sound—and blasts of power. I'd learned that this was where all those diamonds were made, from Paladin who could channel their power into streams of blue flame, so hot that if they managed to maintain it long enough, it turned mere rock into the valuable stones. Well, valuable in *my* world. Here they were too abundant to be worth nearly as much. "I think you landed three hits for every one of mine."

Sharmaine laughed, a light, contagious sound. "Two days ago it was at least five to one, so you see? You *are* getting better."

"Gee, thanks." I couldn't help but laugh with her—just like I couldn't help but like her, regardless of the way she looked at Raidyn, and he at her. When they were together, they seemed to gravitate around one another. They each had an awareness of the other that made me almost embarrassed to watch them, as if I were witnessing something intimate—private. The little glances, the almost unconscious touches at the elbow or hand. I knew of jealousy in theory, having read about it in stories and believing I'd experienced it when Halvor had shown more interest in Inara than me, but I realized I'd never truly experienced it before . . . until *now*. That's what the helpless yearning inside me was when I saw them together, the hurt that was part anger and part longing.

Almost as if I'd conjured him with my thoughts, the door banged across from us and Raidyn and Loukas walked into the arena together, Loukas grinning as always and Raidyn nodding with a half smile at something he'd said.

"Oh, perfect—I needed to ask him something." Sharmaine quickly unwound the last of the wraps on her hands and shoved them in a knapsack where she kept her sparring supplies. "Great match, Zuhra. I'll see you soon, yes?"

"Oh, um, yes. Thanks," I responded lamely as she hurried away with a little wave in my direction, her knapsack slung over one slim shoulder, her eyes bright and her cheeks flushed from the exertion of our match.

She was breathtakingly lovely and so nice. So *good*. And she was a Paladin. She *belonged* here.

I forced myself to look away, rather than torture myself by watching them greet one another, talk to one another. I didn't know why it mattered so much to me. It shouldn't have . . . But all of mother's lessons on attracting a man, on capturing myself a husband if I was ever given a chance, crowded my head . . . and my heart. Though it felt cruel to admit, knowing that he most likely hadn't survived the rakasa attack, I realized now how little I'd actually felt toward Halvor Roskery. He'd been kind and friendly and a boy, and only the last had ever been a requirement to warrant thinking of him as a potential husband, according to my mother. But it had taken meeting Raidyn to truly *understand*. Part of me wished I could go back to *not* understanding, because it hurt a lot more on this side of the equation.

"Shar says you got some good hits in today."

I glanced up at Loukas's voice in time to see him taking a seat beside me on one of the benches that were set up around the outside of the training ring. My grandfather was gone, and Raidyn and Sharmaine were nowhere to be seen. I'd hoped he'd been coming to get me to go flying, but maybe he'd forgotten . . . or changed his mind.

"Yeah, I guess so," I finally responded, with what I hoped passed for a smile.

Loukas's eyes narrowed, and I quickly busied myself with finishing removing the pads. One of the ties had grown knotted during the match and my shaky fingers couldn't get purchase to undo it.

"Here, let me," Loukas offered, reaching out to the mess.

"Thanks." I turned slightly to give him better access.

His fingers brushed my ribs as he worked, but other than an awareness of how close he sat to me, it did nothing else to me—it would have been no different if Sharmaine had been the one to help. Not like Raidyn, who could set my nerves on edge with a mere look. *Why?* I wondered, not for the first time. Loukas was every bit as attractive as Raidyn, maybe even more so with his brilliant green eyes and midnight dark hair. He was also kind, and he was *happy*—funny, lighthearted. So why couldn't I have felt this way about him? Was it the *sanaulus*? Was that the only reason? Or was it something more . . . something *deeper*?

"There you go. Free at last," he announced a moment later, but his fingers still lingered at my side.

"Thanks," I repeated, shifting slightly, but still, he didn't move.

"I've been told you were raised in the Paladin citadel in Vamala without a single male around your entire life." Loukas bent a little closer, so that the warmth of his breath brushed my ear.

I stiffened, alarmed but not sure what to do about it. I didn't want to *offend* him, but—

"So you are probably supremely unaware of how useful a tool jealousy can be," he continued, getting even closer, his hand slipping beneath my padding to rest on my hip, and his mouth close enough to my ear to brush it.

"Louk, *what* are you—"

I twisted, the rest of my confused rebuke dying on my lips when I saw Raidyn staring at us from across the ring, his face a mask, but his lips thin. My stomach clenched into a sudden knot.

"Just trust me," Loukas whispered with a soft snicker, his face bent toward mine. I flushed, my eyes still on Raidyn, who stared right back, his irises flaring dangerously as his long legs ate up the distance between us. Loukas finally pulled back with a louder laugh, as if I'd just said something hilarious instead of my angry half shout that I hoped Raidyn hadn't heard. But he waited until Raidyn was only a few feet away to slip his hand out from under my padding with agonizing slowness, as if making *certain* Raidyn couldn't miss it.

My cheeks flamed hotter than any fire I'd ever sat beside.

"I . . . I don't . . ."

Before I could even form a coherent thought, Raidyn halted a few feet away and bit out, "I'm sorry to disturb you two, but I came to see if you still wished to go with me or not, Zuhra."

"Oh, did you have plans with Raid, already?" Loukas jumped

in before I could answer and it took nearly all my self-control to resist using the training I'd engaged in over the last few days to close his mouth for him. "It's up to you, Zu."

Zu? I gaped at him in mute shock.

Something flashed in Raidyn's eyes but he merely clamped his teeth together, a muscle in his jaw flexing from the force of it. With a tiny nod, he turned on his heel and stormed away.

I stared at his retreating form, dumbstruck and . . . *furious.*

"What is *wrong* with—"

"Now's the part where you go after him," Loukas cut me off, with a little push in between my shoulders, forcing me to my feet.

"What?"

"Go *after him,* Zuhra. And enjoy your flight!"

I snarled at him I was so mad, but Raidyn was already halfway across the ring again, so I did as Loukas suggested and rushed to follow him before he disappeared.

"Raidyn—wait!"

He paused at my shout, but didn't turn.

"I wanted to come," I called again, running to catch him, heedless of anyone else who might see or hear. Loukas was right, I had no experience in these matters, and I certainly had never heard of using jealousy as a tool, but I did know one thing—Raidyn had saved my life, and he'd done nothing but try to help me, and I couldn't bear to see him mad at me.

Though I didn't know why he *would* be.

When I reached his side, I had to push a hand into my side to try and stem a cramp from sprinting so soon after a long match. "I'm sorry—I, uh . . ." My apology limped to a halt when I realized I had no idea what to apologize for. It seemed arrogant to assume I'd hurt him. Maybe I'd read it wrong. Maybe he was relieved by Loukas's supposed interest and had seen the opportunity to shake me.

"You don't have to come, if you don't wish to," he said, not looking at me. "I don't want to interrupt."

"You aren't—you *weren't*—I just—" I lapsed into uncomfortable silence for several long moments while he just waited. "I want to go with you," I finally finished, quiet and miserable. *Thanks so much, Loukas.* If thoughts were capable of being sent mind to mind, I would have shot that one straight into his skull like a blast of my father's power, knocking him to the ground.

There was a baited pause, but then finally he sighed and said, "All right. Then let's go."

He continued forward, still not looking at me, and I scrambled to follow.

We were silent the entire way out of the training ring and as he marched across the fields toward the gryphons' stables, me struggling to keep up without breaking into a jog. His legs were just so *long*. How did anyone walk that fast?

"Raidyn, I know you probably don't care," I finally summoned the courage to at least try to salvage the situation before we were trapped on a gryphon together, "but that was all Loukas. I don't know what he was trying to do, but—"

"You might be innocent, but you can't be *that* naïve," Raidyn immediately responded.

"I-I'm . . ."

"Surely even *you* can understand what it means when a man has his hand on your body and his mouth on your ear."

I reeled back, stumbling to a stop, stunned by the caustic bite to his words that I'd never heard before.

"I-I'm s-sorry," I stuttered, humiliated to find myself near tears.

I don't know what made him stop and turn, looking at me at last, but when his gaze met mine, the hard set of his shoulders softened. He closed his eyes for a second before taking two quick strides to reach my side, lifting his hand as though he would touch my arm before letting it drop once more.

"No, Zuhra, it is *I* who am sorry." This time when he spoke, his voice was low and grave. "That was cruel of me and uncalled for. You couldn't possibly have known—" He cut off abruptly, but before I could even form a question, continued, "Regardless, if you and Loukas are growing . . . close . . . I am happy for you."

"No, you don't—"

"And I'm happy you still wish to go with me and Naiki. I already told her you were coming and she seemed excited about it." He smiled at me, a real smile, one of the first with teeth and everything, and yet it somehow didn't reach his eyes, where an infinite sadness shaded them almost navy. They weren't as bright as they'd been earlier, as if he'd already drained some of his power at some point this morning.

I wanted to protest more, to demand he explain himself, but instead, like the coward I was, I merely asked, "She can understand you that well?"

He lifted one shoulder in an approximation of a shrug. "I like to think so, and we've had enough experiences together that lead me to believe I'm right."

When he turned to continue on to the stables this time, there was no more anger in the strong lines of his body, but the strange cloud that hovered over him now was worse for some reason.

With a sigh, and a mental reminder to beat the fire out of Loukas at the next possible chance, I slowly followed after.

"I think this will be easier if you sit in front of me. That way you can hold on to the reins and you'll probably feel more secure," Raidyn suggested when we stood beside Naiki in the field a little while later, after saddling the gryphon and leading her out from the stall where she'd been finishing her lunch. After six full days of training and little else, I'd forgotten how huge the creatures were.

"All right," I agreed hesitantly. I'd been eager to fly, but now that the time had come, I found myself nervous for some reason. Possibly because the last time I'd nearly died. But I wasn't in shock this time, so I didn't anticipate falling off again.

"Do you want some help getting up?" Raidyn offered politely, sounding completely cordial, as if speaking to a near stranger. For some reason, it cut straight through me.

I stared up at Naiki's haunches, barely within reach of my hands if I stretched, and swallowed. "Um, yes, please."

Raidyn nodded and moved to stand beside me. "Lift your leg, like this." He demonstrated, creating an angle so that his shin was parallel to the ground. "I will grab your leg and help hoist you in the air. Then you can get hold of the saddle and pull yourself up."

I inhaled with a little nod. "All right."

"Ready?"

I nodded again.

"Give me your leg, then."

I did as he'd shown, bending my leg and turning to face Naiki, who waited patiently on her back haunches, wings outstretched to the earth so we could access the saddle without trampling over them. Raidyn bent beside me, and wrapped his hands around my leg. His touch seared me, even through the leather of my boots. I could feel the strength in his grip even before he counted to three, told me to jump, and then launched me into the air, sending me high enough to easily swing my other leg over the saddle and grab on to the reins, settling into place. He grabbed the pommel in front of me, his arm crossing over one of my thighs and the back edge of the saddle, and vaulted himself up into the seat behind me. On the ride here, I'd been aware of his body against mine, but with everything else that had happened that day, it had been a mere drop in an ocean of emotions crashing over me.

Today, as his arms circled my waist, one of his hands closing over mine on the reins, his powerful thighs squeezing Naiki tightly right behind mine, I found it hard to even breathe normally. Each nerve and muscle in my body seemed attuned to his every movement and touch, rather than minor things like making my heart beat normally instead of galloping in my chest, or reminding my lungs to inhale and exhale without my breath catching somewhere in my throat.

"Ready?" he asked as he settled into his seat behind me.

I nodded, afraid he would hear the effect he had on me in my voice.

Little sparks of heat ignited at every point where his body met mine—my back, my waist, my belly. One of his hands suddenly splayed across it, holding me tightly pressed against him as he made a whistling noise to Naiki, signaling her to clamber to her feet and charge forward. Her wings stretched out as she took one powerful leap, and then we were airborne.

I gasped as we quickly gained height, the ground dropping away as we climbed and climbed into the air.

"I love it up here." Raidyn bent forward so that his lips were in my hair when he spoke.

"How did you become a Rider?" I turned my face slightly so he could hear me, inadvertently making his mouth brush my cheek. He didn't immediately pull away; in fact, in the periphery of my vision it almost looked like his eyes closed briefly, his head dipping forward so his nose gently touched my temple. The closest thing I'd ever felt to the Paladin's fire ignited deep in my belly, tightening every muscle there. It was second nature to lean back more fully into his body, so that his arms tightened infinitesimally around me, his biceps pressed into the sides of my rib cage, and his hand on my belly slid further around me, coming to rest on my hip instead.

"I always wanted to be a Rider," he answered at last, his mouth moving against the skin of my cheek where it still rested. "But not everyone who wishes to be a Rider gets to actually become one."

Naiki coasted over the city, high above the gleaming rooftops of countless Paladin homes as he spoke, her wings outstretched and her face upturned to the sun. I felt no fear anymore, only exhilaration: it was just Raidyn and the wind and my heart thundering beneath the cage of my ribs.

"The gryphon has to choose you, when it is born. The bond between Rider and gryphon is sacred," he continued, his hand moving against my hip, almost as if he wasn't even aware of it, the tiny stroking of his fingertips against the strip of bare skin where my tunic had pulled free from my breeches sending waves of delicious heat through my body. I gripped the reins in suddenly trembling hands. "I was lucky that Naiki chose me. She knew, somehow, that I . . . I *needed* her. That without her . . . I would have been lost." His voice was slightly hoarse, and his fingers on my waist dug into my flesh more fully, making me think he was fully aware of what he was doing now.

I tried to absorb what he'd shared with me—what it meant—but I could barely think of anything other than the heat of his body wrapped around mine, of the feel of his fingers on my skin, and his words from earlier ringing in my mind. *Surely even* you *can understand what it means when a man has his hands on your body and his mouth on your ear . . .*

I knew what it had meant to Loukas—*nothing*. A game . . . a wicked game for some reason. But what did it mean to Raidyn? To this gentle man who held me in his arms, who could speak and touch with such tenderness, but who held himself so controlled at all times, so much of him hidden—so much hurt and pain buried deep within that he could destroy a leather bag with one brutal hit?

"I'm glad you have her," I said at last, hoping the wind masked the shakiness, the breathlessness.

"I am too." His mouth moved against my skin with every word and I had the sudden enticing thought that if I turned my face just a bit more, his lips would brush mine.

And suddenly I'd never wanted anything more than that—to have him kiss me. But I didn't dare . . . as much as I *wanted* to, I couldn't bring myself to move.

Up there, on Naiki's back, it felt as though we were the only two living souls in the whole world. Everything else faded away, until it was just me and Raidyn and Naiki and the endless expanse of sky above and the mountains below. The clouds from earlier had broken apart, letting the peaks soar through once more, dark and hulking but not terrifying as they'd once been. I'd never felt safer than I did in that moment, with Raidyn's arms wrapped around me, his strength holding me tight.

But instead of cresting the mountains, or slipping through the small crack we'd originally come through, Naiki banked and began winging her way back toward the city glittering on the hill in the distance, across the valley from us. A ping of disappointment punctured the euphoria of the ride . . . I wasn't ready to go back yet, to have my feet on solid ground where Raidyn kept his distance more often than not, and where Loukas would no doubt be waiting to ask how his attempt to use jealousy as a tool had gone.

Was that why Raidyn held me so close—why his fingers pressed into my hip and he kept his face turned toward mine? Because Loukas had succeeded in making him jealous?

I was confused, and hot, and aching in a nameless way I couldn't quite describe, and I needed Raidyn to want me the way I wanted him, and I was afraid that once we landed, he would walk away from me and I would never again experience the feeling of having his arms around me like this.

We were silent most of the way back, but occasionally his fingers moved on my skin, or he turned his face slightly more into mine, so that his nose brushed my temple again. Once, it even felt like his lips pressed against my cheekbone. I closed my eyes and just let myself feel . . . trying to absorb and memorize this moment, to hold it inside me forever, to take out and cherish after whatever reality awaited us back on solid ground.

And I couldn't help but wonder if he was silent because he was doing the same.

All too soon, the gryphon banked more sharply, tilting downward toward the field and stables below, forcing Raidyn to straighten fully, separating from me.

"Remember, the landing can be a bit rough," he reminded me, his face a respectable distance from mine now. And when his arm tightened around me, his hand was no longer on my skin. His fingers had curled into a partial fist as though he were trying *not* to touch me. The heady exhilaration of our ride evaporated as quickly as the rush of wind against our faces when Naiki extended her back paws for the earth that had come up to meet us all too soon.

She landed with a thud, throwing me forward just enough to unseat me. Raidyn grabbed my arm with his other hand, only for a moment to make sure I was steady, then he pushed backward, so that there was space for him to swing his leg over and jump to the ground.

"Can I help?" he asked, lifting his hands to assist me, his voice cool, nothing more than solicitously polite, but his eyes flamed as bright a blue as I'd ever seen them when they met mine, scorching through me as I nodded and let his strong hands close over my waist. I grabbed onto his biceps as he helped pull me to the ground, setting me down gently in front of him.

I fully expected him to immediately let go and step back, but he stood still, his fingers curling more tightly into my body again, his eyes never leaving mine—an unspoken question that I wasn't sure how to answer. I stared up at him, my hands still on his arms, the sunlight turning his hair golden and his eyes to pure fire—the same fire that his touch ignited in my veins. When I swallowed, his burning gaze dropped to my mouth and I almost stopped breathing entirely.

"Zuhra . . . I . . . I want so much to . . ." His voice was a rasping whisper, and out of some instinct born deep within me, my lips parted slightly and he bent toward me—

"Raidyn!"

The shout was like surfacing for air after being submerged under water. Sound and light and awareness of something *other* than Raidyn slammed into me all at once as we sprang apart and turned to see Sharmaine sprinting toward us from the direction of the castle. I was afraid to look at her—afraid of what she'd seen and what she would think.

But she wasn't looking at me at all. Her eyes were only on Raidyn when she skidded to a halt, panting as though she'd been running for far longer than just the stretch between the door and where we stood beside Naiki.

"The council—there's an emergency meeting—the gateway—" she panted, hands on knees.

"What meeting? What happened with the gateway?" And just like that, Raidyn was all business, all traces of the moment before erased in the blink of an eye as if it had never happened, leaving me chilled for more than one reason.

"Sachiel's patrol came back early—something happened at the gateway. A flare of power. Raidyn—someone's trying to *open* it."

He turned to me just as my legs gave out and I collapsed to my knees on the field.

"Zuhra—are you all right?" Sharmaine's question echoed dimly through the rush of blood in my ears.

"*Inara*," I breathed, staring up at Raidyn. A sob tore through my chest and my eyes filled with tears. "She's alive. She's *alive*."

THIRTY-SIX

INARA

Silence.

I blinked and exhaled. It was gone. *It was gone.*

But something was still wrong.

I was lying on my back, staring up at a ceiling far, far above me, a cool wind blowing the damp hair off my cheeks.

"Inara! Are you all right?"

"How did it *not* work? I don't understand!"

Voices, footsteps, someone dropping to their knees beside me.

Slowly, I realized where I was—*who* I was. We were in the Hall of Miracles. Halvor knelt at my side, Sami right behind him, her face pale and drawn, and Barloc stood at the base of the stairs that led up to the door where I lay . . . where I'd grabbed the handle, where I'd tried to open the gateway . . . and failed.

It didn't work?

It didn't work.

The realization knocked the breath from my lungs. I'd lost myself to the roar again, after the humiliating afternoon when Halvor had tried to come up with a plausible excuse for the burns on his lips. They still weren't entirely healed; the edges of his mouth were cracked and scabbed. I hadn't used my power once, not one tiny bit. Toward the end, I'd had to go lie on my bed, squeezing my eyes shut, drowning in the pain and agony of holding it all in, until finally, *finally* the roar consumed me once more and took me away on a wave of blissful oblivion. I only had vague recollections of what happened after that, the last of which was grabbing the handle to the doorway, feeling my power ignite and surge out of me and into the door just like last time, my back arcing, the excruciating agony of having it ripped from me so quickly, so completely, being unable to let go—

Except that *unlike* last time, the gateway hadn't opened and Zuhra hadn't pulled me free. I'd eventually passed out, collapsing, only then breaking the connection.

"Inara, can you hear me? Are you all right?"

I turned toward Halvor, who had lifted one hand to my face, gently wiping the tears I didn't even realize had leaked out onto my cheeks. Sami knelt beside him now and took one of my hands into hers.

"It didn't work" was all I said, my throat raw, as if I'd been screaming.

Halvor's eyes closed and his head dropped. Sami squeezed my hand tighter.

"We must not have waited quite long enough," Barloc said gravely. "You were so close, my dear girl. Another day or two, that would have done it."

"How dare you. How *dare* you!" Sami dropped my hand to stand and whirl on the older scholar. "Did you not see what that just did to her? She can't do this again. It might kill her!"

"No," I protested, weakly pushing myself up to sit. "He's right. I must not have waited long enough. Next time give it another two days to be certain."

"There will be *no* next time," Sami bit out, two bright spots of red flaring in her pale cheeks.

"Sami." I climbed to my feet on shaking legs and reached one hand toward her arm. "I *have* to. I have to at least *try* to get to Zuhra. What if she's alive somewhere through there? What if she's lost . . . what if she's sitting there waiting for me?" I blinked back more tears as Sami's eyes welled up.

"You know I love Zuhra," she said slowly, her voice thick, "but from what Master Roskery has said, she was seriously hurt already, and if she was pulled through by another one of those monsters . . . chances are she didn't—"

"*Don't,*" I snapped. "Don't you *dare* even say that. She *has* to be alive. And I am going to open this gateway and find her." Strength had quickly returned to my body, my power flaring, sparking within me to heal the minor damages from my fall and whatever the gateway had done to me. The roar was far away; it would take days before it returned. But it didn't matter. I would wait. "We do it again."

Barloc nodded at me, his expression inscrutable, as I stormed down the stairs and out of the Hall of Miracles.

I went straight to my mother's room, rapping sharply once and then pushing it open without waiting for her permission. She sat at her desk, staring out the window at the gray, stormy day, a cup of untouched tea gone cold in front of her and a plate of vegetables beside it.

She startled at my intrusion and turned; when she saw it was me, not Sami, she blanched.

"*Inara?* You're . . . *here?*"

I wasn't sure if she meant physically or mentally, but since both applied, I merely raised one eyebrow. "Why didn't you come?" I demanded. I'd never had much experience with anger. I'd been so focused on survival, on trying to stretch the brief interludes of lucidity as long as possible, that I refused to acknowledge the burning heat of it inside me—every time I asked *Where is mother?* and Zuhra would make up some excuse and try to turn my attention elsewhere. But I had plenty of time now, and once I opened that gateway I would never be lost in the roar again. And if Sami was right about Zuhra—if my deepest fear that haunted all my dreams, turning them to terrors, was true—I needed my mother to be a *mother.* "Why do you *never* come?"

She flinched as though I'd physically struck her. It hurt, to see how diminished she was, how slight her frame, how thin her wrists were beneath the faded fabric of her dress. Her knuckles were white on the cup she gripped and she didn't look up when she said, "I wasn't feeling well and—"

"*No,*" I said. "That is not a good enough reason to hide in here when you knew what I was attempting to do today. When we were trying to go find Zuhra—your *daughter*."

"I *couldn't*, Inara. I . . . I can't go in that room. In *any* of those rooms."

I stared at her, shocked past words when she reached up to swipe away a tear.

My mother was . . . *crying*.

"I tried to be strong for you girls. I know I failed, trust me, I *know*. But I *tried*. I didn't know how else to . . . to *be* strong . . . when I left . . . *everything* . . . for him—and then he . . . *he left me*." Her voice kept breaking, she could barely force the words out. And then my mother, who I'd never seen even get choked up, curled in on herself with a shudder and . . . shattered. All that sorrow and grief and guilt had finally broken loose and it *ravaged* her in great gasping, gulping, body-wrenching sobs. I stood frozen, staring.

"He *left* me," she repeated again and again in between gasps and shudders that convulsed her entire frame. *"He left me."*

And I just stood there, helpless and pathetic and . . . ashamed.

I'd vaguely known my father had left us; it was a story, a hushed secret. But *this* . . . this was real pain, this was a heart *torn apart* by the agony of his leaving. And I had no idea what to do.

Hesitantly, I took one step toward her, then another, until I finally reached her side. I haltingly reached toward her shaking back, gently brushing it with my hand. She flinched but didn't pull away. I was strangely nervous, my heart pounding in my chest, as I inched closer and slowly wrapped my arm all the way around her narrow shoulders. My mother stiffened, her sobs halted momentarily. She lifted her head and glanced at me, her bloodshot eyes and tear-streaked face so familiar and so foreign all at once.

"I'm . . . sorry." My voice trembled, uncertain and afraid that she would push me away—again.

But instead, for the first time in my life, my mother wrapped her thin arms around me, pulling me close. "No, Inara. I am the one who is sorry," she whispered.

Everything was still broken and *wrong;* my father had still left and my mother had pushed me away for fifteen years and Zuhra was still missing . . . but right now, my mother was hugging me.

My mother had said she was *sorry.*

I only wished Zuhra, who had borne the brunt of her pain and anger, had been there to hear it.

"I have two brothers," Mother said haltingly, as if it was still difficult to make the words leave the hidden recesses of her heart.

We sat in her room, eating dinner together. Well, I was eating. She was moving her food around her plate and taking a small nibble here and there. I wanted to push her to eat more, but was afraid if I pressed her to do anything else she would snap back into her old self and shut me out again.

And that was unbearable to consider—not when she was actually *talking.*

"They were younger than me," she continued, "and it broke their hearts when I left. Brycent cried and cried . . . but I didn't have a choice. My father disowned me for choosing Adelric, for refusing to turn him in to the garrisons."

I didn't understand everything she told me, but I didn't dare ask for clarification, in case it made her stop. Instead, I just listened and tried to make sense of what I could.

"Your eyes . . . they're just like his," she admitted, glancing up at me. I flushed, embarrassed for some reason, knowing that when she looked at me, she saw him. Which was probably part of the reason she'd always pushed me away and not Zuhra. That, and the power he'd also gifted to me. "Adelric . . ." The name stuck in her throat after more than a decade of trying to erase it from her memory. "He was . . . my everything. It was like I had lived my life in the darkness of night but he brought me out to stand in the sun. He made everything brighter, more beautiful. He'd sacrificed so much to help our people, and had only been handed back suffering and violence . . . yet he remained so . . . *positive.* I'd never known anyone like him. Even the pain of leaving my family and home on such terrible terms was bearable because of how happy he made me."

I was transfixed, my food forgotten.

"We fled the garrisons and the death decree, traveling under the cover of night and hiding during the day, only to find the gateway shut when we finally arrived. He convinced me we'd be safe here, that the citadel and the hedge they'd planted would protect us. He was one of the last, you see. And the villagers . . . they didn't turn us in, but only after he begged and bribed them not to report us to the garrisons that came every few weeks to check on the citadel—to make sure it was still abandoned. It was dangerous and lonely living here, but there was nowhere else for us to go. He was all I had, Inara."

For some reason, I felt as though she were trying to explain herself, trying to justify what had happened since then. But I was not the only one she owed this story to . . . or her apologies. And as much as I wanted her to keep talking—to keep telling me about what had brought her here, had turned her into what she was . . . I'd originally come to her room with a purpose.

"And then he left me . . . after everything I gave up for him. And we were trapped, and I couldn't even take my daughters and return home. Even if we *weren't* trapped behind the hedge, I don't know if I could have, because of . . ." She trailed off, her gaze flickering up to mine then lowered again as silent tears trailed down her cheeks, the violence of her earlier breakdown passed, leaving this quieter but no less painful regret in its place.

"Mother," I began, soft but firm, "I need you to tell us what you know—and I need you to be with me when I try to open the gateway again. I know it's hard for you," I rushed on when she started to protest, "but Zuhra is out there somewhere. Only you have known a real Paladin before—only you know what he told you about his home and his people. And," I added, "she's your *daughter*. If she survived, she deserves to hear this story—to hear your apology."

Mother was quiet a long time. I made myself wait, though my instinct was to fill the silence with more reasons to try and convince her.

Finally she closed her eyes and nodded. "Tomorrow," she whispered. "Tomorrow . . . I'll try to tell you what I can remember. But I can't promise anything else."

Halvor squeezed my hand, the pressure of his grip reassuring but doing little to assuage the strange flutter of nervousness in my belly. "I still can't believe she told you all of that," he said quietly, too low for Sami or Barloc, who sat across the room at a small table playing a card game, to hear. The day had dawned gray and wet yet again, the sky leaking, dripping, slow and constant and forcing us to stay inside.

"I still can't believe it either," I whispered back. I hadn't told him that she'd agreed to come out of her room today and share what she knew of Visimperum, the home of the Paladin, with us—for fear she would lose courage and go back on her word. But that didn't stop me from eagerly turning toward the door every time there was a creak. So far, it had been nothing but the citadel's normal noisiness.

Halvor's thumb moved back and forth across the top of my hand, the methodical touch distracting and comforting all at once. It was strange how my stomach could be twisted into knots with worry about my mother and Zuhra while my chest was tight with the memory of our kiss and the longing to repeat it—without the disastrous results of the first attempt.

After this is over, I told myself. *If Halvor is still around, if he still wants to . . . maybe then.*

I glanced over to find him watching me, his eyes darkened to umber in the somber light from the storm. Or, perhaps it was something else. His gaze dropped to my lips momentarily, forcing all other thoughts to flee my mind and making me wonder if he wished as much as I did that we were alone.

And of course, it was in that moment of distraction that the door finally opened and my mother marched into the room, her hair perfectly coifed, her dress pressed, and her shoulders thrown back—the strong, dominant woman I'd always known entering the room, not the weak, broken thing of the last week since Zuhra's disappearance.

"Good morning," she announced loudly to everyone, lifting her chin and ignoring the twin looks of shock on Barloc's and Sami's faces. Sami recovered more quickly than Halvor's uncle and jumped to her feet.

"Good morning, Madam. Can I get you anything?"

"No, thank you, Sami." Mother's eyes met mine across the room, hers widening slightly when she noticed Halvor sitting so close, holding my hand. "I know you've all been trying to get Zuhra back and I . . . I've decided to help. If I can."

If Sami and Barloc had looked shocked before, their twin expressions could only have been described as flabbergasted now. Even Halvor's mouth fell open beside me.

I smiled at her, encouraging.

"My . . . husband"—she nearly tripped over the word, but continued on—"told me quite a few things about the Paladin, this gateway, and their home, before he . . . before he left." She almost shrank into herself again as she spoke, but when I stood, releasing Halvor's hand, and walked toward her, she reset her shoulders and exhaled, visibly regaining control of herself. "I hope some of it might help."

"Thank you," I said, reaching out and taking her hand in mine, squeezing it tightly.

She stared down at our clasped hands for several seconds, then nodded, a little of that old stubborn spark back in her eyes. "I hope it helps . . . I hope we can get her back."

"Me, too," I said, and then closed my eyes for a moment. "Me, too."

THIRTY-SEVEN

ZUHRA

I stood sandwiched between my father and grandfather, trepidation turning my hands cold. I crossed my arms and pushed my fingers beneath them to try and warm them—and to hide my trembling. The council was gathered around the circular table; this time Raidyn had insisted I be allowed to stay for the proceedings, and despite Ederra's protests his request had been granted.

I was still stunned at the sudden turn in events. I'd gone from having only a thin thread of hope that Inara had survived to almost irrefutable proof that she *was* alive—and that she was trying to get through the gateway. When I looked at Raidyn, across the table from me, memories of our morning flight rushed back up, the heat of his touch, the brush of his lips against my face, the hints at his past that he'd given me . . . but if the council finally decided to go to the gateway and open it, to keep Inara from doing it herself and allowing more rakasa through to Vamala—or the king's garrisons to come here—then none of it would matter by this time tomorrow. I would be back home and he . . . he would be here, with Sharmaine, and Naiki, and Loukas, and the morning flight would be exactly what I'd decided it *had* to be—a memory to cling to and nothing more.

"This council will come to order immediately." Ederra stood and pounded on the table with a gavel, the sharp rap breaking over the rumble of voices in the room. "We have been called together again because the matter previously decided upon has new . . .

developments that require us to revisit this motion." Her gaze remained forcefully focused on the Paladin sitting around the table, refusing to stray to her family standing together off to the side, watching silently. My father's arms were also folded, tension radiating off him in waves, his jaw set as he watched his mother. My grandfather's expression was more musing, softer, as he looked at his wife, a deep sadness in his eyes that I only partially understood. They'd lost their daughter to my world, and nearly their son, leaving them childless for a time. Though he had been nothing but kind and welcoming to me, I wondered, if given the choice, whether he would willingly allow any of us to go back to Vamala again, knowing we'd never return. If they agreed to let me and my father go through, that would be the cost. *We* would never see Visimperum—or anyone here—ever again. The risk of opening the gateway was just too high.

"Please report on what you witnessed," Ederra commanded another female Paladin. She looked to be about my father's age, the sides of her head shaved, all except a braid down the center of her skull that continued to her waist. She was dressed all in black riding leathers, and was still dirty from her flight. This must have been Sachiel, the general who Sharmaine had told us had witnessed the flare of power at the gateway.

Sachiel stood, and nodded at the other council members. "As many of you are already aware, my battalion was on duty monitoring rakasa activity in the outer lands when we felt a surge of power from the vicinity of the gateway. We rushed there as quickly as possible to find rakasa amassing in the area, obviously drawn by the power surge as well. We weren't able to land, not wanting to engage with the monsters, but it was quite obvious even from the sky that somehow Paladin power was flowing through the gateway. It hasn't opened—yet—but it is definitely unstable."

"Thank you, Sachiel, you may be seated," Ederra said the moment she finished, her voice clipped. "In light of this new information, the motion to reopen the gateway has been submitted for reconsideration."

"Ederra, if I may, I have something to say." Raidyn pushed back his chair and stood, directly across from my formidable grandmother, power and purpose emanating from him. My heart swelled at the sight of him and suddenly, as much as I wanted to get back to my sister, a part of my heart felt as though it were splintering. Without waiting for her permission, he continued, "In our last meeting, we established that your granddaughter Inara is in residence at the citadel in Vamala and that she possesses immense untapped and untrained power. If she is now consciously attempting to use it to open the gateway, this poses a great threat to the safety of both worlds."

Ederra speared him with her icy glare. "Young man, you have a seat on this council because of the untimely and tragic death of both of your parents, but until you gain more experience and wisdom you are more of a—"

"Ederra." All eyes turned to my grandfather with a low ripple of shock, leading me to believe his interruption was unheard of.

Her words to Raidyn echoed through my mind alongside a swell of sheer grief through the gossamer chord of connection between us, stretched to where he stood across from me.

"He is a full member of the council, and deserves your respect. Let him speak."

The look she aimed at my grandfather sent a shudder down my spine, but she nodded once, a short, violent movement that spoke of retribution to befall him later.

Raidyn inclined his chin toward Alkimos for interceding on his behalf, but somehow still retained all his dignity when he continued, "I vote that we immediately move to action—to open the gateway and allow Zuhra and Adelric to return to their family and their home, as they wish. I believe the only inducement Inara would have to attempt to open the gateway is to reach her sister—as their bond seems to be unspeakably strong. If her sister were to return to her, I believe she would have no cause to attempt to open it again—and by allowing Adelric to return to his family, he would be able to train his daughter and make certain she is not a threat to us or Vamala."

Ederra looked at Raidyn silently for a long, tense moment.

"I second his motion." Another Paladin also stood, an older man, who looked to be my grandparents' age. Ederra blinked.

"I third it," Sachiel agreed. "I was there—that gateway is not stable and the rakasa are swarming it. If we don't do something to stop this, we might be looking at a full invasion again."

"Then let them invade," Ederra suddenly burst out, slamming her gavel down with a thud.

"And allow hundreds if not thousands of people to be slaughtered by them?" someone else burst out.

"We made a vow to protect them," the older man who had seconded Raidyn's motion reminded everyone.

"And how did they repay us?" Ederra looked to him first, then slowly let her burning gaze travel round the table. "The humans *turned* on us. Hunted us down and murdered as many Paladin as they could. They tried to invade our world and bring their destruction to *our* lands! That's the thanks we got for our vow to help. I gave *everything* to them and I will *not* do it again." Her knuckles on the gavel were white but her neck was splotched red.

Watching her, hearing the suppressed pain in her voice, drove home the stories my father had told me in a way I hadn't let happen before that moment. It was one thing to think about her losing her daughter, to have almost lost my father, too . . . it was another to hear the taut grief in her voice, to see the agony-induced anger flash in her eyes. My grandfather suddenly put his arm around my shoulders, pulling me into his side with a gentle squeeze. At first, I thought it was to lend me his support, but then I felt the tremble in his hand, and I realized it was partially for his own comfort, too. I'd only known him for a week, but I'd already come to love him. And I knew he loved his wife—that he, too, had suffered and lost his loved ones beside her. What made the difference between his reaction to it and hers? What had made my mother become what she was, as opposed to how my father had dealt with their separation—after losing his sister, and his family?

"You know we need to do this, Ederra," Sachiel said. "Yes, they did terrible things to us. But *we* did this to them—we brought our horrors to their world. We can't decide how they react to us—we can only keep more innocent people from suffering."

"They managed to murder plenty of Paladin when they put their minds to it. Let them turn that determination against the rakasa instead. We stay here. I will not lose any more Paladin to their malice. And we have no proof she can open the gateway again. If she failed this time, I doubt she can repeat the event." Ederra sat down, apparently done with the discussion.

A few council members murmured to each other. Raidyn remained standing, his face a mask. Our eyes met and a fist of regret clenched my stomach. I wished there was a way to get back to my sister without losing the chance to know him . . . to be near him. Even if he never came to care about me in the way I was afraid I was beginning to feel about him. But the only way to Inara was to sacrifice the friendships and family I'd found here.

I reached up and squeezed my grandfather's hand and then stepped forward, out of his embrace. I cleared my throat and hesitantly began. "Ederra . . ."

She remained staring forward, ignoring me, as she had for the entire time I'd been in Visimperum.

I exhaled, my heart thumping in my chest, and took another step forward.

"Grandmother," I tried again, the word a twist of pain in my chest. She flinched but kept her eyes on the rest of the council. "I . . . I know you've been hurt. I know you don't want to look at me, or talk to me, because . . . because I make you remember things you don't want to, I guess. But . . . you're not the only one hurting. My sister . . . I've always been the one to protect her, to help her. The night she was born my father disappeared and the hedge you left behind trapped us in your citadel, blocking us off from both worlds. When he never returned, my mother thought he'd left us deliberately. She never recovered from that shock and she can barely stand to look at Inara, let alone take care of her." I felt my father stiffen beside me; I didn't dare glance at him to see what my announcement had done to him. I should have warned him, I should have told him, but it was too late now. "I was afraid she'd died in the first rakasa attack, but now I know she's alive and I'm *begging* you . . . please, let me go back to my sister. Raidyn is right. If I return, she won't try to open the gateway again."

Ederra finally turned to me, her unblinking gaze cutting straight through me. "Do you understand what you're asking? It's no small feat to open the gateway for more than a few seconds. Rakasa are drawn to usage of our power and they are already swarming the area, according to Sachiel. Paladin could die attempting to let you back through—rakasa could break through no matter how hard we try to stop them. This is *not* merely a question of whether or not I want to let you go back home."

I swallowed, my knees trembling beneath the force of her full focus on me. "I . . . I don't really know what it entails," I admitted. "But if Inara opens it on her own again, the consequences would be far worse than if you were there to control it, wouldn't they? Maybe . . . maybe one battalion could create a diversion of some sort to draw off as many of the rakasa as possible?"

"My battalion could do that," Sachiel immediately volunteered. "If we concentrated our efforts about a mile away, it would be close enough to capture the majority of the rakasas' attention in the area, but far enough to clear the way to the gateway—at least briefly."

"My battalion could protect the gateway while the council opens it." My father stepped up beside me, taking my hand in his. His palm was cold, but he squeezed my fingers tightly. "While my daughter and I hurry through. Then you could immediately close it behind us."

A muscle at the corner of my grandmother's eye ticked and it looked—for just a moment—as though her lip trembled. But with a clenching of her jaw it stopped. "After all these years, that is still your wish? To leave?"

The silence in the room was fraught with tension as all those assembled looked to my father—with me at his side.

"I have never wanted to have to choose between my family and home here and the one I left in Vamala," my father began slowly, his voice heavy. "But just as you made a vow to protect Vamala, at all costs, I made a vow to love, cherish, and protect my wife. And instead, I abandoned her—whether I chose to or not, it doesn't matter. She knows no different—only that I left and never returned. My daughters were raised without me . . . without their father . . . never knowing how much I . . . how much I loved . . ." His voice broke, and he had to stop to clear his throat, his hand shaking even through the tightness of his grip on mine. "I don't want to leave you, Mother. But I have to go back to them. *Please.*"

My grandmother's grip on the gavel slackened and she visibly shrank in on herself, her gaze on the table. "Fine." The word was so quiet, I wasn't sure if I'd even truly heard her speak.

"Ederra votes yes." Sachiel jumped on the chance. "Everyone else in favor?"

A chorus of ayes went around the table.

"Any opposed?"

She barely even waited a beat before she announced, "The motion passes. We will begin planning immediately and depart as soon as possible. I suggest you both go pack your belongings and say your goodbyes," she said to me and my father.

A rush of relief washed over me. I was going back. Inara was alive and *I was going back to her.*

"It *passed*," my father repeated quietly, dumbfounded. "I'm going home."

Raidyn stood still, his gaze on me, a tall, stoic beacon in the midst of a sudden flurry of activity and movement all around him. I couldn't tear my eyes from his. A sharp pang hit me, right between my ribs, below the suddenly strained beating of my heart. We were leaving—going to open the gateway and return home.

And then I would never see him again.

THIRTY-EIGHT

The light of the *luxem magnam* danced in front of my eyes, washing over me. That same pull I'd felt before still there, tugging at my navel—and my heart. But no matter how hard I'd tried while I was in Visimperum, I'd never been able to access any Paladin power. And now I was leaving in the morning and I'd never be able to come here again—to *feel* this again. As excited as I was to see Inara, even to see my mother (and her reaction when *she* saw Adelric), I couldn't deny the pang of regret when I thought of never coming back.

"I wondered if I'd find you here."

I turned at the sound of my grandfather's voice. He walked slowly toward me, his eyes on the lustrous light beyond the balustrade where I leaned.

"This has always been my favorite place to come when I needed to think," he continued, stopping beside me.

We were silent for a moment, standing side by side, as if he knew I needed time to gather my thoughts. I had so many questions, and so little time to ask them . . .

"I never did find my power like you promised I would," I finally said, surprising a laugh out of him.

"Oh, Zuhra." He put his hand over mine. "I am going to miss you."

"I'm going to miss you, too."

"I wish there was a way for you to be able to go home and still be a part of my life. I would have liked to be able to get to know you better." His fingers curled around mine. "I knew I had two grandchildren, but I never let myself *truly* think about it. You have to understand, I never thought I'd have the opportunity to meet either of you—to be a grandfather. And now I . . . I find that I quite like it."

I was shocked to find myself blinking back tears.

"I'm coming with you to the gateway tomorrow," he added. "And so is your grandmother."

"She *is*?" *That* took me by surprise.

"She won't admit it, but I think she's hoping to have the chance to meet Inara too. Or maybe just to say goodbye to you—in her own way."

"She can't stand me."

"No, Zuhra," he gently disagreed. "She's afraid of letting herself love you. Especially now that we're going to lose you again. Something that I think she knew was inevitable, no matter how hard she fought against it."

I was silent for a moment, digesting this. "I wish there was a way for me to go home without losing you . . . I wish I had more time," I admitted.

"Life is full of lost time. I suppose one of the best lessons we can learn is to never put off for tomorrow what we can say or do today—because that chance may never come again. It never came with our daughter Anael, and for so many years we thought we'd never get that chance again with Adelric. When he returned to us, it was a day of rejoicing for his mother and me, but our joy was only possible because of the pain it caused both our son and the family he left behind. The pain it caused *you*." My grandfather shook his head with a heavy sigh. "Listen to me ramble on. The musings of an old man." He patted my hand and then straightened. "I should go—there is much we have to do before leaving tomorrow. I suppose I wanted one last chance to speak to you alone, to tell you that . . . that I am proud of you. And . . . that I love you."

I blinked rapidly to clear my eyes and impulsively threw my arms around him. "I love you, too, Grandfather."

He hugged me for a moment, then pulled back. "I think someone else might be looking for you," he said with a wink.

My heart leapt into my throat as he turned and headed back the way he'd come, crossing paths with a tall figure, limned by the light of the *luxem magnam*. But my hope died as quickly as it had come when I recognized Loukas's dark hair and bright green eyes.

"Don't look so happy to see me," he teased, after he nodded in passing to my grandfather and then continued on to take his place at my side by the diamond bannister.

"Of course I'm happy to see you," I protested, but it sounded halfhearted, even to me, and I winced.

"You don't have to lie to me. I know you were upset by my . . . antics . . . the other day, and I wanted to say I'm sorry."

I shrugged and turned back to the *luxem magnam*. "It doesn't matter, especially now that I'm leaving."

"Doesn't it, though?" Loukas shifted so that he faced me fully, but I kept looking forward.

"No, it doesn't," I reiterated more forcefully, refusing to let myself think of the feel of Raidyn's fingers on my hip, or his lips on my cheekbone. "After tomorrow, I will never see any of you again and you'll all forget me and go back to . . . whatever it was you did before I came and complicated things."

"What, exactly, do you think you complicated, I wonder?"

"I don't have the energy to do this, Loukas. If you have something to say to me, just say it." I finally faced him, clamping my teeth together and crossing my arms across my chest.

The teasing light went out of his unique green eyes and he nodded. "That's fair." He sighed and pushed a hand through his thick, dark hair. For the first time since I'd met him, he looked . . . uncomfortable. Nervous, even. "Here's the thing. Raidyn and Sharmaine . . . they've had this thing going on for most of our lives. The three of us were raised together. Our parents were all best friends growing up, they were all Riders, and it was always assumed that we would all be Riders too. It's hard, though, when two boys both like the same girl."

My eyebrows rose but I stayed silent, letting him talk.

"At first we were so young and it was mostly silly kid stuff anyway—so it didn't really matter. But then the war came and our parents left to fight and suddenly we had to grow up all too fast. She always preferred him, even as kids, of course, because who wouldn't?" This he said with a little self-deprecating laugh that cut me to my core.

"No, Loukas, that's not—"

"I'm not telling you this to gain your pity," he cut me off, a bit more sharply, and I flinched. "I guess I just don't want you going back to Vamala without . . . understanding a few things. And one is this: our parents all came back—except for Raidyn's. When the gateway was shut, they hadn't made it back. All Paladin left in Vamala were presumed dead—because if they weren't already, it was assumed it was only a matter of time.

"We were nine when your grandmother told him his parents were never coming back."

I stared at Loukas, but he no longer seemed to see me, trapped in the memories that he'd decided to share for some reason. "Raidyn was devastated, and nothing and no one—not even Sharmaine—could reach him. He shut her out, he shut *me* out, he closed himself off. The only time I've seen him truly happy since the day he was told his parents were never coming back through that gateway was when Naiki chose him. Raising her, training her, flying with her—those were the only times he seemed truly at peace. I hoped that he'd get over it with time, but we grew up, and nothing really changed. Raidyn's had feelings for Sharmaine for years, and she definitely has fallen completely in love with him, but he's never acted on anything with her, much to her dismay and my frustration. If you think loving the same girl is hard when you're kids, it's infinitely worse when you're adults, but she loves *him* back and *he* won't do anything about it because he's still so lost, even after all of these years."

He paused and I could do nothing except stand there, my hands hanging heavy and useless at my sides. He didn't want my pity and I didn't know why he was telling me this and I was *leaving*—

"And then you showed up," he continued, his focus suddenly snapping back to me.

I swallowed, unaccountably nervous. I wasn't sure I liked where this was going.

"Your father asked him to heal you—and of course he said yes.

Your father is the closest thing Raid has had to a father in his life for the last fifteen years. He would do anything Adelric asked him to do. Even a healing so intense it would invoke *sanaulus* with his daughter—the daughter who just came through a gateway that was supposedly shut for good. The gateway to the world where his parents were trapped and presumed dead but maybe, just maybe had somehow survived—the way Adelric had survived."

A hard knot began to form in the pit of my stomach as several pieces of a puzzle I had no idea existed until now fell into place. "And you think he saw my plight as an opportunity," I supplied. "You think he's been fighting so hard to reopen the gateway 'for me' because *he* really wants it reopened—so he can go through it and search for his parents?"

Loukas's shoulders lifted and fell once. "I think that is a distinct possibility, yes."

"And *you*," I bit out, "saw me as an opportunity—to make Raidyn jealous, to possibly take his interest off of Sharmaine for a bit, so *you* could have a chance to use me to break her heart and be the one to win her over, by comforting her while he was off being enticed by me."

"No, that's not—"

"Well, I hate to break it to you, but it didn't work. He wasn't enticed, she wasn't jealous, and now I'm leaving for good, so the three of you will have to figure it out on your own." I turned on my heel, furious that I was blinking back tears once more—*why* couldn't I just be angry without it making me cry?—and stormed away from Loukas and what I had hoped would be a peaceful last goodbye to the *luxem magnam*. He couldn't have been content with just ruining my belief that Raidyn had truly only intended to help me get back to Inara. Now he'd ruined my last moments here, too.

"Zuhra, wait! I didn't mean *that*—"

"Goodbye, Loukas. Thanks for the enlightening information," I spat through gritted teeth without turning back.

"Are you ready?"

I faced Naiki, my stomach clenched into a twisted mess, surrounded by every gryphon and Rider in every battalion in the Paladin army, except for one that was to stay back and guard the city, and the two assigned to patrol over the other towns and cities beyond the circle of mountain peaks that I hadn't even realized existed. There was still so much to this world I didn't know, and now would never learn about or see.

I'd only caught a couple of glimpses of Raidyn in the two days it had taken to prepare for this moment, and the times I had I'd been afraid to speak to him—afraid it would be too much or not enough, and so I didn't say anything, which was infinitely worse, and now we were out of time.

And instead of all the things I'd *wanted* to say, Loukas's final words were what were ringing in my head as I stood there, with Raidyn behind me, asking if I was ready to go.

After the tumultuous storm of emotions I'd been through here, the time had come to leave this place, to leave my grandparents, and Loukas, and Sharmaine . . . and Raidyn. When I'd learned Raidyn had volunteered to fly me to the gateway my first reaction had been excitement—but, in light of what Loukas had told me, it quickly gave way to distrust, even anger. Before that conversation by the *luxem magnam*, I might have hoped that he wanted one last chance to be together before we were separated forever. But now I was afraid he was only using me to be as close to the gateway as possible—so that he could dive through it when the chance came, to go in search of his parents.

Could he truly still believe they were alive after eighteen years?

Could he truly have been using me?

"Zuhra?" He sounded a bit uncertain when I didn't respond the first time, and I had to squeeze my eyes shut momentarily to regain my composure.

"Yes, sorry. I'm ready." I lifted my leg as I had the last time we'd gone on a ride together, desperately trying *not* to think about any portion of that day, or what I thought I'd felt . . . what I'd hoped we'd *both* felt when Naiki had taken us away from everything except for each other.

I felt the concern, the bewilderment, in him as he bent and grabbed my leg and then boosted me into the air. His touch still set off a conflagration of emotions, especially when he swung into the saddle behind me, his arms wrapping around me to take the reins in his hands, his biceps brushing my ribs. He'd already explained that this ride would be much more technical and that unlike last time he needed full control of the reins. The easiest way to do that was to let him hold me in place with his arms, with mine over top so I could grab onto him if I needed to.

The heat of his stomach and chest on my back, the soft *whoosh* of his breath near my ear, and his arms braced around my body as Naiki stood fully, stretching her wings out to the side of us, were almost more than I could bear. I had to close my eyes again, clamping down on the traitorous thundering of my heart and the hot pulse of blood in my veins.

There was a loud whistle ahead somewhere and then the very earth rumbled beneath us as hundreds of gryphons all galloped forward as one and took off, ascending into the sky—a sea of wings and Riders spreading across it like a sudden massive cloud passing over Soluselis and the castle below us.

It struck me then how dangerous this truly might be, if it required such an immense force.

Raidyn's arms tightened around me as we lifted off the earth, his powerful thighs squeezing Naiki's flanks, and even though we were surrounded on all sides, I couldn't help but remember our last ride—and what he'd told me, about Naiki, about flying . . . it made sense now. She'd chosen him shortly after he'd been told about his parents; that's why he'd been lost. She'd saved him, he'd said. That had been truth. Had any of the rest of it? He hadn't *said* anything about how he felt toward me, but it had been implied, hadn't it?

It doesn't matter, I told myself as the huge cliffs grew ever closer, and the city of Soluselis shrank behind us. He wouldn't be allowed through the gateway, even if he tried. And soon, all of this, including Raidyn, would be nothing more than memory.

"Here comes the gap. Hold on tight!" Raidyn warned as he shortened the reins and guided Naiki toward the frighteningly narrow space between the two cliffs that I'd been terrified of that first day. I knew it was still just as tight a spot to squeeze through, and just as dangerous, but I also knew Raidyn now—and I felt no fear as we soared toward it, as he guided Naiki to tilt, one arm wrapping around my waist to hold me in place. He bent forward, pressing us both against her neck, and we slipped through the gap.

When we came out the other side and straightened out, I felt an indefinable loss to realize that had been my last glimpse of their valley—or the castle on the hill and all it held. The wind whipped the tears from my eyes before they even fell.

The ride that had felt interminably long on the way to Soluselis passed in a blur on the way back to the gateway. Each wing flap brought me closer to my sister, but was one fewer second I had with Raidyn.

We'd been silent the entire time; I'd forced myself to sit as straight as possible, refusing to give in to the temptation to lean back into him. But that didn't stop my heart from thumping or my breath from catching, just as it had a few days ago when it had been just us in the sky, instead of a swarm of Paladin closing in on whatever awaited us at the gateway.

"I always believed she was alive." When Raidyn finally spoke, it took me so off guard I jumped and nearly unseated myself. He let go of the reins with one hand to grab onto my waist reflexively, but even after I was resettled, he didn't let go. "I'm really happy for you—that you get to go back to her."

I nodded, afraid to speak, afraid of what would come out. I was a tumult of questions and wishes and wants and regrets.

"And your mother. . . . I didn't realize she was there, too," he added, referring, I supposed, to the comment I'd made in the council meeting. I hadn't spoken of her much to anyone—not wanting to try and explain her and the complicated mess of feelings I had toward her.

I merely nodded again.

Raidyn's hand flexed against my hip, his thumb brushing the skin just beneath my shirt, and I couldn't keep from shivering at the touch of his skin against mine. He said something else but it was whipped away by the wind.

I turned my head slightly and shouted, "What?"

He leaned forward to put his mouth closer to my ear. "I know it's not fair to use the connection we have and I normally wouldn't even comment on it, but . . ." The thunder of Naiki's wings beating matched my heart when he paused. "We're almost out of time and I don't want things to end like this if they don't have to. Zuhra . . . what have I done to make you mad at me?"

I stiffened, my breath catching in my lungs. Did I admit what Loukas had told me? Did I confess my fears to him? Or did I brush it off? It wasn't fair that the *sanaulus* gave him that insight into my feelings, without my permission. Did that mean he could feel *everything* else I was right then too?

"Zuhra, please. Tell me what has upset you."

Naiki even tossed her head with a small cry, as if she, too, could sense the turmoil roiling within me.

I almost did it—I almost told him what Loukas had said and why I was upset. I would have, if my grandmother hadn't flown into view at that moment, with my grandfather riding behind her on her gryphon, my father at her left flank. She looked right at me, then past me to Raidyn. Her eyes narrowed, and my fears doubled. Did she know—did she suspect?

Maybe Loukas was right and I had every right to feel this way. To feel used.

"Nothing," I finally answered, my eyes still on my grandmother, who guided her gryphon to pull up alongside us. "I'm just worried—hoping this works."

There was a beat of silence—when I could actually *feel* him withdrawing from me, even though his hand didn't move—and then he said, "Well, I'm glad you're not upset at me. And don't worry, this will work. You'll be back with your family before you know it. Where you wanted to be."

There was an odd note to his voice—a hint of bitterness, underscored by a pang of hurt. But I wasn't sure if it was caused by my lie or by his own pain at losing his family in my world all those years ago.

Another whistle sounded, loud enough to overscore the wind and beating wings, and the great mass of gryphons broke into two groups—the much larger one continuing forward to the gateway, while Sachiel led her battalion slightly to the west, to do just as she'd volunteered and attempt to draw off as many of the rakasa as possible.

Naiki and the other gryphons in our group began to angle lower, closer to the ground, and my heart leapt into my throat. I knew we were deep in the rakasas' lands now, and we could be attacked at any time from any quarter. The hesitation to come to the gateway and open it wasn't just because of the threat in Vamala—this side of the gateway was far more dangerous and could very well prove deadly, even today, even with this massive force of Paladin all primed and ready to fight to protect us.

"Don't be afraid," Raidyn murmured. "No matter what lies ahead, I promise, I won't let anything happen to you."

And despite everything, including my own misgivings about him and his motives, I couldn't help but believe him.

Two short, loud whistles sounded and Raidyn released my waist to grab onto the reins with both hands again.

"That's the signal. The first group is going to land and clear the field of threats, then the council group and our group will land, to open the gateway so you and Adelric can go through."

I swallowed and nodded. This was it. It was actually happening. I had no idea what awaited me back in the citadel—what I would find, *who* I would find. But I knew Inara had to be there, waiting for me. There was no one else who could have tried to open the gateway.

Hold on, Nara. I'm coming, I thought, bending forward slightly to watch the first group of gryphons dive toward the trees below and the field where a gateway stood—the one that would take me back home.

THIRTY-NINE

INARA

I am gone.

Who am I?

Who am I?

It's back . . . faster this time . . . and I am . . . *lost.*

Pain.

Pain.

I am *pain.*

Roaring and roaring and *roaring.* And in my dreams, she's there, calling for me, beckoning to me, *needing* me.

I will go to her—I *must* go to her.

In a room with a door to nowhere and everywhere.

The roar will take me to her.

She calls for me and I will go.

Doors and darkness and roaring and voices calling to me, but I must go to her. I must go.

FORTY

ZUHRA

Naiki touched down lightly, barely even jarring me this time, and within moments, Raidyn had vaulted from her back and quickly helped me down. His hands lingered at my waist for a fraction of a heartbeat, but then he released me with a mumbled "Looks like it's working so far."

He was right—so far the plan had worked shockingly well. The field had been cleared of the few remaining rakasa from the last power surge, though it was full of gryphons and Riders, all facing outward in concentric circles around the gateway, prepared for an attack, and when I turned to look, a group of six Paladin—including my grandmother—formed a semicircle around the gateway. I watched her for a moment, conflicted. What *could* have been time for us to get to know one another had instead been wasted, with her too intent on ignoring me. But I hadn't made an effort either, I realized. I could have sought her out, forced her to acknowledge me.

"Ready?"

I turned at the sound of my father's voice behind me. He stood a few feet away, Taavi, his gryphon, behind him. The creature's head was lowered, its beak gently pressed into his back—as if Taavi knew his Rider was leaving him. I hadn't even considered that. Raidyn had talked about the special bond between Rider and the gryphon—how the gryphon chose its rider, the lifelong bond that was created. So what happened if the Rider left? Father had already lost one gryphon in Vamala. What would it do to him to leave Taavi behind?

"Yes," I finally answered his question. "I think so." I didn't let my gaze flicker to the side, where Raidyn stood by Naiki's saddle, his hand resting on her flank, though that tug between us seemed to be pulling tighter and tighter, like someone coiling a rope, hand over hand, trying to draw us closer together. Since neither of us moved toward the other, it only made the tension grow thicker, stronger, more unbearable. "Will Taavi be all right?" The question burst out with more force than I intended, and I quickly followed up with a more gentle, "Since you are leaving him?"

My father turned to look at the gryphon, who had inched closer to him, dropping his head down to Adelric's shoulder, his eyes half-shut. He lifted one hand to stroke the creature's feathered head, a shadow of grief clouding his expression. "It won't be easy, for either of us," he admitted quietly, and Taavi made a low keening noise in his throat.

Out of the corner of my eye, I noticed Raidyn watching them. My father must have noticed as well, because he added, "It won't be easy to leave any of those I care about here," and lifted his other hand to clap it over Raidyn's shoulder, pulling him into an embrace. Raidyn stood stiffly for a moment but then he lifted his arms and embraced my father back, his eyes squeezed shut tight.

Adelric has been like a father to him—that's what Loukas had told me. And now he, too, was leaving Raidyn, to go back to Vamala. Back to his *true* family.

"They've begun," someone nearby said, their voice hushed with awe.

The whisper spread across the field as I turned to see the six Paladin standing with their hands joined. Their veins glowed with power that continued to build and grow, brighter and brighter, until it surged out of them, encompassing their joined hands and bodies in blinding light, and then, finally, surging toward the gateway, rushing over and *through* it. The stone archway drank in the light of their combined power greedily. I could feel its need, could sense the draw . . . the *pull* . . .

A distant shout echoed over the field and was quickly followed by three loud whistle blasts.

The field exploded with activity as the outer ring of Riders vaulted onto their gryphons and immediately took off, while others tightened their ranks around the gateway—and us, standing a little way behind it, waiting.

"What is it—what's happening?" I spun toward my father and Raidyn, who both stood facing the forest instead of the gateway, tense, eyes roaming back and forth. Neither of them looked to me.

My father merely said, "Rakasa."

There was no ignoring the intensity of the pull from the gateway behind us; everything in me yearned to go to it. It called out to me—to *all* of us, I was certain. It wanted more power, *needed* more . . . and *I* needed to go to it. As strong as I'd thought the tug was between me and Raidyn, this was ten times that. A hundred, maybe. I had to physically fight the urge to turn and rush to the gateway, to grab it with both hands and let it drain me.

No wonder the rakasa were drawn here when the gateway was open.

But what could it possibly want with *me*? I had nothing to give.

And then there was no more time to think or wonder—the rakasa came, and they came in droves. Waves of monsters broke through the trees, and the once peaceful field exploded into battle. Flashes of Paladin fire and explosions of power met with roars and snarls and blinding, searing flashes of rakasa fire to meet the Paladin's. They were on the ground, they were in the sky. Some as big as the gryphons, some small and vicious, just as I'd read about in that book I'd managed to sneak from the library what seemed like an entire lifetime ago, when they'd been nothing more than drawings and printed descriptions.

Nothing could have prepared me for the *reality* of these beasts in person. A whole herd of Scylla, with the bodies of horses, leathery wings, and heads at least fifty percent mouth full of razor-sharp teeth to our left—the same monster that had broken through when Inara opened it the first time; a pair of Chimera straight ahead that were part lion, part goat, and part snake; more Bahal like the one that had seized me; and many others of all shapes and sizes.

I stood there, beside Naiki's quivering flank, and stared, frozen with horror—with unadulterated terror that flooded my veins like a poison that caused paralysis. Raidyn held her reins tightly, keeping her there, though I knew her instinct was to go join her brothers and sisters and fight. But he was part of the innermost circle, the ones who had to stay on the ground, closest to the gateway—the last wall of protection to give the council time to open the gateway entirely and let us through.

The earth shook, reverberating with explosions and bodies of rakasa slamming to the ground; screams and shrieks of agony—of *dying*—sounded all around us, and not just from the rakasa. My grandmother had warned me, had tried to tell me how dangerous this was, and I hadn't listened—hadn't been *willing* to listen. Would other Paladin die today so my father and I could return to Vamala? Had I truly been selfish enough to demand that?

A scream—a Paladin scream—from the sky sent claws of guilt and horror raking down my spine. I looked up in time to see a gryphon spinning, free-falling toward the earth, its Rider hanging limp from the saddle. My vision blurred and I blinked furiously as other Paladin on the ground shouted to each other in their language. Suddenly a shimmering blue blanket of power spread out between three Paladin, hovering just above the earth only a moment before the gryphon and its Rider would have crashed to the ground. Instead the net of power caught them and then slowly lowered them. Not Sharmaine, or Loukas, or anyone I knew, but a Paladin nonetheless, who had come here, had risked their life—for *me*.

The three who had created the net rushed toward the fallen pair, one calling over his shoulder. I only understood one word: *healer*.

Raidyn started forward, but my father put his arm out to stop him, saying something quietly to him in Paladin. They usually spoke in my language around me and it only drove home the direness of the situation that neither of them seemed to remember I was even there.

And through it all, the gateway called and *pulled* and then—

"It is done!" Ederra's exclamation was barely audible but it struck me to the core.

My grandfather was suddenly there, grabbing my arm, yanking me away from Naiki and Raidyn. "Come quickly! *Now!*"

"Wait—*no*—" I stared at the gryphon—at *Raidyn*—who wheeled around to stare back at me, his face stricken.

There was to be no goodbye then. With the frenzy of the rakasa attack, we'd missed our chance.

"Zuhra, you must go now! We have to close it and get our people out of this place!" My grandfather's hand was like steel around my bicep, immovable, and he dragged me away with surprising strength. "Adelric—come *now!*"

I glanced over my shoulder to see my father pressing his forehead to his gryphon's, and then with one last squeeze of his hand on Raidyn's shoulder, he turned and rushed after us, where Grandfather was already pulling me up the slight incline to where the gateway shone almost as bright as a sun. I couldn't even look directly at it.

Behind us, a shriek exploded through the air—but this pain was not from a wound inflicted by a rakasa. It was Taavi, keening at the loss of his Rider, and it nearly broke *my* heart. My father reached my side and grabbed my hand in his, his chin lifted, but I didn't miss the tears shining in his blue-fire eyes.

The six Paladin who had opened it stood in a row, watching us, my grandmother closest to the gateway.

"Go, my son. Hurry. We must leave this place." Grandfather spoke in my language as he put his hand on my father's shoulder, much as he had to Raidyn moments earlier. Then he added something else in Paladin and my father nodded.

"I will always miss you and hold you in my heart," Father replied thickly, but there was no time and we had to move on. I didn't know how the six Paladin were standing there, resisting the gateway. Its pull was almost a physical thing, reaching for me, grabbing at the very fibers of my being.

Ederra stepped forward at the last second, her eyes dulled from the draw on her power to open the gateway—and from the sorrow that etched deep grooves into her already lined face.

"Mother—I—" My father tried to speak, but his voice broke and he had to stop, letting go of my hand to grab his mother into an embrace instead.

She whispered something to him. I could hear her voice but couldn't understand her words. Her hands trembled where they clasped him close to her one last time. It almost tore me apart—as I was tearing *them* apart.

When he let go, she turned to me. We stared at one another for the space of a heartbeat, then two. Then she actually lifted her hand toward me to brush my cheek, swiping a piece of hair behind my ear.

"I'm . . . sorry, Zuhra." The words were tight in her throat, barely escaping her mouth, but they were said. When her hand dropped to her side once more and she looked away, I could have sworn she blinked back tears.

"I'm sorry too . . . Grandmother."

Her eyes flickered to mine and then away again, but she nodded, once.

It was as much as I was ever going to get. Our time was up.

I reached out for my father's hand and we turned to face the brilliant gateway.

"Together," he murmured with a squeeze on my hand.

I squinted my eyes partially shut against the brightness, and we stepped into and then through the light—out of Visimperum and into Vamala.

Into the Hall of Miracles.

Where the scene that greeted me turned my blood to ice in my veins.

"Inara!" I screamed, and then I ran.

FORTY-ONE

INARA

The pain inside is light.

It is power.

It is *me*.

But something else is there, calling, calling, *calling*.

Slumbering before, now awake.

Bright, too bright, bright enough to pierce the roar.

And it *pulls* . . . I *need* it . . . and *it* needs *me* . . .

I go to it. I stumble and get up and walk and all is darkness and I'm alone.

Am I alone?

There are voices.

There's a roar.

There is someone there . . .

"Inara!"

"Inara . . ."

"Inara . . ."

The brightness is blinding, the pull is demanding.

I try to go to it, but I can't. Something has me, something holds me back.

Something digs into my arm, into my side, into my neck—

Pain.

Blinding, searing, excruciating pain.

I scream and scream and scream and suddenly—

The roar recedes like a blanket being pulled away from a window—shoving me from darkness into light in the blink of an eye. But I didn't use my power—I'm *not* using my power—and there is still terrible, agonizing pain and something still has me—no, not something . . . some*one*. Someone is holding me down and it hurts—*it hurts*—and my power is sparking, it's trying to heal—but it's leaving me—it's being *ripped* from me—sucked out of my body—torn asunder from my very soul and I am being torn apart with it—

"Inara!"

I hear my name as if through a dream, a voice I only hear *in* dreams. I'm screaming and he's holding me and my power—my power—my *power*—

FORTY-TWO

ZUHRA

My vision cleared to see Inara lying on the ground, a man bent over her, his mouth on her neck, his hands trapping her arms against the stone floor, and blood—*so much blood*—

I screamed her name and ran to her. I was fury reborn as muscle and bone and flesh, and all my training finally came to use when I kicked him so hard he lost his grip on her. I kicked him again and he rolled away and then I was on top of him and my fists were flying and I punched and punched and *punched*—

But he looked up at me and—*his eyes*—his eyes stopped me for just a moment, long enough for him to shove me in the chest. I landed on my back on the ground with a thud, my head slamming into the stone.

"Zuhra!"

I blinked and tried to sit up, in time to see my father lifting his hand, his power coursing through his veins, gathering in his hand—he was aiming at the man—

"Master Barloc!"

Another shout, this from behind us—a voice I thought I'd never hear again. *Halvor was alive?*

The man with the glowing blue eyes—the one who had attacked Inara—turned toward Halvor and bared his teeth at him. "Stay back—or I take you with me," he snarled and Halvor slammed to a halt, his own eyes wide with horror as he took in the entire scene: his master's glowing eyes, his blood-rimmed lips, and Inara lying on the ground, her neck ripped open and her chest barely moving.

I didn't understand—I couldn't make the images make sense. I only knew my sister had been alive and now—now I was back and she was *dying*.

"No—*Inara*!" I rushed to her side and put one hand to her neck, pressing it against the wound, and the other to her chest, feeling for breath. "I'm back, Inara. I'm back. So you can't leave me. You hear me? *You can't leave me!*"

"Don't move or I will dispense with you." My father's threat rang out in the room and I glanced up to see his hand glowing with one of his Paladin fireballs, aimed directly at Barloc.

But rather than cowering, Barloc merely laughed. "Oh, you can try. But you know as well as I do that I will just absorb all that power and add it to my stores if you hit me with it right now."

My father blanched. And then, to my ever-escalating horror, he slowly *lowered* his hand.

No! What was he *doing*? Why wasn't he attacking?

And Inara remained unmoving, her lips bloodless, her chest barely rising and falling.

"She can heal herself. She'll be all right—she can heal herself," Halvor repeated, dropping to his knees on her other side, pale and trembling.

"No . . . she can't," my father said quietly, tears streaking down his face, backing toward us as Barloc lifted both his hands in the air with an unhinged laugh. "She's powerless now. He *stole* it."

And suddenly, a horrific story came back to me—another story that hadn't seemed quite real to me until that moment—of how Anael, my father's sister, had died.

"No," I whispered. "No, no, *no!*"

Raidyn.

My head jerked up and I stared at the gateway that was still open. He could heal her. He *had* to heal her. I couldn't lose Inara now—not after everything we'd been through.

"Thank you for doing her job for me, by the by," Barloc spoke as he moved toward the gateway. "It was kind of you to open that gateway so she didn't have to use up so much of her power to do it first. It left so much more for me."

"You wish to go through the gateway to Visimperum?" My father had backed up to stand in front of us, his arms outstretched as though he were trying to protect us from Barloc. *"Why?"*

Barloc paused, and a shudder went through him, his veins flashing blue—a blinding pulse—and then going back to normal again. "Because it is my rightful home—just as this power is my rightful inheritance."

"That is not your power—you stole it." My father's voice was low and furious.

"It is *mine* now," he snarled. "I took back what should have been mine to begin with."

"What are you talking about?" When Halvor spoke, his voice was barely above a whisper. He, too, pressed his hands to Inara's still chest. His fingers trembled and the look on his face when he gazed at her . . . I recognized it, I knew it—he loved my sister. And now, because of his uncle, she was dying.

"Do you still think the Five who came here all those years ago were truly the first to do so since the original closing?" Barloc laughed, his glowing eyes on my father. "My grandfather was a Paladin—one of the last who came through the gateway with a small group over a *hundred* years ago. He was eventually murdered for what he was, just as so many have been murdered again this time. But I am going to change that. It's time the weak, pathetic people of Vamala learn what the *true* might of the Paladin unleashed feels like—and *I* will be the one to bring it upon them."

We all stared at Barloc, in varying degrees of shock.

"You might be immensely powerful right now—but it won't last. And then they will merely hunt you down and kill you as they have so many Paladin before you." My father's hands were clenched into fists at his side, but he still didn't attack. *Why didn't he attack?*

"Which is why I needed the gateway opened *before* I acted." Barloc edged closer to it, his veins pulsing blue over and over again. "When I come back, it will be with an army ready to take their place as masters and lords over all Vamala."

And then he turned and plunged through the gateway, disappearing from sight.

A little sigh escaped from Inara and I looked down at her, my eyesight blurred from tears. And then I remembered—my father was a healer. "You have to heal her," I whispered, then repeated myself again, louder. "You have to heal her!"

"Why did you let him go?" Halvor accused, his face ashen.

"There are hundreds of Paladin on the other side of that gateway. The council will recognize him for what he is immediately—and he will be executed. Not even a *jakla* can absorb the might of a hundred Paladin at once."

"Father—you have to heal her—*now!*" I jumped to my feet, to grab his hand and pull him to Inara.

"If she's had her power ripped out . . . that is not something that can be healed." My father turned to face Inara, and his hand tightened on mine. "Her only hope is if you stopped him in time, before he drained her entirely." He stepped toward her and then knelt by her head, reaching out to stroke her cheek once, softly, his hand trembling. "Inara," he whispered. "My little girl. My sweet little girl." He gently pressed his hand to her chest, his power flowing down his arms, into his fingers and out into her body. There was a pause and then he glanced up at me and shook his head once, stricken.

I stood there, staring, cold with shock. There was nothing we could do? I didn't believe it. I didn't believe him. He didn't know—he was *wrong*. If he couldn't do it, then Raidyn could. He *had* to heal her. *Someone had to save her.*

"Adelric?"

The gasped name was followed by a thud. I looked up to see my mother at the doorway on her knees, staring at my father, her eyes wide and her face white.

"Cinnia." When he uttered her name, it sounded like a prayer.

"Where were you—*how* are you—" Her voice was choked. She lifted shaking hands to her mouth to press them against her lips, holding back a sudden, violent sob that rent through her. But then her gaze dropped and her eyes widened even further. "Inara!" she cried, and that was finally what induced her to scramble to her feet and rush forward. "What happened? Inara! Adelric? I . . . I . . ."

My father crawled over to where she knelt at Inara's side and took her in his arms, holding her so gently, so tenderly, it made my heart constrict.

But I didn't have time to watch their reunion—Inara was almost gone, and I had to do *something*. Taking advantage of their distraction, I turned and ran for the gateway—and Raidyn.

"Zuhra—*no*!"

I was on the second stair, the third . . . I hit the landing and stretched forward—but instead of me going through the gateway, someone else barreled out of it, directly into me, knocking me backward. We tumbled down the stairs, a tangle of bodies and legs and arms. I landed on my back with another crack of my head on the stone floor, the Paladin on top of me. I stared up at him, the pain receding as my eyes met his familiar blue-fire ones.

"Zuhra?"

"Raidyn?"

"Raidyn?" His name was echoed from behind me, but my father sounded furious—not relieved.

Raidyn scrambled off of me, and jumped to his feet. "Sir, there is a *jakla*—he attacked your mother—I tried to stop him, but—"

Before he could say anything else, the gateway flared and Barloc burst through it again, running full speed down the stairs to leap over me. And right behind him were my grandfather and Loukas on foot. Then Sachiel, her long braid swinging behind her, one side of her shaved head bloody, rode through it on her gryphon, followed by Sharmaine on hers. Then Taavi, bursting through the doorway and immediately letting loose a screech of fury. Naiki followed right behind.

"Stop him!" someone shouted as I jumped to my feet, ignoring the pounding in my head.

Barloc's entire body flashed blue, his skin lighting up from head to toe, then went back to normal, as he sprinted across the Hall of Miracles and out the door.

"Sachiel—go through the window!" My father shouted the

command. "Cut him off—but be careful! Taavi and Naiki, go with them!"

The gryphons cawed again, a roar of sound that vibrated through the hall, and then they wheeled and headed toward the window—the *broken* window, followed by Sachiel and Sharmaine.

I didn't understand fully what was happening, only that Barloc had to be stopped and the Paladin couldn't use their power against him, or he'd merely absorb it. I glanced to the wall where a huge assortment of weapons hung.

But surely, cold, hard steel would work on anyone, even a *jakla*.

I rushed to the nearest weapon—a long handle with a chain attached to it and a ball covered in spikes at the end of the chain—and pulled it from the wall. The weight of it was a shock, but I hefted it back up and then took off after Barloc.

"Zuhra, are you out of your *mind*?" Raidyn's shout in my language almost made me pause—but not quite.

"Heal my sister!" I yelled back as I ran after the man who had done this to her—the man who was going to pay for stealing her power.

FORTY-THREE

Inara

Pain.
   Silence.
I'd never had both at the same time before.

The roar was gone, but so was the flicker deep within me. The one that had always been there.

There was only reaching, grasping darkness. Thick, thick darkness that clung and sucked and pulled, and I couldn't break free. It was dragging me under.

Somewhere far away, as distant as thunder all the way across the mountains, was a murmur of voices . . . a stroke of a hand on my cheek . . . a trembling memory almost too weak to be recalled of faces I wished to see.

Something entered the darkness, a sudden light that snaked through it, searching, reaching . . . but there was nothing for it to grasp, nothing for it to cling to, no way for it to take hold of me and bring me back.

It searched, it reached—

And I slipped further into the deep.

FORTY-FOUR

ZUHRA

I was slower than he was, especially hefting the increasingly heavy weapon over my shoulder, but the hedge would stop him—the *custovitan* hedge would be my saving grace. I reached the stairs of the main entrance just in time to see him stretch out his hands and blast the doors open with an explosion of power that reverberated through the entire citadel, even sending me stumbling backward.

"Zuhra—don't! He'll *kill* you!"

Loukas's shout did little to deter me, but my grandfather was suddenly there by my side, as Loukas rushed past us.

"Zuhra—Raidyn needs you. Right now," he said, soft but insistent. Grief darkened his eyes and turned my blood to ice, scraping through my veins. "Your sister . . . she's not—"

"He healed her. He was going to *heal her*," I insisted, but my grandfather just shook his head mutely.

The metal ball crashed to the ground where I dropped it.

"Go to her. I will stop him. I will stop the one who hurt my Ederra," he vowed, stooping to grab up the weapon I'd abandoned.

His words glanced off me as I turned, running as fast as I could back the way I'd come. Raidyn couldn't have failed—he *couldn't* have. Inara had to be alive. She *had* to be.

Every step felt like a hundred; every breath burned like fire in my lungs, like the Paladin power I'd never been able to find within myself. If I'd had any, I would have given it to her—I would have given it *all* to her, if it meant she would live.

I sprinted down the hallway, toward the doors of the Hall of Miracles that gaped open, like a dark wound torn through the heart of the citadel. More Paladin rushed past me but I barely even acknowledged their presence in my world—what it meant, what it *would* mean. All that mattered was Inara.

I burst into the room to see all four of them gathered around her body—my mother, my father, Halvor, and Raidyn. And Inara, lying on the ground, unmoving.

They all turned to look at me, all except Raidyn, who had one hand on her chest and one on her throat, his head bent toward her and his eyes closed. His whole body was shaking, and yet she was completely still.

I dropped to the ground beside him, almost blinded by tears.

"He's trying." My father's voice shook, his words heavy with sorrow. "Because you asked him to, he's *trying* . . . but I *told* you . . . this is not something he can heal, Zuhra. And if he doesn't stop soon, he will lose himself."

I just shook my head, my tears spilling out onto my cheeks. "No," I whispered thickly. "Inara, no . . ."

"You *have* to tell him to stop, Zuhra. Hurry, or we'll lose him, too."

I looked at Raidyn, at the beautiful face that I'd come to know so well, his eyes squeezed shut, all the veins in his body glowing brightly as he bent every ounce of power he had to do what I'd asked—to do the impossible. Even as I watched, his power flickered and my heart lurched into my throat.

I couldn't lose him, too.

If Inara was beyond our reach . . . if I was never to see my sister again . . . I couldn't lose Raidyn at the same moment.

I swallowed, looking at my sister's lovely face one last time—at the brush of her lashes against her cheeks, her lips slightly parted, and I wished I'd seen her eyes open—that I'd seen her burning blue irises one last time. I bent over and pressed a kiss to her cold cheek and brokenly whispered, "I love you, Inara. I love you and . . . and I'm . . . I'm *sorry* . . ."

I felt my father's hand on my back, a warm, reassuring pressure as I forced myself to sit back up and then turned to Raidyn. "You can stop," I choked out. "Raid, you can stop."

But he was beyond hearing.

I reached out and put my hand on top of his, opening my mouth to repeat myself—but before I could speak, something ignited in my veins, my hand clamped onto his, and then heat exploded out into my body. It was just like when I'd grabbed Inara's hand on the door handle, when I'd felt her power surging through me, burning through my veins, before the rakasa had burst through the gateway and knocked us both free.

Raidyn's power surged into me, through me, turning my veins to fire and binding me to him. Instead of pulling him free, somehow *I'd* been sucked into the abyss *with him*. Dimly, I heard voices calling to me, but they quickly faded, further and further, until it was just me and Raidyn . . . and Inara.

I could hear the slow, steady beat of his heart in my ears. I could feel his presence beside me—*within* me—within *her*. I recognized the touch of his soul against mine from when he'd healed me. I *felt* him recognize me, almost as if his power—his *soul*—sighed in relief. Deeper, more intimate than any caress of his fingers against the skin of my hip, this most sacred, innermost part of who he was intertwined with *my* soul, with the fire burning through my veins, soothing it, calling to it, wrapping it up in his power. Images flashed through my mind: a woman and a man, hugging one another while he watched; the man putting him in the saddle of a gryphon, one I'd never seen before; the woman ladling something into a bowl while Raidyn sat at a table watching the man sneak up behind her, to surprise her with a kiss on her neck; the woman sitting on his bed, singing softly to him, his room softened by the settling darkness of falling dusk; my grandmother putting her arm around him and the crushing sadness that felt as though it were suffocating him; Sharmaine laughing, running her hands through his hair; coming around a corner and finding Loukas and Sharmaine half-hidden by my grandmother's flowers, kissing; flying high above Soluselis, nothing but the wind on his face and the sun above and Naiki below; flying again, but this time, with me in his arms, and wanting so badly to kiss me—

It was *so* fast, over in one beat of his heart, but every one of the memories imprinted onto my mind, as if I'd experienced them myself. And then, somehow, I felt him guiding both of us toward her—toward Inara. I felt the moment we reached her soul, *together.* The same thing happened again, but this time it was flashes of Inara we saw, together. The roar, the *pain,* but also the joy—moments with me in her garden, moments with Sami in the kitchen, reading a book together in her bed, a kiss with Halvor, even a conversation with our mother. In another beat of his heart, it was over, and he and I were pushing onward, further into the core of who she was, where she was.

And all we found was the barest flicker of life, huddled in a corner of so much darkness, bringing back the light felt insurmountable. Somehow I recognized that she was almost gone, that this tiny flame was all that was left of my sister before she left us—forever.

He stretched toward her, but she was out of reach, he couldn't stretch that far.

So I did.

I wound myself through him, *with* him, combining our will and might into one, and together we pressed toward her, toward that last flickering ember that was Inara's life force in this dark, cavernous space, where I realized her power had once resided. It hurt, oh, how it *hurt,* ripping, tearing, burning—but I refused to give up, refused to let her go, and then—

We reached her.

Raidyn and I, together, wrapped our essence, our very souls around hers and slowly, gently coaxed it forward. I felt him doing something, as if he were stitching her back together, filling this terrible void with something else, *patching* it almost, so it wasn't entirely empty.

And, for some unfathomable reason, every stitch felt like someone stabbing me.

But I knew, somehow, that this was the only way to bring her back—to save my sister. And so I grasped onto him and I grasped onto her and he continued his work, reeling us backward out of this dark, terrible, empty place, stitch by stabbing stitch.

Until finally, finally, when I felt as though I would soon lose the ability to hold on to either of them any longer, he pulled even further back, fast, fast, fast, unspooling from her, withdrawing into his own body, so it was just me and him once more, and then with the strangest sensation, as though he'd run a finger over my cheek, except soul to soul, he unraveled himself from me, as well, and with a gasp of pain that flared like an explosion of fire through my body, I was slammed back into myself.

Trying to peel my eyes open took an inordinate amount of effort. When I finally managed to do it, I realized I was lying on my back, staring up at a sea of faces surrounding me.

"She's awake," my father breathed, and my mother reached out to brush my face with her fingers, her own face wet with tears. My mother was . . . *crying?*

"Zuhra?"

I gasped and tried to sit up, but my head swam, forcing me back to the ground.

"Go slow," my father warned. "That was . . . quite the feat."

And then she was there, kneeling at my side, well and whole and alert and lucid and *alive.* But her eyes . . . her eyes were a plain, dull blue.

No spark of Paladin power left.

"Inara," I whispered.

And then I began to sob.

She bent over to pull *me* into *her* arms.

"I . . . I . . ."

"You saved me, Zuzu." She squeezed me even tighter and I finally was able to force the strength into my arms to squeeze her back. "Just like you always have."

"I don't . . . I'm not sure . . ."

She released me enough to pull back. Halvor hovered behind her, his hand outstretched toward her, though not touching her, as though he still couldn't believe it. Inara glanced to her left and I followed her gaze. Raidyn knelt a few feet away, his hands on his knees. He was pale and trembling, his hairline damp, and his eyes were dulled, only the faintest glow left as he watched me gravely.

"Thank you," I choked out. "Thank you for healing her."

Raidyn's gaze never flickered. "I am not to thank. *You* are."

I shook my head, halting and unsure. "I don't understand . . ."

"Go ahead, Raidyn. Tell her what you told us," my father prompted.

I looked back to him. When our eyes met, I remembered suddenly what I'd experienced—what I'd felt . . . what I'd *seen*. My entire body ached, but my heart most of all. The connection from when he'd healed me—the *sanaulus*—I think I understood, at last.

"Zuhra . . . what you just did . . ." His expression was unreadable when he said, "I wasn't able to heal Inara by myself—it wasn't until you touched my hand, until you joined your power with mine that we succeeded."

"My . . . *what*?" A pulse went through me—a stab of want so strong, I could barely breathe.

"Zuhra, you're an *enhancer*." The way he said it, breathing the word as if he could barely believe it, sent a thrill down my spine.

"Apparently it's incredibly rare," Inara added, "and it's the only way Raidyn could have saved me—because your power enhanced his, allowing him to bring me back. I told you—you saved me. Again."

An enhancer. Grandfather had been right after all. I *did* have power within me, I just hadn't found it yet.

Grandfather.

My joy and relief dissipated. "Where is Grandfather—where is Barloc?"

Before anyone could answer me, a blast of light exploded out from the gateway. With a cry, I ducked—but the room had fallen silent. Nothing else happened.

When I uncovered my head and glanced up, the gateway had gone dark.

I immediately turned to Raidyn. He stared, slack-jawed.

The gateway was shut.

He was trapped here.

And he looked genuinely horrified.

Could Loukas have been wrong?

Loukas . . . he was here, too. *Trapped* here.

And *Grandfather.*

"Where is my father—Zuhra, where did he go?"

I snapped back to attention to find both of my parents on their feet, staring at me.

"He—he went after Barloc. He said something about making him pay for hurting Ederra—"

I barely finished the sentence before my father took off at a dead run, my mother right on his heels. Inara rushed after them, Halvor at her side, clutching her hand, leaving me and Raidyn. I scrambled to my feet, even though I still felt humiliatingly weak.

"Zuhra, wait—take it slow. You just drained yourself to heal your sister." He lifted a hand, took a step toward me, but then paused . . . stopped . . . let his hand fall.

My heart fell with it.

"I'm all right," I insisted. "I can't just *sit* here. That's my family out there."

He winced, and too late, I wished I could recall my words. The memories I'd seen—the pieces of his life the *sanaulus* had given to me, flashed through my mind. I flushed and turned away, unable to run but hurrying as fast as I could after the others, not wanting him to read my emotions on my face—or sense them from my proximity. How much stronger would the connection be between us now that . . . *that* had happened? I'd seen so much, felt so much of who he'd been—who he was. His parents . . . that's who the man and woman had been. They'd loved him so much—and each other—it had been so evident in every memory. His heartbreak when he'd been told about them being trapped here . . . And Raidyn catching Sharmaine and Loukas *kissing* . . . Loukas had left that little detail out of the story he'd told me.

When I heard him following after me, I clamped down on the memories—*his* memories. Did he know what I'd seen? How did it work if he was the healer whose power mine had latched onto and enhanced?

My power. I still couldn't believe it.

I hurried through the hallways, managing a strange half-jog, half-speed-walking pace with my legs that still felt like they'd been physically beaten, Raidyn on my heels. He, too, had pushed himself to the brink, nearly losing himself trying to save my sister. We had so much to talk about—but we both remained silent as we rushed through the citadel. I sensed his awe—his curiosity—but also his fear, his panic. A riotous mixture of emotions that collided with my own.

What would we find when we finally reached the courtyard? Surely the hedge wouldn't have let Barloc through, but then again . . . how had he gotten inside the citadel to begin with? And now with the power he possessed—and the Paladin's fear of attacking him . . . *What had happened?* My dread grew stronger with every not-fast-enough step. Especially when I could hear no sound of battle . . . or any sound at all, for that matter, other than the slap of our boots on the stone floors.

"This is where you lived your whole life?" Raidyn finally spoke as we reached the top of the staircase, where my grandfather had taken the strange metal ball weapon from me. The double doors were missing—I vaguely remembered Barloc exploding them open—but there wasn't anyone in the small sliver of courtyard visible from where we stood. The only thing we *could* see through the windows was the hedge, as massive as I remembered. "Just you, your sister, and your mother?"

"And Sami." Where *was* Sami? There was no time to wonder, as I grabbed the banister for support to hop-run down the stairs, my legs nearly giving out more than once. *Curse this blasted weakness!* I needed my strength back. It was a small price to pay for saving Inara, but I'd never felt so helpless.

When I reached the bottom and got a better view of the courtyard, I slammed to a halt, my hand going to my mouth.

My father, mother, sister, and Loukas all knelt around a body on the ground near a huge, gaping hole ripped through the hedge—or blasted through it. Tendrils of smoke still wafted up from the blackened, wounded leaves that had been impermeable my entire life.

"Alkimos," Raidyn breathed beside me, and then rushed forward, somehow finding the strength to run.

That's when it hit me—the body on the ground. There was a large spiked metal ball next to it. And blood. Lots of blood.

"Grandfather!"

I took off after Raidyn. Loukas heard us coming and when his eyes met mine, the bleakness in his turned my body to ice.

No, no, *no.*

When I reached my family, I realized my father was holding Grandfather's hand in both of his, tears streaking down his cheeks. A large gash had been torn through his chest and abdomen. He lay on the ground, the light stolen from his eyes, staring unseeing up at the stormy sky.

He'd tried to avenge Ederra, and instead Barloc had killed him.

He'd killed my *grandfather*—one of the most powerful Paladin in Visimperum.

"H-he . . . he said Ederra was hurt . . ." I could barely force the words out, my gaze moving to Loukas once more.

"She's alive," Loukas said, but the bleakness hadn't left his face. "But . . . she is gravely injured. They'll need your help healing her, I'm sure," he said to Raidyn.

"It's closed," was all Raidyn said back, and Loukas's eyes widened, the blood draining from his face.

"How hurt is she?" My father still clutched Grandfather's hand when he turned to Loukas. *"How hurt is she?"* he yelled when Loukas didn't immediately reply.

I flinched—I'd never heard him yell before.

"It's bad, sir." Loukas's eyes dropped to the ground. "Shar threw up a shield, but it was too much power—Ederra took the brunt of the *jakla*'s blast when he realized he was surrounded by hundreds of Paladin."

My father curled in on himself, lifting his father's hand and pressing it to his forehead. He began to rock back and forth, a low, keening noise coming from his throat. My mother hesitantly reached out and put a trembling hand on his shoulder. I'd never seen her attempt to comfort anyone before—and the sight of her and my father together, with my grandfather lying dead on the ground beside them, was almost more than I could bear.

Nearly blinded by the tears in my own eyes, I turned away from them—away from the hole in the hedge—and stared at the citadel, rising toward the blackening clouds above. I crossed my arms over my body, trying to hold myself together.

I felt him step toward me, felt his uncertainty, his pain, his longing. "Zuhra . . . I'm so sorry." The low murmur of Raidyn's voice thrummed through my body.

I needed him—I needed his strength, I needed him to want me for *me*, not as a means to an end. I needed to be able to *trust* him. Who did I believe—*what* did I believe?

When I didn't respond, he stepped even closer and gently eased an arm around me, pulling me into the strength of his embrace. I let him hold me, folding my body into the planes of his. He gently reached up to stroke my hair, and my eyes squeezed shut as I listened to the beat of his heart against my ear where it was pressed against his chest. His warmth leeched into me, pushing away the chill that had seized me, sinking past my skin, deep into my bones.

I wasn't sure how much time passed before my father spoke again.

"Where did he go? Where are the others?"

As loathe as I was to do it, I pulled back slightly, enough to turn and look at the small group still gathered around my grandfather's body. Halvor had shrugged out of his jacket and draped it over my grandfather's torso, hiding the damage, and his eyes had been pressed shut. Loukas pointed at the hole in the hedge.

"The *jakla* escaped through that, and the others followed him. I stayed back to try and help him . . . but it was too late."

"What does that mean—*jakla*?" Halvor asked hesitantly, as though he were afraid to speak at all and remind us of his presence.

"It means 'cursed' in our language. It is the name for someone who performs the ritual to steal another Paladin's power, as he has done," my father answered. "Something that is normally fatal if

not stopped before all of the Paladin's power is ripped out of them."
His gaze flickered to where Raidyn and I stood, his eyes going to
where Raidyn's arms were still encircling me, and then back up to
our faces. "At least we aren't facing two deaths here today," he said
at last, his voice hoarse as he turned to Inara, who stared down at
Grandfather, her expression unreadable.

With everything else that had happened, I hadn't even had a
chance for it to sink in.

My sister was alive. And she was standing *right there.*

As if he could sense the turn in my thoughts, Raidyn quickly
dropped his arms, and I ran—on my still trembling legs—to grab
her into the tightest, longest hug we'd ever shared.

"You're alive. You're *alive.*" I couldn't stop repeating myself, sudden sobs surging up and consuming me, making my whole body
shake.

But she was crying too when she said, "I was so afraid . . . that
you . . . I thought . . ."

"We're *both* alive," I amended with a tiny laugh, a sound that
held no amusement, only soul-deep relief—and gratitude.

When we finally broke apart, it was to find our parents standing there, arms around each other, their faces streaked with tears.

"Inara," my mother's voice trembled, "I want you to officially
meet your father."

Inara wiped at her face and exhaled slowly. I took her hand and
squeezed it encouragingly. "He didn't leave us on purpose," I told
her. "When you were born, a power surge went through the entire
citadel, and the gateway sucked him through to Visimperum—and
though he fought to be allowed to return, the council never agreed
to open it for him."

She still just stared at him, and thanks to the *sanaulus,* I could
sense her trepidation—the war between the anger our mother had
instilled in us toward him and the longing she'd always felt to meet
him—the man who had given her the power that made her so
different.

My father's face was haggard with grief and pain, but his burning eyes were full of love when he lifted one hand to her—an in-
vitation, allowing her to choose.

And after a moment, Inara stumbled forward a step, then two, and then she rushed into his open arms. I followed after her, wrapping my arms around both of them. And my mother's arms came around me—something I couldn't remember ever experiencing before.

We stood there, the four of us finally a family, and held each other, and cried.

Until there was a low thud behind us and Raidyn cried out, "Loukas!"

We broke apart and I whirled around to see Loukas lying on the ground, unconscious, his stomach covered in blood.

FORTY-FIVE

INARA

The stranger—Loukas—lay on the bed, unmoving. Sami sat beside him, mopping his brow with a cool compress, one of her poultices on the wound he'd concealed from us. Not life-threatening, they claimed, unless it grew infected before Raidyn—the other stranger, the one it seemed my sister had feelings for—regained the strength to be able to heal him.

Not me. Never again would it be me.

I stood near the doorway, silent, listening. Halvor had left an hour ago, going through the hole Barloc had blasted through both the hedge and the iron fence it had hidden. He said he was going to slip down to the village below, listening for any word on the whereabouts of Barloc and the other Paladin who had followed him. There was also the fear that the garrison was still nearby—especially now that there was a hole in the hedge. One it didn't seem to be able to repair itself.

I'd never hated anyone before—had never wished violence upon anyone before.

Until now.

Now, I had to forcibly lock away any thoughts of Barloc. But despite my efforts, they kept slipping free—memories and feelings made of panic that turned my palms slick with cold sweat and sent my heart racing at such a speed that I grew light-headed. Terror seized my throat—right at the spot where he'd sliced it open to *drink* my *blood*, and white-hot rage curled my fingers into claws that ached to rip him apart.

Zuhra sat on the other side of Loukas's bed, Raidyn beside her. Both of them were stiff, tension swirling between them so thick it radiated past them to the rest of the room. I didn't understand it—I couldn't figure out the reason why Zuhra's hands were clenched together in her lap, and his arms were folded over his chest, his fingers curled in tightly to his palms. Why, when they even leaned slightly toward one another—as though the draw between them was so strong they couldn't even sit up straight—did they fight it?

My father—*my father*—walked into the room, pausing to hug me briefly, something that still took me off guard. Both the having a father who wasn't the villain, *here*, in the citadel, *and* the hugging. Mother was right behind him, still seeming dazed by his reappearance. She was never more than a step or two behind him, as though terrified that if she left his side he would disappear for another fifteen years.

Apparently, she'd forgiven him. And based on what Zuhra had told us, he'd deserved the forgiveness after all.

Zuhra looked up at them, her eyes bloodshot and her face ashy. "Nothing?" she asked, and they both shook their heads.

They'd been in the Hall of Miracles, hoping for it to live up to its name.

"I just need a few hours. Then I can heal him," Raidyn said, his voice that was so melodic, yet deep and somewhat smoky, breaking across the room like thunder from a summer storm. I noticed Zuhra's fingers tighten—if that was possible—at the sound of it. It was a remarkable voice. One that was somehow both gentle and commanding.

"I can do it, Raid," my father offered, as he had twice already.

"No," Raidyn refused yet again. "It's not life-threatening. You save your strength, so we aren't *both* depleted, in case . . ."

He didn't have to elaborate. We all knew the danger we were in. Especially if the garrison was still close by and realized there was a hole in the hedge.

"This is all my fault." The words burst out of Zuhra's mouth, as though they had been building and building inside her and could no longer be held back. "If I hadn't pushed so hard—if the council hadn't said yes—no one would be hurt, no one would have *died*—"

And then she crumpled, folding in on herself.

I lurched forward, unused to being the one able to offer comfort to her, rather than the other way around, but before I could reach her, Raidyn hesitantly unfolded his arms and I paused, waiting—

He gently wrapped one around her shaking body, while the rest of us watched.

"That's not true, love," Sami said quietly from across the bed. Poor, sweet Sami who had been knocked unconscious by Barloc in the morning room and left there, until she woke up to find her world in upheaval yet again. "Inara would have opened the gateway eventually; she was just waiting for her power to build up, and that . . . that *monster*," she spat, "would have come through and taken the Paladin unaware. And *Inara* would have died."

"No," my father said slowly. "She wouldn't have."

My gaze snapped to his, at the same time Zuhra straightened, her face splotchy and tear-streaked, and said, "*What?*"

"Inara wouldn't have opened the gateway—not by herself." He turned to her. "You told me that she was in so much pain . . . that even though Halvor was blasted backward from trying to pull her free of the door, you still grabbed her hand to do the same—except you weren't blasted backward, were you?"

Her eyes grew wide and then a look of utter horror overcame her—*why?*—and she shook her head.

"It took *both* of you to open that gateway. Inara alone would never have been able to do it."

Now it was my turn to stare at him. "It wasn't just me that did it?"

"No," he confirmed gently. "It took your sister's power *joining* with yours, and enhancing it, to open the gateway, and even then, only for a brief moment."

I didn't know why that mattered, especially now, but for some reason . . . it did. I'd held the blame of what had happened that day—and everything following it—squarely on my shoulders, *knowing* that it had been my fault, *my* power, that had opened the gateway, brought destruction to us, and stolen Zuhra.

But it had never been just my fault after all. And for some reason . . . it was just too much. Without a word, I turned and left the room.

I vaguely heard someone ask if they should go after me, but Mother murmured, "Let her go. I think she needs a minute alone."

As I walked through the citadel blindly, hazy memories of Barloc dragging me toward the Hall of Miracles resurfaced. I had been lost in the roar, so it was only brief flashes, but it was still enough to summon waves of panic that broke over me, alternatingly between ice-cold terror and fire-hot rage. Until Halvor had quietly filled me in, I'd thought Barloc had dragged me there to *open* the gateway. It was only later that I found out it had already been opened, and they'd all felt the shock wave of power, even across the citadel. He'd reacted quickest, snatching my wrist and yanking me out of the drawing room, knocking Sami out because she was in the way, and blocking the door behind us before any of the other two even realized what he was doing, trapping them in there, unable to reach us or stop him, until they'd managed to break down the door using a fire poker.

I tried to clamp down on the memories, but the horror of what he'd done to me rose unchecked, and suddenly it felt as though the very walls of the citadel were closing in on me, crushing me, *trapping* me. I ran, stumbled, tripped my way to the front entrance.

I had to get out—I had to *breathe*—I had to—

I burst through the ruined doors, out into the cool embrace of the rain that had begun to drip from the weeping sky, and had to bend over and grasp my knees to keep from passing out. My blood was hot and cold all at once, rushing through my veins. But as I stood there breathing in and out, in and out, slowly, slowly, sense returned to me and I was able to lock away the terror once more.

For now.

When I finally straightened, I was facing the singed hole in the hedge.

Silence.

There was nothing but silence.

I swallowed and forced my feet to carry forward, toward the massive, wounded beast of a plant. A *Paladin* plant that I, and *I alone*, had learned how to control.

The hole ripped through it had jagged, burned edges that matched the unseen wound within me. The gaping, torn cavern left where my power had once pulsed.

I lifted my hand slowly. It trembled in the small space between me and the hedge, the droplets of rain that fell onto my skin shivering and rolling off it. With a tiny exhale, I pushed it forward so that my fingers brushed the large, uninjured leaf closest to me.

Nothing.

There was nothing to feel.

Nothing to sense.

Nothing to *be*.

Who was I?

I was nothing.

I had been many things: daughter, sister, monster, savior . . .

But now I was . . . *empty*.

I knelt down on the ground, dug my fingers into the soil, and tilted my face up to the sky so the rain could wash away my tears.

FORTY-SIX

ZUHRA

The citadel groaned, a sound that was at once familiar and foreign after spending more than a week away from what had once been my entire world. The candles on the table guttered when a draft snaked through the room. The fire Sami had tended to before leaving to make supper—the one thing she said she knew how to do to help—burned greedily across from the window where I stood, staring out at the wounded hedge.

"She will be all right," Raidyn spoke softly from where he stood one step behind me. "With time." I could *feel* him—both the warmth of his body just out of reach and the thread of emotions that stretched between us and had only grown stronger since healing Inara together.

Fear, panic, grief, want, exhaustion . . . a tangled morass that trapped us both.

"Will she?" I didn't question his knowing where my thoughts were. When I turned to face him the firelight limned him in gold. His eyes, growing ever brighter as the time slowly passed, flashed in the falling darkness of dusk.

"If she has even half the strength you possess, then yes. I'm sure of it."

His words should have warmed the chill that gripped me, but no amount of kindness could erase the horrific events of the day— *because of me*—the repercussions of which we were still just beginning to see.

Loukas moaned on the bed, but still didn't wake.

"This is not your fault." Raidyn lifted one hand, slow, hesitant. When I didn't flinch away, he gently brushed my cheekbone with the back of his fingers. I squeezed my eyes shut to hold back sudden tears and leaned into his touch. His hand opened to cup the side of my face.

"Yes, it is," I whispered, broken. Like my grandfather, like Inara, like the hedge.

His hand dropped away but was quickly replaced by both of his arms coming around me and pulling me into him, cocooning me in his warmth and strength. "Inara is *alive* because of you. Your parents are reunited *because of you.*"

And my grandfather is dead . . . and my grandmother might be dying. And a jakla *is loose in Vamala.* I didn't speak any of those crimes out loud, but his arms tightened around me as if I had.

"Your father always said there are only two options with grief and guilt." His mouth moved near my ear, in my hair. "You can either let them drown you, or let them drive you. It's your choice."

I stood there, in the protective circle of his arms, the memory of his grief that I'd experienced through the *sanaulus* combining with my own. His words—my father's advice to him because he'd been trapped there with Raidyn instead of here with me—struck through them both. *It's my choice.*

Raidyn suddenly stiffened and let go of me.

"They're back" was all he said, and then he turned and rushed from the room. I glanced out the window to see four gryphons soaring over the hedge—Sachiel and Sharmaine in front, with Taavi *and* Naiki, both riderless, behind.

No Barloc to be seen.

But at least they'd all returned, whole, unharmed. At least Raidyn's gryphon had made it through and was here with him in Vamala and not left behind, separated by the closed gateway.

The fire snapped behind me. Loukas sighed from the bed again. I glanced over at him, at the bandages tightly wrapped around the wound he'd sustained when he'd selflessly followed Barloc through the gateway into my world and then chased him down, heedless of the danger, his only thought to protect others—even a world that had rejected his kind, putting out a death decree because of one king's fear of the power they wielded.

Power *I* wielded.

Loukas had done that, and my grandfather, and Raidyn, and my father. Sharmaine, Sachiel, and so many others. Risking their lives, *losing* their lives, to protect and help others.

Guilt and sorrow still threatened to pull me under, but I couldn't let their sacrifices, their bravery, be wasted. *Let them drown you or let them drive you. It's your choice.*

Drown you or drive you.

If she has even half the strength you possess . . .

What strength did Raidyn see in me? Did I truly possess any? And could I find the amount I needed to push through this—to face whatever was coming? To still find hope and purpose as my father had, despite everything he'd been through? My mother had let it drown her, but my father had chosen to be driven by his suffering, to keep trying, keep fighting. Could I be like him?

Yes.

I would *find* the strength. I *had* to. I refused to drown.

Out the window, I saw Sharmaine jump from her gryphon just as Raidyn exited the citadel, running across the courtyard toward her. She threw herself into his open arms. The hug, though brief, still punctured the fragile hope in my chest. Naiki folded her wings to her side, her head rising in greeting, and hurried toward the embracing pair—toward Raidyn.

They were lifelong friends, and her life had been in danger. Of course he would greet her with relief, with affection. Plus, it wasn't like I had any claim on him. I turned away before he could glance up and see me watching their reunion.

Let it drive you, not drown you.

I would be strong, and I would face whatever was coming with dignity, with courage, and with hope.

I would help Inara find her way forward without her power.

I would figure out how my newfound power could be used—how it could help.

And somehow, I would find a way to right the wrongs of this day.

With a deep breath, and one last glance at Loukas still sleeping on the bed, I left the room and went in search of my family—and the answers that we could only hope Sharmaine and Sachiel had brought back with them.

ACKNOWLEDGMENTS

Every time I get the chance to write these it is both an immense blessing and immensely terrifying! I just know I am bound to forget someone. But I will do my best and if I fail, please forgive me! You know I love you!

Thank you to my agent, Josh Adams, for always believing and continuing to make dreams come true. And the entire Adams Lit family—I am so grateful for all of you!

A huge thank-you to Melissa Frain for falling in love with my sisters (and their boys) as much as I did, and for turning this story into a book. I am so grateful for you! And the entire team at Tor Teen, thank you for the support and excitement for my book. Thank you, Jim Tierney, for the gorgeous artwork for the cover. Thank you especially to Kathleen Doherty, Liana Krissoff, Elizabeth Vaziri, Lucille Rettino, Eileen Lawrence, Sarah Reidy, Peter Lutjen, and Lauren Hougen. I appreciate all of your hard work and belief in this book—SO MUCH!

Kathryn Purdie—you are always there for me, no matter what, no matter when and I will always be forever grateful for that and for YOU.

I went through some difficult trials during the process of editing this book, so a huge thank-you to everyone who helped me through that time, especially Katie Purdie, Sarah Cox, Janessa Taylor, Lauri Lund, Kim Hoggan, Cathy Blake, Jen Appel, Natalie Lund, Jamie Kirkham, Jessica Knab, Andrea Taylor, Candy London,

Julie Tomsich, and many others who reached out, supported, prayed, and cared. The tender mercies that got me through were in large part due to all of you. Thank you will never be enough. You know who you are.

As always, a huge thank-you to my amazing family. My parents, Henri and SuZan—you are always there for me, always so supportive and loving and helpful and I can't thank you enough! My sisters . . . I wrote this book because of how much I love you all. Thank you for being there for me no matter what, no matter when. I'm so grateful to have you in my life! And my in-laws, Robert and Marilyn, thank you so much for all of your support and help. You are always willing to drive kids places and help whenever we need it and I am so grateful for that!

To my writing/author friends who understand, who uplift, who commiserate, who KNOW. THANK YOU. Erin Summerill, Emily King, Lynne Matson, Tricia Levenseller, Charlie Holmberg, Valerie Tejeda, Erin Bowman, Susan Dennard, Shar Petersen, C. J. Redwine, Stephanie Garber, Mary Pearson, Ally Condie, The "Vals," Sarah Maas, and so many others. My life is better for knowing you all—even if it was just a timely message I needed right at that moment. I'm so lucky to not only get to read your incredible stories, but to learn from you and call you my friends.

Brad, Gavin, Kynlee, Addie . . . and Trav. You five are my everything. I love you with all of my heart and soul and I hope that I make you proud. (Even though I know you wish I wasn't on my computer so much when I'm on deadline!) Thank you for supporting me and loving me. I'm the luckiest girl alive to have a husband like you, and our incredible, beautiful children.

To all my readers—those who have been there from the start or ones who just found me—thank you. Thank you for loving my characters and these worlds that I get to create. Thank you for going on these journeys with me and for allowing me to do what I love because of your support!

And to my Heavenly Father. Everything I have or am is because of You. My gratitude is eternal and unending.